The Secret Life of Rosie Mauer, Wallflower

Shay Lawless

The Secret Life of Rosie Mauer, Wallflower— Copyright © 2017 by Shay Lawless

ISBN-10:1-940087-26-0

ISBN-13:978-1-940087-26-9

21 Crows Dusk to Dawn Publishing, 21 Crows, LLC

Chapter 1

I suppose it all started with a crumpled section of an old newspaper. The newspaper probably would have gone unnoticed in my rush to get out of the crowded Laurel Grove Holy Trinity Church choir room after we finished the eleven o'clock service, had I not felt a sudden tickle in my nose. Not two seconds later, I had an attack of five, impressive dust-expelling sneezes just as Rocky McDaniel, my sister's boyfriend and a hulking bull of a man, blows past with a stack of dust-infested hymnals in his beefy arms tucked all the way to his chin.

"Sorry, Rosie," he mutters in passing, with an almost impish grin that makes me wonder if he didn't make a quick bypass of the old ladies in the corner just to irritate me. "Kind of ironic, though, that the school librarian is allergic to books. Ha ha."

"I'm not—" I begin, turning to watch him pass while I sneeze twice more and fumble for a tissue to swipe beneath each nostril. "I'm not allergic to books, necessarily," I finally manage to mutter, but my words fade away as fast as he is disappearing into the crowd. "It's the dust mites," I divulge to his back. "They are microscopic arthropods, relatives to the spider." By the time I finish, I'm talking to the air; Rocky has already blended into the crowd—twenty-two choir members stuffed elbow to elbow inside canary yellow walls.

We all bustle about, trying to get our robes off and hung up so we can get out of the parking lot before the Methodists, and the Baptists on Third Street, get out at noon, followed by the Catholics on Second Street, who disperse about twenty minutes later. We church-goers gunk up the streets with traffic; it is nearly impossible to get out on to High Street in front of Laurel Grove Holy Trinity Church.

I stuff my fingers inside the royal blue choir robe pocket for the crumpled pink tissue I stored there earlier to swipe beneath my always-runny nose. *Bingo*! I feel the rumpled softness. But I also feel something more like paper. When I remove the tissue, I see the irregular-shaped scrap of newspaper flutter towards the floor. I try to catch it, but it just tickles the tips of my fingers as I miss. I have to kneel to pick it up.

I turn the folded bit of newspaper over in my fingers, then gingerly unfold it. It is a ripped section from the front page of an old Laurel Grove Tribune, dated Wednesday, May 23, 1979. It reads: *LOCAL GIRL, 2, MISSING*. The date catches my attention. It was close to when my seventeen year-old aunt disappeared. I peer up out of my thick glasses, see if anyone is looking at me. I'm curious. Certainly someone must have put that into the pocket of the choir robe specifically for me. However, I know the odds are slim, considering it's not my usual robe. This morning, I couldn't find the one with the little tag held on with a safety pin with SIZE SM-R. MAUER written on it in black indelible marker that I usually wear. I quickly grabbed this one with EDNA PAULSON written on the tag instead. Of course, I'm not Edna. Our robes are hand-me-downs from an Episcopal church in Columbus. Edna must have been a pleasantly plump, big-busted opera singer, because it is five sizes larger than my scrawny, flat-chested one-hundred and ten pound frame.

"Hey, what you got there?"

"Nothing," I grunt, snapping to attention at the deep voice and rising a little too quickly, like a three year-old with a chubby hand caught in the cookie jar. The bottom hem of my choir robe flips over my head and nearly drowns me in an ocean of soft cotton.

"You going to live in there? Looks like you're in a bit of a pickle."

Oh, God. I hear that through the tunnel of choir robe. And that's Rocky McDaniel passing through again who saves me from sinking too deep in the darkness of the frumpy robe. I'm desperately flapping my arms, trying to make it to the surface. I feel a tug somewhere near the top. When I come out the hole for the head again, I'm blinking wildly upward through thick, black glasses at laughing blue eyes.

"I'm okay," I mumble, red-faced, while I start to fumble-stuff the newspaper clipping back into the choir robe pocket. I can't get the tiny gap open, so I secret it into the cleft of my palm. "Leave me alone, Rocky."

"Hey," he sniffs a laugh. "I was just trying to help, favorite surly sister of my Nicky." *My* Nicky. Who calls a girlfriend that? Only Rocky. "You know where that term comes from—*in a pickle?*"

"Yes, but I'm her *only* sister," I reply. "I'm not surly, and you're not helping." He's staring at me. I know he's waiting for an answer to his question so he can make fun of me; it is belittling, at best. He makes me feel like a pup whose master teases it by dangling a piece of meat in a circle above its head to make it dance. I close my eyes, take in a breath, and answer him anyway. "Okay, pickle comes from the Dutch word *pekel,* which means the brine, or salt water and spices used to preserve vegetables. If you're in a pickle, literally sitting in brine, it would be an uncomfortable situation that you would want to get out. William Shakespeare used the term in *Tempest*. You should know that since you teach Freshman English."

"I don't know," he shrugs lazily. "It's just grammar stuff I teach and not literature."

"*Just* grammar stuff." I shake my head, roll my eyes.

Let me just say something quickly, so it is clear why a beauty-challenged girl like me would shun what my mom's book club, between cupped palms and a few tittering old lady giggles, refers to as *the most delightfully handsome man this side of Texas*. Since we're nowhere near Texas, so it says a lot about his stupid perfectness. Rocky's my sister's go-to guy. That sounds strange, but I don't know how else to describe their relationship. They aren't *exactly* a couple, but they go out all the time and my mom hints, at least once a week, that my sister should be wearing an engagement ring by now. If it isn't with Rocky, she remarks, with a finger wagging in the air, there's a whole lot of other fish in the sea for her beautiful, smart, and eligible daughter.

But Rocky doesn't see it. I think when he looks in the mirror, he still sees the same self-conscious, pudgy guy with thick red hair who followed my sister around like a loyal puppy throughout high school. They went their separate ways in college. But when they returned five years later, they seemed to resume where they left off—still hanging out together, although their relationship has cooled. The two seem more like an elderly, platonically married pair than a couple in their twenties, enjoying the splendor of young romance. They both have jobs at Laurel Grove High School. However, now Rocky has lost about forty pounds and hides his red hair under Never Guess Men's Hair Color Deep Chestnut Brown. Instead of holding hands like they always used to do, my sister and her kind-of boyfriend act like a really, really old couple, bickering or looking bored at each other on the couch in front of the TV.

That said, you would think Rocky and I would get

along, considering we share my sister and, as mentioned, he's easy on the eyes. Not so. Insinuating he was saving me a moment ago was a bit of an overstatement on his part. On his behalf, I think smart girls infuriate him; he's always grilling me on a subject, then teasing me about it when I answer correctly. So saving me from drowning in a sea of blue robe was simply Rocky finding yet another way to point out I'm a blundering idiot hiding behind my sizeable vocabulary, the ability to calculate high numbers in my head, and having a brain that sops up words from a book like a mop soaks up water on a linoleum floor. I, on the other hand, don't like haughty men who fly through life by the seat of their pants and who can get anything they want with a wink, a flirty smile, and in a pinch, taking off his shirt to expose his perfect abs.

Our lack of enthusiasm in embracing our differences doesn't end there. You see, my sister and I have different daddies. And there's been a bit of a feud going on between *my* daddy's family and Rocky's daddy's family for well over one-hundred and forty years. We're forced into these situations daily because he and my sister have their thing. However, we have an unspoken agreement that my mom's house and church are common ground and off-limits for battle. We still stumble across each other in certain circumstances and not because we want to have any contact. He's the freshman math teacher, freshman English teacher, and coach at the Laurel Grove High School, where I'm the librarian, lunchroom attendant, and after-school detention monitor.

I can't even look him square in the eyes. I suppose, instinctively, my mind is telling me he's an alpha male, the dominant one, and I need to show my submissiveness as a lower member of a pack. Because that's the way it is at Laurel Grove High School where we work. If there is a pecking order amongst the ranks of students, it is nothing compared to the social order laid out by the staff. In a nutshell, he and the seventeen other teachers are one step lower than the vice principal, and I'm one step above the parents who say they are going to volunteer to work the concession stands at the games, but don't show up at all. I know my place. So, I just swallow hard and shrug. Anyway.

I make a quick turn to avoid Rocky's chuckles and to slip the newspaper article into the pocket of my well worn, favorite black sweater sitting on the table and waiting for me to shove my arms into its safe embrace. Then just as I wiggle out of the robe, I feel a bump against my shoulder. The jostling sends me forward two steps and I nearly bump into Marvin Cunningham, who is probably eighty-something but still manages to help me right myself with a smile that screams that I'm about as graceful as an elephant in a room full of blown glass. At least he notices me. Most people don't even perceive I'm actually there when I step on them with my clumsy feet.

"I'm sorry, Mister Cunningham."

"That's okay, dear. Do I know you?"

Yes, he has known me for over twenty-six years. His granddaughter is a teacher at the same school I work for and his son is the principal. I don't say that, though. Mom says they find him once in a while at the grocery store, wandering around. He can't remember why he's there. So instead, I nod and remind him. "I'm Gracie Mauer's daughter. Bobby Vandevenne is my stepdad. I'm Rosie. I sing alto. I'm in the back corner."

"Oh, the quiet one from Troublesome Creek."

Ug. Of *course* he managed to remember that. Yeah, the quiet one from Troublesome Creek. It's not much in the way of a character description. But, yes, it does describe me.

Because I got the shy from being around my mom and sister. I got the redneck from coming from my dad. And while my sister got the monopoly on being the pretty one, the smart one, and the athletic one all balled up into the perfect woman; I got stuck in her shadow and thrust into the worst of both worlds. At least from the perspective of those living on this side of town. Because what most people won't say aloud is that I'm the shy, *redneck* one. It is a way of pointing out what makes me different on this side of the creek. On the other side, I am the quiet, dorky one. I don't quite fit into either. If you pass me on the street, you probably won't even take a second look. I tend to blend with whatever surroundings I'm in, like my little brown gecko, Godzilla, blends into the grungy plastic trunk of the fake tree he is clinging to with his sticky, little toes inside his terrarium.

And, it shouldn't be that difficult to stick out in Laurel Grove, Ohio—population, 3,310. Most of the residents of this little town, plopped in the raggedy hills of southern Ohio, are either over the age of sixty-five or under the age of fourteen. I don't know what makes me invisible. I walked into the gas station to buy a candy bar last Tuesday and the man stepping through the doors in front of me slammed them in my face. At Reynold's Hometown Grocery Store yesterday, I had three people cut right in front of me in line to the cash register. It's like I don't exist. I should stick out like a gangly pink giraffe in a trailer park. I've got long mud-brown hair I usually keep tacked on my head with a bun. I've got dull-green eyes that I cover with thick-lensed glasses. I'm on the tall side, just short of five feet and eight inches with knobby knees and bony elbows. All of this leads to feeling lackluster and self-consciousness enough that I walk slightly keeled forward with my chin tucked to my chest.

"Oh, maybe next time I'll remember you." He pokes a finger right on the right lens of my glasses. I blink, stare past the little smudge his forefinger leaves. "Your lenses are pink. It's like you're looking at life through rose-colored glasses."

I sigh and nod in silent agreement. Rose colored glasses. Mom picked these out for me and now I am sure her intentions were not simply that the glasses brought out the ocean green from the grungy green my eyes truly are. Am I so unattractive she has to hide me behind rose colored glasses?

"Rose colored glasses," Margaret Williams chuckles while she weaves past and gives me an eye roll and double elbow-nudge in Mister Cunningham's honor. "Does your wife know you're down here still?" she grills Mister Cunningham. His wife's friends all have to look out for him, when they are out and about. I see his head fall like he's almost embarrassed by her words. He's ashamed he's so bad at remembering that his wife has to drag him around on an invisible leash of her friends. Margaret slips past me with her robe in hand and cackles. She takes a second robe from another choir member who is following close behind. Mary Stamper. I cringe when she brushes my shoulder while she follows Margaret. I can't help it, even if I feel a little bad for it. She has been the school counselor for what Rocky exaggerates as being almost a hundred years. They are finally forcing her to retire at seventy-two. Imagine that. I spent a lot of time in her office, working through what she called *mommy issues*. She gives me a wink-wink when she passes by, a code that she *gets me*. Sadly, I suppose, if anyone does, it has to be the school shrink.

"How you doing, sweetie?" Doctor Stamper asks me.

"Fine," I answer with a squeaky voice resonating like

a child. "Congratulations on your retirement."

"Oh, I don't plan on retiring. I'm still going to see some of my old clients at my home office." She looks around, sees no one is in hearing range. "Your mom says you've been having anxiety issues again. Are you still taking the pill I prescribed in high school?"

"Yes. Every day." I cringe and snap my gaze right to left. I wish she wouldn't announce it as easy as asking if I ate breakfast. What if someone's within earshot?

"Remember what we used to talk about. You can make your own decisions. When your mother starts to make you panicky, just walk away. You know, you can take two pills if you feel stress coming on, right?"

"Yes." I do know that. Every Sunday right before I go to Mom's, I pop two little Adtraxins into my mouth.

"If you want to set up an appointment, I will most certainly fit you into my calendar."

"No. I'm fine."

"If you do, honey, you know I'm here." She gives my shoulder a gentle squeeze. It does make me feel better. It's something she would do every time I left her office, like a little pinkie promise between friends. "Your mother is looking for you." *Wink-wink.* It's code for Mom is in one of her moods today. She started giving me these little hints when I was in middle school, I suppose, to form some kind of bond with me. She used to tell me how I could read the different moods of people through their expressions and stance. I could decipher my mom's emotions and perhaps, duck and cover when she was in one of her overbearing temperaments. *You'll always lose in a confrontation with an adult, Rosie,* Doctor Stamper would say, *but you can avoid confrontations with a few simple tricks.* Well, some of them, not all.

"Remember, it is better to avoid," she whispers and gives me a gentle shake. Honestly her words are a copout. Doctor Stamper knows my mother better than that. Avoiding Gracie Mauer is like a doe stuck on a highway bridge, trying to dodge a pickup truck full of hunters with their guns loaded. She'll pursue her prey, and chase it down until she's got its head mounted to the living room wall. Or it jumps over the edge in a desperate, suicidal attempt to get away.

Chapter 2

That curious reflection, while Doctor Stamper smiles patronizingly at me and scoots away, sits unpleasantly, like a tepid mug of hot chocolate on a freezing day, in my head. I grab my sweater, slip my fingers through the arm holes, and wiggle the newspaper clipping into my pocket. It reminds me of a newspaper clipping my mother had carefully cut out of the local newspaper and stuck to my refrigerator door with one of the picture magnets I have of my cat, Mister Baby Cakes, and the fourteen other pets I've got in cages and terrariums around my house.

There were already twelve random newspaper articles, magazine pieces, and two cartoons of an old lady with thick glasses with her cats placed haphazardly from top to bottom on the fridge door. There's probably one for each time I avoided her this month, because my mom has her ways of getting to me, even when I'm not in the same room as she. For example, the newspaper clippings. Each is Mom's awkward attempt to feed the feeble bond she has with me, her awkward daughter, and communicate with me through cryptic messages I am supposed to solve like little puzzles.

Last week, it was a short ditty she had copied from an online blog about the dangers of bacteria in cat pans. Next to it, she had placed the phone number of her chiropractor's son, who had just gotten divorced. Her message? I had mentioned I saw an orange tabby cat on the local pound website who needed adopted. She was trying to scare me into forgoing the orange tabby and finding another form of company that was human, male, and of marriageable age. Ha. Like anyone I know would put up with my ornery Siamese, six hamsters, four geckos, a guinea pig, a milk snake, and two neutered male rats.

I had actually gotten so irritated with her implying I was going to be an old lady with twenty cats, hoarding magazines piled from ceiling to floor, I snapped one day and put a big note at the top of the fridge: MOM'S NOT-SO-SECRET ADVICE FOR THE FUTURE CRAZY CAT LADY as a sarcastic joke. The clipping on my refrigerator was not much different than the one in my pocket. I have to assume it is another one of my mom's ambiguous messages. The headline read: *BODY OF SOUTH MILAN WOMAN DISCOVERED IN QUARRY AFTER A YEAR OF SEARCHING. Those who worked with Angel Rianne Daugherty at her job as a home healthcare aide said the young woman kept to herself. An avid reader and an aspiring writer, she quietly went about her job with great tenacity and went home to a lonely apartment with her three cats. She was well liked by those she cared for at Willis Nursing Home and Rehabilitation Center and will be missed in this small community*—The newspaper picture showed a young, local police officer I went to school with, Timmy Kinney, helping to draw the woman out of the water.

Mom's advice this time? If I didn't find somebody soon, I was going to die alone. But what could she expect? She set me up from birth. My name's Rosie Mauer. If you weren't aware, Mauer is German for *wall*. So, like my name implies, I'm a true wallflower, which my mother loves to bring up at social functions like at this very moment in the little room we use for the choir at church after the service. I've even thought about getting business cards that say: *Rosie Mauer, Wallflower* so she can pass them out while she does her usual spiel about me. Like now, as I catch a bit of her sultry voice from across the room and follow it through the maze of choir members who have yet to get out to beat the Sunday traffic.

"Oh, and that's my Rosie heading this way," her voice chimes above the humble chatter of the others while I dig my fists into my beloved sweater to wrap it tightly around me like a shield that can deflect her blows. "She's what we used to call a wallflower when I was in school. You know, one of those girls who sits by themselves and blends into the surroundings."

My mom waves me over to the battlefield with a handful of well-manicured, pearl-white nails and announces my weaknesses to anyone who will listen as if I have already surrendered to her as foe. If she doesn't realize it, she is distancing herself from me in the public eye. It is a small town and everyone knows everything about everyone. And they know I am the daughter that *happened* between her first husband and her second husband and couldn't be assigned to either. My grandmother calls me my mom's love child, although I don't think there was much love between my birth father and herself. It was more a one night stand when my mom's best friend double-dog-dared her to go bar -slumming with her at the Crazy Fiddle Country Tavern just outside town one boring Thursday night to pick up what Mom would later call *the first hick who walked by*. It was just six days after her divorce. I'm assuming the night got less boring as it went on because I was the product of the evening out with the first hick, who is my dad.

"Honey, can you say hello to Jack Barkley?" She's quick to point out my flaws even to strangers, like the nicely dressed, suited and tied gentlemen who is politely nodding at me. She will also treat me like I'm a four year-old who needs to have her words translated, so she doesn't give away that the daddy who sired me is known as being a bit of a redneck. "Do you remember him from commercials on TV?"

I do. Jack Barkley is a steady icon on local TV, advertising for his country club, golf course, and private residential community surrounding it. It's not far from the airport, so he gets a lot of traffic for his restaurant and bar. Every time there's a local sponsor commercial, it is Don Hamen from Don's Used Cars dressed up like a race car driver and pretending to drive what he calls a *pre-loved* car in front of a cheesy racetrack background. Or it's Jack Barkley's phonetically dubbed voice rolling through a long line of amenities in his gated community and adjoining country club, Crystal Springs, while he holds his hands out toward the God-knows-how-many-million-dollars-it-will-cost subdivision. It's not like anybody in Laurel Grove could afford to live in his luxury-gorged neighborhood with all the frills, pay the five-hundred dollar green fees to golf at his expansive resort course, or eat at the five star restaurant at the club.

Mom leans in and whispers, "He was also the emcee for late night horror shows when I was young. They called him The Ghost Host. He was quite handsome when he was in his thirties." Well, now he is sixty-something with black hair speckled with gray. He has a flighty blink to his buggy eyes, like the little sparrows hopping around beneath my bird feeder, trying to snatch up bites of seeds before my cat pounces hard against the paw-smudged glass window. He keeps tugging off his glasses, swiping them with a blue tissue, and blowing off the tissue dust with two puffs of his breath. Then, he shoves them back up the bridge of his nose with two fingers. He is a bit stocky, but wears a tailor-made, striped gray, freshly pressed suit and pants.

"He's the choir director's brother. He's looking to hire a secretary." Mom pats my arm. "You were suggested as a good fit."

"I'm looking for an *office manager*," Mister Barkley

clarified, clearing his throat. He thrusts a business card at me. I can hardly snatch it with my mom waving his hand away. "I'm trying to find someone who can maintain the books—"

"Yes, an office manager. That's what they call secretaries now, dear," Mom interrupts and rolls her eyes at me as if we share some little secret. I take the card between two fingers. "But I told him you were busy being the librarian at the high school."

"And a wallflower," I add with a puff of air from my lips. I think she wants me to return the business card. All three of us are staring at it dangling from my fingers.

"There's nothing wrong with that, is there honey?" she goes on, as if defending my lack of colorful character. "Wallflowers lead simple lives, no complications. We would rather Rosie became a doctor like my father and brother or a school counselor like her sister," she tells Mister Barkley while she stares warmly with a smile at me. "Perhaps it's for the better. She's the one I never had to worry about—no parties in the driveway, no boyfriends sneaking up the walk at night. Now, my Nicolette, *she's* another story."

"I'm not the one who pointed out to Pastor Neff halfway through his sermon that it was an explosion in an oxygen tank that nearly ended the Apollo 13 space mission." My sister, Nicky, slides in like a breath of warm, spring air that's confident everyone is ready for her after a cold, harsh winter. She's blessed with blonde hair, blue eyes, and is petite without the knobby knees and elbows I have.

"Well, it's true," I retort fervently with arms crossed. "He said a meteor hit it, which is factually incorrect."

"That's not the point, Rosie," she tells me with a know-it-all, patronizing tip to her chin. "His sermon was about the faith the astronauts had that they would get home alive, not necessarily a lesson on space missions." She sighs, and looks at Mister Barkley, who is peering back and forth between the two of us. "She's got a photographic memory from mom's over-achieving side of the family and a big mouth from her dad's hillbilly side. She's the true definition of smart aleck." There's muffled laughter at my sister's remark. She struts up and gives Mister Barkley a healthy handshake, pushing herself between us so her back is to me, emotionally and physically shoving me to the outside. "If my mom hasn't told you yet, I'm the loud one. My sister, she's quiet and meek like a mouse. And besides, she does have a boyfriend. His name is Mister Chubby."

"Mister Baby Cakes," I correct her, leaning to the side so I can address Mister Barkley. Mister Baby Cakes is the Siamese cat I've had as long as I can remember. He's twenty-two pounds, old, grumpy, and yes, the closest thing I've had to a steady boyfriend, I suppose. "And the term *smart Alec* comes from 1840s police slang for a criminal who was what they called: *too smart for his own good,*" I correct Nicky. "There was a pimp named Alec Hoag who used to have his prostitute wife hustle money from her johns. He also paid off the cops, so she wouldn't get put in jail for it. Then he got a bit greedy. He duped the cops of their money and got caught."

"Poppy Rose! You're in church! Watch what you say." Nicolette, on the other hand, is actually my half-sister. And yes, she calls me Poppy Rose all the time, mostly shortened to Poppy. "And you're doing it again, correcting people. Stop. Just let people be wrong for once." I don't even remember when the nickname started. As her name, Nicolette, implies (French for 'people of victory'), she has succeeded in besting me at everything. And Nicky always gets the last word in.

"For all intents and purposes, you're calling me a

criminal, Nicky," is my well-thought-out rebuttal.

"You could be a little more considerate of people's feelings by not pointing out their mistakes," Mom tells me. She got her degree in social work. Although she only worked for four years before marrying my first step-father and becoming a housewife, she still tries to use her outdated expertise on me. Of course, I have a difficult time allowing myself to absorb anything she says. I mean, she's hardly a great role model for relationships, statistically speaking, that is. She's been married four times. After the second husband, Walt Mauer, she just gave up taking a married name. It's like she knows the marriage isn't going to last long enough for her to have to worry about changing all the usernames on her e-mail accounts.

"Even if it isn't true?" I retort, watching Mister Barkley shift uncomfortably like he wishes he could excuse himself from this strange family feud while his eyes bounce between my mom, sister, and me.

"Yes!" Both Nicky and my mom say together.

I know he wants to run. He's got the scared-rabbit look in his eyes. Having a photographic memory isn't the only gift I received because of Mom. I'm very intuitive at reading facial expressions. Nicky's father didn't like me; when he came back into my mom's life for a short time when I was six, he would bully me. I learned quite quickly how to avoid a slap or a pinch, a mean remark or a lie he would tell my mother about me. Meanwhile, Nicolette makes a grand gesture by throwing her hand into the air. "Because mom's right. You *are* a wallflower. A trumpet creeper or something because your constant trumpet nose sniffling and blowing your nose almost ruined Tangy Cunningham's solo." She stresses the name *Tangy*. Yes, it is odd. But Tangy's mom said when her daughter was born, she was tiny and jaundice-orange like a tangerine. So she named her Tangy. For some reason, her mom didn't take into account her daughter would have to explain, for the rest of her life, her likeness at birth to a piece of fruit.

Rocky swoops by with yet another handful of hymnals he's taking to stack on a cart next to me. "Wallflower." He says while he dumps them on the shelf. "Do you know where that term came from, Rosie?" His voice is so incredibly deep it sounds like summer thunder rumbling down the mountains. He tones it down a bit, almost whispers when he talks to me.

"Rocky, come. Quit showing off." Nicky reaches out and wiggles her fingers at him. He automatically comes up to her like a well-trained pup after she has accidently dropped his leash. He lifts his chin so she can unfasten his choir robe. I make a little doggy whistle while I dig my elbow into his side. It's so low, I know only Rocky can hear it because he shakes his head, gives me a lip twitch.

He doesn't let on to anyone else, though, before he continues: "There's a European plant with little yellow flowers that used to be placed along the stone walls of homes," he tells me while Nicky whirls her hand in the air and he turns so she can help him out of his robe. "Girls that used to sit by the walls at parties, because they were shy and didn't have a partner, were called wallflowers."

"Rocky, help me out here," my sister demands. "Did you actually look that up to impress my sister?" She sniggers and snatches the shoulders. Then Nicky starts to tug while Rocky wiggles back and forth.

"Well, maybe if you get the teaching position, you'll step off that wall," Mom says like she's trying to mop up the bloody mess left after her slaughter on the battlefield.

"I'm not getting the job," I announce. All four look at

me in clumsy silence. Meghan Wilder got it. Again, based on the social structure, she was a shoo in. Did I mention even among those in the third level tier below the principal and the vice-principal, there is a secondary social order? Tangy Cunningham, Mariah Patterson, and Meghan Wilder are the pretty girls among the teaching staff. They delegate the dress code, seating in the teacher's lounge, and tasks farmed out to each of the personnel. My application probably didn't even end up on the school board's agenda.

"Maybe next time," Mom mutters with such exaggerated disappointment, I feel like I've failed some big test. Nicky pulls off one sleeve of Rocky's robe, and then the other. They are tight around his biceps and she has to peel them off with her fingertips like she's stripping off the skin from a banana. I hardly look at Rocky, just blink at the shoulder of his button up shirt. Rocky's six feet six inches tall, buff, and the perfect specimen of a man, even if he has that look of the high school jock who's going to be a hundred pounds overweight once he settles down. I watch Rocky, my mom, and my sister all move off. That leaves Mister Barkley and me staring at each other in awkward silence.

"It was nice meeting you," I mumble at the floor. "Thanks for thinking of me for the job."

"Well, to be quite honest, I'm not looking for a *secretary* at all. I'm actually interested in hiring someone to do some—" Jack Barkley takes a quick scan of the room, leans in, and drops his voice, "—research for me, some private investigating. I didn't want to say that in front of your mother. She seems a bit—overprotective."

"Research?" I'm intrigued, however I can't imagine what he could need researched except for advertising cost comparisons or finding new populations of rich people to become members of his club. "Like researching the reputation of companies interested in advertising for your country club? That's more in tune with someone who has a marketing degree. I'm not really trained in marketing."

"Well, I have a company who does my marketing. But you came highly recommended. You're smart?"

"Well, I—"

"Because I was talking to your father at the shooting range the other day and I said finding good employees in this job market is like trying to open a pickle jar without hands. And he said—" Mister Barkley rubs his chin. "Let me remember his exact words. Oh, yes. He told me if I was looking for a person who could figure out how to get a pickle out of a glass jar, just flag down some idiot off the street to open the jar, pluck it out. But if I needed to know how to make a glass jar that could be opened without hands, I should talk to you."

"My—my father told you that?" I ask, with a snicker. "Yeah, it sounds like my daddy."

"Yeah, he's quite a character. He's in charge of my shooting range now, don't know if you knew that. But we were talking about our kids. Said you can cut a target of a boar in his backyard right down the center in five shots. He also said you're off the charts on your IQ."

"I was a straight A student in college."

"He also said you are a teacher at the high school."

"I'm the librarian."

"Oh," he sighs. "I understand we may not be an exact match—your skills versus what may be demanded of you. However, I can't find a researcher that is actually—legit," Jack Barkley continues. "There's twenty-eight in the phone directory. There are a hundreds more listed online in a fifty mile radius. I've hired three. Each of these has taken my money and not provided any results. I've been through one quack after another. I need someone with brains. I need someone who is accountable and not some wannabe private investigator. I'll train you in anything crucial for the job."

"What do you want me to research?"

"Well, here's the thing. I've got a stepson who is learning the business. He needs an assistant—"

"He needs a babysitter." The choir director, William Delgado, interrupts with a chuckle while he walks through the choir room door. "That boy needs someone to follow him around, keep him out of trouble." He's tall and thin with a sparse amount of too-black hair on top of his head combed over to one side. My sister says the choir director looks like a pickle; I'm not sure why. He's bent a little in the middle, but he's always got a smile.

Jack Barkley looks hard at his brother and sighs. He scrubs a hand on his head. "Yes, the boy is twenty-one and spoiled. I need someone who can keep an eye on him five or six nights of the week."

"That sounds like a nanny job." I shake my head.

"There are times that my stepson isn't so busy. That would be a good time to do some—research," he replies evasively. I'm staring at Mister Barkley. Something in his stance, the way he's shifting from foot to foot, makes me believe he's not divulging the entire truth—what my mom would call a sketchy character. I opt out, take a step back.

"I'm sorry. I don't think my mom would approve. She *is* over-protective. Your assessment was correct."

Jack Barkley nods like he almost knows my rejection was expected. "I expect you'll keep this conversation confidential." He reaches into his pocket, pulls out a money clip and tows out a hundred dollar bill which he hands to me pinched between finger and thumb. I look at the money and then at Jack Barkley. "Take this," he says, leaning in and speaking softly. "Hush money." He has a little smile on his lips, like he's teasing me.

"No." I shake my head. Hush money? For what? Is he afraid I'll tell someone he's looking for a nanny for a twenty-one year-old? "I don't need the money. I won't say anything about our conversation." Jack Barkley nods, stuffs the money back in the clip. Then he reaches into his pocket, wiggles out a second business card. He stuffs it into the little pocket of my sweater. "In case you lose the first one. You won't regret it, Miss Rosie. The pay is quite good and you would be a valued member of our staff."

Chapter 3

I have a place I go that makes me feel safe. When I'm unsure or feeling the dread of heading to my mom's house for after church lunch, I visit Laurel Grove Lake Park on my way. It's far from the demanding eyes of my mom. I'm free, there, of a sister who grumbles with embarrassment at having a half-sister. *Half* being half-creepy and half-hillbilly, according to Nicky since ninth grade.

Not many people come to the park anymore, except to fish the small lake fed from Little Muddy Creek or to take a walk along the mosquito-infested trails. It was once a small amusement park called Dell's Fantasy Land, with rides like carousels and even a small roller coaster. Dell Allen Custer was the owner. When he retired seventeen years ago, the place just shut down. The city eventually acquired the property and fenced off the old rides—including a Ferris wheel, swings, and assorted kiddy rides. The humongous and aged sign out front remains, too. It's a thirty-foot tall cut out of a creepy-looking clown with mean, beady eyes, a bulbous nose, and a yellow-toothed grin that used to light up. It stands at the entrance beckoning visitors with outstretched hands and a sign at its enlarged feet that says: RIDES! PICNICS! FUN FOR ALL! DELL'S FANTASYLAND! CLOWN AROUND WITH US! Now it only summons a handful of locals to a huge hill with a view of Laurel Grove below, a path that leads to a cliff, and a small lake.

There's a huge rock at the top of the hill, settled into the cliff I like to sit on. I don't go out far. It makes my stomach jump. I sit prudently far from the cliff wall with my legs bent and my arms around my skirted knees. I can see my mom's house, the town, and even my little subdivision from here. Listening to the silence calms me. At least for a while. Then as I sit there, I always get this terrible sense of loneliness, like some spurned lover who returns to a place where she once met with her beau, know she will never see him again. It makes it no easier when I look down, catch the sweet scent of the tiny bell-like flowers clinging to the honeysuckle vines creeping up the path and on to the stone. Wallflower. While I sit in the middle of the vines, I think I must look like the wallflower queen, blending into the stone, solitary and all alone.

I reach into my sweater pocket and pull out the crumpled newspaper clipping. As I do, Jack Barkley's business card falls out. I miss catching it twice before it falls to the rock near my leg. I pick it up absently, tuck it back into my sweater pocket. Then I carefully unfold the newspaper I found in the choir robe pocket.

LOCAL GIRL, 2, MISSING, I read again. Then I scan down the article. My eyes focus on a couple pictures next to the print. The one to the left is a bit blurry and a full body view of a toddler with a wispy spray of white-blonde hair. She's wearing a two-piece bathing suit and standing ankle-deep in a baby pool, holding a garden hose in one little hand. It looks like it was taken with a Polaroid in a back yard. However, it is the second picture that almost takes my breath away. It is more akin to a yearbook picture, a face staring back at me. It looks like me when I was ten years younger. I squint at the caption beneath the images. *Gina Lee Channel (left), has been missing for two days. Locals are concerned that the circumstances match that of Rosaline McGuire (right), age 17, who disappeared May 22nd of last year. Rosaline has not been found—*

I blink. It *is* my aunt in the picture. She was seventeen and what my daddy calls pugnacious. My mamaw and my aunts and uncles on my daddy's side said she ran away after a fight with my papaw while they were eating eggs-over-easy and bacon at the breakfast table. My daddy says my aunt said she had a stomach ache and didn't want to go to school. My papaw told her she just didn't want to go because she had to ride the school bus. She stood up from the table, walked out the door, and Daddy says she just vanished into thin air. He remembers it just like yesterday— my papaw had poked the white of the egg, then mopped up the yellow yolks spilling on to his plate with a piece of toast folded in half. My aunt said something under her breath. Papaw waved a hand and told her: *You just walk then.*

Nobody talks about her much anymore. Sometimes, they whisper how uncanny it is that I look so much like her. *Oh, do you remember when Rosie used to grin like that?* Or *she tips her head just like Rosie used to do when she asks a question.* Sometimes, they look at me with sad eyes when I do something that reminds them of her. *Rosie used to hold her breath when she got mad.* It's almost like they just want to forget about the girl who vanished like a little, red, helium filled balloon that slips from a child's fingers and disappears into the sky. And sometimes, I feel they wish I wasn't always there to remind them of her.

I scan the article. It is only a paragraph, talking about the volunteer search efforts to find the 2 year-old girl, Gina. There's just two sentences about my aunt: *Local authorities feel it is an isolated incident. Rosaline McGuire is thought to have run away after an argument with her father.*

I survey the two images. I can't quite figure how the clipping got into the pocket of the robe. Maybe the robe was old and someone left it in there from long ago. Certainly two girls missing was a big deal back then. I turn it over. The names Rosaline M. and Gina C. are written in tidy cursive on the back with a red pencil. Still, the goosepimples rise on my arms. What if someone did place the clipping there for me to find?

After my jaunt to the park, I travel about nine miles off my usual Sunday path from church to Mom's house. I take my little cherry red, road-weary car and drive it to South Milan Quarry Park. I pull into the vacant, muddy-gravel parking lot and stare out at the crystal blue water of the quarry. I'm afraid to turn off the engine. Sometimes it doesn't start and I have to call Rocky or my stepdad to come get me. Then I have to feel belittled while one or the other jiggles a few wires under the hood, hops in my car, wiggles the keys and it starts right up.

The park isn't that big. It's maybe ten acres with a couple baseball fields and an old stone quarry with a NO SWIMMING sign tacked to a rickety post. It's quiet here. I pull out my phone, poke in *Gina Channel*. Nothing comes up, not even an old newspaper article to match the one in my pocket. So I sigh and type in *Angel Daugherty* in the little browser screen and read a couple short articles about her death. I try to imagine this shadowy figure driving up to the same place I am parked now and then jumping out to open the trunk of a car. Inside is Angel Daugherty's body, wrapped in a twin-size white sheet, stuffed into three black plastic garbage bags, and tied with a man's leather belt, size 42. Beside her are homemade red bricks laced with lead to weigh her down. The shadow dips down, lifts Angel in his arms and takes her to the water bank. He returns twice to get the bricks, a couple armfuls. Then he bundles Angel up with the bricks. He slinks off to the still quarry water and tosses her into its depths.

In my mind, her body hitting the placid water causes a rippling effect, expanding across the quarry. She floats there in the center, just a moment before folding somewhat and sinking slowly and deeply into the belly of the quarry.

Bubbles rise to the surface, then pop, fading away. After only two minutes, it is like she never existed at all.

The Columbus Weekly Press said she probably lay in the cold waters for ten to twelve months before a fourteen year-old boy snagged one of the deteriorating bags with the hook on the end of his fishing pole. He slowly reeled the cumbersome black-bagged body to the shoreline and when the fetid odor of death forced a gag, he clung to the pole with one hand and texted his mom with the other. She called the police.

I'm not there ten minutes when a sixty-something couple pull in and warily eyes me sitting alone in my car. I vaguely recognize them. Joyce and Ted Winters. Ted is my mom's car insurance agent at Winters Insurance Agency. I wince, hoping they don't recognize me and mention to Mom they saw me here. They stop and stare into the clear waters, once in a while glancing over their shoulders at me. They make me nervous. I shift my car into drive and weave my way back to the main road, feeling strangely bonded with the dead girl. And the image of her slipping beneath the surface hangs heavily on me.

Chapter 4

"Come on, play a game with me, shirts versus skins," Rocky is teasing me, like he does every Sunday afternoon. "You be skins."

I know he notices I keep checking the clock on my phone. It's almost time for me to shift gears and change from the modest Sunday dress and pumps I wear to my mom's completely renovated, two-story home in the historic, upscale section of town and settle into ripped blue jeans and a t-shirt. I do this every Sunday, right before I leave to go to my daddy's house far outside town. Daddy has a much less formal and mostly chaotic Sunday family supper, with paper plates and a crapload of my aunts' and uncles' kids armed with water balloons running amok in the front door and then out the back door, barefoot and like a pack of little wild puppies.

Rocky dribbles the ball around the ample court my stepdad, Bobby, has set up around his four car garage. He does a little circular dance and fakes making a basket over my head. Then, he does this thing where he feigns he's going to toss the ball at me. He stops the ball an inch from my eyes, blinking wildly with an involuntary reaction, not realizing it is a scam.

"You can't leave until you lose a game to me."

"Mom's house is common ground," I remind him as I walk pass him with my shoulders forward protectively. "Quit pestering me." Each time he fakes a toss, I twitch and bring up my hands like I am going to catch it. He finally stops. I hear a giggle and look over to his niece, Gabby. She's found one of my old hula hoops in the garage. She's swinging it around and around on her forearm in the air. He's always got her in tow on Sundays and, it seems, a lot of evenings too.

Gabby's mom is Leah McDaniel. Leah is Rocky's short-tempered, wildly red haired, cousin with a shitty attitude, who works nights as a janitor at the high school. Leah's birthday is only three days from my own. But being the same age is the only thing we have in common. She's been my nemesis since the second day of kindergarten, when she marched her way through the trash in front of her daddy's beat-up doublewide mobile home to the yellow school bus. Once her raggedy tennis shoes crested the top step of the bus, she punched me in the arm in passing to the back seat while I sat in the front seat, singing softly and happily to myself. Consequently, I thrust out my spotless, white tennis shoe into the center of the bus between the seats and tripped a chubby back then Rocky, who was following right behind her. He fell hard and flat on his face to the rubber bus floor matting, ended up with a bloody nose.

Accordingly, so did I when Leah stepped over the prone Rocky, cornered me in the bus seat and punched me in the face thirty seconds later. I learned a valuable lesson that day—if you're half the size of your opponent, it is better to just hit and run and accept the price at the end of the road when you can't run any farther. Or be sneaky, sly, and underhanded and never let the enemy know you are slowly, secretly, and methodically bringing them down. Because I spent the next twelve years avoiding her fists mostly in part in small, well-calculated increments, using Rocky to get back at her.

"My mom got a new job clearing dirty dishes from tables after people eat when she's not working at the school," Gabby announces, to no one in particular. "That's what she's doing today. She's going to buy us a pool when we get rich." She's wearing a flowered dress that is halfway down her shins and was probably out of fashion in the 1980s. "I'm going to be an FBI agent when I grow up." As if to show her determination, she pats one of two breast pockets on her dress. On the pocket, she's got a dollar store, plastic badge with Federal Bureau of Investigation emblazoned beneath an eagle that looks more like Daffy Duck. I'm assuming the dress is something from the thrift shop the churches set up in town with free used clothes. I saw Mom grit her teeth when Gabby walked into church, with her hair uncombed and wearing the frumpy dress and a milk mustache while holding Rocky's hand. I quickly snatched her up with the excuse of guarding the women's bathroom door for me, which doesn't lock properly, and instead, braided her hair and wiped the breakfast off her lip in the choir room.

I ignore Gabby's chatter. Rocky looks discomfited as he tugs on his collar. He knows Gabby's mama isn't going to be able to afford a pool on minimum wage, especially with a forty year-old boyfriend whose sole job is dealing drugs in the local bar parking lot. He also sees Nicky clamp her mouth shut, stifling a laugh.

I settle into a lawn chair with a celebrity gossip magazine hiding Bobby's police books about criminal behavior he conceals on the top shelf of his study. Bobby used to be in the Laurel Grove Police Department before he retired. He's always buddying up with Rocky, teasing him that he should quit his teaching job and join the police force because he's such a big guy. Rocky volunteers on his off-time at the Laurel Grove Fire Department. Bobby says the fire department is for wimps and sissies. The two are always wagering bets on their basketball games that if Bobby wins, Rocky will be a cop. Then Nicky always rolls her eyes and says Rocky's too much of a baby to be a cop or a fireman.

Rocky has removed his Sunday suit and button-up

shirt, and he is making a lazy, soft-core porn flick for me dancing around in his sleeveless t-shirt and well-toned shoulders and chest. His arms are slightly muscled and gorgeous, although I think a half hour per day of dumbbell curls would suit him fine and tone his biceps to a lusty perfection.

"I'll stop bothering you if you tell me what eight-thousand times ninety-four is in less than five seconds." Rocky takes two steps so he is hovering over me and starts to count slowly and methodically. He's blocking the sunshine and it is a bit chilly out. I feel the goosepimples roll down my arms.

"Seven hundred and fifty two thousand," I say without looking up. "Go away."

"Where does the term *piece of cake* come from?"

"It means easy. It's from a fad in the 1870s. Couples danced for the prize of cake. Whoever was best got the cake. Apparently, it was easier for them than their bumbling opponents because they were more graceful."

"God, you're smart." He still stands there and I know he's staring at me with a funny tip to his head. I'm trying to hide the book so I lean it toward my chest.

"Don't take the Lord's name in vain, Rocky Archibald McDaniel," my mom's voice rings from the kitchen window. It sounds like she is talking through a drum.

"And you're dumb, *Archibald,* for not realizing my mother has ears like a moth," I reply, looking up at Rocky whose eyes are veering wildly like a four year-old caught peeing in his grandma's garden.

"I'm sorry, Missus Mauer," he mutters sullenly to the dark kitchen screen. He still uses her surname, the same as he did when he was fourteen. "A moth?" Rocky turns his attention back to me, his face coming back down with a curious tip. My skirt scooted up when I sat down and he bounces the ball on my bare knees twice. "Never heard that."

"Ow, don't do that, Rocky."

"Sorry." He only makes it worse by tucking the ball in the cleft of his arm and patting my knees with his hand like some kind of strange apology.

"It's fine. But as I was saying, the greater wax moth can hear a hundred and fifty times better than you can," I answer, squirming a bit at his touch. "It has evolved to compete with its predators, like bats, which have great echolocation abilities. In fact, males attract females by producing short ultrasonic signals."

"That's sexy," Rocky huffs like I just proclaimed some sultry secret known only by moths. He falls silent except for the pat of basketball while he tosses it from hand to hand.

"It is—quite erotic on insect terms," I look up and Rocky has fixed his gaze on me. "It makes the female's fan their wings, which releases pheromones in the male. Said pheromones entice the females to come within reach. Then they copulate."

"Copulate," he repeats hoarsely.

"Have sex," I translate.

"Rosie, pull your skirt down," Nicolette pipes up from her perch on the side of Mom's hot tub. I didn't notice, but she must have been listening half-heartedly to the conversation. Rocky reels back a little quickly, blushing into a thousand red freckles on his cheeks.

The hot tub is settled easily next to the pool, which is still in its winter cover, a short five steps away. Nicky kicks her feet letting the water splash on her shoulders, chest, and belly in teeny little droplets that look like specks of gold from my vantage point. She keeps smiling like she has a secret. Well, at least until she had to point out my skirt must have risen enough to flash pink panties. Nicky's on a bit of a high. The school year is almost over and next year, she will been awarded the position of head guidance counselor because Doctor Stamper, who has been there for nearly forty-two years, is finally retiring.

I readjust my skirt while Rocky stumbles away, still dribbling the basketball. Sometimes I hate my sister. She'll do anything to embarrass me, even if she has to pull something out of her ass to make it appear I am flirting with Rocky. I wasn't. I know my own face is burnt red.

I turn to watch Gabby's eyes warily follow the voice to Nicky. It is the beginning of March in Ohio. One day it is seventy, the next we're expecting a snowstorm. Today, it is record-warm enough for Nicky to sink her feet into the one-hundred and two degree water of the hot tub and don a bathing suit so she can work on her spring sunburn which, with Nicolette, always turns into a beautiful toast-colored tan. I, on the other hand, always turn a shade of ginger-colored toffee and break out in a hive of freckles. My sister is gorgeous, lounging there in mirrored sunglasses, a two-piece bathing suit, and goosebumps. Her Barbie level perfection mars my sense of self-worth. I'm sure it doesn't help Gabby's either, with her knobby knees, frizzy hair, and ten-thousand freckles.

"Rosie, you need a shut-off valve." She reaches out with one pink manicured, toe, tapping it against a blue floaty full of hot tub chemicals so it bobs away towards the center of the tub. "Rocky doesn't give a rat's ass about the mating habits of moths. Nobody does." Nicky giggles and Gabby turns her head toward me as if she is waiting for my reply. "But I suppose none of us would be able to find said ass underneath that ratty black sweater you've knotted around you again. Rosie, how do you do that without getting heat exhaustion? It is seventy-two degrees out here."

"I know CPR," Rocky offers. He snatches up one of the pool towels and tosses it at me so it falls across my head and magazine. He's making it difficult not to make this a battlefield. I tug at the towel, let it fall to the ground.

"Leave me alone, Rocky," I tell him again. He's like having an irritating little brother around all the time. "You made a deal if I answered the math equation, you'd stop."

"He can't stop. If he quits pestering you, he'll invoke the curse—" Nicky makes a ghostly hum with her lips and wiggles her fingers in the air like she's inducing a spell from them. Then she laughs. "And then everyone in town will bear the brunt of his indiscretion."

"You know you insult us by bringing that up." I glower at my sister from beneath my glasses. It is her way of indirectly making fun of my daddy's family and Rocky's family. It is a bit of a sore spot with me. She can't call them backwards or rednecks or hillbillies to our faces. Instead, she brings up stuff like old local superstitions and rubs our noses in that like bad puppies over a puddle of pee.

"She doesn't offend me. I believe it," Rocky admits with a nod, looks at me with a serious pucker to his lips. Then he does this double eye-blink. Whenever someone mentions The Curse, he gets this facial tic where he blinks his eyes twice. "You don't have to defend me. Call me a watered down hillbilly for thinking it, but you ask anybody and any time a McGuire gets together with a McDaniel, there's hell to pay."

"Bull." I shoot him a glare. "The last time a McDaniel was nice to a McGuire was before the frigging Civil War."

"Yeah. Look what happened. There was a civil war!" Rocky beams with his well-placed argument while Nicky giggles.

"You're blaming the Civil War, not on something as monumental as politics and disagreements on slavery, but something trivial, like your great-great-great grandfather almost marrying my great-great-great cousin? And I'm sure if they had the same genes as you and I have, they fought all the way to the justice of the peace. It's coincidence. It's ludicrous." I roll my eyes. "Look at all the crap going on in the world between that time and now—wars, murders, terrorism. None of that was caused because you brought me a bowl of ice cream from the kitchen the other day so I didn't have to miss the last five minutes of the sitcom Nicky and I were watching."

"It's not ludicrous," Rocky scowls at me like I'm just a silly little girl. "It's true. You believe what you want to believe and I'll believe what I want to believe."

"And he'll never bring you a bowl of ice cream again," Nicky snickers knowingly. Sadly, she's probably right. How can something so nice to behold also be so stupidly gullible?

"I won't. You're right." Rocky nods in agreement. "So, who was the eighteenth president of the United States?"

Nicky shakes her head. "Leave her alone."

"I want to know if she knows *everything*. You're always saying she's a know-it-all, Nicky."

I stiffen. I get what he's doing, pitting me against my sister. Nicky throws a towel at him.

"The eighteenth president was Ulysses S. Grant," Gabby pipes up. Everyone's eyes turn to hers and her freckled face turns bright red from her throat to the tips of her ears. "We, um, we learned that at school."

I look over my magazine at her. She's staring hard at me like she's being all haughty because I didn't know the answer. I do. "Who was the seventh president, smarty pants?" I ask her.

"Andrew Jackson." She wiggles her shoulders, then turns back to the hula hoop and jumps through it.

"If you're so smart, Gabby," Nicky retorts. Oh, now she's my protector. Nobody beats up on Nicky Mauer's little sister but her. "Then why don't you know how to use a hula hoop right?"

"She *is* using it correctly, Nicky," I grunt, absently. "Egyptian children used grapevine hoops to play with just like she is."

"Your sister is right; you *are* a know it all." Rocky grins at me as he pretends to toss the ball at me again. I shrink back.

"And you're a bully." I raise an eyebrow.

"I offered to give you CPR—"

"And one day, she's going to finally get tired of your bullying and kick your pansy ass," Nicky mutters, then shrugs it off when Rocky does his signature chuckle-laugh. "Yeah, Rocky, and you're not so far from being a loser either. You want play fireman with the other boys. We all know that. You do know you don't give CPR to somebody who's overheated, right? You see, this is the reason you're much better off teaching—"

In Rocky's defense, I knew he was just trying to make light of the situation because I see his silly grin drop dead.

"Rocky wants to quit teaching?" Mom asks half-concerned as she steps out the back porch door and stops just short of her garden. I eye her carefully while I peer over the magazine. She takes in a deep breath like she is tasting spring for the first time. "Oh, Rocky, you of all people know how hard it is to get a degree. And you are the only one in your family to graduate from college. Anybody can be a fireman. I hope you're not throwing that all away. What a shame—"

"No, Mom, he isn't," Nicky sighs while Rocky is looking sad-puppy at my mom and sister like they just stepped on his tail. "It's just a pipedream. He's too much of a priss and knows it. He's just going to volunteer and—"

"He's right," I interrupt her, louder than necessary. Everyone turns to me. Silence. "About CPR. Rocky's correct. If someone loses consciousness and goes into cardiac arrest from heat stroke, they *would* need CPR. I mean, if you're basing his ability to work for the fire department on the fact that he answered the question incorrectly, then he—then he could be a fireman. Because he was right."

I don't know why it bothers me. I feel like I should be mean to him for my daddy's side of the family's sake. Rocky's uncle is always shooting at my daddy's no trespassing signs. My daddy is always slipping over to his daddy's land and hunting turkey. I almost feel guilty for being in the same room with Rocky and not being snarky at him when I'm with Mom and Nicky; I suppose he feels the same way. However, if I had to pick between the two that day, I'd rather shit-stare my sister for making me feel like an idiot about the moths. And so I do.

"What are you talking about?" Nicky looks at me with a scrunched-up, questioning face while Rocky thinks he can escape by turning and making some baskets. "Oh, you're still stuck on the ugly sweater thing and being hot." She stops and thinks this out a second. "But as we were saying, Rosie, before you interrupted—" She reels her head around from me back to Mom. "—yes, Mom, he wants to quit teaching and be a fireman. He'd get half the pay." When Mom looks at Rocky with a wary purse of lips, Nicky slaps her feet on the water and turns her attention back to me.

"But humor aside, you got enough cat hair on your sweater to stuff a pillow." She tips her head to the side and looks across the expanse between us, blinking at my hands. "What are you reading, Poppy?"

Crud. I follow her gaze. I am so flustered by Rocky's muscled bare back, I'd let the magazine fall away to expose a wee bit of the cover: *Criminal Profiling: The Minds of Killers.*

"Just—stuff for the library at school."

"What is it, dear?" Mom pipes up, fanning her face.

"It's one of Bobby's crime books." Nicky rolls her eyes toward my mom, then me. "There's no way they'd let you have that in the library for students to check out," she warns me harshly. "You need to think things out."

I follow her gaze back to Mom's. It's Mom's own fault for putting that stupid newspaper article about Angel Daugherty's murder on my refrigerator in the first place. What did she expect? And it's quite possible that her insurance agent is a serial killer. She'll thank me later when she's not enticed into Winters Insurance Agency some dark night on the premise she didn't pay her bill, then dismembered, and settled into the quarry beside six other well-to-do women who pooh-poohed the fact that serial killers are all around us. From the book I'm reading, serial killers can be placed vaguely into three categories: organized, disorganized, and mixed, depending on their characters. Of the thirty or forty characteristics of an *organized* serial killer, Ted Winters fits about eight. He's smart, socially proficient (he talked my mom into insuring both me and my sister on her car, even though we never use it), well-educated with a degree at the local Laurel Grove Community College, and he drives a flashy car. Not to mention, he quite possibly returned to the crime scene to relive the moment of his murder.

"You're not getting obsessed with crime stuff again, are you?" My mom takes a pleading-eye step toward me, her pursed lips offer a bland, concerned smile. I can see Gabby looking a bit fidgety. When we bicker sometimes, it makes her nervous. Rocky told my sister it is because her mostly absentee daddy is a drunk. When he shows up once in a while, he beats up on Leah. "Are you taking your medicine? Mary Stamper suggested to me today that we may need to increase the dosage. We all remember what happened last time you started reading about crimes."

Last time. She says it with such distaste, I sink a little in my chair in embarrassment and tug the magazine over the book. Okay, I got a little carried away when I was seventeen and my cat was missing one morning after I had let him outside before breakfast. In my defense, the old man who lived next door had threatened to poison Baby Cakes if he pooped in his garden one more time. I just knew my cat had been murdered. I called the police and started my own investigation, complete with sneaking into our neighbor's house when I thought he had left for work. I got caught red-handed when I opened the door to his upstairs bathroom and he was sitting on the toilet with a Laurel Grove Tribune in his hands and horror in his eyes. He screamed and I had a panic attack right there in his hallway. Baby Cakes was sitting on the front porch when I got home. The memory haunts me as I look over at Rocky. I know Rocky can hear my mom and I know he thinks I'm sickly. I hate that I take a pill or everybody thinks I'll have what Mom calls *an episode.* It's a classic panic attack—I can't breathe, I get dizzy, and my nose bleeds.

But in my defense about *last time.* I will just comment on one thing, it is that I felt I had good reason. I mean, my family has a history of things vanishing without a trace. Before I was born, my daddy's sister disappeared. Then, when I was fourteen, I was gone for two days. I was supposed to be at a sleepover with some friends from school on a Friday night. They just lived two blocks away. Just before I left, I got in a fight with my mom. I snatched up a sleeping bag and a plastic grocery sack filled pajamas and took off in an angry fit.

Mom didn't think anything was amiss until the next evening. She called the girl's parents and they said they'd been out of town, but there'd been a party at their house. Mom managed to sweep it under the rug—she still thinks that I just got drunk and passed out, then was too afraid to come home. I don't remember a thing, except for swinging my sleeping bag over my shoulder and yelling something to Nicky about staying out of my room. That's where my memories become a puddle of muddy water; from that day at three-fifteen in the afternoon to Sunday evening two days later. Everybody else's account is all I truly distinguish as real. Nicky tells everybody she was sitting on the porch two days later. I just came walking up the sidewalk like nothing had happened at all. Well, except the back of my head was dripping a bloody red.

The doctors at the hospital who put eighteen stitches into the back of my head said it appeared I had fallen off a balcony or simply flipped off a porch railing. It probably knocked the recent memories right out, along with some irrelevant memories of my childhood. Once in a while, a lost moment of my past will pop up and I can't quite put a finger on it—I don't know if I dreamed it or if it really happened. But I haven't grasped anything about those two missing days.

"—and Principal Cunningham pulled me aside today at school. Poppy, are you listening?" Nicky is frowning at me. No, I was lost in thought. In my defense, though, all my sister does is talk, talk, talk. She is grinding her teeth, giving Mom a knowing gaze. "Wake up and listen. Principal Cunningham wanted me to talk to you before you hear it from somebody else."

"He talked to you instead of me?" I peer over the magazine, absently flap my fingers at a housefly buzzing near the cover. I look at my sweater. It *is* covered in Mister Baby Cakes' gray and white hair. I give the sweater a half-hearted swat with my fingers. Boom-pop. I listen to the basketball bounce off the asphalt, then there is silence.

"He was afraid you'd be upset." Nicolette isn't watching me. I can see her gaze shifting toward her kind-of boyfriend. He is standing there with the basketball tucked between arm and ribs. They share a glance before she sighs deeply. "Rosie, they are making cutbacks at school—"

"I thought they hadn't laid the idea in stone yet," Rocky takes the ball in both hands and tosses it up a few times. I look at him. Where did they hear this and I didn't?

"Paul Cunningham said they are ninety-nine-percent sure they are making the budget cuts," Nicolette says. "They're cutting back on staff. Your librarian and your lunch attendant staff positions are among what they are cutting. He said they might be able to keep you on staff for about eight hours a week to work with the at-risk students, but you'd lose your insurance."

I know my sister and Rocky are staring at me. I feel suddenly washed-out and dizzy. I've got a house payment, student loans, a car payment, and I've got to eat.

"Poppy, Mom said she could help you out until you get another job," my sister reminds me softly. "Your job at the high school doesn't pay that much anyway, right? You can find something—what about the country club? Didn't I hear Mom say Jack Barkley offered you a job?"

"Oh, no. Stop right there, Nicky. That's the *last* place any daughter of mine is going to work," My mom's voice slips up along the little garden between pool and sunroom of her house. "Don't put that in her head. Those Barkleys are always stirring up scandal. Jack Barkley preys on young women, you know that, right? He always has a pretty, young thing riding on his arm. His last wife was *nineteen*, for heaven's sakes! Did you not read the latest Celebrities Up Close Magazine?" She's wagging her hand at the magazine dangling in my fingers. "One of them is a Sunday morning preacher in California. He was put in jail for embezzlement. He had an eighteen year-old mistress."

My sister giggles, stands up and walks across the expanse between us. She wiggles the edge of the magazine to show the book beneath. "She's not reading the magazine, Mom. I'd be more worried about her working on this."

I can't see my mom; she's on the other side of the screened-in porch now. I hear the back door squeak open and see the mirror image of Nicolette standing there. They could be sisters, my sister and my mom. I'm the odd one out, with my brown hair and eyes the color of bland green-yellow, late fall grass.

Regardless, she ignores my sister. "Sweetie, you didn't want to be a librarian anyway, did you? I mean, really, books are going the way of floppy computer disks and bellbottom jeans. You've got a degree in English, math and computer sciences. I know you took the librarian position because it was simple, safe, and close to home—"

"I took it because they already had someone teaching English, math, and computers."

"Dear, really?" Mom says dismayed. "You took it because you like to hide in the dingy corners of a dark room with a book. Honey, I'm just being honest. There are plenty of jobs out there. You can take one close to home. I can talk to Neal at the real estate office or—"

"Don't, Mom. I know what you think. I know what all of you think." I take all three of them in. My eyes stop on my mother's hard gaze. "I'm dispensable. If I disappeared right now, nobody'd even know I was gone. You think I take after my daddy, some backwoods hillbilly who can't keep a job. You're embarrassed I look like him, act like him. I'm just a constant reminder of the mistake you made in the backseat of a pickup with some dirtbag when you got stupid drunk one night with the girls after your divorce."

"Don't you say that, young lady." I hear my mom's Sunday pumps clacking along the landscaped bricks until they stop just short of me. I start to rise. Just as I do, I see a little speckle of blood dribble on to my sweater. It lays there, a round droplet, while I automatically draw my fingers up to my nose and press them there. Blood on my fingers.

I take in a breath. I know the drill. I get these nosebleeds when I get one step away from a panic attack. Doctor Stamper, who was my counselor in high school, said it was from anxiety. She always alluded from our sessions, my mom and my older sister were the main source of my stress. I'm not a psychologist, but I completely agree.

"Oh, God." I just want to get out of there. I plop the magazine down near my chair, feel the warmth of blood oozing between my fingers. I look around wildly. I always feel a little numb and prickly, like when my leg falls asleep if I sit on it too long.

"Here, Rosie, hold this to your nose and sit down." Rocky's right there. He's holding his wadded up white t-shirt and shoving it to my nose. "Sit. You're fine. You're going to be just fine. Look at me." I do look into those baby blues and stare hard while he drops a steady hand on my shoulder and pushes me toward my chair. "Easy, just sit and tip your head forward." Then he tells Mom and Nicky to run inside and get a couple washcloths and an ice pack. "What's the square root of—of nine-thousand and twenty-five?"

"Huh?" I narrow my eyes.

"What's the square root of nine-thousand and twenty-five? Just answer me. Breathe easy."

"Um," I think hard and try to keep my breaths from coming too quickly. "Ninety-five."

"What's four-hundred and fifty times thirty-six?"

"Sixteen thousand and two-hundred."

"What is the largest animal in the United States?"

"The bison. It can weigh over two-thousand pounds as an adult."

"What does *can't judge a book by its cover* mean?"

"You can't accurately judge by outward appearance." My breaths are more even and I'm almost sleepy as I feel myself calming down. Rocky's hand on my shoulder is firm and calming. He asks me twenty more random questions before Mom comes running out of the sunroom door and I'm already tugging the shirt from my nose.

"There, all better." Rocky is smiling at me. I feel like I accomplished some huge task and he's proud. I've got mixed emotions, considering he's usually shitty with me. But he's the only person that seems to be able to walk me through these attacks and keep everybody else at bay and away from me by running for ice, and water, and towels when I throw up. "You just need to think of other stuff, alrighty?"

"She just needs to take more of her anti-anxiety medication," Nicky corrects softly. "Doctor Stamper knows what she's talking about, even if your idiot doctor said you would grow out of them." I don't expect anything less from Nicky. Most little girls idolized teen boys in fad magazines in high school. Not my sister. Nicky worshipped Doctor Stamper. Doctor Stamper basked in Nicky's reverence, even made her an assistant during the summers she was in college. "Look. She was right. You didn't."

I push the icepack Mom is handing me away and rise. I pull my eyes from Rocky and tell him with a bit of embarrassment that I'll wash his shirt and get it back to him. Then I make a quick escape through the house to the front door. Away. I just need to get out of there. It's like a frigging battlefield and I'm on enemy territory.

"Everything okay, honey?" That is Mom's newest husband. He's as lackluster and bland as the high-priced brown recliner in front of the TV. Still, he's a nice guy.

"Yeah, fine, Bobby," I grunt as I stomp my way to the front door. I am surprised he saw his invisible stepdaughter at all. "Just fine."

Chapter 5

"All right, you're just going to have to run, Rosie. I can't get it unstuck."

"I can't, Rocky. I won't leave my dad's ATV! It's custom-made." I grimace beneath the football helmet I'm using as head protection and clench my fists on the handlebars and try to push. It doesn't budge. "It's got an adjustable suspension, four-wheel disc brakes, and a thumb warmer! A thumb warmer! He'll kill me!"

He gives me a sideways glance, his eyebrows arching; I identify this expression as easily as I can count to ten. It's a classic Rocky way of revealing what I am saying is completely out of his realm of thinking because it is far too much simply unneeded information. "So translated, it means he doesn't know you borrowed it, does he?"

"No, not really." Heck, Daddy calls the ATV Baby. At least he did when he tugged the protective storage cover from atop and showed it off to me last month when he finally saved up enough cash to have one of his buddies finish it. He and Greg Eaton custom built the entire all-terrain vehicle from engine to body. Well, my daddy can't put together a child's puzzle, but he told Greg what he wanted, and held the wrenches while Greg worked his magic. For the man who can't even change the oil in his truck, it's like he's the original architect for the White House. "It's got power steering and—" I stop myself from overwhelming him again with a detailed list of accessories I'd read when Daddy handed me a stack of manuals on the parts he used. "—stuff, Rocky." And stuff—*Baby girl,* my daddy told me while he walked around his brand new, cherry red ATV with arms wide like a salesman displaying a Lamborghini to a rich, perspective customer. *Look at this.*

It's my pride and joy. Well, next to you. I ain't never been able to afford a new truck. I ain't got a nice house and I missed going hunting the last two years because my ATV was broke. My old ones, they always been your uncles' hand-me-downs—

"How can someone be so incredibly intelligent and so damn scatterbrained all at once?" He swipes sweat from his brow.

"How can somebody be so damn pretty and so incredibly insensitive at the same time, huh, Rocky? I'm not leaving!" I spat back. He tips his head, looks at me intently.

"You think I'm pretty?" His lips are twisting smugly. I don't answer. I can hear the police car sirens screaming up the dilapidated gravel of the old road, just up the rise from where I'm leaning, shoving the back of the ATV. One of his cousins is still shooting the air with his shotgun. The ATV is stuck—the back wheels are so settled into the ruts on the McDaniel's side of Little Muddy Creek, they're not moving even with Rocky shoving it hard with his fingers wrapped around the handlebars and putting all of his strength into it. I'm halfway across a muddy creek bed and covered from head to toe with brown, sticky muck. I can't see Rocky. He just looks like another smear of dirt on my glasses. But if it wasn't for him, his big brother would have shot me dead being the last in the long line of my family members hauling butt to get out of there.

"Would you rather my brothers and the cops catch you? Because Timmy Kinney was the first cop on the scene. You know that little pissant has spent his entire life trying to impress Tangy Cunningham and he knows she's got it out for you. If he doesn't try to put a snare trap on you, the rest will tear you apart like wolves on a teeny weeny bunny," Rocky scolds. "Please go. Your dad would rather you were safe. I don't want to see them rip you to shreds."

I know he's right. It makes me mad. But Tangy has held a grudge since fourth grade, when I snuck a half bottle of hot sauce into her snack milk at school to get her back for tattling to the teacher because she thought I stole her pencil. Honestly, I know if he didn't have to do the same thing I do every stupid weekend, go to his uncle's house where his family meets like I have to go to my dad's, I'd probably be in handcuffs and marching into the police station escorted by Timmy Kinney. Because there would be nobody else helping me get out of this misunderstanding including a little bit of gunfire and a lot of trespassing.

Yet, I got stuck. I called Rocky on my cell phone because nobody on my daddy's side knew I was missing yet and he's the only one in a ten mile radius right then who isn't from his uncle's side that would lynch me. "Hey, I'm in a bit of a pickle," I had admitted in a desperate tone.

And he says in a too-laidback and sassy tone: "I don't know what the means, a *pickle*? What?" Like he suddenly doesn't know what that means. I know he saw me ride past. I'm the only one wearing a safety helmet.

So I answered: "I explained that to you. I'm sitting in brine. It is an uncomfortable position. You used the term to describe me stuck in my robe this morning at church."

"Huh?"

"Rocky, don't be an idiot. That was me at the end of the line of ATVs that just went past. I was the only one wearing a helmet." It was my dad's old football helmet. I couldn't find any other head protection and although Ohio is not in the top five states with deaths from ATVs, I wasn't taking any chances. "I was the one who got stuck."

"Imagine that. I should have known," Rocky answered sarcastically. Still, he jumped in front of his

Uncle's truck. I know he was playing stupid so I had time to get away. Then I narrow my eyes, realizing the truth. No, he's not saving me in this crazy game of steal the flag our families play. He might be saving my ass to stay on my sister's good side, but now he's got my daddy's ATV for the warring rivals. Honestly, I know why. It's that damn curse. His family has filled his head with so many darn superstitions, he really believes he has to even the odds with something mean each time he's nice to me. He probably considers himself a hero for saving my life earlier helping me overcome my panic attack.

Ug. I hear somebody yelling on the hill above. Rocky leans around and gives me a bear-paw shove with his hand. I trip-walk three steps. I stare at Rocky for one second through my eyes no longer covered by rose colored glasses, but mud-covered ones instead. He looks like a smudgy bear.

"Dammit, go!" he growls. "And take off that stupid helmet." I wonder how the hell I get into these situations. Oh, well, this time I know—

It all started after I left Mom's. My daddy's name is Ray McGuire. He had quite a reputation when he was younger. I've heard him called *a lady's man*. Mom used to tell me he was the most handsome boy she'd ever seen with his chestnut-colored hair and deep green eyes. She said when he walked into a room, the girls would just stop to stare at him. She said he was poor and redneck, but none of them cared because he just had a certain something— charisma, charm, a swagger emanating from him. Even now, my mom gets this silly twist to her lips when she runs across an old picture of him. I know he's the only one in the world who seems to realize his lackluster, geeky daughter is there when I walk into a room.

He lives up on Troublesome Creek Road, in an old 1920s house with the white paint chipping off the exterior and six junked trucks settled deep in the raggedy lawn. Brown shag carpet lines the inside held down by a ragtag assortment of furniture and a TV set that must weigh a ton. It's cozy and warm and he lets me walk around the house in my shoes instead of taking them off at the door to walk in stocking feet. He doesn't care if I put my soda cans on the sofa table without a coaster and he likes lying under my car with me while we fiddle around and pretend to fix it. Daddy's as good at being a car mechanic as me. Still, we like getting our hands greasy and pretend we know everything there is to know about car maintenance. We stare up at the engine, poke around, and talk about our week.

I spend Sunday evenings with his side of the family, eating Sunday supper. I'm stuffed to the side of my Aunt Kay, who smells like talcum powder and old books, and who is adjusting my papaw's chipped green oxygen tank by jiggling the handle back and forth.

It's a completely different world. I have to believe that's why my mom shoves her Sunday lunch back so late—I have less time with my daddy and this world so alien to her. Most of the time, I feel like I'm leaving an elegant wedding through a magic door and walking into a dusty, rustic barn. There, I slip off my posh high heels and trade them in for a comfy pair of muck boots. My grandmas becomes mamaws and my grandpas are papaws. Instead of sitting around the hot tub, sipping wine my mom gets in the mail from her Wine of the Month Club, somebody usually hands me a clammy aluminum can of cheap beer with droplets of condensation on the outside from a six-pack my Uncle Teddy picks up at the gas station then plops into a cooler of melting ice on the back porch.

"Can you breathe now? Papaw, listen to me." Aunt

Kay keeps saying louder and louder. His breathing is fine. It's his hearing that's going out. Besides, Papaw is more interested in the TV blasting out the Cincinnati Reds baseball game and fanning her away with his hand. When he gets excited about a good base hit, he takes off the mask and yells, then starts to cough. He doesn't realize it's a DVD my dad put in with a winning ballgame from twenty years ago. My Papaw gets really upset if the Reds lose so Daddy tapes a bunch of games and just plays them over and over.

Daddy's house is crammed full of family and it is frenzied and loud on Sundays. I've got more cousins and aunts and uncles on his side than I can count on my fingers and toes three times over. My Aunt Jo keeps trying to plop her stinky two year-old in my lap because he needs a diaper change. He's got snot running like a faucet out of both nostrils and his fingers are covered in something that looks like brown applesauce. She thinks it's funny I gag when she dangles his malodorous butt in front of my nose.

My cousin Charley, who is wearing a ballcap with a Confederate flag on the front, is sitting in a recliner across the room. He's gangly and already too-tan from working for a roofing contractor this spring. He keeps firing a Nerf gun randomly at the side of my head. It makes a funny twanging noise each time he sends one my way. I still fail to steer clear of its target. *Twang.* "Two points, Dorkbilly," he says every time he almost knocks my glasses off. It is at least twice a minute. Dorkbilly is short for dork and hillbilly, his nickname for me.

"Leave me alone. I had a nosebleed today," I warn him, covering my nose with a cupped palm. Of course, this only pushes a wider berth between us because it provides evidence I am not cool and redneck, but nerdy and sickly.

"What'd you do, bump it on a book?" And it usually

doesn't bother me, his picking on me, but what my sister said about me getting laid off is making me a bit testy. I can't focus on the only thing my daddy has to read in the entire house, which is an old crossword puzzle I'm trying to figure out. Charley isn't making it any easier because he's hit the pencil in my hand twice.

"Charley, leave the girl alone. The only thing touching that face are those goofy glasses. When she gets nervous, she pansies out. She starts spurting blood everywhere." My cousin, Renée, lobs a raggedy throw pillow across the room at him and misses. "Let Dorkbilly work on her crossword." I didn't see her come inside. She's stocky and built like a weightlifter. She's got a horse farm up the road and helps my uncle with his logging company. "Remember when you had to sing a song in tenth grade and you got on the stage and your nose was bleeding so hard, you puked up blood on Josh Carlton?" She's not defending me. She's like an alpha female wolf who is moving in on a coyote kill, I'm the coyote.

"Yes. Thanks for bringing it up."

"You're welcome. It was *so* gross! It was like that Stephen King movie—what was it? Oh, yeah, Carrie." I don't remind her it was a bucket of pig's blood that caused the mess on the gymnasium stage on prom night in the movie, held aloft by a string and dumped by her schoolmates. My own was puking nosebleed blood during a Christmas concert. She is correct that the premise was the same. Carrie was a shy girl from a small town and the butt of jokes. In a classic horror sense, I share her pain.

Regardless, it is just Renée's way of letting Charley work me down until I'm exhausted, then she'll move in for the kill. They haggle back and forth between themselves for about five minutes, then Charley hunkers down in his seat and makes wary eyes at the kitchen doorway. Renée plops down on the floor and leans back against the couch. The alpha male, my cousin Jeremy, is stomping around the corner with a plate full of my mamaw's fried chicken stacked six inches high. He keeps the ornery pups at bay.

"Hey, Dorkbilly," he says to me while he chomps hard on a chicken leg leaning into the doorway between kitchen and living room. He's what my grandma calls 'burly'; big armed, barrel-chested, and beefy. I would describe him as a big black bear because he's hairy too. "So what's up with the dead girl Junior found off Federal Road? You know that was him that found her, right? He's the guy that used to work at the hardware store in town. Junior—" He thinks about this hard while he slaps his lips in unison to a couple bites of chicken. "Hell, I don't know his last name. It's Junior something. At least, that's what Cindy Lawson, at the grocery store, told me the other day when she was cutting some ham at the deli. Junior was out looking for a place to set up his deer blind in the fall. He almost stepped on her head! That stepdaddy cop of yours said anything about it?"

"I don't know anything about a girl on Federal Road. Junior who? I don't know anybody named Junior. It sounds like gossip to me," I mutter, looking up. He's not as hairy as he used to be. He shaved his head, but still maintains a short beard. He's wearing a t-shirt, blue jeans, and boots. Another dead girl doesn't even pique my attention. It's probably one in the same anyway. Once rumors start flying in Laurel Grove, there's no telling where they'll end. A dime dropped on the sidewalk on Tuesday is a thousand bucks hidden in a treasure chest off the highway by Friday.

"It wasn't. It was real. Her name was Annie or something. She worked at the country club." He drops the chicken leg on the plate. It isn't anything but bone. He picks up another and holds it up in front of his face, eyes it carefully. "I figured you'd know because you read so much. Uncle Ray said the cops should be looking into it. Maybe whoever killed her did something to his sister."

"I just heard about Angel Daugherty," I say. "They found her at the quarry. But she'd been missing since summer of last year. She was *real* dead."

Charley thinks that's funny and chuckles. Jeremy shrugs. "So was the girl Junior found, that Annie girl. He said she looked like a mummy with skin hanging off her. That's two dead girls last summer."

"The newspaper said the girl found off Federal Road was a waitress," Aunt Kay adds. "Her name's Alaina, not Annie. Officer Kinney was interviewed at the site. He said it was an isolated incident. I heard at church they think some guy from the country club did it. His name was Liam. Ruthie Reynolds heard over the scanner they pulled him over to question him. Maybe he killed the girl at the quarry too."

Jeremy wiggles the chicken leg at me. "What are you reading? You're like Einstein or something, right?"

"It's a crossword puzzle. And not entirely." I shift so my Aunt Kay can turn to eye me like a bug under a microscope. "My IQ isn't as high as his." I pause for dramatic effect, roll my eyes. "But almost."

"And you're a girl." Jeremy sniffs a laugh.

"Yeah, I'm a girl." At least my cousin recognizes that fact even if every guy who slams the door in my face going into the Laurel Grove Speedy Gas and Carryout does not.

"So, you're smarter than that cop, Timmy Kinney, right? The dumbass we went to school with?"

"Hell, yeah," I scoff at him with a snarky look of disbelief that he even asked that. I think sometimes I'm the only one who can get away with talking back to Jeremy. He's considered the hardass of our family. I haven't quite figured out if it is only because I'm my daddy's only child and if he kills me, my dad has no heirs, or if he simply feels sorry for me because I'm so out of place here.

"You're offending your cousin, Jer," Aunt Kay sniffs a laugh. "Comparing her to a cop? What are you thinking? Wasn't his grandpa the same cop who used to sit outside the Crazy Fiddle and wait for your daddy to drive home at midnight so he could give him a DUI?"

"Yeah, that's him." Jeremy scratches his back against the corner of the doorframe. "But it's like this, Aunt Kay. I'm thinking, if she's so damn smart, she should figure out who's killing girls around Laurel Grove. Because I think—" He stops and licks his fingers, leans in a bit with a quieter voice. "—I think that's what happened to Aunt Rosaline. The cops, they are either too stupid or don't care if they find anybody." He turns to me and shrugs. "Just saying, Billy. I'd like to talk about something other than Aunt Rosaline coming up missing at the Sunday supper for once. So I also hear-tell Johnny McDaniel's logging up Sugarcreek Road, right up to your dad's property line. You hear anything?"

No. I understand Johnny McDaniel, Rocky's uncle, has a logging company called McDaniel and Sons Logging. Jeremy and his dad also own a logging company, McGuire and Sons Logging. If it isn't bad enough the McGuires and the McDaniels have battled for over a century, but of all the companies each could choose to operate, they both settled on the exact same business, with the same name idea. Regardless, logging has never come up in any conversation I've had with anyone on Mom's side of the family, including Rocky. But my daddy's side of the family seems to think I'm like some undercover agent Daddy sired with an outsider solely so he could send me out to infiltrate the enemy and obtain all their secrets; Rocky is my hostile informant.

I try to nip it in the bud right off. I hold up my hand. "Rocky McDaniel and I do not speak more than two words to each other." I know they don't mean to, but they alienate me, make me feel like an outsider when they act like I hold the secrets to the enemy. "He's got it in his head that stupid curse will end the world if he's more than lukewarm to me."

"You can laugh, but *I* believe it." My Aunt Jo swoops in with a diaper and her stinky baby and sets it down on the coffee table in front of us. It about starts World War III with Charley griping at her about changing the stinky diaper right in the middle of the room. The fact she's using the coffee table we just had our plates on as a changing table for a bare-butted, poopy baby is not even brought up.

"Hey, so I've got an idea," Charley stands and waves a hand in front of his nose before he takes the gun and points it at me. *Twang. Twang.* It's right then he lets loose a double shot at my head. "Let's get the ATVs and go for a ride over along the property line—"

"Ow, dammit!" I yowl at him when my glasses abruptly stomp across the bridge of my nose, not once but twice in quick succession.

"Quit being a baby, Dorkbilly," Renée snickers while I adjust my glasses back to the proper position. "Or Aunt Jo will put one of those diapers on you. Yeah, I'm game. Let's see if they're stepping over the line." I see Aunt Kay roll her eyes like she agrees with Renée's description of me.

"I'm not a baby," I grunt to no one in particular. "You're going to break my glasses and they are expensive."

Renée looks at Charley, then waves a hand toward me. "You get to lug around Dorkbilly on your ATV this time. She's dead weight and whines at every bump."

I hate not fitting in. Just once, I'd like to be the one

who everybody wants to ride on the back of their ATV. "I don't whine," I mutter. "I can ride my dad's ATV. I'll ask him." I never asked him. I just snuck the keys from the kitchen drawer; I don't know what I was thinking.

It's only thirty-two minutes later, I'm running through the woods as fast as I can. I stop to catch my breath at the top of the hill in the cover of the trees. The cops come down and linger around my daddy's ATV, like Rocky just killed a polar bear with his bare hands. I watch them tow it away on a trailer to take to impound and then I take the long, long walk back to Daddy's house. I stop out by the garage where he kept his ATV. I toss stones at the wall, trying to think of what to say, trying to figure out how I can make my daddy not think his only kid is a complete screw up and can't even keep up with the ten year-old who was in front of me. Because I'm *sure* he's heard the story.

"I mean, how does somebody get an ATV stuck?"

I jump, turn and it's my daddy standing there, with his arms crossed before he jabs a thumb behind him.

"I don't know," I whisper, hugging the football helmet in the cleft of one arm. "We decided to go over and check out Johnny McDaniel's property, see if he's logging on your side. Somebody got the bright idea of cutting across his field. Charley accidently shot an electric box with a gun."

"I hear tell somebody got the bright idea of borrowing her daddy's ATV without asking."

"Yes, sir."

"And you weren't smart enough to tell them all to turn around? Girl, how old are you? Six?"

No, but I'm the girl who wants to fit into, at least, one of her two worlds, but can't seem to figure out how *not* to screw up both at the same time. But he doesn't get it. He's cool and charming and a part of Troublesome Creek.

"You know I can't go down there and get that out of the impound, don't you? It will start World War III between me and Johnny. He'll know it was one of my family who shot at the house." He's mad. I can see it in his dark eyes while he growls at me. I sniffle and start to cry.

"Don't you think he knows? They'll run the tags."

"Ain't got no tags on it. I rebuilt the whole thing from scratch. I ain't got a serial number. If I go down there, the cops will think I stole the parts and I ain't got no receipts. Johnny, he'll think I'm posturing."

"I'll go. I'm so sorry, Daddy. I'll talk to him—"

"Oh, no you won't. That's even worse. He'll think I sent you, like I'm too much of a coward to do it myself!"

Chapter 6

It's seven-fifteen in the evening and almost two hours earlier than I usually leave my daddy's on Sunday. But it is quiet now, like a funeral after my epic failure. I decided I couldn't take the humiliation of all my daddy's family giving me sad, doleful eyes like somebody died. I figured I could sneak out the back door of the kitchen without anybody noticing. I was wrong.

"So did Jack Barkley get ahold of you about the job?" My back is to him and I'm one step away from my car. The hardest thing about being so perceptive about other people's behavior is I know when they are hiding being angry or—in my daddy's case, disappointed. I see it in his forced smile, the way the corners of his lips are pushed upward too tightly. He blinks a lot. I wiggle the lanyard holding my house key and my car key.

"Yeah."

It's just like my daddy to say nothing about something important until three minutes before I leave. It's his M.O. I suppose that's where I get my phobia of confrontations, his genes. Once when I was thirteen, he told me he was getting married in a week to a lady he met at a bar. It was five minutes before Mama picked me up. I remember standing there, blinking up at him. Now, I'm staring at his arms with coal black hair that he's rubbing with his hand up and down. It's a good sign he's been putting off saying this because he thinks there might be some reason I didn't tell him in the first place; either I didn't tell my mom or I'm hiding something from him.

I don't say anything for the count of ten. I'm thinking of going into another round of sorries, but I know I'll start crying again. Instead, I scratch a mosquito bite on my bare shoulder and cringe.

"Your mama don't approve." He doesn't step lightly, like he already knows the answer.

"No, daddy, she doesn't. It doesn't matter. I'm not good at anything. I'd probably screw it up too."

"That's not true. You are good at a lot of things, baby girl." He forces a sad grin. "Just maybe not driving an ATV."

I grunt, roll my eyes. "How can you joke about that?"

"Too soon?"

"Yes. And no, Daddy, I'm not. I couldn't even get the teaching position over Meghan Wilder who didn't even finish her teaching degree yet." I sigh. "I have a degree. They are letting her take online classes while she teaches. I'm stuck in the library and the only people there are the kids skipping class. The staff make me do all the dumb jobs nobody else wants. I even had to get my notary so I can sign the stupid legal documents at the school. Nobody else wanted it because Principal Cunningham waits until three-thirty and he's walking out the door to dump anything like that in someone's lap. I can't even write a book. I'm two sentences in and my mind goes blank."

"What kind of book are you writing?"

"That's just it. I don't know. I try to write something girly-girl and it's stupid. I try to write—"

"Write about what you know," he grunts. "You know girly girl stuff? I'm not sure girly-girl is what you're all about. You're smart. Write something smart." He stands there as I stare at the outline of his face. I suppose he's probably the last person who would understand my woes, considering he's never even left Laurel Grove in his life, never went to college, never kept a job more than a couple years. He knows it. I know it. We just don't say it. Sometimes when I'm deep in a conversation, he looks a bit glaze-eyed. I get mad because I don't think he's listening. He puts up a hand, saying something like: *sweety, you got to dumb it down for your daddy. I'm just a stupid, ol' hick.* And I feel bad because I make the only person who has my back one-hundred percent feel like he's stupid.

He's tan and has tiny freckles all over his face. His hair is still dark brown and his eyes have laugh crinkles at the corner. I try to imagine he isn't my daddy to see if he is really as handsome as Mom says he is. He just looks like Daddy and he looks like me in the same way Nicky looks like Mom. "You're good at everything you do." He flicks a fly away. "Write about stuff you know," my own personal daddy-cheerleader tells me. "Will you think about the job for me?"

"Can I ask why you're so interested?"

"I just hate seeing you always getting overlooked at that stupid high school." Daddy gets this long look and turns his attention over my shoulder. "I can't give you much, never could," Daddy says softly. He reaches into his pocket and tugs out a little silver chain necklace. He lets it dangle in his work-calloused fingers between us until I take it. I can see from the sadness in his eyes, the necklace means a lot more than money to him.

"What's this?" I ask him. I push up my glasses, study the necklace. It isn't an expensive one, just a silver chain with a little B and two different size keys hanging on it. One looks like it is an old skeleton key. The other looks like the key to a little jewelry box I used to have.

"I found that in a drawer. It was your Aunt Roo's. She hardly ever took the thing off. I remembered it. Don't know why she didn't have it on the day she disappeared. She was wild, but when you was her friend, she'd walk through fire for you. And she had lots of friends. I don't know where she got it. Not even sure what the B stands for. I just figured she'd want you to have it because she liked it so much and you're her mirror image. You remind me so much of her, you know that right? You look like her. You act like her, all smart and pretty and ready to take on the world. You got the same kind of softness that bubbles over to mean and stubborn just like her—"

"I'm not mean and stubborn, Daddy. I'm backwards, that's what my sister says." I unclip the chain and slip it around my neck before I wiggle the clasp on. "But you didn't answer my question. Why do you want me to work for Mister Barkley?"

I let it fall to my chest and pat it. Aunt Roo. Her real name was Rosaline, just like me, but when Daddy was little, he couldn't pronounce her whole name, such, Roo. She was my daddy's sister and was two years older than him. In 1978, she was seventeen. Daddy said he just remembered her blow drying her hair when he ran past the bathroom door that morning she vanished. She had on brown corduroy overalls and a t-shirt. She screamed at him because he'd peed on the toilet seat. During breakfast, she walked out the front door and nobody ever saw her again. She just—disappeared.

"We was just talking." He looks at me long and hard. "Working at the country club would be better than sitting in a boring library. You could meet folks your age. I always look at you and I think maybe you're a bit like your Aunt Roo. She always liked an adventure, even if it did land her in trouble most of the time."

"Tell me something else about her, Daddy," I beg him, trying to change the subject.

He just shakes his head. "I don't know, Rosie. It hurts to say stuff about her." He smiles softly. "Especially when I look at you and it's like she's standing right here in front of me."

"Just one thing."

"Okay." Daddy sniffs and runs a knuckle under his nose, then he leans back and folds his arms across his chest. "She liked them shark horror movies and she carried around a little plastic shark in her pocket that squeaked. I told her I won it for her at the county fair. I didn't, really. I won it and I was so damn proud of that thing that night. I was walking around, scaring the girls with it at the fair and feeling a bit high about it. She was with a bunch of her girlfriends and I passed her and those girls was so pretty, I just got stupid all of a sudden and gave it to her, like I'd won it just for her. She really thought I did and all her friends were patting my head and saying how cute I was. It was worth it."

"I bet she liked it, like the things you give me. They make me feel special." I scrub my nose with my palm, something I can't do with Mom around. Daddy doesn't even seem to notice. "Like the ice scraper for my windshield you got at the flea market. I think of you every time I use it." He interrupts, "I'm going to find you a pistol at the flea market. Will you carry it with you, if I do? And make somebody walk you to your car if you leave your school after dark, stuff like that? They never found Aunt Roo, not even a body. Then these two girls come up missing. I can't help—" He stops, rubs the late afternoon stubble on his cheeks.

"I know. Okay, Daddy," I affirm. I do know. It's his way of telling me he loves me, even if I just cost him twelve-thousand dollars for an ATV. It doesn't come easy for him. I know it rattled everybody on Mom's side of the family when I was two weeks old and he knocked on my grandma's door where Mom was staying with me. He'd gotten a job at the

Tilton Gas and Pump and hired a lawyer; said he was asking for permission to help raise me, but he'd play hardball if he needed to so he could be a part of my life. Mom doesn't say it, but I know up until that point, she was just going to say I belonged to her ex-husband, as to not cause a scandal. So it was a bit of a battle for him. There were times when I was a teenager, I thought the only reason he claimed me was because he liked the competition with my mom, liked to give her pokes now and then to make her sweat. But I still remember him tucking me into the cleft between ribs and elbow and reading me stories about princesses on Friday and Saturday nights and buying me the dollar store tiaras to wear while he read. I adored him, still do. And I remember the sad-puppy gaze he'd give me when he had to take me back to Mom's on Sunday morning before Sunday school.

"Tell me one more thing about her, Daddy."

He heaves a big sigh. "I guess I can do one better." He wheels around, walks to his garage, a rickety white building filled with boxes and crates, a mattress or two, and now an empty space where his ATV had set. He returns with a small, square trunk in his arms. It is decorated in old fashion magazine cut outs with girls wearing 1970s clothing. There's a cut-out piece of an old sign on the top that has white writing added in an unfamiliar hand: POSTED NO TRESPASSING. He doesn't set the trunk down, just nods his head toward my car.

"Rosie, I was cleaning out the garage the other day and ran across this," he explains as we walk out to my car. He kicks the back of my car with his muddy boot, so I'll open the trunk. "I was going to toss it, then couldn't. I thought you might want it."

"What is it?" I'm jamming my key into the trunk lock and turning it. The trunk lid pops open and he grunts when he leans to place it inside.

"It's something else of your Aunt Roo's. Maybe you can take a look and get to know her better." He looks up at the house cautiously and my eyes follow. No one is there. He uses his palm to lower the lid. "I didn't think it was for my eyes, being a man and all. My mama and daddy must have kept her trunk; stored it, just like all her stuff. I think for a long time, they thought she'd just show up out of the blue, just as strange as she left." He swallows hard. "She used to keep all her stuff in it. It was way in the back of the old shed, had a bunch of your mamaw's sewing stuff on it. Maybe you can go through Aunt Roo's stuff. I couldn't."

"It clearly states *no trespassing,*" I laugh softly and point to the scrawled words in indelible ink on the top of the chest just as it disappears into the shadows of the trunk lid when Daddy closes it with an abrupt shove of his hand.

"Yeah, well, I think it has her diary and personal stuff, sweetie." Daddy leans over and gives me a peck on the forehead. Then he chucks me on the arm. "You got somebody that can carry that into your house for you?"

"I do." I don't. I puppy-punch him gently on the arm back and it is always awkward for me when I leave because Daddy always just stands there quietly and stares at me with sad eyes. It's like the birds stop chirping happily and the sun is getting ready to set. The house looks lonely and vacant, even if there's a whole houseful of people left. I guess it doesn't take a genius to figure out the reason. I would suppose it's because he sees Aunt Roo in me and maybe, I'm going to drive off and he'll never see me again too.

"Olive Bluff," Daddy says, like he always does as I get in my car and roll down the window.

I smile. It's our secret code. Daddy knew I liked

puzzles when I was little, so he showed me how to make a reverse alphabet code. He had me write down all the letters of the alphabet in pink on top. Then directly underneath the letters, I wrote the alphabet backwards in green. I LOVE YOU spelled using the top pink letters is OLEV BLF using the green beneath.

"Olive Bluff." I return before I drive off. I watch him stare at my car until he disappears from my rearview. I wonder how long he stands there, staring at the vacant road and the settling dust after I'm gone.

I can't sleep. I had a bad dream. It seems a few times a month, I get this same ugly nightmare. I can't breathe. There's the scent of dead things, like a deer on the hot August highway. And I'm running fast and blindly because I suddenly cannot see. I wake myself up with closed-mouth screaming, a muffled and drawn out wail. To make matters worse, I'm haunted by the sad look in my daddy's eyes. I get up from bed and lug the trunk in from my car. I figured I'd have to twist the lock open with a hammer. But just when I'm about to wiggle the claw end between the clasps, I pat the keys on Aunt Roo's necklace. The old skeleton key opens the lock. I kneel down next to it at the end of my bed so the top is even with my waist. My floor is wood and I've got three or four little pale blue shag carpets tossed around. One of these, I use to kneel on.

The trunk is crafted in decoupage—countless 1970s pictures of girls in bellbottoms and wispy dresses, overalls and roller-skates. Aunt Roo must have cut them out of teen magazines, glued each to the surface, and then covered the trunk in a light varnish. They are all smiling, young, and full of life. I struggle with the strange sensation my aunt had been the same age as these cut-out girls when she disappeared, probably died.

I flip the little latch and wiggle my fingernails under the lid, lift it up. It opens with the sucking sound of a plastic food container long left in the refrigerator. It has the same kind of muggy odor of a fusty old washcloth, tossed under the sink and forgotten. I wrinkle my nose, peer inside. Three magazines are carefully stacked at the bottom. There's a little ballerina jewelry box. When I open it, there's a ring inside with an oval stone. I take it out, slip it on my forefinger. Ah, a mood ring. It has picked up my mood with incredible accuracy—black.

I sigh and poke aside a glasses case and expose a little round pillow with a smiley face, and a leather bracelet with a snap and DIES IRAE hand tooled on it. There's a pair of carefully folded short-shorts, a peach-colored puka shell necklace, and three pale troll dolls with orange hair. There's some pieces of lined school paper folded to palm-size rectangles, hundreds of little notes with flowers and hearts and tic-tac-toes. There's a magic 8-ball that I shake. It says: Try Again Later. I see lilac eye shadow and a pair of worn, white leather roller skates, and a suede purse made with four thick rows of deep red and sky blue leather.

And then, there's a small baby blue book just a bit bigger than my palm. I pull it out, see the little clasp and lock on the side. The second key on my necklace opens the book. I tug it open, recognize it as Aunt Roo's diary. I turn to the first page and it says:

August 14th, 1977

To Whom it May Concern:

My name is Rosaline Dianne McGuire. I am 15 and almost 16. I live in a white house at 101056 Troublesome Creek Road, Laurel Grove, Ohio, United States of America. Earth. I have five brothers—Billy, Junior, Kelsey, Ronny, and Ray and three sisters—Linda, Kay, and Rita. I like collecting troll dolls, reading magazines, and playing softball. I also like Barry Metzger (hee hee) who is in my

fifth period class. I hate math and my math teacher, Mister Simms. That's all. What more can I say? I'm done. I'm finished— I wonder what's inside a magic 8-ball.

I stop there. I feel almost ashamed like at any moment, Aunt Roo is going to come clambering through my bedroom door and shame me because I've pried into someplace where deep secrets were kept. I sigh, flip through to the very last page that has writing.

May 19, 1978

I don't know where it all started going wrong. Nobody listens to me. They act like I'm crazy. I just want to die. I don't want to go to the doctor.

It stops there. I'm mesmerized, I can see the blue ink of the pen is smeared. I roll my index finger across the page. I wonder if the smudged ink is from teardrops. What happened? I know it was sometime in May when she disappeared. I skip back a few pages.

Paul came over to listen to music. We made out. The only reason I did it was to make B mad. He says I'm too good for such an idiot. My favorite song is Roll with the changes by REO Speedwagon. Dad and I got in a fight at supper. I asked if he'd pass the mashed potatoes and he told me he wouldn't until I said Please. I hate him sometimes.

B. I clutch the necklace to my chest. Who is B? I don't see any more mention of him. I sift through the diary, back and forth for twenty minutes, couldn't find any reason things went so bad for Aunt Roo. Was she sick? Each carefully marked date was all just simple remarks and observations about her day to day activities.

This place is the most boring on earth. Today I had to wash clothes. Walked to town. Got a green Popsicle. Walked back. I wish I had a unicorn.

I'm not even sure why I'm digging in there. It's almost creepy, like I'm peering into a bathroom window while someone takes a shower. It's so personal, private. Am I looking for clues to her disappearance? Because if no one has found her by now, I doubt we ever will. Then I wonder if they ever found Gina Lee Channel, who came up missing after my aunt. I drop the diary, snatch up my computer and begin the search. There's three or four newspaper articles, but none stating she ever showed back up.

I look up, hearing a noise, and see Mister Baby Cakes staring down at me from the bed. "Hey, Baby Cakes." He's the king there and I am merely his jester, entertaining him once in a while with a gentle pat on the head or a scratch under his chin. I honestly don't know what I'd do without him. He's been with me through good times and bad, two stepdads, getting bullied in high school, and six schools I've gotten turned down for teaching positions. And he's here now while I bask in another evening alone, or I suppose not alone because I've got him.

Then the landline phone rings. It is loud in the stale air. I jump and feel goosepimples rolling up my arm and shivers racking my body.

"Is this Rosaline McGuire?" A croaky, old voice asks on the other end while I scrub away the goosepimples with my palm. It's a private caller. I can't tell if it is a man or woman. The voice is low and gruff.

"Excuse me? Um, no, this is Rosaline. But my last name isn't McGuire." I am absently rubbing my arms and wondering why I divulged that information. My sister is right when she says I got a whole lot of brains and that doesn't leave much room for common sense. There's a long pause of complete silence, then: "Can you keep a secret, Rosaline with the last name that isn't McGuire?"

"A secret? What do you mean?" Silence. So I answer what I think they want to hear. "Yes, I can keep a secret." My heart is racing. The voice is hoarse, strange and choppy like whoever is speaking is having a hard time spitting out the words.

"I know who killed those girls."

My face blanches. Okay, maybe this is a practical joke by one of the students from the high school. Even wishing that, my heart doesn't stop its drum-like pounding. "Why—why are you telling me this?"

There's a creepy huffed laugh. "Because I know your secret. Now you know mine."

"My secret—?" I ask. Then whoever called hangs up.

The phone rings again not two seconds after. I nearly jump out of my skin. I let it ring and ring. I finally pick up on the third round and jerk it to my face.

"What?" My breath is huffy. "What do you want?"

"Rosie, are you alright?" The voice is deep. It's Rocky.

"Yes."

"Your mom and your sister have been trying to call you. They figured you weren't picking up because you saw their number. Nicky suggested I try to call you."

"What did they want? It's two in the morning."

"They've been trying to get you since seven this evening. I didn't know until I got home from Uncle Johnny's. They are freaking out because you had a nosebleed. Then I started getting worried because of your dad's ATV. Your nose didn't start bleeding again, did it?"

"No. I'm fine. I was here. I didn't hear the phone ring."

"You sure you're all right? You sound... odd." He draws the last part out. "They took your dad's ATV. They didn't know whose it was and they put it in the impound. Timmy Kinney was ticked off and prancing around like a buck deer in rut. I'd let things simmer down before—"

"Rocky, I'm not discussing this with you. Goodnight."

"Don't hang up. Please."

It's like he's holding his breath. I have my finger on the little red button to end the call. "What, Rocky?"

"We're not so different, you and me. You know that, right?"

I sniff a caustic laugh. "Yeah, the girl they call Weird Wosie and who can't even fit in with her own family does not have anything in common with the guy who is probably first in line to be the chief firefighter in any state, if he simply fills out an application."

"You—you believe I could do that, really?"

"Rocky, please don't be an idiot to try to make me feel better." I hate when he's nice, because he thinks I'm going to cry. "It confuses what little common sense I have. But Y-E-S," I enunciate each letter clearly. "If I have to spell it out for you. I'm fine. Somebody made a prank phone call. It just scared me. Just tell Mom and Nicky I'm fine, I had the phone turned off or something."

"A prank call?" he asks me, suddenly sounding not so

tired. "Like the kind they ask you if your refrigerator is running and you better go catch it, or the kind that says I'm a crazy clown looking in your window. I'm going to eat you."

I peer toward my window. Shit, I hadn't thought about the curtains being open. Somebody's probably watching me right now. "Rocky, don't. You're scaring me."

"Is that the kind you got, the scary kind?" he grills me. "It's probably some goofy kid from school. Your number's listed online and in the phonebook."

"How do you know that?"

"I don't know. I just do."

"Was it you calling? Are you a creepy killer clown?" I slide down the wall, peer at the window, and wonder how I can make it across the room and dim my lights. I'm scared.

"No. But I'm coming over and sitting in your driveway until morning."

Rocky really does pull into my driveway ten minutes later. He calls me, tells me he's there. It's peculiar our situation, bound by my sister. In the fifteen or so odd years he's been close friends with her, we've hardly surpassed polite chit-chat when Mom's around and something akin to sibling rivalry when we're alone. I don't know why, out of the hundreds of guys that went to Laurel Grove High School and who weren't related to Johnny McDaniel and my dad's sworn enemy, she chose him to be best friends. I know Mom and Nicky use him way too much doing stuff they don't want to do, like making sure a killer clown isn't hovering around my front door or cutting my lawn when my mower breaks down.

We don't really talk in public; that might overstep certain warring country boundaries between his uncle and my daddy. Like him sitting in the driveway and not coming into my house and flopping on the couch. And me peering out the curtain and feeling safe, seeing him making a sloppy job of trying to get comfortable behind the steering wheel.

Safe. I can't sleep. So I pull out my phone, flop on the bed, and text Rocky:

Hey, Rocky, do you remember catching frogs in the pond at Laurel G. Park?

He doesn't answer for about twenty seconds. I think he's asleep. Still, I stare the phone, hoping he's not.

Then this comes in: *Yeah, goofy, I showed you how to put them on their back and make them sing.*

You showed me how to skip a rock 2. You don't have to b here. I know you no like.

Do you feel safe?

Yes.

Then I like.

I stare at the last message a long time. Then I write: *I like you, Rocky. I don't care what my daddy says.*

What does your daddy say?

I don't know how to answer him. My daddy tells me that Rocky and his family are good for nothing. They are poor white trash and trouble. I don't need to answer though. I suppose my long lull explains it because he answers before I do:

It's ok. I like you too. You're smart. Maybe I can show you how to ride ATV good and you can help me study for fireman test.

I can ride ATV just fine.

He doesn't answer. I wait and wait; I don't notice when my eyes close and I fall to sleep.

Chapter 7

Laurel Grove High School is an ancient, two-story brick building, about a hundred years old. It is filled with dank hallways with linoleum floors, yellow rooms, and gray metal lockers. It has a certain scent, not unlike the smell of a kitchen cabinet sink with a leaky pipe, old damp dishrags tossed in a bucket, and dry erase markers. In 2007, the school was set to be demolished, along with its ancient furnace, leaky roof, and rusted water pipes. The students would be bussed to the new county high school. It didn't happen. Instead it became Laurel Grove Village Exempted High School. Too many parents had too many memories of going to the school. So instead of demolishing the building, the state allowed the town of Laurel Grove to keep their school as long as the town funded the maintenance of the building.

I suppose having an old school was a bit of luck for me. It meant that Laurel Grove actually still had a spacious library, with a carpeted floor and shelves filled with books, instead of just a bare room with little more than tables with computers like the new county high school. The downside of the cozy atmosphere is that a handful of the teachers use the room for a coffee break mid-morning.

This morning, it is Tangy Cunningham and Mariah Patterson settled into a couple beanbag chairs near a large bay window, overlooking the back of the school and the baseball fields. They are utilizing the special breaks from the classroom they get during lunchtime. The two are sipping hot teas out of Styrofoam cups and pretending to go over teaching notes. They're not, I note while I absently tap my finger on the lone book I'd pulled from the return box that sits outside the library doors that the students can use to drop books off before classes start. Instead, bleach-blonde, big-eyed, perfect-complexioned Tangy is four minutes into a bitch session that bubbled up from a short notation that Kendal Murphy had taken one of her bottled waters from the teacher's lounge refrigerator. The one sentence: *Kendal stole a water from me* exploded into a lengthy conversation criticizing the man for every point possible.

"—he's always, like, staring at my boobs," Tangy is whispering behind a cupped palm to Mariah. I personally don't know why he'd stare at her boobs. Yes, they are big—however, they are long, saggy, and dangle like cow's teats almost to her naval. I can only assume Kendal is trying to figure out how Tangy doesn't fall face first with every step she makes with those butt-ugly boobs putting so much weight on her chest. Tangy has the brown-orange tanning bed tan and teaches advanced placement math.

Mariah is her mirror image with a size larger boobs (believe it or not), and a size larger butt, who teaches advanced placement English. Both have manicured nails, last year's style khakis and blouses, and the kind of short haircuts that only churchy women over sixty wear. "He's *so* gross," Tangy goes on. "How do you get hired on as a science teacher and be so creepy? He weighs like three-hundred pounds and smells like cat poop."

"Cat poop. That's funny," Mariah hisses while I gently readjust my flowered knee-length dress. "God. He's as bad as—"

I think they are just mean. Kendall Murphy doesn't smell like cat poop at all. And he got hired because he's really good at coming up with ideas to make science fun for the students, which is more than I can say for Mariah or Tangy. They are both Laurel Grove alumni and Tangy

Cunningham is the daughter of the high school principal.

"Are you eavesdropping?"

I don't realize I'm staring at them from over top my computer. I am eavesdropping, but not necessarily on purpose. I know my eyes get wide behind my huge glasses when Mariah's squeaky voice ripples across the room. I duck down enough only my glasses and forehead show up over the screen. Then, I drop my gaze back to my computer where I am actually snooping around.

My mom's husband, Bobby, worked for the police department. He hooked my sister up with access to the criminal database, so she could check any would-be boyfriends for potential sex-offender risks. Of course, when he handed Nicolette the little card with all the background check information on it at the dinner table, I saw him look up at me with an embarrassed intake of breath at his blunder. He made an awkward slip of hand into his pocket, said that he'd thought he'd brought two, and must have lost mine. Fibber. I don't think he'd even prepared to give his backward, invisible step-daughter the information. Not that he didn't love me. He just didn't think I'd ever find a boy that would like me, not even a sex offender. Nicolette had laughed, though, tossed the card over to me and said she'd known Rocky all her life and that's who it appeared she was stuck with for eternity. If there was something weird about him, she already knew what it was.

"Hello, Weird Wosie, are you in there?" Mariah asks of me in a baby voice, with her lips pursed and her head wagging back and forth.

"Or are you too busy *weading* your book up there?" Tangy giggles. Weird Wosie. Tangy gave me that nickname my freshman year, when my English teacher made me come up and sit in the front of the room because I couldn't see the writing on the dry erase board. She whispered it each step I took. I was mortified. Everybody laughed. It stuck like glue.

I let my eyes drop to where my finger is still tapping. Book? What book? Oh, *Winsome Falls*. It looks like a goofy love story. I'm not into love stories. I'm more a non-fiction, scientific read sort of person. I'll fall asleep reading *Romeo and Juliet* in six seconds flat. Give me The *Forensic Science Primer* and I'm biting nails in excitement at five-thirty in the morning to get it finished before I have to get ready for work. It embarrasses me they think I'm reading a romance because well, I don't have any in my life. I give it a quick shove with my fingers away.

"No, it's not mine," I mumble and shake my head, push the glasses up the bridge of my nose. "I mean, yes, I could hear you. No, I wasn't eavesdropping. I was just— thinking."

I'm not really thinking. I'm looking at Angel Daugherty's criminal record. It appears the cat-loving, bookworm home healthcare aide had a wild side. She'd been arrested twice at the Crazy Fiddle Country Tavern six miles outside of Laurel Grove for drunk and disorderly. She had seven unpaid speeding tickets and did a three day jail stint after hitting a cop with her purse at a wedding. None of this was ever printed in the newspaper after she died. I speculate sex might have been the motive—she'd flirted with the wrong horny cowboy. Or she bought insurance at the same agency as my mom. Ted Winters as a suspect has still not left my mind. I make a note to myself to find out if the insurance-selling couple visited the local bars.

"God, you're really weird." Mariah huffs. "You should marry that creep. Kendal. You're the perfect match with your beady eyes and those stupid pink glasses. You'd have the most freaking creepy kids ever."

"Well, actually, we're not the perfect match," I point out softly and stop myself from pushing up the glasses along the bridge of my nose. "According to some scientific studies, attraction is based on behavior and hormonal responses, and how our personalities react to these factors. Kendall is imaginative, cautious, and calm. I am logical and impulsive. We conflict."

The two just stare at me, unblinking. Finally, Tangy turns her head slowly and opens her eyes wide at Mariah and they both burst out laughing. My face turns crimson. I hear muffled laughter from the back of the library, a few students who are supposed to be studying are actually playing video games. Tangy's head makes a sharp snap to her right. I don't think she knew we weren't the only ones in the room within earshot.

One of the students is Rocky's cousin and Johnny McDaniel's son, Colton. He should be sitting with me working on his reading, which is at an eighth grade level and not an eleventh grade level. He's not. Colton McDaniel always does the opposite of what I ask him to do, then stares at me with these quarrelsome, I-dare-you-to-make-me-bitch, eyes. I have learned to ask him to do the opposite of what I want him to do like fifteen minutes ago when I asked him to sit with me and go over his homework. Instead, he snatched his phone out of his back pocket and swaggered off to the back of the library; it is exactly what I wanted him to do. He annoys me.

Like now, I can see his thick, more-blonde-than-red hair bobbing in and out of my view once in a while. He's playing games on his phone and entertaining two girls with funny videos of cats. Then sometimes, he leans out to see if I'm looking. If I am, I get an eyeful of his skinny freckled face before he mouths something I think is *biiii-tch* all drawn out with the last half said aloud echoing in the room.

One of my jobs is to work with the lowest level of what the school calls, *At Risk Students*. These are the kids who are one step away from being in prison, have been in prison, or are simply so disruptive in class, the principal doesn't know what to do with them. Just like I'm in the lower ranking of the school system, these kids who are dropped in my lap are what Principal Cunningham, in the confines of the teacher breakroom, calls *the bottom of the barrel.*

Colton would be considered the actual bottom of the barrel. However, one of the two girls beside him is quite the opposite in the school system's eyes. To the unexperienced and naïve school authorities, Mindy Carter appears to be the classic hipster-geek—drab brown hair that's always a bit oily and covered with a slouchy hat, unbuttoned red flannel shirt over a blank t-shirt, capris, and big, fake glasses. She has double-income parents, her family is well-established in the community, and by all intents and purposes, she is an A student and is expected to thrive in college and life.

However, to those of us who can see past the image she portrays, Mindy Carter is heading down a dark path because she isn't getting enough stimulus with her schoolwork. She smokes joints behind the school and out at Colton's truck. She spends most of her classroom time on her phone and is probably texting some middle-aged man who she thinks is a seventeen year-old boy. And sometimes, she copies the answers out of the backs of books just so she doesn't have to actually go through the steps to get the answer to a difficult problem. Is she *my* problem? Nope. She is my sister's riddle to solve. Nicky co-heads the counseling department at the high school along with Doctor Stamper. Both only see what they are allowed to see, a facade that is handed to them by those higher up on the school board.

I sigh, look down to my computer again. The business card belonging to Jack Barkley is laying between my computer keyboard and monitor. Normally, I would have tossed the card. I suppose, up until I lost my daddy's ATV, I was used to being who I am. I'm comfortable in my sister's hand-me-down pumps, thick granny sweaters, and knee-length skirts at school. But the moment I laid down in bed that night and my mind started sucking up the horrible events of the day, I realized I was as close to rock bottom as I could get. So I'd sat up in bed, worked the card from my pocket and held on to it like it was some lifejacket that could, at least, keep me afloat. I'd stuffed it in my pocket this morning and then laid it on my desk to stare at all day. Now, I pick up the business card, twirl it around in my fingers.

Then my eyes flow a little lower to something scratched into my desk. It is fresh. It says: I'M WATCHING YOU. I know who did this. I'd stopped at the school on my way home from Daddy's last night, so I could pout a little in the darkness of my library. *My* library. I thought I'd circumnavigated the cleaning staff, and one plump and sassy Leah McDaniel who is Colton's five feet and eight inch carnivorous Tasmanian devil sister and on the nightly cleaning staff. I did not. They had come in on Sunday night to do the atypical polishing of the gymnasium floors.

"This is a bunch of shit."

I jump, a bit rattled that I'd shifted into a daze, rolling the little business card in my fingers. Right now, Tangy Cunningham is hovering over Colton McDaniel with his phone in her hand. I suppose she's mad because he overheard all the bitching she was doing with Mariah.

"What's the matter, Colton?" I ask flatly, looking back and forth between the two. Let's see, who am I more afraid of—Colton or Tangy?

"Miss Cunningham just took my phone."

"You're supposed to be studying in here, not playing with your phone. You know the rules. No phones during classroom time. You'll get it back at the end of the term in a month," Tangy says with a head waggle. She looks up at me. "And you're supposed to be babysitting him."

I can see Colton gritting his teeth. His jaws are working back and forth. Oh yeah, he's the scarier of the two. Tangy might attack me verbally, but Colton's probably got a shotgun hanging in the rear window of his truck. "Tangy, he's supposed to be looking at his phone," I lie. My stomach jumps and quakes. I hate confrontations. "He's working on an assignment for me."

"On cats running into walls?" she hisses. As she sees it, I'm supposed to be on her side.

"Yes, please give him the phone. The cat videos have titles. He's supposed to read the titles."

She's not going to call me a liar in front of the seven or eight sets of eyes staring at us. I push my glasses up on my nose and beg my eyes not to turn away. Instead, Tangy sails around Colton and drops the phone on my desk near my elbow. "And this is why your job position is getting terminated." She leans in, whispers with a snotty waggle of her shoulders. "This is why you don't teach here. You have to *cover* the other teacher's backs. You don't side with the students." Tangy pokes the desk in front of me. "I hate to bust your bubble, but when the cutbacks came up at the dining room table, I was first to raise my hand and tell my father which positions I thought were as useless as those who held them. So what do you say to that?"

"Burst," I reply.

"What?" she snaps, pulling back in surprise.

"It's *burst* your bubble, not *bust* your bubble," I correct her. "It comes from blowing bubbles and popping them. Once you pop them, they are gone. So is the fun of watching them. Just like you assume I'm disappointed you sabotaged my job. But it doesn't matter anyway, my bubble isn't burst. I expect no less of you."

"Holy shit. Miss Mauer is feisty today!"

I could throttle Colton McDaniel. When I look up, I see him and every person in that library staring wide-eyed at me. I bite down on my lip. "You can't be out of here soon enough," Tangy hisses. I watch her waggle her hand at Mariah who rises. Both make an exit while I wiggle Colton's phone in the air. I watch him rise, saunter up to the desk.

"I don't owe you nothing," he informs me, snatching the phone from my hand. "You know that, right?"

I don't get to correct his improper English. Right then, Rocky McDaniel comes charging through the doors of the library, taking a half second to open them for Tangy and Mariah who bustle past him in a whirlwind. At first, when I see his hulking shadow on the glass partition between hallway and library, I think he's coming to yell at me about the ATV incident. I automatically sit erect.

"What's up with Tangy?" he asks as he stomps up to the desk, still following her shadow with a craned neck. "She looked mad." He turns his attention to me.

"I don't know," I lie, shrug my shoulders. "She's always uptight." He looks a bit uptight, too, at the moment.

Rocky returns my shrug. "I'm going to kill her."

"Tangy?" I ask. Rocky is drumming his fingers on my desk. I try not to stare at them. Even his hands are nice, with long fingers and enough callouses to show he works hard.

"No, my cousin. Did you see Leah put something in

my desk?"

I blink at him innocently. "No. She's gone when I get here in the morning." It's true. I avoid her at all costs. Back in school, I let her copy my homework from kindergarten and all the way through twelfth grade. That's where we should have parted ways forever. I went to college, Leah had Gabby and went to work. Not so. Now, I work in the school during the day, she is one of the dark creatures of the night on the janitorial staff, coming in after hours. For the most part, we don't come into contact. I take great strides to avoid her entirely.

"*You* didn't do it, right? Because the last time when I pulled down the projector screen in the front of the room, and there was a fake snake in it, she said you were the only one who was around before school."

"Rocky, no, I didn't do it." I'm shaking my head, putting on my wide, scared eyes. Rocky falls right into it.

"Nevermind." He holds out a hand like it is going to keep me from crying. "I know you wouldn't. It was a dumb idea believing Leah. Are you *sure* you didn't see her?" His face is red with anger. His jaws are working hard. "Because all my drawers to my desk are glued shut. They are completely glued tight. I can't open them."

"She must have been in a bad mood last night," I say. I have to hold back a smile. It took two bottles of Locked Tight Super Glue to glue his drawers shut. Through trial and error and over the course of many years of study, I figured out that the safest way to get back at Leah McDaniel for years of torture has been to play practical jokes on Rocky and persuade him that Leah is the one who is to blame. Then I manipulate Rocky into seeking justice by pranking his cousin. It is fun watching them deny the blame and play practical joke ping-pong back and forth. "She carved this in my desk." I poke my finger in the *I* of *I'm watching you*. "She scares me sometimes. Who does that kind of stuff?"

"Not normal people." Rocky waggles his head. "She's in for a big surprise, that's for damn sure," he tells me poking a finger on my desk. "I'm not letting this one go. It's something new every week and she denies it like I'm stupid or something." He starts to turn, puffs out his lips, then comes to a standstill. "By the way, they took your dad's ATV to the impound at the police station. Timmy Kinney said they aren't going to release it until someone admits they were trespassing."

"I'll just go down there and tell them the truth."

"You're kidding me, right? Then everybody will know I was helping you push it out," Rocky looks right to left. "And if you go down there, you'll get a fine and go to court. If you get in trouble, they are going to put you on administrative leave and you could lose your job. It's costing a few thousand to fix the electric you guys shot out. You could get jail time, you know that? Think it out, Rosie. Just let it go."

"I can't." I tell him. But he's probably right. I don't need jail time. I don't wait for his reply. Instead, I reach under my desk and pull out a book with a plain blue cover and EASY MATH FOR STUDENTS printed on the front. I designed it myself; it's a dummy cover. I hand it to Rocky.

"What's this?" he asks, turning it in his hands.

"It's the Crystal Springs Firefighters Study Guide, incognito, of course," I tell him with a slight smile and point to the cover. "Since you have experience with the Laurel Grove Fire Department, you qualify to test out of Crystal Spring's initial five week recruiting course where they weed out any persons they deem unqualified. If you pass the test with ninety percent or higher, they will train and send you through their full program for free. I laid out a study guideline for you based on a three month schedule. That's when the next test is scheduled."

"How did you get this information?" He's gingerly opening the book, rolling a finger along a page in the front. He's staring at it like it is Christmas morning and this is the gift he's been begging Santa for all year. I swear, for just a split second, his eyes have the subtle hint of a book nerd because there is a moment, I think he is going to sniff the pages, take in its essence so he can cherish the moment. Instead, Rocky looks right to left warily as if he is concerned we can be overheard.

"I picked up the phone and called the Crystal Springs Administration Department. Then I drove there and picked up the booklet. That's all it took," I tell him. "Take two days, read the first chapter. I'll quiz you on the third day."

I'm expecting him to ask me the reason I did it. He doesn't, just closes the book slowly and clasps it firmly in his hands. I think he's going to make some stupid joke and plop the book on my desk. He doesn't. This is a turning point for Rocky. He has the same panicky set to his eyes that my sister got the first time she rode a roller coaster. Then it suddenly drops from panic mode to surrender, just like Nicky's face did when she realized at the top of the first hill, just before the roller coaster careened down its first flight, that she was seat-belted in and she couldn't turn back.

"Okay. I'll start tonight. As soon as I get home." Rocky says, more to the floor than to me. I think, you know what? It's time for me to fly too. I pick up my cell phone and wait for him to take a few steps away. I type in the number for Jack Barkley with a text message that says: *Is the job position still open?* Even though, in my mind, I'm wondering if I need to be a loser at one more thing. Maybe I should just stick to what I'm good at already—being a wallflower.

Just as Rocky gets to the first set of bookshelves, I clear my throat. "Oh, by the way, about Leah. To get her back, you could fill her sweepers with that red sand from the baseball diamond and turn the hoses around so instead of pulling in the dirt, it blows it out. When she turns the sweepers on, she'll get a face full of sand."

"Good idea, Rosie," Rocky stops long enough to give me a thumbs up. "You're way too good at this."

Oh, if he only knew how good I was at this, he'd just die. He struts out of the room. I see him ten minutes later, filling up a garbage can with scoopfuls of sand he's digging up with a dustpan at the varsity baseball diamond. I smile to myself. And they think *I'm* the goofy one. I suppose I could say it is my way of keeping their curse from coming back.

It is only fourteen minutes later, I get a return text. It says: *Meeting tomorrow 10 am. Crystal Spring Private Country Club. 15503 Crystal Spring Road.*

Chapter 8

I slept in the next morning. It is a Tuesday. I called in sick. It is the first time I've ever missed a day of work at Laurel Grove High School. I should have been feeling incredibly guilty while I lay there, tucked beneath a cozy pink flowered comforter with fat Mister Baby Cakes lying on my belly. Instead, I'm feeling a bit antsy. I'm sure it isn't helping that I didn't take my prescription anxiety pills today. Or yesterday, I forgot. However, they make me a bit sick to my stomach and I certainly wouldn't want to throw up all over Mister Barkley at my interview.

I think I hear someone in the driveway. I get up, thinking it is my mom coming to check on me. It isn't. Instead, I discover a little package. Thirteen roses. They are baby blue and carefully wrapped in brown craft paper and twined with lacy, red ribbon. The bouquet of roses is sitting on my porch and I almost kick them stepping out of my door. I pick up the package and turn it over. There's no tag, no note. I spontaneously sabotage any idea that someone sweet left them for me. I'm not into weepie romantic gestures. Besides, I tend to think roses are incredibly overused as a way to display affection. Still, I sniff them and they smell sweet. I swallow back a smile. I call the local florist and tell Kayla Betts, who owns the shop and who is also in my mom's garden club, someone must have accidently dropped the flowers at my house. When Kayla asks me what my exact address is, I tell her. She says they haven't had a delivery anywhere near my house today.

"Are you sure?" I ask. "Because they have to be expensive. There are thirteen, and they are blue. I've never seen blue roses before."

There's a long hesitation and then a light chuckle on

the other end. "Hmm, you must have a secret admirer, Rosie," she says. "Thirteen roses means you have a secret admirer. Blue, that's not so good. I'm looking at my rose color chart as we speak, and it says that blue roses means it is for an impossible love, one that is unattainable."

Well, that solves that, then. Secret and unattainable. Thirteen blue roses is kind of a waste of time and money, isn't it? Why would someone send something like that? I don't say it, though. I just know nobody would spend that kind of money on me. It is either someone playing a joke on me, my sister trying to make me feel better with one of her endless remedies to my backwards behavior or— I just sigh. "Okay, thank you," I mumble. "If someone calls and wants them back, leave a message. I'll be gone for a while."

I leave at eight-thirty for the Crystal Spring Private Country Club. Of course, I make a short stop at the Laurel Grove Lake Park for my usual pep talk from the mosquitoes and crickets. It doesn't help. My tummy is as jiggly as my sister's soupy cherry Jell-O with pieces of pineapple bobbing inside that she makes for Sunday dinners. So I sit there and wiggle around, fidgeting and wanting to get this day over. I finally leave feeling, once again, like I'm missing something there. It only adds to my jitters.

It is a forty-five minute drive and I'm a half hour early. I keep checking my nose in the rearview mirror and poking a tissue underneath to make sure it doesn't start bleeding right in the middle of the interview. I think Doctor Stamper was right about what causes me to stress out. Mom and Nicky always seemed to be around when my nose starts bleeding. There, I sit in my little two-door, older model car and flip through my contacts on my cell phone, all six of them, which includes my daddy, my mom, Bobby, Nicolette,

Rocky, and now, Jack Barkley.

It isn't that I'm going to contact anyone. It's just something to do. If I look up at the building, built of timber so it is like a gargantuan lodge, my stomach starts to feel jumpy. Of course, I don't turn my car off because I'm afraid it won't start again. I can't call Rocky or Bobby. And I'm afraid to leave it on because sometimes, it overheats. I'd die if it started smoking holy hell in the parking lot of the country club and I had to get it towed away. I almost bolt. I know Mister Barkley knows I'm here because I had to check in at the security gate to get clearance. A clean-cut, buff security guard with NATHAN H. engraved on his name tag took one look at my 2002 compact car and I could see him cringe, ready to turn me away. He stops me, slips inside the gazebo-like building and I can see his mouth flapping for about three minutes before he comes back.

"Okay, help me out here. Mister Barkley just ripped me a new asshole because I didn't ask your name. He asked if you were the *eccentric one*. I'm not a rocket scientist. I don't know what that means. I'm assuming you are Rosie Mauer?" He sloughs it off with a red face as I nod.

"Eccentric means odd," I reveal with a shrug.

"Oh, okay." He looks relieved while he eyes me up and down. "Then he told me to send you to his office. Kim will meet you at the door."

"Who is Kim?" I almost whisper. He eyes me up and down with the same criticizing purse of lips my sister gives while she peers at the cat pan when she comes over. I look in the rearview mirror. Okay, my hair is mussed a bit. I've got it held back with a spare hair scrunchie, a few tendrils have slipped out of their hold. I'm wearing a sparse bit of makeup and my usual gray skirt and flowered blouse.

"Kim is Mister Barkley's assistant. Brown hair,

snooty attitude, but don't tell her I said that. You'll recognize her." I see his eyes roll right before he pats the back of my car like it's a horse that he's herding toward a stall.

My hands are shaking as I get out of my car and take the long walk up the landscaped path to the building. I'm wishing I'd taken my anxiety pill and I'm hoping I don't go into freak out mode. *Don't think about it,* I keep telling myself. *Don't think about it.* There's a second security checkpoint just inside the doorway where a younger woman with brunette hair pulled into a bun and wearing a perfectly pleated, white blouse and short-skirted uniform meets me.

"Miss Rosie," she greets me. "Welcome to Crystal Springs. Mister Barkley is waiting for you in his office. Follow me, please." She waves a hand. I follow her along shiny wooden floors lined with tan walls filled with pictures of personalities who have visited the golf course and facilities.

There are two men seated. I instantly recognize Mister Barkley. He is settled into a huge wooden desk with piles of papers sloppily splayed around a laptop computer.

"So you changed your mind," he says it like he expected me to eventually come around to his way of thinking. It's the same kind of attitude I got from my mom when I asked to go to a prestigious university in California to study forensic science but eventually settled on the small community college two towns away from home to get the general degree in education she suggested. "This is my son, Liam." Liam. Right, the one who my aunt said might be a suspect in a murder. Great. He does have that hottie, rich-boy murderer look indicative of every women's network horror movie on Saturday afternoons. Barring I have another suspect for my list, I'm not happy with this situation.

The younger man stares at me hard, almost looking disappointed before his expression drops to bored and detached. He's twenty-something and styled like a business magazine cover model, with bleached blonde hair and a shock of black along the sides, and a suit and tie. The one thing sticking out on him is uncompromising blue eyes while he slides deeper into his chair, brings a hand up to rub across the grizzled hair on his cheeks. He scoots up a little, rests elbows on knees, and slips his cell phone out of his pocket. Then, he starts tapping away.

"So, here's how it goes," Jack Barkley shoots his hand out, offers me the seat next to his son. I slide into the leather chair, watch as he sits down across from me. "My stepson needs an assistant, someone who can—"

"—babysit me," Liam grunts from his seat and doesn't look up. "Let's be honest, Jack, that's what you're looking for—a nanny for your twenty-one year-old stepson. You're lying to her. You've lied to all of them. That's why they don't stick around."

Jack Barkley looks at his stepson long and hard. I can read the expression easily. It's pretty simple; he's thinking there are a lot more reasons his nannies don't stick around. However, I clamp my mouth shut, imagining my mom's pursed-lip glare when I open my mouth and relate my opinionated opinions aloud. "Liam, I really don't need your input right now," Jack Barkley sighs. "We *both* know why they don't stick around."

"Then why'd you have me come to this meeting?" Liam sits up quickly, eyeing first the man at the desk, then me. "My honest opinion is this idea sucks. If you want to hire somebody for me, hire a bodyguard and not some weird *chick* who looks more like a stupid librarian than security."

"I *am* a librarian." I look at Mister Barkley and back to Liam again, confused. "I've never been a bodyguard."

"Really, Jack?" Liam laughs out loud, a long huff-huff that ends in a snicker and eye roll. "You've got to be kidding me."

"We want to keep this confidential, Liam." Jack Barkley closes his eyes for a long moment before opening them again. "If you are dragging around a team of bodyguards, you attract attention. The attorneys state that is the *last* thing we need right now, not only for the country club, but also for your well-being. Do you want to be a target for a crazy person?"

"Crazy person?" I interject. "There's someone stalking you?"

Liam swivels his head to look at me. "You don't know who I *am*?"

"I know you're Mister Barkley's son," I answer, but I don't outright divulge what I'd heard my Aunt Kay call him. I'll let him tell me. "Should I know more?"

"*Step*son. I'm Liam Dubois. Good God, you do read the newspapers, don't you?"

No, newspapers tend to be biased and only print what people want to hear. The only newspapers I've read recently are tacked up on my refrigerator or the obituary I found in my pocket on Angel Daugherty. So no, I haven't been keeping up with the newspapers. I shake my head, feel a burning on my cheeks. He draws his cell phone close, pokes it a couple times, and then shoves it under my nose. "Read."

I adjust my glasses, hesitantly take the phone in my still slightly shaking fingers, and drop my eyes to the copy of the Laurel Grove Tribune on the screen. There's an article in the center with the caption: *SECOND BODY DISCOVERED. FOUND ALONG RAILROAD TRACKS AT FEDERAL ROAD. Remains found in Stone Creek Hunting Area are believed to be those of missing college student, Alaina Faye Windowski, who disappeared ten months ago after leaving her job as a waitress at Crystal Springs Golf Course Dining Lodge. The death is being treated as a homicide after three bullet holes were found in the skull. Police say a resident discovered the decomposed body while hiking the public use land looking for a spot to set up a hunting blind. The body was found in a ditch less than twenty feet from Federal Road. Although the police have not identified the murderer, several persons of interest have been brought in for questioning—*

"I am the main suspect they are talking about in the newspaper." Liam rolls his eyes to the ceiling, looks at his stepdad, then back to me. "My stepfather is using you to infiltrate the ranks. He's hiring you to mix in with the other employees and then suck out information from them. He's hiring you to babysit me, be my alibi. I didn't kill her. He's trying to figure out who did, or at least hold my incarceration off until they find the real killer." Liam Dubois rubs a hand across his forehead. "I keep telling him he's barking up the wrong tree, trying to get idiots to perform the task of professionals. He can afford the best lawyers, the best detectives. You're a prime example of what he shouldn't be employing—ugly, stupid, uptight girls only hired because he knows I won't sleep with them."

"The article says they only have persons of interest—"

"Yeah, so what? I'm one of them."

"Persons of interest are just people the police are questioning that might know something. Suspects are those the police believe are involved in the crime."

"So?"

"So they don't list you as being a suspect—maybe they don't believe you did anything."

"I still don't get your point."

I chew on this a moment while Liam stands up and shoves his chair back. "I don't know how to make it any simpler," I say. "Do they have evidence against you?"

"I don't know. I'm done. I'm out of here," he snaps. "This is about as useless as hiring that bunch of private detectives who took the money and ran."

"I'm not stupid," I mutter as he has his back to me, walking to the door.

"Oh, sure," he sniffs a laugh.

"No," I retort, thinking out my words carefully. "And I'm thinking that if you get yourself into a situation where you are a suspect in a murder and you're not utilizing every tool available to prove the police are wrong, you're obviously not that clever at all. Or at least not as smart as me. Because I *do* see what your stepdad is doing."

He turns on his feet, narrowing his eyes until they are nothing but two tiny blue sparks of anger. "You're fired. The staff doesn't talk back to the owners of this establishment or call them idiots."

"I'm not staff. You can't fire me," I point out gruffly, swallowing hard. My heart is pumping. "I didn't say you were stupid, just not—perceptive. I compared your IQ to mine. Mine is about a 138, give or take." I don't tell people my true IQ which is 142. Nicky says it makes them feel stupid around me. "You're showing that you're perhaps in the 40 to 50 range by making such rash decisions based on appearance."

He stops, pivots on his feet and stares at me like he is trying to swallow the words I just said and they are pieces of spoiled meat. "I absolutely *hate* arrogant, smart women." His head is tipped slightly to one side. Then Liam grunts. "Listen, I'm just telling you that you're being hired with ulterior motives. It's probably better that you don't get involved. I'm bringing it out in the open." He turns to his father, throws his hands out. "Do I get a say? I don't want her. She's a freaking dork!"

I would ask myself why I took the job three minutes after Liam Dubois left the room. His father was pale when I turned back to him with the slamming of the door.

"I suppose I can guess your answer, Miss Rosie," he sighs as he pats his desk with his hand and starts to rise. "I should have hired another private detective. It was hard enough to hire a nanny when he was six. Now that he's twenty-one, it is ten times as bad because he can just walk away. If I hire a bodyguard, they just end up buddying up with him. I find out Liam's out at the bars all by himself because he's paid off a driver or a guard. And women? He's ended up sleeping with every one I've hired or he scares them off. It's difficult to find any that aren't afraid of him or who aren't—" He chuckles blandly. "I really feel someone on my staff knows something about Alaina Windowski. I know we can dig deeper and find a better suspect than Liam. They are either too afraid to tell the police or they are a part of whatever happened. I know my stepson didn't kill the girl." He stops, hard-sighs. "My Liam needs a babysitter, someone to follow him around and keep him out of trouble. I need someone to dig around and see what the staff knows. I just thought he wouldn't give me too much crap if you were cute."

I stand too. I'm trying hard not to tuck my chin. "What makes you so sure he didn't kill her?" I ask bluntly.

"I have my reasons." Jack Barkley comes around his

desk, pushes his hand up toward my shoulder steering me toward the door. "I thought we might be a match. My stepbrother told me you were offered some kind of a scholarship for forensic science in high school and your mother persuaded you to turn it down. You're a nice girl. You're smart. I'll give you an office, buy the computers, and pay you well. In return, you can babysit Liam for a few hours a night, be his alibi until the police figure out who killed those girls. What do you say?"

"Was your son abused as a child?" I ask.

"Excuse me?" Mister Barkley reaches up, adjusts his tie. "Well, um, he would say he was, but no. He had a pretty normal childhood."

"Is he anti-social, does he have any friends?"

"No and too many. He doesn't know an enemy. Except you because he feels threatened by your beauty and intelligence. Why do you ask?"

"I'm not pretty," I say honestly. "Please don't try to appease me with compliments. I am smart. I can figure that out. Regardless, I just read that there are twenty-five to fifty serial killers working at any given time. Is he a Taurus or a Sagittarius?"

"Excuse me?"

"Men born between April and May or November and December are more likely to be serial killers."

"His birthday is in late February."

"So, he's a Pisces, which is way down the list on the month of the year people are born who end up being murderers or serial killers. Is he manipulative?"

"He's lazy," Mister Barkley offers.

"Does he spend a lot of time looking at himself in the mirror?"

"He's more interested in looking at girls—"

"Does he lack empathy—?"

"Oh, dear, I don't know, why?"

"These are traits that show up in people who are the murdering type. I've been reading up on it." I sigh. He doesn't sound like somebody who would kill a bunch of girls. Mister Barkley is looking at me questioningly. "I already have a day job as a librarian in our high school. Your job offer sounds like a twenty-four hour a day deal."

"Not really. I've got others covering a lot of the bases. Of all the jobs in the world, why'd you end up taking a position as a librarian?"

"My mom pushed me into doing it." I smile. "I wanted to be a professional photographer for a while, then an artist. I can't take a picture that isn't fuzzy and I can't draw a smiley face. I wanted to be a writer and a police officer. My mom, she says those are fun things to do as hobbies. Police jobs are too dangerous. She suggested I can volunteer down at the police station, maybe file paperwork. She says I've got the wrong personality for all that anyway. I can make you a list of reasons—"

"—why your mother didn't want you to be something you wanted to be? Something safe for her? There's nothing wrong with a little adventure, a little danger that you can't get out of those rated G books in the school library." He pauses at his office door. There is a young woman already waiting to escort me out. "If you change your mind," Jack Barkley tells me. "I'm willing to help you prove your mother wrong." He gets a smile on his face. "Don't let Liam hurt your feelings. He was spoiled and angry at the world even before this happened with the Windowski girl. You know, if you just tweaked a few things, you could be quite pretty."

"Okay." That's what I say. It suddenly occurs to me I

will go to any length to make my daddy proud of me. If I make enough money to buy him a new ATV, then I can fix everything. Mister Barkley smiles, doesn't realize I'm taking the job. And although it may be hard to believe, I wouldn't mind being pretty. Perhaps, Mister Barkley knows how I can tweak a few things and be pretty.

"Thank you anyway, Miss Rosie." He starts to close the door. I put my hand out, stop it, press it open a few more inches.

"No, I meant okay, I'll take the position." Then I lean in, take in a breath. "He's right about me. I am uptight and I'm not very pretty. Do you really think you could—tweak me?"

Chapter 9

I'm standing in front of my car on Federal Road with my rear resting on the bumper. It's not a major roadway. However, it is a shortcut for locals not wanting to take the highway from Crystal Springs to Laurel Grove. I'd guess twenty or thirty cars drive through here on a normal day. In October, during deer hunting season, there's probably ten or more cruising through, heading for the state lands on either side. It's mostly ten year-old asphalt. However, there are a few spots where township maintenance crews have tried to pad places where old pipes had rusted away beneath the road and the asphalt has begun to sink. It's a pebble and tar mixture they use and it leaves a dingy spread of gravel.

Alaina Windowski's body was found along one of these pebble-tar patches about twelve steps from the road. There's a gravel pull off for hunters right before a slow moving creek. That's where I've stopped. I'm looking out over the small grassy meadow leading into a thick wall of pines, trying to get a feel for the area. It is remote, but not so much that it wouldn't be a careless gesture on the killer's behalf. I look behind me. There's a small hill. And in front of me, the road turns slightly. You can't see cars coming from either direction. On a windy day, you probably couldn't hear them either. Alaina's murderer was either arrogant or unthinking. Considering nobody saw the body being dumped, I'm assuming it is the former—the killer is intelligent, likes the excitement of possibly getting caught, maybe finding ways to toy with and outsmart the police.

I've decided to develop a list of any suspects identified on a piece of paper. I obviously don't have the advantage of evidence collection, like the police do. I figure I'll have to either talk to suspects or find others who knew the victims. I've already jotted down Joyce and Ted Winters and Liam Dubois. I figure I can start with them. I can probably pick up a few others by perusing the social networks, figure out who was friends with Alaina Windowski and Angel Daugherty before they died.

The news account I found online listed Alaina as unaccounted for beginning May 21st of last year. She left her job at the country club. No one saw the car she got into. The gate attendant was busy with incoming traffic, but he did state that Alaina walked past his booth as if she had not driven to the country club, but was getting a ride at the end of the road. She didn't wave, but was talking to someone on her cell phone.

It was a man by the name of Harold Tyrone Clayton Junior who found the body almost a year later. It wasn't difficult to check out my cousin, Jeremy's, account. I just couldn't figure out the identity of Junior. He wasn't listed in the newspaper except being dubbed *a resident*. However, my daddy knows all the hunters in the region. I offhandedly asked him who hunts turkey in the fall. It came down to three of his buddies he used to work with at the quarry, ten years ago. I called two and on the third, got ahold of Junior.

Junior told me he'd just gotten out of his truck and put on his rubber boots. He was cutting down the ditch line because there was a pretty big rain the day before and he couldn't get around the creek. He said he kept smelling something rank and he thought it was a dead deer that had been hit on the roadway. He was just getting ready to jump the ditch when he saw something pale white hidden in the tall grass. One step and he saw the body on the opposite embankment, something he describes as looking gray and patchy like a mummy without the cloth wrapped around it. *She wasn't wearing one of those waitress suits like they wear at the swanky country club,* he told me over the phone. *You know, the black skirt and white blouse with a vest. She had on a tank top and shorts. It was creepy. She looked like she'd laid down and fallen asleep. But her clothes was falling in where her skin had rotted. Her hands was tucked under her head. Looked like a 'coon had been snacking on her too. It had to be something small because only her ear was gone and part of her foot. The rest of her, though, it was parched and dried up just like a dead mouse you find behind a refrigerator six months after it died.*

"Sweetie, are you broken down?"

I'm so absorbed in thought, I take no notice of a car coming up next to me. I jump a bit. I'm what my Mamaw Willy, on my daddy's side, used to call a Nervous Nelly. I'm anxious and insecure. I'm scared of taking risks. And when I do the simplest new thing, I'm hesitant, ready to bolt. So when the car stops and I just figured it would pass, my heart starts beating wildly. Still, I'd had three others slow and ask me if I needed help—Harris Trenton who works as a bagger at the Laurel Grove Grocery, a guy named Benny, whose daughter is in twelfth grade at the school, and one of Rocky's buddies, Zach, from the garage in town. But I turn to my left and see three elderly woman in the front seat. I recognize them instantly—Doctor Stamper, whose voice I heard, along with Margaret Williams, and Essie Cunningham. Crud. Of all people, Doctor Stamper is waggling her head and looking back toward my car like she's expecting to see someone with me. They are all in Mom's garden club, bible study class, and choir group.

"No, just thought I'd get out and take a hike." I lower my head a bit to address each. "It's a pretty day." I give Margaret a little wave.

"Oh, by yourself, dear?" Missus Cunningham asks me. It's Tangy's grandmother and Marvin's wife, the man who wanders off all the time. She's got a weasel-face with a long nose and chin.

"You shouldn't walk alone out here in the middle of nowhere." Doctor Stamper straightens herself in the seat.

"Well, I'm all done anyway." I smile and nod politely and pretend like I'm leaving by turning and taking a few steps until I come up next to my driver's side door. I pray they don't tattle to my mom.

As the three drive away, I try to analyze the area, figure out if it has any points in common with the quarry where Angel was found or if there is anything similar to when my aunt came up missing. Nothing. I sigh and question my ability to solve a crime when I can't even drive a stupid ATV fast enough to keep up with my ten year-old cousin. Still I feel like I should gain *something* for my drive here. So I hastily add six more possible suspects to my list: Mary Stamper, Margaret Williams, Essie Cunningham, Harris Trenton, Benny Wheaton, and Zach Matthews. Perhaps one of them is returning to the scene of the crime.

I turn slightly as the sound of the car fades into yowl of wind whipping over the field, the birds, and a hound dog baying far off. I catch a glimpse over my driver's seat and to the back seat of my car. A book. I squint, cup my hand, and peer inside. It's the same stupid romance book someone had dropped in the return box at the school library. Is it a joke? I have to assume Tangy stuck it in there. I roll my eyes, turn my back on it.

My phone tings. I reach in the window, grab it from the seat where I left it. It's Nicky. *Can you babysit Gabby? Leah's working to 10. Rocky got called out. I'm sick of kids.*

I text her back. I don't know why she always tells Rocky she'll watch Gabby when he's on call at the fire station. At least once a week, she drops her off at my house to entertain. I suppose I wouldn't mind it so much if Nicky didn't take all the credit for watching Gabby and then disappear without a trace. Gabby likes putting together puzzles and petting Baby Cakes. She plays with my hamster and isn't afraid of my snake. She's a good excuse to make the high calorie double fudge brownies I love to eat. We call them Gabby No-Cry Brownies because when she was little, they distracted her from missing her mom when I baked them.

I tell her yes. A half hour later, Gabby is settled into my couch on one side reading one of my old kid's mystery books. She's still dutifully carrying around the FBI badge. I wonder what her mom's deadbeat, drug dealer boyfriend thinks about it. I'm settled on the other side, reading *Notorious Kidnapping Cases of the United States*. We've got a bowl of popcorn between us. She is giggling because we keep reaching in to get popcorn at the same time.

"So, how'd you get that shiner?" I ask her.

"Shiner?"

"Your black eye." I point to it. "That's what people used to call a shiner." I really don't need to ask. Nicky says she thinks her mama's boyfriend hits her. It is just not said aloud, though. There's always one excuse or another.

"Oh, the swing hit me when I jumped off." Gabby's hand comes up and absently rubs along the FBI badge.

"The swing." I nod my head in agreement. "Yeah, that hurts." And I tell her a story of how I got hit with a swing because Nicky wanted on and I got on before her when I was seven. Nicky picked up the wooden bottom and just let it fly at my face.

"Yeah, T's like that." She gives me a knowing look, rubs the badge again. "We get to camp out in the car a lot because he hits Mama." She looks sad and maybe a little guilty when she realizes she might have said too much. So I just smile at her. "I slept in my car a couple times when I locked myself out of my dorm room in college." I didn't really lock myself out, per say, although I did sleep in my car. My roommates always had their boyfriends over. "I'm hungry for brownies. You want to make some?"

She lifts up her thumb and uses my geek signal, pointing it toward the ceiling. "Yeah, Gabby No-Cry Brownies!"

As I reach to open the refrigerator door, I freeze, blinking at a new newspaper article tacked with one of my picture magnets. I stop so quickly, the magnet detaches, sending the newspaper clipping fluttering to the ground. It lands face up. I stand motionless, staring at the newspaper article. I can see it even from my vantage point. It is a front page display: *MISSING COLLEGE STUDENT, ALAINA WINDOWSKI'S, DEATH PRONOUNCED A HOMICIDE BY COUNTY CORONER.*

I lean over, snatch up the paper before Gabby sees it. "Did Nicky put something on my refrigerator?" I ask nonchalantly. Gabby peers at the paper, shakes her head.

"Nuh huh, not that I saw. I mean, maybe. I don't know. She had her purse and I went to the bathroom. The front door was open when we got here."

"My front door was open?"

"Uh huh," Gabby opens the refrigerator, reaches around me for the eggs. "Nicky called your mom and told her you needed a babysitter."

"I suppose you're my babysitter." I roll my eyes at her and force a smile. Gabby giggles. I take the newspaper clipping, tack it up with a magnet next to Angel Daugherty's article. I'm thinking Nicky stuck it up here as another warning. Well, at least I'm *hoping* she did. It leaves me uneasy, though, and I make my way to the living room and cautiously lock the door.

Chapter 10

Jack Barkley is anything but frugal when it comes to his business and providing his employees with ample training. He says he wants to cover all the bases. He also tells me if he doesn't do everything he can to protect me, should it arise he hired me for more than an office manager, he does not want to get sued. "I mean, I am hiring you as my son's babysitter. If he was seven, I'd have you take CPR. He's not. Tell me now if you've got a problem with that, because I'm not wasting money—"

"No, sir, that's fine. I'll do whatever it takes," I'd answered quickly. However, I told him twenty-three days into my training that he might get sued if Norma Edwards, his cardio-kickboxing coach, beats the crap out of me again.

"Ow, ow, ow." I'm lying on the floor, staring up at Norma and Mister Barkley. He wasn't there a moment ago. However, I was standing and seeing clearly one second ago. The next, I see her gloved fist making a hundred-mile-an-hour jab right between my eyes. POP! For just a moment, my world was a blissful state of stars and black blobs and Norma poking me in the face. Now, my cheek just aches where she punched it.

"Did you knock her out?"

"Yes," Norma announces. If I wasn't seeing double, I would think she had a proud tip of her chin. "In my defense, she fights like a girl."

"I am a girl," I blurt out, but it sounds more like *my yam ya girl* with my mouth guard in. I blink upward through my sparring helmet, stretch my glove out toward Mister Barkley's extended hand. "She'th gonna break me. I get nothe bleedth. I could bleed to death."

Mister Barkley grabs my wrist and tugs me upward.

Norma's got biceps that are as big as my thighs with one, well-defined, muscled bump on each. She's sleek and toned, with a long, blonde ponytail under her headgear. Norma teaches cardio-kickboxing at the country club to the wives of middle-aged men and their daughters and now, me. I'm learning kickbacks and strikes and not to run away when I see Norma go into her fighting stance.

"How's my son'th nanny doing?" he asks her. Yes, I know he's making fun of me with the lisp. His lip is twitching while he wipes his fingers on his suitcoat. "Do you always sweat that much?"

"Yeth, thee thares me," I mutter and Mister Barkley looks at Norma for a translation.

I intervene, spit out my mouth guard into my glove. I think my lip is bleeding. "I said, yes, because she scares me. I can't go to my other job with black eyes. Tell her I'm not her human punching bag," I whine to Mister Barkley. I am getting the feeling the word *nanny* is going to be exchanged with *bodyguard* somewhere down the line. I think he's probably sick of my complaining. I asked him yesterday afternoon and this afternoon why I hadn't been able to do the two things he asked me to do for him—investigate Alaina's murder and sneak-ask questions from his staff. He just waved me away like I was being silly and told me to be patient.

"I've got bruises on every part of my body. And I get nosebleeds. I could bleed to death with one carefully placed punch," I divulge with a heated gaze at Norma, like a kid sister who finally has daddy around to protect her.

"And where would that be, my little pansy," Norma asks while she feigns a couple dry punches at the center of my face. "Just so I know."

Like I'm going to tell her. Ha. I'm sore. As soon as I

get off work at Laurel Grove High School, I drive home. Then, depending on the night, I either drive to the country club or Mister Barkley has a car waiting to pick me up. I spend two hours working out and running the Olympic sized track and three hours learning self-defense because Mister Barkley requires it of all the females on his staff. At ten o'clock, I'm shoved into a waitress uniform for an hour and told to help the staff with seating customers, which are more what I'd expect in a gentleman's club—old men with big wallets and young men with wandering hands. Tonight I still have to try to fit an old metal desk, chair, and an empty file cabinet into a tiny closet office next to his. I was so sore and tired last night when I got home at midnight, I fell asleep in the bathtub.

"I thought you were putting up a good fight there for a second." Liam Dubois is leaning against the workout room doorway with his arms folded across his chest. He always wears this bored-with-life look, like he's one step away from yawning because the world around him is an old, dull black and white movie and he'd rather be in a new Technicolor one. But right now, he's not so stiff. I also wonder if he's not drunk yet. He reaches up, wiggling his hands in the air like a frightened cartoon character. I thought I'd heard snickering when Norma wiped the floor with my face the fourth time. Liam's got this *hyack-hyack* laugh. It's pretty distinct. It is like the sound Baby Cakes makes when he hacks up a golf-ball size hairball.

"You are confusing her fighting with trying to get her balance while she turns to scurry away, like a scared squirrel." Norma picks up the laughter. "I hope she waits tables better than she hits." I roll my eyes. One day, I'm going to wipe the floor with her face and she'll know what it's like. Okay, maybe not.

"Don't you have a line dancing class or something I

can take instead of kickboxing?" I ignore Norma, who is banging my hand with her gloves, so I will put my mouth guard back in. I'm stalling for no other reason than I need to catch my breath.

"Miss Rosie, I require all my girls to take self-defense and go through training." Mister Barkley waves a hand at Norma while he pivots on his feet toward his son and the door. "I think she's okay. Just a little concussion. Don't break her in the next hour. She starts working for my son in a few hours."

"Tonight?" I'm not sure I'm ready to deal with Liam.

"Yeah," Liam sidles up behind me. I can't see him with my headgear on. I turn, blink at him through the sparring helmet. "Jack wants me to show you where I last saw Alaina." He's got a funny twist to his lips as if he just told a joke.

"Oh. Okay."

Just before I leave the gym, Norma pulls me aside, wrapping her arm around me like we're old buddies. I eye her cautiously.

"You take some sort of ADD medicine?" she asks softly.

"Huh?" I certainly don't want anybody here to know about my anxiety medication. "I don't know. No."

She eyes me cautiously, nods. "Okay. Because you got this dull look to your eyes like my little nephew, Luke, sometimes." She points two fingers at her eyes. "He's got Attention Deficit Disorder, gets kind of wacky sometimes. But what I'm getting at is that you're delayed when you punch. Luke was like that, turtle-slow when he was taking his old meds. I see it. They had to take the boy off them because he just wasn't functioning right. You get me? I don't want to hurt you because you're drugged up."

Chapter 11

I should have questioned Liam's intention when his driver dropped us at the front of Downtown Sally's Adult Nightclub twenty-two miles south of Crystal Springs. It's settled into a drab, dark parking lot off the highway and overlooking a couple family restaurants. He's got six of his buddies waiting for him and he starts doling out wads of dollar bills into each of their outstretched hands before they get to the door. He laughs, tries to hand me some pocket change, and I roll my eyes, push his hand away.

"Oh, come on," he taunts me. "It'd be sexy watching you stuff a few fives in stripper panties." I'm wearing a knee-length, blue-flowered skirt and a dingy blouse, so I know I shouldn't be surprised when Liam jabs a thumb behind him when I reluctantly step out of the car.

"Hey, this is my cousin. I've got to drag her everywhere," he announces our relationship like he's been working on that excuse for weeks.

"Listen, your stepdad didn't say anything about going to strip clubs." When I start to protest, he leans into me and with a far-too-sly smile says, "Jack told me to take you to see where I last saw Alaina. And here it is." He waves a hand, then walks toward the door.

"She was a stripper?" I ask his back, too loudly I assume, because Liam turns and throws his hands into the air and tells me to shut my mouth. He turns back and I don't have much of a choice but to follow into the darkness.

I'm not exactly uncomfortable with four, mostly naked, bleach blondes gyrating three inches from Liam and his buddies' noses. However, it is awkward. They have a private table, so I can smoosh back in the corner and watch the boys giggle like seven year-old schoolgirls on their first sled ride while the girls smash their boobies into their faces and a bigger show plays out up on the stage. Liam keeps dishing out fives and tens to his friends, buying rounds of drinks, then eyeing me with this devious smile. I just roll my eyes at him. I excuse myself to go to the restroom. But it isn't the bathrooms I'm looking for when I slip past the little door into the hallway housing the women's facilities.

It's not a girls night, so it isn't busy back here. There's a young woman smoking a cigarette at the far end of the hallway in a pair of red, white, and blue shorts and a skimpy half-top. She's got the back door propped open and she's holding her cigarette out the door and taking quick, wary puffs. I pass the lady's restroom door that says SALLIES and saunter down to the girl. She's got a cagey twist to her lips. "Customers got to go out front to smoke."

"I don't need a smoke. Can I ask you if you knew Alaina Windowski? Did you work here last May?" I cut right to the question and she just stares at me, then drops her eyes to the cigarette. She's not that rough, has soft brown hair, and a sweet set to her lips.

"You a cop?" She looks me up and down. Her face is stone cold.

"I'm not a cop. I'm not talking to cops."

"Why you asking then?"

"I'm looking into it for a guy who is paying me."

"Is it the guy you came in with?"

"Yeah. I guess I'm kind of a—private investigator." She just stares at me and I know she's not going to tell me anything. There isn't any trust. I'm a stranger that could be a cop or a creep. "Okay, so here's how it is—" I reach into my purse and pull out the only bill I've got inside. "In a nutshell, I was riding my dad's ATV on private property and

I had to leave the damn thing because it got stuck in the mud and the cops were coming. They impounded the ATV. So I'm trying to get enough money I can bail out my dad's ATV and some guy's paying me to figure out who killed Alaina. I obviously don't like cops too much." I sigh. "I'll give you twenty bucks if you can tell me anything that would help."

"You got to be kidding me."

"You think I could make up a story like that if I was?" I don't wait for her to answer. "Do you remember if that guy I came in with was here the night Alaina came up missing?"

"He used to come in every Thursday and Friday Alaina worked. So I suppose he was." She closes her eyes for a moment, then looks up at the ceiling. "Yeah, I know he was here. He tipped me a hundred dollar bill that night so I'd introduce him to another girl."

"So was he here when she left—?"

She nods her head. Right then, a thick door to the right opens and a bald man comes out, points to the girl. "Your break's over. Get out there. This your sister, the religious one?" He doesn't appear to think I'm much of a threat. "What the hell? You having a family reunion, Riley?"

"She's going." She waves him away. He gives me a sideways glance before he disappears back into the door. Riley takes a quick last puff of her cigarette and flicks it out into the darkness.

"So Alaina worked at the country club. There's no mention of her working here at Downtown Sally's. I'm assuming the cops didn't know, haven't questioned anybody here. How's that happen?"

"Ask Bill in there. Some of the girls do it under the table." Riley stops and grins. "That's funny, right? They *do it* under the table. Because some of them do."

I smile and nod. "You think Bill might have killed her?" I ask.

"Bill?" she snickers. "He's a dick, but he never leaves that office. I know the night she left and didn't come back, he was in there. He's a slave driver, doesn't want to lose a dime so he's always going back and forth making sure we're all not sitting around. So Alaina worked here on Thursdays and Fridays under the table and for her sake, in the back room and in some of the creepier guys' cars. She was paying off student loans," she says. "She had a stage name—Haylee Haines. That's what Bill put on her tax forms. He says it's her problem if she files or not. But—her car was a piece of shit, kept breaking down. The last couple weeks she worked, Bill there—" she waves a hand toward the closed door. "—he said she was fired if she missed another night. The last two nights she worked, some old man dropped her off and picked her up. I thought it was her dad or her grandpa. She said it wasn't. It was just some guy who'd stopped by the side of the road to help her fix her car a few days earlier. She was desperate enough to take a ride from anybody. Figured that's what she did and why she ended up dead."

"What kind of car was it? Did you get a license plate number?"

"It was a big, black thing," Riley answers, tugs on the door. "No, I didn't. I was smoking a cigarette like this and looked out just as it pulled in. I closed the door real quick thinking it was somebody trying to sneak in the back door."

"The guy I came in with—"

"Liam Dubois," she says. "I know his name."

"You're *sure* he was here after Alaina left that night?"

"Uh huh."

"Will you sign a statement that says you saw Liam Dubois in the strip bar that night after she had gone?"

"For what he paid me in twenties that night, yeah, sure."

I walk out with a statement on the back of a beer order that I notarized on the spot. It's probably the first time I appreciate being the one who had the school notary position dumped on her. The office was always needing somebody to notarize documents. Nobody else wanted to do it. Now Liam's got an alibi that will, most likely, hold up in court for Alaina's murder.

However, the table where Liam was sitting is empty. Empty? A wave of apprehension grips me as I tug my sweater around me. Gone. My eyes make a wild scan of the room. He's nowhere in sight. I ask the bouncers at the front door and they point to the parking lot. That, too, is devoid of Liam's car.

It doesn't surprise me. As I hover there, I see Riley with a second girl and pointing to me.

"Hey," She calls out to my back while I'm hoping to God Liam hasn't ditched me. I turn half-heartedly. I realize it's one of the girls who was dancing at Liam's table.

"That guy you were with tonight, he was here that night Alaina came up missing. Riley said you were asking."

"You saw him too?" I ask. I take her in and she snatches my arm, tugging me into the shadows. "I remember him. He kind of sticks out in a crowd, you know? Most of the guys coming in here are old, fat, or ugly. Everybody was fighting to dance at his table. He was doling out twenty dollar bills. Tonight was no different." She holds up her hand and there's a couple hundred dollar bills sticking in her palm.

"Was he still here when Alaina left for the night?"

"You aren't going to the cops, right? I got a boyfriend and a four year-old kid."

"I'm not. But he needs an alibi. What would it cost me to get a signed statement?"

"I'd do it for five-hundred."

"You got an ATM around here?"

"Yeah."

"My name is Crystal Glass. I was in his car with him that night." The girl divulges sheepishly when she returns from getting her driver license so I can check her ID to notarize her statement. I shove the first of my debit cards into the ATM at the door. "You know, a hundred bucks is a hundred bucks, no matter how you get it. I needed the cash."

"I'm not judging you," I tell her while she looks me up and down, takes in my prim outfit. I've got to use two debit cards because I'm limited to three-hundred a night.

"I'm not worried about you. You think this will go to court? He kind of paid me for the blowjob." I look at her ID and she's telling the truth about her name.

"You don't have to reveal certain specifics in your statement. I'd stick with details pertaining to what you saw and who you were with at a precise time and not necessarily the reason you were there."

"Okay, I saw Alaina leave through the windshield of the car. I was kind of watching for her. She'd get mad if we stepped in on her regulars. And Liam's a regular. She had a little red backpack purse. Nobody else here has it. I ducked down. It was raining. There were dribbles on the windshield, but I saw her. She left and didn't come back. Listen, we need to get back to work. Can we make this fast?"

I had nodded and only five minutes later, Crystal and Riley are back to bumping and jarring against smudged poles to the beat of crumpled dollar bills stuffed into their skimpy outfits. I'm outside with eyes making a panicked skim of the parking lot only to find Liam and his friends have vanished. The restaurants are closed with empty dark parking lots. There's ten or twelve cars in the Downtown Sally's lot. Not all of them are empty. It's the last place I want to be. I suppose it is dangerous even for an invisible girl like me, a parking lot with the kind of creepy men who get off on girls dirty dancing on poles and who leave horny and looking for a way to vent their unfulfilled lust.

There's only the lights on the highway while I wrestle desperately with the idea I've got nobody to call to pick me up. *Hey Daddy, I'm at a strip club. Can you come get me?* That's not happening. I poke Mister Barkley's number in the phone, but I can't quite push the little green button. How can I tell him the girl with the high IQ is stupid enough she can't babysit a twenty-one year-old for an hour without losing him?

"Hey, sweetie, you looking for someone?"

I'm standing next to a car and I skitter back two steps. The door starts to open. I swear it is old Marvin Cunningham from church. Shit. Shit! What the heck is he doing here? I see him start to wiggle his long legs to get out, his arms using the steering wheel as leverage. *He's an old man. An old man picked up and killed Alaina!* With that thought in mind, I don't know what comes over me, but I screech and in a mindless knee-jerk reaction kick his door closed with my foot. I just don't do it once, because it hits his knee and whips back open, so I smash it a second time before I take off at a dead run to hide in the shadows of two empty cars. And I'm more worried about him telling my mom I was hanging out in the dark parking lot of a strip club than about what the heck he was doing there.

I try to calm myself down, kneeling in the shadows and peering left to right, trying to see if he followed me. I have three dollars in change in my purse and I'm not even sure which direction I should start walking to get out of my predicament. I'm thinking maybe Liam will turn around and come back for me.

Ten minutes of leaning against the parking lot guardrail later, I get a text. I snatch up my phone. Is it Liam? No. It's Rocky McDaniel. He never texts me. Never.

Hey, where are you? He writes.

I'm busy. I text back, thinking maybe I want to ask him to come get me really bad, but I know he'll see me in this parking lot and the crap will hit the fan because he'll tell my mom.

You were supposed to be at choir practice tonight. Your mom's worried.

I went someplace with friends.

Are you home?

Yeah.

Because I'm sitting in your driveway and you're not answering the door.

Why are you sitting in my driveway? Go away.

Because your sister is freaking out because you've been acting weird. You're never home. Your mom thinks you're on drugs. You didn't go to choir practice.

I'm fine. Go home.

No, not until I know you're safe.

I just stuff my phone back in my purse. I'm freaking out. I just beat the crap out of an old man who goes to Laurel Grove Holy Trinity Church and whose son is my boss at the high school. What if he calls Mom and tells her he saw me in the dark parking lot of a strip club and I slammed his door on him? Grrr! I rub my face with my palms in frustration. Then I stand there and stare at the sky that is now swelling up with big, black puffy spring storm clouds. I stuff the urge to cry in the back of my mind and dig my phone back out, and swallow my pride.

Rocky. I'm in a pickle again. Do I need to explain what in a pickle means again? Can you come get me?

His response is almost immediate. *Where are you?*

Downtown Sally's, off the highway. I pull up a GPS map and hit the location button. Then I copy and paste it in the text. *Here.*

There's a long pause during which I assume he's punching the location into his truck's GPS system and then staring, flabbergasted, at the locality.

B there in 45 min.

I'm sitting on the guardrail in the restaurant parking lot below Downtown Sally's when I see Rocky's big red truck thirty-one minutes later. He must have kicked it into high gear to get here. It's loud, like a dragon grumbling, when it pulls off the road on to the shoulder.

I climb in. I see him staring at me, then over my head at Downtown Sally's. He rubs a hand on his jawline, doesn't say a word before he turns his attention to the windshield.

"Say it," I huff. "Just get it out now, McDaniel. Lay it out on the table before you start moving so I can jump out before you get too much speed built up—"

"So, here's a joke you might like. Two strippers walk into a bar—"

"Stop."

"Okay." Rocky pushes the truck into gear and presses his foot to the gas. It is awkward and silent except for the *zing-zing* sound my phone makes when I set the ringtone to vibrate.

"Don't judge me, Rocky," I grunt. It is muffled inside my purse. I hear it *zing* probably thirty times.

"I'm not. I'm just curious. So was it a weird date?"

"No."

"Job interview?" He gets the tiniest of snarky twists to his lips. "You're not *working* there, are you?"

"I swear to God, Rocky, don't go there."

"Friends?"

"Yeah," I lie. "New ones I obviously didn't know." The phone is going crazy with texts.

"That's probably your mom or Nicolette," Rocky observes flatly. "You might want to let them know you're not dead in the ditch or the quarry or wherever else girls who disappear get dumped around here." He clears his throat awkwardly. "You know not to date guys from the internet, right?"

"Are you assuming I'm desperate? That I found some guy on a random site looking for a girl to murder?"

"No—no, I mean, you were at a *strip club*, Rosie," he stutters. "I mean, it's not a bad thing—dates, not strip clubs. Just check them out. There are sites that do background checks. Bobby gave Nicky a whole bunch of information about looking up people before we started dating."

Oh, my. I rub the red from my cheeks. He thinks I'm so awkward that I'm desperate. I suppose when you date a girl like my sister, who has guys lining up to open the door for her, I probably come off as the geek who'd dig up a guy on a social network just to feel alive. I keep wondering if Mister Cunningham will remember me. Or maybe I should call someone to tell them he's there. Mom said he wanders off sometimes when he takes too much of his medication. I sigh, reach into my purse and tug out my phone. There are three texts from my mom, one from Nicolette, and while I scroll down with my finger, I can't even count the number of texts from Liam. He must have a hundred, all of them demanding: *Where the hell are you?*

I don't answer Liam. I do, however call my mom. I tell her I was just tired after school and fell to sleep. She asks me if I'm sick or if I'm having one of my old dreams. *Old dreams.* It isn't just the ones about running blindly and I smell the reek of something dead. Sometimes I wake up after a hard sleep and I've dreamed about something specific from the two days I disappeared. I mean, it isn't a long expanse of time that's wiped from my mind, probably just a few months. But the memory slides in and I used to ask my mom if something really happened or not until I realized it freaked her out. So I don't anymore. Like now, I tell her no. She asks me what the sound is she hears. It is Rocky's truck. I tell her it's my refrigerator. When I push the little disconnect button two minutes later, I don't look up at Rocky because I know he is judging me in the silence.

"Don't make me a part of your lies, whatever they are," he tells me bluntly, snapping his gaze from windshield to me. "Don't ask me to lie to your sister or your mom."

"Then don't ask any questions. I'm not one of those stupid strays you take in," I sigh. Yes, Rocky has the biggest heart this side of Kansas, and it is another reason for my sister to groan. She doesn't have a soft heart for animals. Rocky, he's a sucker for big eyes and a sad story. He still has a pig named One-Eyed Gus he bought from the fair four years ago and saved from slaughter. "Listen, just drop me at the next exit. I don't know what I was thinking. You, of all people, should have been the last person I called. You're like my nemesis. If I was a superhero, you would be the villain."

"I'm offended. I saved your butt the other day at Uncle Johnny's. You could have been arrested. I should be the hero. *You* were the villain for damaging his property."

"I lost my dad's ATV, Rocky. If you were being my hero, you wouldn't have let the cops take it. Drop me off somewhere. I'm going to walk."

"Is that what this is all about? Are you trying to get more money to get it out of the impound?" Rocky turns his head, rubs his chin with his fingers. "And I'm not dropping you off at any exit, Rosie. Don't be ridiculous." Rocky, he's all cocky with this swagger of shoulders and his head thrown back that only comes with boys raised redneck. "It's not happening. You smell like a brewery. I'm going to drop you at your door and it isn't going to happen again."

I sit there. "Screw off, Rocky." He looks at me with a funny twist to his head.

"How much did you drink?"

"I didn't."

"Um." He rubs his chin like he doesn't believe me. "Because you're quarrelsome and yak-yak-yak tonight. You're usually hit and run in less than three sentences."

I slump my shoulders like Mister Barkley says makes me look like a gorilla. I clamp my mouth shut, grinding my teeth. Then, while the radio plays some old country music song low and soft, I stare out the window at the blackness outside. Rocky doesn't say a word.

My house is dark except for a tiny yellow front porch light. I can only think I'm going to have to confront my mom tomorrow and make up a bunch of lies to cover where I've been and pray Mister Cunningham didn't recognize me. I hate battling it out with her. She always wins. I have no clue what Mister Barkley will do about me not being able to handle the one simple task of babysitting his son.

The crunch of tire on concrete driveway with a bit of gravel mixed in is the only sound creeping to my ears until I get out. I think Rocky is going to walk me to my door. I jump out quickly before he even shoves the truck into park.

"Hey," he says just as I'm getting ready to close the truck door. I just look at my feet, pause because I'm unsure what he wants. "If it happens again, I'll come get you, okay? I'll be there. No questions asked."

I don't answer, just shove the door closed with both my hands and walk up to my house. There's something on the porch. I can see the brown paper, just like the paper the thirteen blue roses were wrapped in. I bend down and pick it up. I can see what's inside; thirteen more blue roses.

"Rosie?"

"What?" I throw one hand into the air and pivot so I can see him sitting in the truck, his passenger side window rolling down and Rocky's leaning sideways to see me.

He just sits there staring at me. "What are you holding?"

"Flowers."

"Nice," he says, gives me a thumbs up. "Same guy?"

I don't tell him I don't know who is sending them. I have a sneaking suspicion it is the creepy guy three houses down, Alvin Temple, who walks past my house at least once a night staring at it. I've even nicknamed him Weird Al. I'd add him to my suspect list along with Marvin Cunningham tonight, who is at the top of my list at the moment. However, I don't think Weird Al has a car so he couldn't dump a body at the quarry. Rocky opens his mouth like he wants to say something, doesn't. Instead, he shakes his head, gives me a wave.

"Did you ever read that book?"

"What book?"

"Winsome Falls. The one I put on your desk and you immediately put on the shelf. It is also the one I stuck in your car."

I grimace. So Rocky's the one behind the stupid romance novel showing up. "No, Rocky, I did not. I'm not really into that kind of sappy romance stuff. Please do not let my mother or my sister coerce you into shoving fiction down my throat when they fail at it themselves."

"Well, you're smiling now. Think about it. You might find you like to mix it up a bit."

I'm not smiling. Oh, shit, I am. Frigging what is up with these flowers? They must be tainted with pheromones. He stops and gets that smug twist to his lips, rubs his hand over his stubbly cheek. "I mean, there's another strip club off the highway about ten miles—"

"Go to hell."

"Can't you have a normal conversation with me, Rosie? Damn." Rocky shakes his head, frowns at me.

"You're kidding me, right? You're the one who just made the remark about the strip club. You're the one who believes in the curse."

"Yeah, I guess I did," he agrees like it's no big deal. Then he smiles big at me again. "I'm just teasing you. You take stuff too seriously."

"And you don't take stuff seriously enough. Did you study for your fireman's test?" I toss back. His smile drops.

"Naw, haven't had the time."

I know better. He's like a poor kid standing outside the sport shop, staring at the most expensive baseball glove inside. He thinks he'll never get it because he's not rich enough or smart enough, and his parents won't let him play ball. But he likes to stare at it, dream of that glove wrapped around his hand, dream of playing with the other boys.

"I suppose, then, I am the one who takes stuff too seriously. But you don't take life seriously enough. It wouldn't hurt to mix it up a bit, Rocky," I lecture with a snarky waggle of my shoulders. "You could certainly work a little harder at being a teacher, if nothing else." He hard-stares me a second, then he seems to shake it off. "I didn't mean that," I mutter, feeling like a rapidly deflated balloon. "I'm sorry. It's just that you'd be such a great fireman, you know?"

"I am one now. It's just not full-time."

"You're the grunt and you'll always be the grunt in Laurel Grove because you're from Raccoon Hollow. You sweep floors, cook meals. You get the crappy callouts. You need to expand your horizons. Try applying someplace in Brown County or Alton or Crystal Springs."

"Yeah, I don't think I'm quite qualified."

"Nobody else knows how to make my nosebleeds stop. Nobody. You've got a gift. Use it!"

"A gift." He gives his classic chuckle, a muffled *huck-huck-huck*. "Yeah, maybe I'll mix it up if you do, Rosie." He gives me a snarky smile then. "You know you could have spared yourself a whole lot of agony by just standing down in the restaurant parking lot and telling me you got stood up there."

I stop, let his words sink in. He's right. I groan. I hug the flowers to my chest and stomp inside. He waits until I'm in the house nearly ten minutes before he drives away.

I pick up a tablet of paper and write MISSING GIRLS at the top. Below it, I put *Gina Lee Channel—last seen in bedroom by mother at Laurel Grove Apartments* and *Rosaline Diane McGuire—last seen leaving home on Troublesome Creek Road.*

Then I get another sheet of paper and put DEAD GIRLS on the top. Beneath, I write: *Angel Rianne Daugherty—last seen at home of client for home healthcare* and *Alaina Faye Windowski—last seen at Downtown Sally's strip club.*

Lastly, I tug out one final piece of paper and put SUSPECTS at the top. Underneath, I write: *Liam Dubois.* I scratch out his name. He's got an alibi.

At scene of crime—(Angel Daugherty) *Joyce and Ted Winters-sell insurance.*

At scene of crime—(Alaina Windowski) *Mary Stamper, Margaret Williams, Essie Cunningham, Harris Trenton, Benny Wheaton, Harris Trenton, Zach Matthews.*

Could be old man in parking lot who picked up Alaina: *Marvin Cunningham*

Hell's bells, that's it on suspects. It could be anybody. It could even be Rocky for all I know. Then I take Rocky's advice. I pop a credit card number into an online background check a half hour later when I can't sleep and do a little digging; I only wish I had done it sooner.

Chapter 12

I done made the devil a deal. He's bringing all hell up on my heels. That's one of my mom's sayings. She doesn't use it often. I heard her say it the first time when Nicolette was thirteen and Mom caught her smoking a cigarette out her bedroom window. That's all Mom said and Nicolette burst into an explosion of tears like she'd been exorcised. She'd danced around, crying and carrying on for so long, I swore I'd never smoke a cigarette.

It's like an incantation, I suppose, Mom's saying. I'm not even sure what it means. Still, she said it to me softly last night when I called her before I went to bed. She asked where I'd been. I told her I went out with some friends. She knew I was lying. I expected tears to come to me, the same kind of explosive sobbing that forced the devil out of my sister so many years ago. Nothing happened. I suppose maybe I didn't feel like I'd really made the devil a deal. That is, until the next afternoon—

"Where the hell did you go last night?"

Liam Dubois meets me at the front doors of the country club Saturday afternoon, shoving it open. Rage filled eyes glower at me when he leans hard against the door to let me through.

"After you ditched me at Downtown Sally's?"

"Shut up!" he hiss-whispers. "If my stepdad hears that name, the shit is going to hit the fan." He stops me with his hand. I turn, face him, and return the glare. "It was a joke. We came back. You need to tell him it's your fault."

"My fault? Are you crazy?" I spit back. I'm a little on the irritated side. I get this way when I skip taking a pill. I only took half a one today on Norma's advice so I was more awake. "You did not come back and it was not funny for me.

I was there for over an hour and a half. I didn't see you once. And did it not occur to you it would be legal suicide to show up there again? If the cops had seen you there, if anybody took pictures of you coming or going, they could tie you into the murder."

He gets this funny twist to his lips and snickers.

"What?" I ask him. "It's not funny. It was a jerk thing to do. There was a guy there I can bet recognized me. What's he going to tell people? He saw me at a strip club?"

"*He* was at a strip club too. You think he's going to squeal on you?"

"He's from my church."

"Ah, that would explain the Jesus flyers under the windshield wipers of all the cars in the lot, including mine."

"Great," I mumble. I pinned Marvin Cunningham as a suspect and he's out trying to save the souls of strip club perverts. "So yes, he probably will squeal. Thanks, Liam. Why are you looking at me like that?"

"You're—different than you were last month. You don't look like a scared chick fresh out of its shell anymore. You got this sassy look to your eyes—a spark."

"I'm pissed," I inform him flatly. "You left me at a stupid strip club where a girl disappeared and was later found murdered. I could have been murdered." Liam breaks out in sarcastic laughter at that.

"Yeah, right, because you looked so much like one of those girls coming out of there."

So I shut him up quickly with, "And at what point were you going to tell me you knew Angel Daugherty too?"

He freezes and shrinks back. His face pales. "What—what are you talking about? What makes you think I knew her? And I don't have to tell you everything."

I don't answer him too quickly. I want to make him sweat, like he left me stranded and rattled last night. But I suppose when the police checked out Angel Daugherty's social network pages, they stopped cold at one image. It is a picture of Angel dancing at a wedding at the country club. In the background, Liam Dubois is standing with arms folded across his chest, holding a beer, watching the dancers.

I'm assuming some cop had taken a magnifying glass to all the images showing up on her page, then, and Liam was the only man who appeared consistently. The cop saw him and, in his enthusiasm to solve the murders, simply stopped without digging any farther. I did not stop. I took it a step farther. I called Deborah Winston, whose wedding had been at the club on May 20th of last year. It was the last place Angel had been seen. She told me Angel had never been on her list to come to the wedding. In fact, she said that was what Angel liked to do. She and two other women had a website called *Wedding Crashers*. They would show up at random weddings and take pictures of themselves there, then post them on social media. Deborah Winston was mad, utterly furious really, because Angel had even hogged the dance floor and posed in pictures with the family and wedding group. And, what I can see, Liam who was an invited guest.

She wasn't kidding. I checked out the website. Angel had been to over fifty-two weddings, all uninvited. While I scanned the images, all five-hundred and eighty-one of them, I see none other than Liam Dubois at another wedding, this one outdoors and this time, he's slow dancing with Angel.

However, Deborah Winston told me Liam was an invited guest. Her brother ran in certain circles with him and had actually introduced Deborah to her new husband.

She also said Liam was still at the party when Angel was finally kicked out at one in the morning. In fact, he was in a hotel room on the same property with the maid of honor, Lexie Livingston, who also worked part time at the hotel. He didn't leave until seven the next morning. Sure enough, Lexie corroborated the information. I was even able to get a copy of the hotel receipt she had with his signature on it and a notarized declaration. Then I contacted Angel's two wedding crashing friends and they each told me that, yes, they had dropped a very drunk Angel off at her house at four in the morning. The last they saw of her was Angel staggering up her walkway holding up a beer. I met with them at a coffee shop and they, too, signed statements.

After the long pause and Liam bouncing back and forth on his heels, I whip out my phone. I show him the picture where he is dancing with Angel. He squints at the picture and then lets a slow puff of air from his lips.

"Oh, yeah." He shoves his hands in his pockets, shrugs noncommittedly. "She was this fat girl who kept asking me to dance. The drunker I got, the cuter she got."

"That's all you've got to say for yourself?"

"I didn't kill those girls if that's what you're saying. You're like dragging around an ugly, little sister with dorky glasses and that stinking sweater with cat hair all over it," he growls back. "You know how much my friends made fun of me for that? I don't care if you're like everybody else and think I'm a murderer. I don't give a rat's ass. Just quit."

"Yeah, you think you're fun to be with?"

"My friends seem to think so."

"When you're handing out twenty dollar bills and drowning them in booze. They're so drunk, they'd hold hands with the devil by closing time. I don't want to hang with you. I don't want to babysit you. I don't even like you."

I can see cleaning staff looking up from these little carts they push around with brooms and cleaning supplies. I clamp my mouth shut. Liam is expressionless.

"Well, then, start looking for another job. If you don't quit, I'm going to find a way to get you fired. For one, I'm going to call your mom and tell her you're working for my stepdad. Next, I'm going to tell my stepdad you were the one who wanted to go to a strip club. Also, you will refer to me as Mister Dubois and not by my first name."

"Okay, Mister Dubois, if you want me to quit that badly, I quit. But then you should know this—" I lift up my middle finger, shove it in his face just like Colton McDaniel did to me the other day when I told him to turn down the music on his phone in the library. "Screw you. Screw your stepdad. Screw this whole entire piece of shit country club. I hope they drag your sorry ass down to jail and you rot there for the rest of your life." I pivot on my feet and head out the way I came. "I don't like working here anyway."

My heart is racing while I walk down the sidewalk out of the building. What the hell did I just do? *I need a pill. I need a pill,* I keep telling myself. I think I'm going to faint. I haven't raised my voice in a fight, not even with my sister, since I was fourteen. It's empowering and—irresponsible. I'm not sure if I'm inspired by my actions or so guilt-ridden, I want to dive into the asphalt and disappear.

"Where are you going?" I wasn't fast enough to evade Jack Barkley. "My assistant said you were leaving."

"I quit. Your son said he was going to do everything in his power to get me fired, including telling my mom I work here. So instead of going through the pain, I quit."

"My son has no say in the decisions of this resort facility. I told you that," Mister Barkley growls. "You answer to me, young lady. Our deal is not off. I don't expect he wants a nanny at his age. But he needs one. He has to have one at least until this whole fiasco with the murdered girls goes away. You've got to do it until I can figure something else out. I have a month invested in you."

"No, I'm done. He needs an entire army of nannies to keep him out of trouble."

"No, you're not. I hired you to babysit my son!" He is screaming at me now. His face is red. There's a thick vein popping out of his temple. "You keep his ass out of trouble!"

"No, I'm done!" I yell right back, then lower my voice. "It's not only emotionally and physically impossible to keep your son out of trouble, I came an inch from murdering him myself. I quit. Period."

"No, you're not. If you quit, then your dad's out of a job. Period." Mister Barkley stands up straight, puts his hands in his pockets.

I stop in my tracks. "You're kidding me. My dad?" My head is swimming. I'm suddenly deflated. "You can't do that. That's not fair." I pinch my temples, wheel around.

"Yeah. It is fair to me."

"I didn't know your son was such an ass—why does my dad's job have to be at stake?"

"*Why does my dad's job have to be at stake—*" Mister Barkley pushes his voice up high, mimicking me. "Because I'm a family business. You are a family package. I only hired your scrawny ass because I told your dad I'd give you a try. So what do you say, Rosie? You going to step up and do your job or do I have to hire another girl to babysit my son and another redneck to run my shooting range?"

I stand there knowing what Rosie Mauer, Wallflower would do. She'd nod her head and shed a tear or two. But I'm sick of being the flower that gets stepped on. "No."

"Where are you going?"

"To my dad's, to tell him I lost his job." I don't

recognize myself as I jerk open my car door. Letting my daddy down again is the last thing I want to do. "Then I'm going to find another job where I don't have to get punched for three hours or left in the parking lot of a strip club."

"Strip club?" Mister Barkley is stomping around the hood of my car. "What are you talking about?"

"Ask your son." I sit down hard, push the key in the ignition. "No, don't ask your son. He'll lie. He took me to a strip club, then left when I went to the restroom. And by the way, I found him alibis for the Alaina Windowski and the Angel Daugherty murders. Just saying. Goodbye." I turn the ignition. It makes a sad *wing-wing-wing* sound and won't turn over. I groan inwardly.

"What? What did you say?" There's a knock on my window as I turn the ignition again. *Chug-chugged-chug.* "Jesus Christ! Stop!"

I pause, sigh, and look Mister Barkley in the eye. Then I roll down my window, look up at him. "I'm not sure how credible a judge would find these alibis, but there are six people who can account for Liam's whereabouts the nights the women came up missing. I mean, there is a bigger time frame that somebody being meticulous could ask for more alibis because the coroner can't definitively state they died the same night they appeared to be missing. However, in Alaina's case, she was seen leaving with a stranger that night. In Angel's case, the last people to see her were two friends who watched her walk to her apartment alone." My car pops and bangs finally and sounds like it is getting ready for a drag race. I look up. Jack Barkley's grinding his teeth. I can see his jaw working.

"You're kidding me? You have proof?"

"Six signed, notarized statements."

He stands stoically. "What do you want from me?"

"What?" I ask, pumping the gas with my toes so the car doesn't stall.

"Okay, Miss Smarty-Pants." He leans into the window, looks me straight in the eye. "You said you found him alibis for the murders?"

"Yes." I want to turn away. I want to go home, sit on the couch with my kitty and watch an old, stupid movie.

"Here's a sweet deal for you. You babysit my son for—let's say, two more months. I'll give you twenty-five thousand dollars above your normal pay if you keep him out of trouble. I won't tear up your dad's contract. I'll sign your father on for another two years. And if you think you're so damn smart, then figure out who is murdering those girls so this whole damn thing isn't darkening my reputation. Hell, I'll pay you fifty-thousand dollars if you prove, without a doubt, who did it. What do you think about that?"

"Mister Barkley, Liam doesn't want to drag me around. He says I'm dorky and ugly. I mean, I get it. Even if he didn't care, I don't know if I can do this job without looking over my shoulder every second for someone who goes to my church. I can't go around asking questions because if my mom finds out I'm going into bars trying to dig up stuff on murdered girls, she'll say I'm crazy."

"Well, then, I suppose we can kill two birds with one stone. We'll have to put up a smoke screen so she doesn't find out, eh?" he says. "We'll have to tweak you a bit. Good God, I'll even throw in a car if you figure this out."

A car. Fifty-thousand dollars. I could buy my daddy a new ATV, make him proud of me again. That's two years' worth of wages at Laurel Grove High School. Mister Barkley holds out his hand for me to shake. I can't think this quickly. I reach out my hand and feel his hand in mine and for some reason, I hear the echo of Mom's voice in the back of my mind: *I done made the devil a deal. He's bringing all hell up on my heels.* I feel like I just made a deal with the devil as our palms touch and he moves our fingers up and down. Maybe I did.

Chapter 13

Snap. I yelp, feel a sting of something like a pebble hitting the tender flesh just below my right butt cheek and the cut-off fringe of my jean shorts. I wince. I'm thirty feet up a tree on my dad's back property. I'm peering at Johnny McDaniel's house through a pair of Mom's cheap binoculars she got free for signing up for some birdwatching magazine.

"What the hell are you doing up there, *McGuire*?"

I'm rubbing the raw skin just above my right thigh and looking down at Rocky balancing on some roots sticking out at the bottom of my tree. I try to tug my old sweater around my legs for protection. It doesn't work. "It's Mauer and I'm looking at birds," I lie. I hold up the Southern Guide to Local Birds book I'd also borrowed from my mom to use as a prop should someone get nosey. "See? Birds." I rock a little on the flimsy limb. "Go away. I think there's a rare bluebird on the far side of the fence."

"Liar. Bluebirds are all over this hillside." Rocky holds up something in his hand. I can't quite make it out. "You're spying on my uncle. Did you not learn your lesson when you trespassed last month?"

He is right. I am lying. My Aunt Kay texted me and told me she heard over the scanner on Friday that the cops dragged Johnny McGuire down to the police station to question him about the murders. Then, on Sunday morning, she found out why. While she was teaching Sunday school at Holy Cross Church, the preacher's wife told her when the two officers went to Johnny's house the day my cousin shot the electric box, they saw where Johnny'd used a backhoe next to his house to dig. There was a woman's shoe there. Maybe he was burying girls.

I'm not sure if he was or not, but as soon as I gave

the signed statements to Mister Barkley, he must have given them to his lawyers. Because now, although Liam isn't entirely out of the picture, they're pointing fingers somewhere else—Johnny McDaniel. He's just made it to the top of my suspect list, too. Not necessarily because I believe he murdered anyone. It's more that I'm still a little tetchy about Johnny calling the cops on us and Daddy's ATV being in the impound. I push on my glasses, lean in to see what Rocky is holding up. Aw, crap, it's a slingshot.

"Bugger off, Rocky. I'm on my dad's side of the land."

He's lifting his weapon up, putting a shiny something in the little pocket, and getting ready to shoot again.

"Yes, and the ATV still sitting in the impound lot of the police station was on my uncle's side not long ago."

"Go to hell."

"My, you're churlish." He wiggles his eyebrows like he is trying to impress me with his big word. I roll my own. It annoys me. Everybody keeps calling me cranky since I took Norma's advice and cut back on my pills. I feel slightly emancipated by it. Well, except on Sundays. I still take them before I go to Mom's. "I heard somebody called to see what needed to be done to claim that ATV."

"Who?"

"Me," Rocky says. "And they aren't going to release it. They are holding it for evidence."

"You're lying."

"I'm not. I got the word from Bobby. Just thought I'd give you a head's up because I figured you were going to take the step and ask about it. I'll save you a couple days in the county jail and tell you they aren't releasing it until somebody confesses. If you walk in there, they're going to want a confession. I figure you aren't going to rat out your cousins, but the cops are sure going to try to coax it out of you. By the way, I heard gunshots over at your dad's house this morning." Rocky's got this sly smile on his lips. "You two get in a fight?"

I'm sure his tiny target is the bare flesh of my right butt cheek sticking out of my underpants and jean shorts. I'm getting the feeling Rocky is on to me. I'm not as backward as everyone believes. I mean, I fell into it when I was fourteen. I kind of became a turtle that hid in its shell; it became something of a pattern. Whenever I stray from it, Mom and Nicky freak out and Mom makes me go to a therapist. Such, the turtle goes back into hiding. But hearing the news about my dad's ATV makes me crankier than I already am. Bobby mentioned the same thing to me the other day, said it had a big tag marked: EVIDENCE.

"No, I was target practicing." I was. "Daddy got me a pistol. It's pink and cute." Daddy did get me a little pink pistol with a matching pink shoulder holster at the flea market, just like he promised. Daddy decided since there are so many dead girls, I should know how to protect myself. He said I should carry it with me and make sure I get someone to walk me to the car *after I work my hosting job at the country club*. Hostess? He thinks Mister Barkley hired me as the hostess who seats guests? I didn't correct him, simply nodded. "It's my weapon of choice." So he dragged out a bale of hay from Papaw's barn and tacked a couple targets he got from work on them. Then we spent a couple hours wasting bullets. It was fun. "And I'm not beyond using it on you if the slingshot becomes *your* weapon of choice." I hold out my forefinger, aim it at Rocky and cock my thumb like a gun before I wink and make a clicking sound with my tongue. "Just saying."

"Damn, you're spot on today." Rocky cocks his chin and makes a wolf whistle. "So let the games begin." He holds up the slingshot and closes one eye to aim.

"Don't! Now, stop!" I yelp again when it pelts the soft skin on the inside of one bare thigh. "I don't have my pistol on me." He's not very good at his aim, but I'm not going to tell him that. "Besides, you're going to upset me and make my nose bleed."

"That's the worse excuse I've ever heard. You can't be all sassy to me and then hide behind your nosebleeds."

"Yes, I can. It might start bleeding and I'll faint up here and fall. Then my daddy's going to have to hunt you down and kill you."

"With your pink, girly-girl pistol?"

"You won't call it girly-girl when you're crying the tears of a two year-old *boy* when I shoot your butt, Rocky McDaniel. Stop."

"Then get down out of the tree."

"No, go away!" I growl at him. He looks like he just got out of bed. His hair's sticking up on top. He nibbles on his bottom lip. I know that means he's working up to something and when I realize that, I'm also a bit caught off-guard at how well I can read him.

"You are going to get more than a marble hitting you in the ass if he sees you snooping around." Rocky sighs, loads another marble. "Don't make me do this."

"Don't *make* you do it? You act like you're not enjoying it when you do. I know better. Just *don't*. Ow!" I stand up, try to grapple with a limb to slip to the left out of his range and to use the tree trunk as a shield. Rocky just shifts to the left. I think it just makes me more vulnerable while I try to tug my short-shorts down at least to the panty line for protection. "Dammit, I think you like this."

"I do, *McGuire*. And you know, I can see your pink underpants." Rocky says while he reaches into his pocket and tugs out a handful of little, shiny marbles. "God, if you only knew how much I enjoy pelting you. Because I get the feeling *you* were the one who glued my drawers shut. Leah said she found two glue bottles in the library garbage can."

"I told you. My last name is Mauer. And it is Leah. She's lying. Why would I be so stupid to leave Super Glue in my garbage if I did it?" Twang! Pop! "Ow!"

"When you're on your daddy's hill, you're a McGuire and you're fair game. When you're at your mom's, you're a Mauer and it is common ground. I'll be nice." He pauses and taps his chin. "By the way, I didn't say it was Super Glue." He tugs back the sling while I rub my bottom where it hit. I watch while he pulls it upward and lets another round fly. It misses.

"Na na na na, boo boo," I chant and tug my sweater. "You missed." I wiggle my butt, waggle my head and fling my fingers in the air with the taunt. I probably shouldn't thirty feet above the ground with a rabid dog beneath me. Not to mention it's hard to hold the binoculars, book, and wrestle with my sweater at the same time. Rocky seems to let this soak in. I see his eyes narrow and he gets this certain cock to his chin. Now *he's* being a bit surly. Arrr. I know him way too well to be his enemy.

"You know what? I'm seeing through your stupid act. You can make your mom and Nicky think you're this sweet and innocent girl. I know better. So are we going there, Rosie?" he asks me hoarsely like he has to push the words out. "Because I'm not kidding. If Uncle Johnny sees you here, he will get out his gun and fill your rear with buckshot. That white little butt of yours will be a deep shade of pink."

"It already is!" I yowl at him. "Butthead."

"Yeah, I know. I can see your pink panties and your pink butt cheeks right now." He's wearing a cocky grin. "I don't know why you are spying on him, but you've got to stop."

"It's none of your business." I look down at the limb I'm balancing on. It is hardly bigger around than my wrist. It bends slightly when I shift my feet like a drunken trapeze artist doing a balancing act on a wobbly string. "How'd you know I was here?"

"Because your mom saw her binoculars and bird book missing. You were sneak-reading a crime book and borrowed six more just like it from Bobby's shelf." Rocky loads another marble. I move the book under my arm for better balance. "Everybody at church is talking about the big pile of dirt Uncle Johnny dug up. You took it one more step pegged him as a murderer. Just so you know, he's putting in a garage. The size seven shoe belongs to Leah. By the way and for future reference, I would suggest next time not leaving a huge open space in the shelf. It was obvious. Your mom also said you're acting weird lately. That can mean only one thing. You're doing that obsessive thing again and I saw your car parked down in the gravel pull off." *Twang.*

"Ow!" I try to step back, which is the wrong thing to do. "Stop it, shitass!" I'm already barely hanging on to a little stubble of a branch. "Why are you so mean to me and nice to everybody else? I'm only half-McGuire. You can be half-nice to me so you don't get your stupid curse."

"I'm not being mean, I'm saving your life. And I use up my half being nice to you when you are at your mom's. Here, I can be one-hundred percent mean. If my uncle sees you here, you're dead. And *shitass*? That's a new one. Are you twelve? Because you sound like it."

I feel the book slide out of the cleft of my arm between elbow and ribs. Foolishly, I snap to attention and try to catch it. *Twang. Smack*! Now that one hurt. It wasn't that I was in an incredibly defenseless position. He hit me right on the boob. I feel my left foot make this strange little kilter to the left. I reach out, trying to snatch a twig hanging there to balance and the next thing I know, I'm smashing down through the branches and leaves, banging off the big limbs with my ribs and getting slapped in the face by the smaller ones.

Two seconds. That's all it took for me to end up dangling by my buttoned-up sweater six feet from the ground and two feet from Rocky's head. I'm like a helpless bass dangling off a fishing pole with my arms stuck in my sleeves and Rocky looking up at me with wide, startled eyes. Then, the idiot has the nerve to start laughing hysterically at me. He gives me a gentle push with one hand and I sway back and forth, like a swing.

"Well, look who's in a pickle again," Rocky taunts me. "You look like one of the dead does my dad hangs up outside the house during hunting season."

"Get me down, jerk!" I'm screaming and trying to swing and kick him with my toes when I come forward.

"I'm a shitass, remember?. And I'm not letting you down." He stops to take a breath. "You're like that little white bunny Leah got for the county fair; it went wild and started chasing us around and trying to bite our ankles." Then he bellows another round of laughter until he's bent over with his hands on his knees.

"Oh, Rocky, you don't know the half of it, right now. If you don't help me down, I swear to God it won't be your ankle I'm biting."

He finally heaves this huge sigh and grabs me around the legs, tugs me up and down. I can feel him trying to detach the back of the sweater from the limb, then I'm free falling downward to my knees with my butt up in the air and my sweater still dangling over our heads. For one more humiliating moment I get to hear Rocky sniffling chuckles.

He's wiping tears from his eyes when I look up, for heaven's sakes. "Now, see? I saved your life," he starts. I feel a little tingle start at the nape of my neck and work its way downward to my belly.

"You almost killed me!" I shout at him. It feels really good, like a cork popping off a bottle of champagne that had been shaken. "Look!" I turn around, pull up the back of my shorts to expose two, tiny welts on my butt and then point to one on my inner thigh. Rocky's eyes waggle toward the sky. He pulls up a hand, rubs his chin like he is swiping a beard and I know he is trying to hide another round of laughter by the giddy smile dancing across his lips.

"Now you're killing me, girl," he says in a sexy voice.

That sent me over the edge. I go at him with both my hands, shove him back a half a step. Then I lay into him with a couple slaps on the chest that don't even make him wince. He has this silly grin on his face as he takes one step back and then another. Wow. I'm really not me today. I *do* feel like a feral bunny.

"Calm down."

"Don't tell me to calm down!"

"No, seriously. Are you all right, Rosie?" he asks me, suddenly concerned and talking down to me like I'm a baby. Calm down? I want to murder him. If I had my pistol at that moment, I think I just might load it and shoot at him.

"Screw off, Rocky."

"Or what?" His concerned expressions shifts easily to a snicker. He takes two steps forward and he's towering over me. I think he's going to put out his hand and give me a little push backward. Instead, he drops the snarky twist to his lips and just blinks down at me.

"What?" I'm waiting for him to say something to irritate me.

"I don't know. Nothing." His eyes are narrowing, like Rocky's sizing me up. He's close and so much so, he's blocking the tiny bit of wind between us. I see his hand rise. My eyes snap downward, watch it work its way upward. For some reason, I can't read him now. Is he going to flick me? Is he going to give me a push? I'm rigid when his fingers alight gently on my shoulder, just lay there tickling the skin. I look up from his hand to his face, my eyes working back and forth between his own. Hells bells, I can't figure out his tipped-head, glassy eyed expression. And yet, I'm not sure how to react—push his hand away, step back, or just stand there forever and wait for his next move.

It's right then, Rocky takes one more step forward and his fingers slide down my arm, slipping slowly to my elbow. It is soft and gentle, like a feather slipping along my skin. I feel the tickle of the hairs of my arm rise and I snap my attention downward, try desperately to blink away the embarrassment that he made me break out in a rash of goosepimples.

"What are you doing?" I jerk my eyes upward again and I swear Rocky is leaning down like he's going to kiss me. A quick step backward and I feel my back bump into the trunk of the tree. Rocky takes a step forward and I swallow hard.

"I've almost tamed the wild bunny now," he whispers, low on his breath. "Didn't I?" He's got this smug tip of chin.

I grit my teeth so hard, I hear them grind while I look for an escape route. "I hate you, Rocky."

"That's harsh—"

"Did I just hear you disrespecting my daughter?"

Oh, no. Daddy. I hear the crunch of leaves beneath feet far too late. I'm staring at Rocky when I hear Daddy's voice. I see his face lose color at the same time he sees my eyes get wide. He turns a hazy shade of pale green while he takes two giant steps back. My head snaps to the sound of the voice and behind me.

"No, Daddy," I sputter quickly. "He—he just came up to tell me Nicky and Mom were worried about me."

"That ain't what it sounded like to me." Daddy's eyes get dark when he's mad. His jaw churns like he's chewing something hard. I see him eyeing Rocky with the wary airs of an alpha lion staring down at a younger male. "If you got a problem with my little girl, you can take it up with me."

"I don't," Rocky answers. He holds up his hands, takes a step back from me.

"You know how Mom is," I sputter quickly. "Daddy, she won't let me walk ten feet from the house without calling in the National Guard. Or in this case, the closest line of defense, which is Rocky."

"You tell her to call me next time," Daddy says. "She ain't got no reason to call Rocky McDaniel when I can take a walk up the hill."

"Okay," I mutter. I turn and snatch up the bird book settled on the ground. I look up. My sweater is still caught ten feet up in a branch.

"What's your sweater doing up there?" Daddy asks, following my gaze. He takes a couple steps and stands on his tippy-toes, trying to reach it. For some reason, Rocky knows not to walk up with his full height and tug it down. He just takes three steps, then climbs up the tree, wiggles the sweater free where it is wrapped on a broken twig.

It falls. Daddy catches it. I see him look up at Rocky. I don't know if he notices I see him give Rocky the deepest, darkest of warning gazes. But I do hear this: "Stay away from my little girl, Rocky. She don't want no part of you, don't want no part of the McDaniels."

When I get back to my car a half hour later, I see a book on the passenger side. I get in, pick it up, and hold it between me and the steering wheel. *Psychology of Detecting Deception, Clues to the Truth.* I know immediately that Rocky put it there. It's his sarcastic way of telling me he knows I'm hiding something, I know it. It irks me even more. I shouldn't have defended him. I open the cover slowly. It looks brand new. I figured he'd took it off my stepdad's bookshelf in his study. Not so, maybe. A little piece of paper falls out next to my thigh.

Rosie, I saw this book when I was at the bookstore in town. I thought you might like it. It might be another book you can hide in a magazine.

"Maybe you can be a super woman or something and I can be a fireman, huh? I mean, you almost had the flying thing down a half hour ago in the tree—"

"Cripes almighty!" I jump so hard in surprise, I nearly drop the book. Rocky laughs aloud, that chuckle-huff he does. He's standing there, his hands on his hips, staring off into the air like some super hero getting ready to take flight. The wind blows his hair and he plays it off, tosses his arms skyward. I feel my face turn deep red. "Rocky, how long have you been standing there?"

"Just a second." He drops his hands, but not his silly grin. "Before you get mad again, I could have compared you to a witch taking flight. I didn't."

"I didn't have a broom. It wouldn't make sense."

"You're sassy *and* surly outside the confines of your mom's house." He loses the smile and shakes his head. I can still feel his fingers touching my arm. It irritates me that I liked the way it felt. Then he points to the book in my hands. "It's about interpreting body language, you know, like telling if somebody's lying by their facial expressions. Like you the other day when your mom asked why you had a bruise on your arm. You said you bumped into a table." He fans his fingers over his eyes. "You did this eye flutter thing. I figured you were lying."

"Is this some kind of game?" I ask him warily, watching his hand fall.

"No, Rosie. I'm just hoping you're not dating some guy that's hurting you."

"Worse than getting my butt pelted with marbles and making me fall from a tree? You can have your stupid book." I thrust it toward him. He looks hurt, backs away.

"No, I got it for you. No ulterior motives. I'm just—" He lets out a breath, does this shrug and shake of his head. "Did you read Winsome Falls?"

"The silly love story?"

"Yeah, we read it in your mom's book club. It was—"

I sniff a laugh. Mom's book club is eight or so fifty-something women who sit around each other's living rooms and drool all over PG rated saucy romances while they sip hot tea and nibble on homemade cookies. "*You're* in my mom's book club?"

"I am," he says, narrowing his eyes. "You could stand to read something other than—hardcore technical stuff." He wags a hand at me.

"I *like* hardcore technical stuff. Did Mom put you up to this?" I ask.

"No." Rocky loses expression, just looks bored. "Just take a chance and read it. Hell, I'll read it with you. I'm not like my Uncle Johnny, you know? Not that he's bad, just a little crotchety."

"So, did you read the test book I got you?" I ask gruffly. "I mean, you can hardly expect me to explore the sappy side of romance when you can't even open the pages of the book that will help you achieve your dream."

"Okay, that's fair." Rocky pats the window edge, with an inviting nod. "But the difference is that you're smart, I'm dumb. It's easy for you. I barely got through college with Ds and tutors sitting with me for every subject, every single day. Rosie, I barely passed the teaching exam the *third* time I took it. And I honestly think they knew I'd taken it so many times, they felt sorry for me and let me slide on that one."

"Why do you teach, Rocky?" I ask him. "Be honest."

"I don't know. Your sister and I were going out. She said it'd be cool if we both work at the same place after we graduated. I teach. She could be a school counselor."

"So, it's easier to achieve someone else's dream than your own? Why? You're afraid you'll fail the one thing you've dreamed of your entire life." I eye him carefully.

"I know."

"You won't fail." I say matter-of-factly and Rocky starts to say something. I hold a hand up. "But if by some fluke you do fail, you pick your sorry ass up and try again, and again, and again until you get that dream. You wanted to ride a bike when you were a kid, so you rode a bike. You probably fell twenty times, skinned a knee or two. But you got back up, bruised and bleeding, and climbed back on, and peddled your little legs off until you got it. It's common sense that you try it. You might fail. But you keep trying. You should know that, Rocky. I get it and everybody tells me I don't have a lick of common sense."

"Rosie, we don't have to be enemies all the time."

"Then I would suggest not hitting me with marbles

from that stupid slingshot." I sniff a sarcastic laugh, know he's thinking about that stupid curse even as we speak. Rocky gets a little half-grin. "Really? Because that was kind of fun."

Chapter 14

"It's amazing to what great lengths she'll go to avoid a conflict with her family." That's Kim at the country club, talking to Mister Barkley. I've already told them twice I'm standing right here and they don't need to talk about me like I'm not here.

"Did you find her another name, something sexier than Rosie?" Jack Barkley asks his assistant.

"I found a couple names online, sir," Kim is handing him a small sheet of paper. "Jasmine, Lillian, Lily, Pansy, Poppy, Posy, Ginger, Violet—"

"Violet," Mister Barkley seems to taste this with his lips while he rolls his tongue around the name. *Violet*? I'm thinking. *Who is named Violet except self-consumed, gum-chewing Violet Beauregarde from Willy Wonka who needs de-juicing after swelling into a giant, purplish blueberry?*

"Won't someone with the name of Violet stick out like a sore thumb?" I interject.

"Miss Violet Popovich," he whispers, ignoring me and seeming to taste it on his tongue. "That's it. Get her some contacts. Make her eyes—violet. And some different clothes." They both scan me with the kind of puckered lip frown my sister gives to dead animals on the highway when she passes them. "Make sure her new name's in the computer for taxes. She needs a license, birth certificate—"

"Birth certificate? Do we really need to give me an alter ego?" I try to see if they are joking, making fun of me for being so paranoid. I don't think they are.

"You said you didn't want anyone knowing you worked here so your mom doesn't find out. We might as well cover all the bases," Jack Barkley says curtly. "You got a problem with that? Because I don't do things half-ass."

"I guess not—"

"Good answer. Do you have any background in infiltrating possible suspect's homes?"

"Excuse me?" I croak. "Like breaking and entering? ? No, I mean I've never broken into anybody's house barring our neighbor's when I thought he stole my cat. I've never even had a parking ticket. That's not part of our deal. You didn't say anything about breaking the law."

Jack Barkley twitches his chin between forefinger and thumb, turns to Kim. "Let's plant a mic on her and have her talk to the cops or something to see if she can get more details."

"I'm a bad liar," I warn.

"Flirt a little. They'll be more interested in your smile," Mister Barkley suggests.

Kim pats my arm, smiles smoothly. "He's just kidding. He's having fun doing this. Let him play. I think he's like a kid, wanting to play spy."

"But *I'm* the one he's playing spy *with*," I huff. "And you're tossing me out in the open where everybody can see me. I know people who come here from my church—"

"And when I get done with you, they aren't going to recognize you." Kim reaches into a plastic grocery bag that is sitting on a nearby desk. She wiggles out a little box and holds it up high. "What's this say?" she asks me.

"Um," I squint at the box. "Taggert's Allergy Medicine. Stops Runny Nose. Watery Eyes—"

"Yeah, dump the thousand tissues you lug around and use this once a day instead. That red under your nose will clear up. You won't spend another dime on Kleenex."

I take it and watch Kim roll her eyes at Mister Barkley. I'm trying to digest the information, blinking at

Jack Barkley and Kim when my cell phone tings. The only people who normally text me are my mom and Nicky. But it's Rocky so I open the message.

I told Nicky I was thinking about fireman test. She laughed. I told my mom, she told my dad. He wouldn't talk to me for two days. Asked me where I come up with such stupid ideas. Nobody likes their job. Sorry. I appreciate the help. But I can't. I hate being laughed at and called stupid.

I don't know how to answer him. I'm kind of unfocused because Mister Barkley is droning on to Kim about an upcoming event.

"Are you listening to me?" Jack Barkley grunts at me, slaps the top of my phone. "Or are you more interested in texting your little friends? Because you can go and hang out with them instead of getting paid here."

"I'm sorry." He's so short-tempered. I nod, shove the cell phone in my purse. I'm not listening. I don't tell him that, though. I'm just thinking about Nicky always criticizing Rocky, always scolding us like bad puppies when we don't sit on cue or bark on cue or heel on command.

Ting. I cringe, knowing Rocky's wondering why I don't text him in return. *Ting.* I try to ignore it while Mister Barkley grumbles and gripes about employees and their cell phones. However, I suppose, realistically speaking, getting a little bit of attention from the frigging prettiest man in a million mile radius is making me boy-stupid.

"DAMMIT, WILL YOU EITHER TURN THAT DAMN PHONE OFF OR ANSWER IT!" Mister Barkley screams at me and I jump. He throws his hands into the air and stomps across the room. *Ting.* I'm not sure if Mister Barkley was just being sarcastic when he told me to answer it or not. So I throw caution to the wind, hope he wasn't being sarcastic, and mutter, "What if it's Liam? He has my number."

"Oh, my God, answer the damn thing!" Mister Barkley grunts. "You kids and those damn phones."

My eyes waver questioningly at Kim who lifts her shoulders and give me a *go-ahead,-but-you-might-get-fired* look. So I reach into my purse and gingerly pull out the phone.

Are you ok? Rocky texted three times, as if I might be in the middle of a kidnapping or mugging simply because I didn't answer him immediately. So under the watchful and lip-twitching gaze of Mister Barkley, I answer:

Dammit, Rocky. I'm at work! I'll text later.

Work? At school?

Oh, shit. I was so discombobulated between Mister Barkley's berating stare and Rocky sounding downtrodden, I didn't even think my text out. Oh, sometimes I wish I could trade in some of my smarts for common sense. Mister Barkley shakes his head. "You understand I was being sarcastic about answering your phone." Mister Barkley wags a finger at me. "I've got a phone conference. Don't make the same mistake twice, young lady. No playing around on your shift." Then he turns to Kim. "Get her a work cell phone to use here. Keep your personal one at home." The last line was aimed at me.

I wait three minutes after Mister Barkley stomps away before I call Rocky back.

"Rocky, you've got to stop texting me tonight," I tell him when he answers. "I—I started a job—waitressing at a restaurant in Crystal Springs," I stutter over my words. Oh, crap, *why* did I say Crystal Springs?

"Is it the country club?"

"No." I shake my head. "Just an old restaurant off the highway. Now let me get back to work. My boss is watching me."

Chapter 15

It rained all day on Wednesday and into Thursday. I spent Wednesday night babysitting Gabby again for my sister. It left me with a double fudge brownie tummy ache. And the rain left a layer of thick fog oozing out of the valleys in tiny twists and spirals driving back from the country club at ten o'clock Thursday night. My sister called after school, asked me to see if Gabby left her FBI badge and could I drop it off if I went to town. I tucked it into my glovebox and made a mental note to drop it at her house.

It's a slow drive along the backroads. The ground is saturated with water. The flooded creeks are creeping up and over the roads. I'm a creature of habit. I make my usual bi-weekly stop at the Laurel Grove Speedy Gas and Carryout to top off my tank, drive over to the pumps and jam my credit card into the machine for twenty dollars' worth of gas.

A mist is slipping past the bright lights of the gas station that ease out until their beams meet up with the four roadway lights along the intersection of a county road and the two-laner. The road is still busy this late—semi-trucks taking the quick route to the highway and workers at the Benson Tire Company coming and going from the factory. I can see all the way out to the highway, hear the swish of car tires when they roll along the asphalt in passing. I suppose it is just as I grab my little receipt from the printer I hear the man's voice on the loudspeaker at my pump. "Pump Six. Can you please come to the register and get your receipt?"

I look up the gas pump and my eyes alight on the huge 6 marking the pump above me. I look down to the damp receipt clutched in my fingers. Still, I huff a muffled *uh huh* at the ceiling where the voice is booming from and make my way to the counter. I'm a little off kilter about it. I'm hoping I'm not in trouble. A couple days after I found the article about Gina Channel in my choir robe pocket, I put up a little note on the corkboard bulletin board at the back of the gas station, where people put up things for sale. There's also a rag-tag handful of missing persons posters tacked there. The guy at the register that day had asked: "Hey, is there anything in particular you're looking for?"

I had craned my neck around at the voice of a young man at the register and shook my head. He had brown hair stuffed into a beanie hat and wire-rimmed glasses. I couldn't see his name tag from here, but I knew it said *Bucky T* on it. I always used to stare at it instead of looking him in the eye when I paid for my gas if I used cash.

"Oh, no." I had answered. "I put up a flyer asking if anybody knew a little girl named Gina Channel. I read about her coming up missing in 1979. Nobody seems to know what happened to her. I thought maybe somebody would remember her or have a newspaper article. She disappeared and there's absolutely nothing about her. Now the flyer's disappeared."

"Some guy came in and took it."

"Oh. Do you remember what he looks like?"

"Homeless. He had long, dirty hair and a long beard. He wore a ballcap." Bucky T patted the top of his head. "He looked like he hadn't taken a shower in a year. You have your cell phone number or anything on the flyer?"

"Yes."

"That probably wasn't such a good idea."

So now, I'm a bit leery. I've got my eyes set on the t-shirt of the same twenty-something hipster at the register as soon as I walk through the glass doors. This time, I catch Bucky T's eyes. If there's surprise in his returned gaze, like everybody else lately who is used to me shyly looking anywhere but at a face, the only evidence is a slight narrowing of his eyes before they make a quick snap to the right. My gaze follows. There's a shabby looking man at the end of the candy aisle with a scruffy beard, blue flannel jacket, and a dirty, red ballcap. His brown pants are dingy and riddled with holes. He's hugging a grocery store-size crumpled brown paper sack in his arms. I look back to Bucky T uncertainly. He holds up a finger as if telling me to wait. I come to a standstill and awkwardly linger there in line behind the man to whom he is handing a receipt. The gas station is quiet except for the sound of country music playing softly from a boom box near the register and the ting-ting of someone paying for gas.

"He's got something for you." Bucky T's finger comes up and he makes a lazy point to the man, then turns away and makes himself busy behind the counter. Bucky looks as unsure as I feel right now.

"Rosie—McGuire?"

I stop uneasily before the man at the aisle. "Rosie McGuire was my aunt." He's staring at me, then looks disappointed. It is an uncomfortable kind of stare, like he's drinking my entire face in before he thrusts out the sack.

"Oh, I thought you—I mean, I thought she came back," he stammers, taking a step forward. I glance toward Bucky T who is eyeing the man as cautiously as I am. "I sat outside and watched to see who put that paper up about Gina. You got gas every other day. You went inside every other day at exactly three o'clock, when you got done at the high school and before you take off down the highway."

I probably should be more concerned that he just admitted he was stalking me. However, as my mind works— less full of common sense and more full of rational thinking,

I only focus on the connection he has to my aunt. "My aunt? You knew her?" I ask. He doesn't answer, so I extend my hand. "What is this?" I hesitatingly take the sack. I catch a whiff of BO and I force myself not to wince.

"I know'd I shouldn't of kept it. But I thought you was Rosie, the *old* Rosie, and thought you'd want it back. I kept it like you said—like *she* said. She were so pretty, lying there. I thought you'd want to know she weren't hurting no more. Just don't give this to Johnny. You told me that. Until it was okay. I guess it isn't okay. Because you're not back. But I got to go." He starts to turn.

"Wait. Who—who was—lying? My aunt? Who?"

"I got to go. You probably should just let it go. Don't get your hands dirty with it. Don't go tacking stuff up so they see it, inviting them in. They'll find you. And they'll come after you! If you're dead, you can't talk. And they don't know your secrets. Don't let anyone know her secrets."

"Who?" I ask with a wispy breath. "Wait, please," I'm talking to his back and then the glass door when it shuts slowly behind him. I just stare at him, watch him walk across the black asphalt parking lot. I glance at Bucky T who is doing the same, watching him leave. "Do you know who that was?" He just gives me a shrug of his shoulders right before his eyes snap upward.

"No. He came in and asked me to call you in here. He's stopped in a couple times this week. This was the first time you were here." Bucky T's eyes are narrowing. He's leaning hard on the counter. "Oh, what's he doing?"

I turn slowly, follow his gaze past the bright lights above the fuel pumps, then farther into the more oozy depths of the highway lights. I step toward the door, stop just short of the glass. I can see the man who just handed me the sack. He is running—arms pumping, legs sprinting, heading right toward the guardrail on the highway. He uses both hands on the guardrail to push his legs over like a gymnast jumping a pommel horse. Then he makes a jerky run right out into the road.

I hear a gasp. It is my voice. The front end of a semi-truck smashes into the man. Boom. Or maybe it is more a *pfoot*, muffled by the glass window doors and followed by the screech of tires on wet asphalt and the blast of truck horn seconds too late. *Pfoot*. He is there, then he is gone. I waver there with my palm cupping my lips, wishing this is a bad dream. *Pfoot*. I'm glued to the spot, mouth dropped as the truck comes to a sideways skidding stop.

"Oh, my God!" I didn't even hear Bucky T come around the counter. He lays a hand on my shoulder and I jolt. He's shaking. "Why—why'd he do that?" he huffs like he's out of breath and like I have an answer. "Holy shit. I mean, holy, holy shit!" I can't even speak. "Did you see that? Did you see him—?"

I sat on a stool next to the counter for at least forty-five minutes while a firetruck, an ambulance, and two police cruisers arrive out on the highway. I'd clutched the sack in my hand, working the paper back and forth in my fingers. My mind replays the scene of the dull thud of semi-truck smashing into body over and over. I'm in shock. We watch the lights and keep telling each other how weird the whole thing was.

"He just said not to get involved," I hiss. *"If you're dead, you can't talk. And they don't know your secrets."*

"Who was he talking about?"

"I don't know." I look up at Bucky T. His face is bleached white.

"Why don't you get out of here?" He points to the

door. "Just—maybe let's pretend you weren't here. Something's not right. I got a bad feeling about it."

"Hey, Rosie, you all right?"

It's Rocky coming across the little section of grass between the parking lot and the highway just as I get to my car. He's got on his fireman safety uniform when I start to get in my car. I'm closing my door, peering out the open window. I nod, try to pretend I'm not numb inside. "Yes. I'm fine."

"Were you here when that happened? They're questioning the people who stopped, asked me to come down here and see if anybody else saw what happened. I saw your car." He puts his hand on the window, leans in hard and looks down. "Oh, you're pretty pale."

"I'd gone inside," I say to his expressionless face. "I didn't see much. He just walked right on to the highway. I mean, that's what I saw through the doors."

"That's what everybody else is saying. You want to tell that to the police?"

"No," I whisper, still clutching the bag on my lap. "I just want to go home."

He looks at me long and hard. His gaze lingers about two seconds, eyes going back and forth between my own. Then Rocky gives me the slightest of squints. I realize right at that moment, Rocky might be my archenemy by default, but he knows me better than my own sister. And he can read me better than my own mom. He knows I'm freaking out about something. He knows—

"What's up, Rosie?" he says, looking over his shoulder at the scramble of red and blue lights. I want to lie and tell him that there's nothing going on. I know better.

"Rocky, I need you." Why the hell did I whisper that?

I know it wasn't more than a wispy rush of words against the chatter of the police radio on the highway and the sounds of traffic moving around the scene. But I don't want to go home in the stifled quiet and sit and think about it over and over.

He pats the roof with one hand. He's hard-staring me without expression. Then he takes in a healthy breath.

"I didn't mean that," I blurt out. "I don't know why I said that. You don't have to be nice to me."

"Give me five minutes to drop my uniform. Most of the fire department crew has left. I'm getting ready to leave. I'm just finishing up that ol' grunt work you were talking about." He smiles gently at me. "I'll ride home with you, sit with you for a few. We can watch a show or something."

Chapter 16

Beneath the amber lights in my kitchen, I open the brown paper sack while Rocky pulls up a chair and settles in across from me with a fresh cup of coffee. The mug he's holding has a dancing pig on it. I wonder why he picked that one out of all the others on my shelf.

"Do you want me to do a drum roll?" he asks, holding both his forefingers up before he makes a beat softly on the table. I roll my eyes. "I'm just trying to make light of a *really* unnerving evening, Rosie."

It looks like a stuffed animal is in the bag. I reach in, feel the fur and tug it out. It's an old, worn monkey backpack, with pink and blue faux leather straps and a little zippered denim compartment where its tummy would be to hold stuff.

"It looks kind of old," Rocky observes. I nod. I wiggle the zipper, gently tug it open. I see Rocky lean in so our heads almost touch. A few crumpled and folded pieces of lined paper fall out. I snatch them up, carefully unfolding one.

"What is it?" Rocky asks eagerly, his deep voice is soft. I keep waiting for him to make a salty remark. He doesn't.

It's an English assignment paper with a red A– written on the top. "It looks like somebody's homework," I answer. The writing below has an uncanny resemblance to my own. *Rosie McGuire.* I blanch. My hand goes to my lips.

"What?" Rocky asks.

"It's my aunt's backpack. I mean, I think."

He says nothing, just blinks like he is digesting what I said. Rocky watches my face like he is evaluating my reaction. I look down, stare at the little monkey flopped down in my lap. I open a second paper. It's another assignment. Another A. There's a little brown leather wallet too. Inside, Aunt Roo's driver's license stares back at me. There's more—a roll of a couple dollars' worth of bills, a tiny troll doll, and a cat keychain and a handful of change. Oh, and a small, plastic, great white shark squeaky toy.

"Oh, Rocky," I murmur. "Daddy told me he got this for Aunt Roo at the county fair. She never went anywhere without it." I must look like I'm going to cry because Rocky swallows hard and his eyes get big. "It's okay," I say hoarsely, but I think Rocky knows what's going on in my head. If she doesn't have the shark, it means she is dead.

"I think I'm going to cry," I warn him. And the tears just pour like a March rain. I can't do more than sob into my hands while he pats my back awkwardly. Then, while my nose runs, I ask him to get me a tissue. He jumps up like a scared rabbit, snatches a paper towel from the roller above my sink. Just as he snaps his wrist to separate the first from the dispenser, the square doesn't release. As he whips his hand out, the towels unroll one by one until he's got them spilling out in a sea of white to the floor. A stunned expression crosses his face as he snatches up a wad and dumps them in my lap; I can't help but laugh like a hysterical lunatic. Rocky looks like he doesn't know if he should laugh along or wait for me to burst into tears again.

Finally, the tears stop and I push the hair out of my eyes. I keep picturing the man who handed me the sack at the Laurel Grove Speedy Gas and Carryout. I see his eyes, light blue and almost white. The scraggly beard. The dirty hair. He was wearing a flannel jacket and dirty pants. He just *looked* like a serial killer, right? But my mind, it peeled away the exterior. I look deeper than the dirty clothes and the unkempt hair. I see a man who has given up taking baths and cutting his beard because he has no reason to look good. He has no reason to live. His stance wasn't arrogant. It was sad, his shoulders sagged as if the weight of the world was upon them. *If you're dead, you can't talk. And they don't know your secrets.*

"You've never seen this man before, Rosie?" Rocky interrupts my thoughts. "He just handed you the sack, then walked out on to the highway?"

"No, I haven't." I shake my head back and forth. I get this feeling he thinks that's probably the guy who sent me the roses. It would have to be someone creepy and suicidal. But he doesn't say that. Rocky sits back in his chair and takes a sip of his coffee. "I put up a flier on the bulletin board at the gas station, asking about Gina Channel. You know, the one by the bathrooms. He saw—"

"Rosie," Rocky groans, tossing his head back. "What were you thinking?" He lets a long line of air from his lips and then rubs his temples between thumb and forefinger. "You should really go to the police about this."

He must see my faraway look at him. He knows that remark will force me to distance myself from him.

"No. Not yet," I answer. "Rocky, I think they know something. If I take this to the cops now, it will disappear."

"What makes you think that? You have to trust somebody," he tells me. Rocky leans in a bit, tries to grasp my eyes in his. "You've got to let somebody know there's something going on."

"I'm telling *you*," I say to him. He nibbles on his bottom lip, leans over so his elbows are on his knees and his hands are folded between. Rocky's staring at his thumbs twiddling back and forth. I know he's deep in thought, trying to figure out a way he can sabotage the reason I am trusting him right now. The curse. That damnable curse is going to kill him trying to elude it before it strikes misfortune on the world. "You're thinking about the curse, aren't you?" I gripe. "You know you double-blink whenever you think about it. It pops up in your head so often when I'm around, your eyes look like Gabby's doll that got stuck in the screaming-mama mode. It made Mom so crazy, she put it in the garage when Gabby was visiting."

Rocky looks up, ignores my words. "You are tampering with evidence to a crime. I work part time for the fire department, Rosie, and I'm a teacher. I will never get a job if I am a part of this. You'll go to jail. I'll go to jail."

"Okay, then walk out the door right now, Rocky McDaniel." I point to the door. "Just pinch me so it hurts a little and that stupid curse won't follow you. I won't hold it against you." I hard-sigh. "But just so you know, I honestly believe the police are trying to pin this on somebody from Troublesome Creek or Raccoon Hollow. I think they will try to pit us against each other and sit back and wait for the fight to begin. We'll all battle it out. My daddy will deny it. Your uncle will deny it. Then they'll freak out and start turning each other in for one thing or another—"

"If you turn that in, though," he interrupts. "Maybe they will find out who that man was and maybe he did something to your aunt. Maybe he was the one who murdered the girls. His backyard could be full of graves!"

"*Maybe*. Or maybe they'll just say he did it long enough for some other poor girl to get murdered. Then, they'll point a finger at me like I made the whole thing up. And if not and they decide to pin it on somebody else when the dust settles, whoever loses will get sent to jail. Your uncle or my daddy, which will it be, Rocky? Your mama or my granddaddy. You or me?"

When I say the last part, he snaps his head up to mine. "Now you're being silly. Why would you say that? We're too young to be blamed for all those murders. "

"Fine," I hold out the bag, shove it towards his chest. "Take it. Hand it in to Timmy Kinney so he can arrest me. While you're at it, tell him I was the one driving the ATV. It ought to cover that stupid curse for at least a hundred times to the refrigerator at Nicky's to get me ice cream."

He rolls his eyes. Then Rocky pushes the bag back. "I don't want it. You're manipulative, you know that, right?"

"Manipulative, my ass. I'm pointing out the reality of the situation! They are going to blame somebody. They are looking for those who are the least likely to fight back and that everyone in Laurel Grove would expect to commit a crime."

"Well, it wouldn't be you so I don't know why you're worried. Nobody would ever think you would commit a crime. You don't even have a parking ticket. And yes, you are manipulative."

"I am not!" I stand up, slap the monkey backpack on the table and fold my arms across my chest.

"Yeah, and that's why you did those things with your eyes." He waves a hand at my face.

"What are you talking about?"

He rolls his own eyes, then blinks his and tries to look coy, "*Oh, Rocky, I need you,*" he says in a high-pitched voice before it drops again. "What you should really be saying is: *Rocky, I want you to be an accessory to a crime.*"

"That's not fair. You don't have to be here. And I *did* need you." I step back, let his words sink in. "And if you really want to point out flaws, you're so damn ignorant and superstitious, you've given yourself a tic disorder, you understand that, right?"

"Bullshit! You think because you're smart you know everything but you don't, you—"

"The curse," I say that one phrase and he blinks

twice.

"Stop it."

"The curse." Blink-blink.

"The curse, the curse, the curse—!" I say louder and louder each time so I'm leaning over my table with my hands flat on the surface.

"Enough!" Rocky yells those words and his hand hits the coffee mug when he rises and it goes flying. I swear, I've never heard him full-body, deep-voice shout and I know my own eyes get big and I freeze when he stands up to his full height. *Oh, God, this is where a McDaniel kills a McGuire!*

He just stands there, arms folded across his chest and his chin in the air like he thinks he's holier and mightier. Then all of a sudden, it is like I'm being pulled through a pipe and the Rocky I'm staring at is at the far end. Between, there is a gray ooziness. And then, I see it. A car. A shovel. Rocky when he was fourteen, with a black eye. I reach up, touch the back of my head. *Just so you know. He always forgets to tell the girls that it's going to hurt for just a second.* I hear a woman's voice tell me. *At least the first time. Sometimes it takes him a couple times. I'll try to get him to be quick.*

"Rosie, I would never hurt you."

I jump when I feel Rocky's hand barely touching my shoulder. I keep stepping back and back and back until my bottom hits the stove. I stop there with my jaw slack. I'm sure I look like a stunned doe staring hard into truck headlights.

"You had a black eye?" I whisper.

"What?" Rocky leans in, like he can't quite hear me. His hand doesn't leave; I feel his warmth on the skin of my shoulder. "A black eye?"

"When you were a kid." My voice is hoarse and soft,

and barely makes it over the sound of my refrigerator. I feel a tear on my cheek. I'm ashamed of myself. If my daddy knew I was showing weakness in front of Rocky, in front of a McDaniel, he would disown me. Well, at least he'd sit me down and give me a lecture. "I just—remembered it. You had a black eye when you came to school. It was the day you told me we weren't friends anymore."

Rocky looks dumbstruck for a moment. Then he stares at the floor. "You're right. I did. You remember that?"

"I didn't come home. It was Kylee Wren's sleepover. Her parents were out of town." I feel woozy, lightheaded. "I remember." I say to no one in particular. "Did the woman do it to you? Did she give you the black eye?"

"What woman, Rosie?" Rocky's voice is soft. He looks discomfited and concerned.

"I remember a shovel at my feet in a car. She told me that it would hurt—I hear her voice, but I can't see her."

"She?" Rocky's temple is beading with sweat. What is wrong? I shake my head.

"I don't know. I heard the voice in my head. It was a woman. It sounded familiar—but not familiar. It's like I know who it was, but I know that it might not be that person because I was just thinking about her?"

"My cousin gave me the black eye for—"

"—for hanging around with me. I know." I take in a breath, let it out slowly. Oh, he's right. A bit of memory creeps into the back of my mind, teases me with just a hint of remembrance. "We used to ride bikes—one summer. You and I hung out a lot."

"Yeah, Rosie. Friends. We both liked riding bikes up at the old amusement park. Kyle and some of my cousins found out. They—"

"—they beat you up. Told you that you were going to

bring the curse down on your family. You sent me a note in fifth period at school and said I was weird. You didn't want to hang out with me anymore."

"I was afraid they'd hurt you too."

"What did I do? Why do I remember a shovel?"

"I—I don't know." Rocky swallows hard, rubs a finger along his lips. "You were so angry. I remember you leaving school. It was seventh period, gym. Your mom said you came home and got a backpack and filled it with clothes to go spend the night with a bunch of friends."

I look at Aunt Roo's backpack. I shake my head. "Mom used to act like I fell and bumped my head. Nicky said I just wanted attention and got drunk and passed out. I wasn't supposed to drink because of my anxiety medications. I think I did. I think they came up with this story about me partying at Kylee's house and between my pills and the beer, I passed out and fell or something. When I bumped my head, I conjured up the story and confused it with Aunt Roo's disappearing."

There's a knock on the door. I jump. Rocky turns toward the living room and to the front door. "You got somebody coming over?"

"Not that I know of."

I get up slowly, make my way to the front door. There's a figure on my porch. There's a car in the driveway; it looks like Leah McDaniel's little beat up compact. I tug open the door and sure enough, it is Leah standing beneath the porch lamp.

"Is Rocky here?" She grunts at me.

I hear the chair in the kitchen make a creaky groan as he stands up.

I don't even have to answer her. She leans around and takes in Rocky walking across the room.

"What's going on?" she demands, looking from me to Rocky. Rocky's running his hand through his hair over and over. "Are you babysitting again tonight?" she grills Rocky, pointing at me. She looks cranky, has a twist to her lips and she's tugging at the bun on top of her head. It's not a good sign. Every time she dug a knuckle in my back in junior high, she played with her hair. "Dad was looking for you. He was wondering what went on up at the gas station. He called the station. They told him you never came back. I stopped in and Nate Turner said somebody in a little car gave you a ride."

"What do you need, Leah?"

"I told you, Dad's looking for you."

I can see the two of them glaring at each other for almost the count of ten. Rocky is the one who breaks, looks somewhere between sheepish and distressed.

"Yeah, Rosie saw some guy get run over by a truck," he says. "I'm sitting with her until her sister gets here."

"They need to put a leash on her," Leah sneers. I feel my hackles rise. Rocky holds up a finger, points Leah out to the porch, then steps outside after her. He closes the door behind them. I can hear the two whisper-yelling back and forth.

Five minutes later, Rocky opens the door. He doesn't step all the way inside, simply stops right at the threshold. I see how this is going to go. Even when he reaches out a hand and latches on to my fingers.

"I'm going to give Nicky a call so she can come over and spend the night." He waggles my fingers. "Leah's taking me home." I know Leah told him his family was shitting bricks because Nate Turner told them Rocky went with me.

"No, don't call Nicky. I'm fine." I tug my hand away and stretch my fingers out in front of me like I'm holding him at bay. Then I reach out and grab on to the door knob. "I know the drill. I've been through this with you before. We need to draw the line, build a wall—whatever. I'll make it easy on you. Here's the first brick, don't come around," I whisper. For some stupid reason, I've got this huge lump in my throat. "There's some things I remember and some things I don't. Most of the stuff I do remember is you coming to school with a black eye and bruises a few weeks after that summer we hung out together." I do recall Rocky getting on the school bus. He'd been sitting behind me for the entire year, poking me in the back of the head, soft-flirting like boys do with girls. But on that day, he'd just walked past. He didn't look at me, just went back and sat down with a bunch of boys and Leah sitting in the back of the bus. "Then that very day, you stopped being my friend. You started being a shit, just like Leah and all the rest of them. It hurt. It hurt—so bad," I almost lose the words to a whisper. "So, let's save the bruises this time, Rocky. For both of us. Here's the next brick in the wall. Just tell my mom and my sister you can't babysit me anymore. I'll avoid you. You avoid me. Don't be nice to me. And the third and fourth brick on the wall—don't come around Mom's house on Saturdays. I'll skip Sunday. It's that easy."

He says absolutely nothing. Rocky just nods his head, stares at the ceiling while I reach out and give him a little push. He folds with it far too easily. I close the door and I hear his footsteps on the porch before they fade away down the little stairs and disappear along the walkway. I lean back against the door, slide down along the bumpy exterior until I'm sitting on the floor. Then I sob into my hands, feeling the same heartache I'd felt that day so long ago again from losing my best friend. I wish the old memories would just stay out of my reach and stay lost in the dark recesses of my mind.

Chapter 17

"How much did he offer you?" Liam Dubois is settled against the wall of the makeshift locker room the staff use before they go to work. It is just down the hallway from the dank little office Mister Barkley had his maintenance staff set up for me. There's an ugly metal desk with drawers that don't quite close, a lamp, file cabinet, and two ergonomically correct chairs across from the desk.

Liam is looking me up and down while I douse my lips in red. It's not like I'm a cherry lollipop, which the guy who was getting gas said he'd like to lick when I pumped the fuel into my car forty minutes ago. It's more like he's not quite sure it's really me beneath the makeup, slinky red dress, high heels, and oh, yes, violet contacts. And I'm not sporting my usual tissue. Kim was right; the allergy medicine dried me right up. "Because I was sure you weren't coming back. You've been gone—" It's tiny and cramped with a men's side and a women's side. Mister Barkley told me the area where the dining room, kitchen and entrance are located now was once the original golf club before they renovated and added a new section.

"—three days," I finish for him. "And I think that is how long it took to get me from Rosie—" I wave my hand in front of me. "—to Violet. Which, I might add, is more for you than me, Mister Dubois. That is, so you aren't embarrassed to drag around your 'little cousin' in a raggedy sweater." It's been three days since Mister Barkley upped his offer to stay. He's good to his word, even if I feel like a fish out of water as Violet. I am focusing on the fact that twenty-five thousand dollars will buy my daddy a new ATV.

Still, it didn't come easily. "I—I don't like this." I had told Kim when I walked into the kitchen ten minutes earlier where she was going over something with the chef. They were both leaning over the table, and looked up at me at the same time. Neither spoke, just gaped at me with wide eyes. "Did—you—hear me?" I asked softly. "I'm not comfortable at all with this."

My mascara was so thick I felt like I was looking through a bunch of bushy trees when I blinked. And my dress, it was halfway between knee and crotch. The woman who came from The Treasure Boutique in Crystal Springs to fit me for new clothes, style my hair, and show me how to put on makeup shoved in fake, plastic boobies to make mine look like two huge cantaloupes. She sprayed on some temporary hair-color to turn my bland brown to chestnut with a little streak of violet slipping in front of my ear. Then she tossed my old black sweater in a paper bag and told me to toss it. Mom would crap petunias if she saw how short this slinky deep red dress was and how much makeup I was wearing. And the lipstick, it's cherry red and makes my full lips look like I just ate a cherry Popsicle. Oh, or a lollipop.

"Oh." Kim finally blinked. "Rosie, I mean Violet."

"Oh, God, grow some balls, Mauer."

I about died right then when I snapped my head to the left and saw a big, thick ball of red hair tied back with a gigantic red scrunchie. Leah McDaniel. She was dropping a bin of dirty dishes on the sink and turning so her back wasn't to me. "What are you looking at, princess?" She'd whispered those words, but they bounced off the walls in a sudden lull in the conversation. I'm not sure if she was surprised her voice had carried past me or if she just realized who I was talking to, but Leah's eyes widened and her shoulders tense. My emotional reaction was something akin to a two year-old peering beneath the bed and actually seeing a monster grinning jagged-teeth back at her. My hair stood on end and I made a nearly voiceless peep of terror.

"What—what are you doing here?" I stuttered, snapped my head to Kim. "What is she doing here?" My heart was pounding and my brow was sweating beneath a mask of thick makeup. I was six years old again and waiting for her to snatch up my arm, twist the skin between her fists, and give me an Indian rug burn.

"I bus tables." She gestured at her outfit. She was wearing a black and white uniform. I don't think I'd ever seen her in a skirt and especially as short as the one she was wearing. She narrowed her eyes, balled up her fists.

"Excuse me," Kim interjected, stood up and looked from me to Leah. "You don't talk to her like that," she ordered. "You don't *ever* speak to Mister Dubois's staff in such a manner. Do you understand me?"

"Yes, ma'am." Leah looked drained when she said those words, didn't make eye contact with me. I should have been cocky about it. Strangely, I wasn't. I could see Leah's jaws churning and her freckles looked like little flecks of cinnamon against white skin. I could only think this would give her more fuel to bully me.

"I know her from Laurel Grove," I whisper to Kim.

Kim made a quick twist toward the chef. "Give me a moment. Let me take care of something." She turned to Leah. "Outside the doors. Leave your apron on the sink."

Leah's face lost a bit of color before she made a quick turn, slipped off her apron, and plopped it on the sink. Kim waited for her to walk out and turned to me. "Mister Barkley doesn't need staff like that working here. I'll take care of her. I'll also make sure this goes no farther."

"You're not going to fire her, are you?" I grabbed Kim's arm. She stopped, looked at my fingers then to me. All's I could think of was Gabby tossing her chin into the air with a proud twist, telling me her mama was going to buy her a pool. It never occurred to me she bussed tables here.

"Do you have a problem with that?"

"I do. I mean, kind of. It's complicated but our families go way back," I shifted uncomfortably. "And maybe it isn't in a good way. It's kind of a thing between us, that bantering. Our families have this historical feud. She's from one side of the fence, I'm from the other."

"Really?" A funny smile passed over Kim's face. It was like I was holding a tasty cookie over her head. "Like the Hatfields and McCoys?"

"Yes. My grandmother believed that the two families were cursed."

"Cursed?"

"Yes," I answered, nodding my head. "I know it sounds silly, but they believe what they believe. It goes way back that when the McDaniels and the McGuires have any friendly contact, marry or whatever, something bad happens."

"Like what?"

"Well, I'll tell you what my mamaw told me—"

"Your *mamaw*?" Kim snickered and I gave her a stare long enough she dropped the laugh and held out an apologetic hand. "I'm sorry. It just sounds funny."

"Mamaw is what we call my grandma. Do you want to hear the story or not?" I ask hotly and Kim nods, so I continue. "Well, in the 1860s, Hannah McGuire, who was my great, great cousin was teaching school at the little Troublesome Creek school house. Troublesome Creek used to be a town back then and not just a couple houses on the hillside. But she was only like fifteen and she had a boy in the class who was seventeen and she fell in love with him. He was George McDaniel. They decided to elope, but their buggy overturned in Troublesome Creek during a storm. It was always a tough creek to cross during a flood. They both died. At least, that's the story I've always heard. It was only a few days later, both families got word that they were looking for troops to recruit for the Civil War. The McGuires blamed George McDaniel for starting the curse, and the McDaniels blamed Hannah. They associated all the bad stuff that came after on each other regardless the war was inevitable and it had been longer in the making than two sweethearts running away from their families to get married. Such, folks started believing that we'd all be better off if the McDaniels and the McGuires hate each other. Bad things might not happen again."

"So, usually there's a way to break the curse," Kim pointed out matter-of-factly. "At least, in all the movies there is."

"Yeah, we have to find a dark haired girl and bury her alive. That's what is said."

"Whoever heard of such a thing in southern Ohio?"

"I was making the last part up, Kim," I scowled. "I was talking about you being sacrificed—nevermind. No. No cure for the curse, except the McDaniels have to be mean to the McGuires and visa-versa."

"Well, curse or not, I would think you'd want Leah McDaniel fired. There won't be any ramifications for you."

"If she tells anybody where I work, there will."

"We have a form all our employees fill out when they start for confidentiality of all other workers. She'll be talking to attorneys if she says anything." Kim said. "But Mister Barkley said to make you happy. You make the call."

Ten minutes after Kim walked out, the two returned. Leah walked right up to me, her face utterly lacking expression. "I'm sorry, Miss Popovich," she said clearly. "I mistaked you for someone else." Kim waited for Leah to leave with the empty bin and she turned to me with a folder in her hand.

"Don't worry about her. She's not going to speak to anyone about you. From now on, when you are here, you are Violet Popovich, a niece of Jack Barkley. She said honestly, she had not turned around, just heard your voice. She thought she was mistaken when you passed her."

Liam didn't recognize me at first either. It's a teacher in-service day, so I came in early to obtain some information from the staff. I got nothing but deadpan stares, even when I try to help fold towels with the laundry service. Now, I'm freshening up, sliding cherry red lipstick over my lips at a little mirror. I had looked up, heard Liam's quick remark. He's not supposed to be on this side. I don't remind him of that. I am just thinking he must have gone through this before. I wonder how many adult nannies he's gone through until me.

"I don't like you." Liam tells me.

"The feeling is mutual," I reply blandly. "But let's be enemies together." I say that with a smart-alecky waggle of my shoulders.

"Frenemies."

"I suppose that's the proper term."

"*I suppose that's the proper term,*" he repeats back in a whiny, high-pitched voice. "You're *such* a geek."

"Do you have *any* friends, Liam?" I ask him hotly. "I mean, really. If your hand isn't out with weed or free drinks or a wad of cash, do people actually want to hang out with you?"

"Oh, you're all pouty, did I hurt your feelings?"

I ignore him. "So where are we going tonight, boss?"

I ask him, taking in his face. "Because I'm all dressed up so I don't, you know, embarrass you." If his personality wasn't so crappy, he'd be downright hot. But he's got that rich boy, hoity-toity, snob attitude with his chin held a little high and the dead-bored look to his eyes. "Spend some money on me. Your daddy bought me shoes, dresses, makeup, and even fake tits," I point to my significantly larger than normal bust. "What are you going to give me?"

"I'll buy you some white lingerie and a sexy nurse's uniform and we could have some fun."

"I'm more the black leather and whips type." I lean in, cock up my chin, and give him a warning purse of lips. "You want to go there with me after leaving me in a dark parking lot at that strip club?" I don't think he does. I've opted out of my anxiety meds again and it doesn't take much to set me off. I think he's noticing it too.

Liam takes a step back, rolls his eyes. "Damn, girl, you put all that stuff on and you're like a different person; you know that right? You're snarky and stuff." I just stare at him until he shrugs. "You're not really going to do this, are you?" He rocks back and forth against the door. "My dad's not going to know the difference. I can have the driver take you home. You get paid. I get to party."

"Yes, I am," I tell him. "And he *will* know the difference because you'll end up getting arrested or someone will get a picture of you. You're stuck with me for two months or at least until the police catch whoever is murdering girls—or I suppose one of us murders the other whichever comes first."

"Two months. So, it's a contract?"

"It is."

"You think it's me just like everybody else. Maybe I *will* murder you. You're ruining my sex life. Just walk away.

My stepdad won't do anything. He's all bark, no bite." His voice scuffs the air like an old tennis shoe on a newly waxed floor, ending in a squeak. He sniffs a laugh.

"You really want me to leave, *frenemy*?" I ask him. "Because I'm the only one between you and the state penitentiary right now. And I know, from certain privileged information, that you're going to get questioned again. Because there was a girl attacked."

"What? I thought you gave my stepdad alibis. You're lying. I know you're lying. I talked to the lawyers."

"Yeah, well, the night when you left me like a lost pup at the strip club, there was another girl attacked."

"How do you know?"

How do I know? I found out when Kim gave me a whole new driver's license this morning. It had Violet Popovich on it. She made my middle name Sofia. It's Ukrainian because Popovich is Ukrainian. She told me Mister Barkley is telling everyone his sister married one of his old army buddies. Violet is a step niece. I asked if the cops would know it was fake and she said no, she had added me to the national databases. And I'm not to ask her how she did it. She wouldn't tell.

She also told me her uncle works for the police department at Crystal Springs as she brandished a newspaper. I blinked at her, dropped my eyes to the big, bold letters on the front page of the Hamford, Ohio Daily Times. *VICTIM THREE? POLICE STUMPED. WOMAN MAULED BY ATTACKER DIES.*

"I can sum it up," she told me. "At one-thirty in the morning, Phoebe Wells was driving home from her job—it's about forty minutes from here in the town of Hamford."

"They released her name?"

"No, my Uncle Donny works for the Crystal Springs

Police Department. He knew I worked for Mister Barkley and asked if I knew where Liam was that night. I told him it was covered. You were with him."

"No way," I hiss. No way. I groan inwardly, try not to show my apprehension right then. Because Liam wasn't with me at all. He'd taken off and was out of my sight.

"Yeah. They didn't find her for three hours. She was lying on the side of the road. They think the guy who grabbed her thought she was dead. She was in the middle of the highway, almost got smashed by a truck."

"What highway?" I ask slowly and not wanting to hear the truth.

"State Route 32. Why?"

Why? Because the strip club was right off State Route 32. So that's how I know Liam Dubois is in a whole lot of trouble. And that's what I tell him—"Because you took off after dropping me at the strip club and disappeared for two hours. They found a girl lying in the middle of Route 32 going west toward Cincinnati and it was less than an hour's drive away. I could have been your alibi for the third murder, which would have proven you weren't involved. But because you were such an idiot, now I'm not."

"You're a bore, Rosie, you know that right?"

"Violet. Here, Mister Dubois, my name is Violet." I sigh, shake my head. He's not going to make my job easy on me. "But I'll tell you what a bore is going to be and that is you sitting in jail." I'm getting the feeling Liam Dubois is just like an overgrown kid who tries every trick in the book to get rid of the nanny he doesn't like. However, he doesn't know how desperately I need this job right now. And I suppose I underestimate his desire to chuck off his stepdad's latest and most frantic attempt to tame his stepson and keep him out of jail.

"You wouldn't lie for me?" he asks. And there is just a moment while I'm standing there staring at him with his half-smile and knowing gaze, I can't help but wonder if he didn't pay off those two girls at the strip club and then the four at the wedding to lie to me. I breathe in, breathe out, and try not to think about that hypothesis.

I also underestimated Liam's hatred of me. I suppose living inside a shell for so long, I was protected from people like this spoiled boy-man who lacked any compassion whatsoever, but could hide it behind a fake smile.

"You know what, Miss Popovich?" Liam rubs his chin, sighs. "We got off on the wrong foot. Let's just put on the brakes, stop, and start fresh. I'll buy you a drink. We'll go out for dinner, how's that?"

Chapter 18

"Miss Mauer, can I see you in my office?"

I'm sitting with my rear on the hard concrete sidewalk in front of the high school, reaching out to grab on to Liam's driver's hand. Liam barely introduced him last night as Rusty Rossi when he pulled into the parking lot in a full-size limo I can bet is usually reserved for high school proms and weddings at the country club.

I am learning Liam likes to be the center of attention. Riding in a limo in small town Ohio makes him appear like a movie star. Rusty doesn't stick out in my mind. He's a bland, buff man with a flat nose, who is nearly always silent and who stuck out as little as a fly high on the wall last night when he peeled off the magnet on the side of the limousine that said *Rossi Limousine—Luxurious, Affordable. Business Trips, Weddings, Bachelor Parties, Birthdays, Airport Transportation* and tossed it into the glovebox. I blink against the bright eight a.m. sunlight and see the shadow of another man behind Rusty. Oh no, it is Principal Cunningham.

The buses are pulling in and I've just tumbled out of the back of Liam's limousine overtop two girls; I have no clue of their names. Right behind, a young man comes stumbling out of the same limo door and does a trip-walk until he rights himself at the curb and looks curiously around. He's black-haired, super tall, and doesn't speak but maybe three words of English. I distinctly remember kissing him on the hood of the car. I'm not sure where we were parked. Oh, my head is pounding.

"Dónde estamos?" he asks, blinking at the even more questioning eyes of students stopping to stare. Rusty is giving me a too-sneaky grin while I frantically rub at my makeup and try to swab away my cherry red lipstick. I must have fallen asleep in the backseat sometime around two in the morning on the ride home from Cleveland. I drank three glasses of wine. Oh, no, maybe it was closer to five or six and I faintly recall holding up a bottle of rum. Liam promised me he'd get me home in time for school this morning. I had no clue he was going to park in the lot and dump me there. But Rusty, his driver, opened the door, and there were ten or twelve people crammed in the back. We all rolled out like the little butter flake crescent rolls that come popping out of their tubes after the paper is peeled back and the tube is banged against a counter edge.

"Yes, sir," I mumble to Principal Cunningham as I rise. Oh, why is he looking at my head? I reach up. Rusty had been wearing a chauffeur cap. How it ended up on my head, I have no idea. I snatch it off, shove it at Rusty's belly. Then I drag my too-short cocktail dress down toward my knees. I can hear the grumbles and giggles of the two girls while they pile back inside. The third, the dark-haired man I vaguely remember, is drunk-smiling at me and shoves a card into my hands. "Por favor llámame."

I'm still only slightly awake. I blink and take a step forward, fumble in my purse for my glasses. Oh, I remember Liam buying rounds at a dance club. I remember him laughing when he kept trying to sneak whiskey shots into my wine. Oh, and I remember dancing on the top of the limo hood with the guy whose card I'm holding. My left foot tips sideways hard downward just as I whip out my glasses, shove them over the bridge of my nose.

"You danced the heel off. Then you tried to get it to stick back on last night with fingernail polish," Rusty chuckles. "It didn't work."

I look down frantically and tip forward. My heel is

broken. My stomach is upset. I groan then throw up right on Principal Cunningham's black business shoes.

Principal Cunningham chewed me out for twenty-eight, excruciating minutes while I pulled my hair back in my usual lazy bun. He lectured me on the importance of being a positive role model for the students while I scrubbed off the last of my makeup with half the box of tissues on his desk. He said, since this is my first infraction, albeit a big one, he wouldn't put me on administrative leave as long as nothing like this ever happens again.

My sister is not so forgiving. "Are you trying to put Mom in the grave?" she whisper-yells at me in the library. There are three students sitting at tables, leaning forward to listen. "If she finds out, you're dead, you know that, right?" I want to put my hands over my ears like I used to when I was six and my sister criticized me for not combing the tangles out of my hair or for hanging around with Lanie Burton, who picked her nose. I don't. Instead, I pull Aunt Roo's little diary from my purse and hold it in my lap. I took it last night, thinking I could read it in the car while I was waiting for Liam in the bar.

"What is that?"

"Nothing."

"Poppy Rose, answer me or I swear I will be the first in line to tell Mom what happened today."

"It's just Aunt Roo's diary." I don't hold it up. I just stare at my fingers.

"Is *that* what this is all about?" She lets out a long breath and leans into the library counter. "Your dad's sister that disappeared, right? Is it her birthday or something?"

"No."

"God, you are harder to wheedle information out of than my ADHD kids, Poppy. Don't think I don't remember all the stories your dad used to tell you about her—that you were just like her and stuff. You got to let that roll off you. Why don't you give me the diary, I'll put it away—"

"No." I say flatly, look her right in the eye. She doesn't expect her backward little sister to push back. She looks shocked while I shove my glasses up the bridge of my nose.

"You're the least normal person I know, you understand that, right?" Nicolette says. "You're normal until you go to your dad's house. But you go and then you come back all weird. I remember mom peeling the dirty clothes off you when you were little, tossing them in the trash and then scrubbing you down for an hour in the bath."

"Don't say stuff about my daddy."

"Fine, then figure out a way to be normal again."

Her idea of normal? I groan inwardly. I feel like a ping-pong ball going back and forth on the table, except I have to change colors every time I cross the net to be normal.

"Okay, I'm just going to say it." My sister's eyes are angry. She takes in a deep breath and stares at me so hard, I swear she can see right through me. "Did anything ever *really* happen back when you were fourteen? Did you really get abducted, or was it just another big, fat lie to cover up something else?"

I blink at her, feel my heart do a flippy-flop. I push my fingers to my nose, just waiting for it to start bleeding. My eyes move to my purse where I've got two emergency pills in a little baggy. It's a habit I don't think I'll ever break. "Cover up?"

"You know what I'm talking about." Her face is expressionless, except for one minor twitch in her right eye while she eyes my fingers patting my nose cautiously. "Quit knuckling your nose. It's weird. I'm going to talk to Doctor Stamper and have her give you a call, see if we can get you into her home office. You never answered me. Was it real?"

I push my hands down, then I jump up really quickly trying to avoid the confrontation. "I don't know." That's what I say. Because sometimes, I really don't know.

"So Miss Mauer parties." Colton scoots up by the library counter. He leans over, tapping a hand in front of me. I'm unsettled after my sister's insinuation that I was *not* abducted. Sometimes I wonder, myself, if maybe I didn't fall that night and used all those stories everybody's stuffed into my mind over the years about my aunt's disappearance to patch together the oozy darkness into a fake memory to fill the void I can't remember. There's a single yellow rose with pretty red tips on the petals on the counter. I groan, shove it into my drawer. "You don't sell weed, too," he whispers. "Do you?"

"No. Go away, Colton."

"Did you put this in my truck?" He reaches into his back pocket, tugs out a community college application.

"I don't know what you're talking about," I lie. I did know. I've got something I do a few times a week. I usually come in earlier than everybody else, after the janitorial staff is long gone and before the teachers and students come into the school. I may not talk to many people, but I hear what they say to others, I see the books they sneak-look at when they are in the library. Like Lacy Wells, who has been searching up keywords like: *phobia, speaking in public,* and *dealing with shyness.* I snuck a little Post-It note into her locker that said: *You are fearless.* Last week, I placed a little note with an incredibly difficult math equation in Mindy Carter's locker. It was the beginning of a scavenger hunt with six clues eventually leading her to a book in the local PG Tucker's Coffee Café in town with a coupon for two cups of coffee and two cookies. At approximately the same time she was on her last two equations, I texted a short riddle to Colton McDaniel that also led him to the PG Tucker's with a seat next to Mindy.

Nicolette confided in me that when kids like Colton come into her office, it's pretty much written in stone they aren't going to do anything more than work at the local gas stations or fast food restaurants. So, I decided to intervene on the behalf of all us who are overlooked. She steers them toward vocational school. *It's a waste of my time to counsel them. It's like they are dumb-coded to just stop in sixth grade. Anything after that is like being in jail to them. Don't you notice that too?*

I don't. I just see their hopes and dreams in the books they peer at and the stuff they look up online. Colton kind of has me stumped. He reads at a middle school level, but he can whip up a tall tale to me with such intricate detail, I find myself leaning in with bated breath to hear the ending.

"Maybe you should give it a try," I growl as he hovers above me. "You've got nothing to lose."

"College? You're crazy."

"What are you going to do after high school?" I snap at him. It isn't my usual retaliation. I always just watch him go. He stares blankly at me for a moment. "Why do you get up out of bed and go to school? You hate it here. Just stay in bed. Don't come to school."

"Screw you. Maybe I'll work at PG Tucker's. Isn't that where your stupid riddle sent me? Was that another hint?"

"No, Colton, I did not send you there to get a job. I sent you on an adventure. I'm thinking if you're nowhere, you've got no place else to go but somewhere. Anywhere. To

Columbus or freaking Brazil. But I guess, minus the money, you're no better than the jerk who dropped me on the school steps this morning." I wave him away with my hand and pull the little blue diary from my purse. I open it, puff out my lips in a grand sigh and start to read. "Go away. I've got a headache."

"You mean, a hangover," he snickers. "And yes, before you ask because I know you are going to, I ran into Mindy. Is that your way of trying to get my ass kicked because you, as a teacher, can't do it yourself without going to jail or something? Because she's got a boyfriend."

"Go *away*, Colton. Her boyfriend is a guy online who is probably fifty and uses a stock photo of a seventeen year-old model." I lean my hand on my forehead and stare at my aunt's diary. I read:

October 10. Mamaw came to visit. I went to the skating rink.

"What's that?"

I let my eyes roll. I'm trying to keep my slinky dress hidden behind the counter so I can't move much. "It's my aunt's diary."

"She's letting you read it?"

"It belongs to my aunt that went missing." I realize my voice drops to a whisper whenever I say that she's missing, vanished, or disappeared. "And no, she's not. I am reading it slowly because her handwriting is hard to read and I feel like there's something cryptic in here I'm missing." I'm not fast enough to shield the book. Colton leans in and gets a snarky expression. Then he snatches up the book and holds it at his chest.

"Bitch can't read it now, can she?" he taunts me, his fingers flipping the pages. I'm not sure if he means my aunt or me.

"Colton, give it back."

"I want to read the sleazy details. That's why you have it, isn't it, snoop?" He stops and narrows his eyes. "*Got my hair feathered today,*" he reads with a high-pitched tone. "*And I'm grounded. Staying in room.*" Colton stops, rolls his eyes. "Boring."

"Maybe it's boring, but I'm not reading it to snoop. I'm reading it so I can try to figure out what happened to her. Look at the last page with writing."

Now, he doesn't say anything, just rolls his forefinger from page to page until it stops. "This? Is it this? *I don't know where it all started going wrong. Nobody listens to me. They act like I'm crazy. I just want to die. I don't want to go to the doctor.*"

"Yeah, creepy isn't it? Now give me the book back and keep it secret."

"What happened to her?" Colton presses his palm to the center of the book. His fingers skim slowly over the ridges left from several pages being torn out. "There's stuff missing."

"I don't know what happened. That's what I said, she disappeared. Nobody knows." I wiggle my fingers, hoping he'll give me the book back. "Go use some of those computer skills and see if you can find anything about her."

"Really?"

"Yeah. Her name was Rosaline McGuire." I work up a smile. "At least until Principal Cunningham finds out and fires me. Do me a favor and keep this to yourself."

"I asked Mindy out."

"What'd she say?"

"I don't know," he answers.

"You have to work harder with some people, Colton," I say while he walks away with the diary. "Bring that back before you leave, you hear me?" I tell him. He doesn't listen. Then I look up the yellow rose online. It means *falling in love*. Falling in love. Who could possibly be falling in love with me? Liam? Mister Barkley? The guy who parks cars? The guy at the gas station? My creepy neighbor? Ug.

Chapter 19

"Hey, if I've got an electrical fire in my toaster, can I put it out with the little hose on my sink?" I'm sitting at a booth with a torn, vinyl seat in a little truck stop diner thirty miles south of Laurel Grove. I'm eating pancakes and an egg over-easy because they serve breakfast all day. Between bites, I'm talking to Rocky, who I called.

"No, no!" he yelps like he thinks I'm getting ready to douse a fire with water. I'm not. I've got one of the firefighter books in front of me. It was one of the questions on the pre-test. "Rosie, don't! You're not, right? Water conducts electricity. You'll get shocked."

"Oh, okay. Did you stack two bricks on my front porch this morning?"

There is silence, then a sigh, "Yes."

"Were you trying to kill me? Because I tripped over them going to my car."

"No, they are being used as an illustration for the make-believe wall you're building between us. See, I can be smart too. I used them as an example. There's two of those bricks we just aren't going to be able to use and you know it is the truth. One, we can't avoid each other. Two, your mom and sister rely on me to babysit you like now. *Is* your toaster on fire?"

"No, I'm just passing the time." And I'm relieved he took the step and put the bricks there so I had an excuse to call him. It's weird not having Rocky around. "My car's not working again. I'm stuck at a restaurant while it cools down. I think it overheated." It didn't. I'm not telling him the truth. "Then I smelled the toast burning in the restaurant and I thought about it and wondered if using water would work."

"You need me to come out and fiddle with it?"

"The restaurant toaster? I think they've got it under control. I'll call 9-1-1 if they don't."

"No, Rosie. You can't code it a 9-1-1 if it isn't an emergency. You get it? I think you're in trouble. You're not, right? Quit being goofy. I'm not used to you being goofy."

"I'm not being goofy, just inquisitive. Are you bringing your surly cousin or my mean sister?"

"No. Why would I do that?"

"They always boss you around. I think you like it."

"I don't like it and no, they don't."

"Oh," I whisper, preparing myself for another lie into the phone. "There's a really creepy guy staring at me. I thought he was following me around. I'm uncomfortable. I think I'll go see if I can get my car started—"

"No, no, Rosie. Stay in the restaurant where it's safe." Rocky huffs. I know his eyes are wide on the other end. "You hear me? Please. I'll be right there."

I know this is the only way I can get Rocky McDaniel to crack open a book and study so he can be a firefighter. I'm going to have to force him. But it isn't just that. I've got an ulterior motive and only three hours and ten minutes between jobs today.

My Aunt Kay told me in the next couple months, the city is going to auction off all the confiscated police items, my Daddy's ATV included. My Uncle Matt works in the sewage department, and he asked about getting the ATV back if he paid the fines. They said under local laws, the vehicle could be auctioned off because it was unclaimed. If he claimed it, he could be arrested for trespassing. He also said that his friend, who works as a clerk in the administrative offices, said if Daddy was to try to claim it, they could bring him in on charges of criminal mischief and could send him to jail. I plan on getting the ATV back, even if I have to pay a million dollars for it at the auction. However, I thought I could butter up Rocky and maybe since he's from the other side of the feud, he could talk his Uncle Johnny out of pressing charges.

I'm right. I think Rocky realizes the trick the moment he bursts through the restaurant doors, swinging his head around like he's looking for the creeps who've got me tied up in some back room with duct tape over my mouth and hands up my shirt. He stops short of my chair, looks down.

"What's all this?" he asks, indicating the table at my booth with books, paper, and pencils scattered about the surface. "I thought you were in another Rosie pickle?"

"Sit," I order. "I ordered you a coffee and piece of apple pie. You're going to need the sustenance while we study for your test." I push over a piece of white paper, turn it so he can read the writing on it, and point to the line at the bottom. "I understand you might think I'm being nice to you and by virtue of a certain curse, you may feel obligated to decline my services. So I have designed a contract between us that allows me to tutor you for the fireman's test. It includes reading, your ability to overcome certain situations, memory, and spatial orientation, so they know you can find your way out of burning buildings. Otherwise, you stay away from me. I stay away from you. Sign here."

"You're kidding me." Rocky leans in and squints at the paper. "You said it was a 9-1-1. What about your car?"

"No, I'm not kidding," I answer. "And my car seems to be fine now." I still have a hard time looking him in the eye. I count to three, force myself to four before I pull away. Blue, oh so damn blue, with dark around the irises. I try not to think how I look to him, beautiful Nicolette Mauer's wallflower sister, hunched over the table with baby-diaper green eyes and big black, rose colored glasses.

"Don't do this again. You scared the shit out of me! A 9-1-1 code isn't something to play with. I was supposed to meet with some buddies for a beer tonight, Rosie, and watch the game," he grumbles. "I don't have time for this."

"Well, that ain't how dreams are made, Rocky."

"What's in this for you?" He sits down, pretends to look at the paper I'm scooting toward him. However, first he scans the room. Most likely, he's praying nobody sees him with me. It's a gut punch. But I'll take it right now just to kind-of be near him. That's when it really hits me. I've got a crush on my sister's kind-of boyfriend. I'm smart enough to know I'm manipulating the situation to be near him. I'm waiting for him to start making excuses to leave while his eyes peruse the paper. "There's nothing in writing. Perhaps you could talk your uncle into dropping the charges for trespassing. Sign at the bottom to continue," I demand.

"I knew it had to be something," Rocky grunts. "I'm not talking to my uncle. Do you still want me to sign?"

"Yes." I look at Rocky. He's suspicious.

"I don't need math for this, do I?" He takes the pen I'm handing him reluctantly and fidgets.

"Yes. They need to know you're good at problem solving and have good numerical reasoning. You need to be able to determine water pressure and hose sizes, just to name a few. You'll have to make life and death decisions and—"

"I'll just guess them on the test, like I did for the SATs," he tells me, tapping his fingers on the table like he's made the decision. "Isn't there some sort of rhyme game thingie you can do that helps you guess?"

"It's called strategic guessing." I look up, glare at him, and roll my eyes. "Or in your case, probably utilizing the simple approach of 'eeny, meeny, miny, moe.' No, it isn't a realistic methodology. The odds you'll pick the wrong one are incredibly high."

"It's cute when you use big words even if you're doing it as a roundabout way to stick a sword in my side because you think I don't get it." He reaches across the table and pats my nose teasingly with his forefinger while he grins at me. I slap his hand away.

"Here's three more big words: *psychological defense mechanism*. It's what you're using right now, teasing me, to appease the anxiety of completing simple math problems."

"It's working, isn't it?"

"And it will also eventually lead you to getting culled by the Crystal Springs Fire Department. Unfortunately, Rocky, good looks are not going to get you a job as a firefighter like they did with your teaching position at the high school. Crystal Springs is looking for the cream of the crop both intellectually and physically. It is not based on beauty. They get so many applications; they've got plenty of recruits to choose from. I'm not going to let you slide like your professors did in college because you can crack a good joke and flirt with them. You don't appeal to me. So either sign the damn paper, McDaniel, or walk away."

"Ouch." Rocky leans back in his chair. He folds his arms across his chest. "The waitress over there likes me." He nods toward the tall blonde who traded serving tables with the girl who'd taken my coffee order. "I heard her telling the other girl she'd give her our tip if she could wait on us." She is coming over with a piece of pie the size of a dinner plate. I know she likes him. She's spilled coffee on three people because she can't take her eyes off Rocky.

"Okay, if you want her to tutor you, then I'll leave," I say as she plops the pie down in front of Rocky. I close the book I'd opened. I turn to her while I rise. "My mind is blank. Can you tell me what six times twelve is?"

"Oh, you mean like multiplication? Or is this a pun?" She starts to count on her fingers, then uses her pad of paper to try to add it up. Finally, she sighs in defeat. "I don't know. It's something like sixty or seventy. Is that close? I don't know fractions." She grins at Rocky who I think is going to stand up and give her a standing ovation for being close.

"That's close enough for me." He winks at her.

"I'm sure they'll accept that *pun* estimate in the testing center, Rocky." I start to gather the books and papers and he sits up quickly and grabs my wrist. The waitress looks confused and Rocky waves her away with his hand.

"I'm just trying to be nice. But I guess a hundred and fifty years of feuding between our families and your incompetence at being human won't let me."

"Screw off."

"Stop, I was just teasing." His smug smile is gone. "You're right. Okay, I'll try. I won't let you down." *He won't let me down?* He leans over, taps the pen twice on the table and eyes me carefully. Rocky shakes his head warily, then makes a scribble of his name on the sheet.

"The only person you're letting down is you, Rocky, if you don't try. I'm not going to judge you." He stares at me. "You're good at so many things. You're not dumb. You've just gotten so used to people letting you skip your way through everything because you're charming, funny, and attractive. You've lost the ability to actually do the work."

"But I don't wanna work," he teases. When I don't react and hard stare him with pursed lips, he rolls his eyes, shakes his head. It's like he's playing hard to get. He nods to let me know he's ready. I'm thinking it's like he's surrendering to me, giving into my advances. And while we work, I see him leaning his elbow into the table and running his hand through his hair over and over, trying to absorb the material. It's incredibly sexy, like I'm breaking out in a sweat kind of sexy. I'm thinking while he scratches numbers on to the paper, trying to please me by getting it right, it's almost like his fingers playing on my skin, trying to figure out what makes me gasp in pleasure. And when he finally gets it right, I react with the same gusto I would in a climax—

"Rosie, is it right or not?"

I blink at Rocky furrowing his brow at me. "Um," I mutter, feeling my face turn a deep crimson. "Yeah. I mean, yes." And me, I'm thinking everybody who walks into the restaurant might think I'm something special for being with such a hot guy. Maybe being pretty *is* over-rated.

Or not. After I close the book and check the time on my phone, I excuse myself to the bathroom.

"Hey, can you give my phone number to the guy you're tutoring?" It's the waitress who slips a piece of paper into my fingers. "Is he single?"

It clearly hadn't occurred to her that he might be with a wallflower like me. Ug. "No," I mutter. "He's dating my sister."

Chapter 20

"I assume if you can change my identity while I'm here, you're good at finding information on people, right?"

Mister Barkley's assistant is walking ahead of me down the hallway with a jacket slung over her arm. She's getting ready to leave for the night. She turns, looks at me.

"That didn't take long for you to figure out." She stops in the dim light and faces me. "Yes Violet, what do you need?" Violet. It takes me a moment for it to sink in she is talking to me. She must recognize my hesitation because she sniffs a laugh. "It's Mister Barkley's orders. He made it clear in the staff meeting that your name is Violet and we are to call you such here. Once you're about thirty miles away and cross the township line, you're Rosie again and we don't know you here. Mister Barkley used to be in the military in the 1970s, the Central Intelligence Agency, to be exact. It's my thought he misses the structure, that's why he runs such a tight ship."

"That would be more akin to the Navy, their ships being neat. The CIA works with foreign entities."

"You would probably make more friends if you simply nodded instead of pointing out flaws in the conversation," Kim chastises me firmly. "Because I think, regardless, you get my point that he runs it in an orderly fashion and with a high level of professionalism. We are a team, Miss Popovich, when we are here. We all cover each other's backs whether it is helping to wait on tables when the servers are overwhelmed or—" she smiles at me, "—in your case, keeping someone's identity concealed to save you from being harmed while you investigate murders." Then she narrows her eyes. "You do realize you squint constantly when you wear the contacts, right?"

"I'm having a difficult time adjusting back and forth between glasses and contacts." But the truth is, I'm actually wrestling with my new identity and it is a subconscious reaction to juggling an introverted and an extroverted personality. I want to cower, run for my sweater. I can't. I purposely leave my sweater pacifier at home. "I need info on the murdered girls."

"What about them?"

"I'm trying to find out if they have any other suspects in their deaths. The newspapers don't list any. I talked to a girl who knew Alaina and she said Alaina left with an old man the night she died. The only old guy suspect I have for her drops off church fliers at the bars and strip clubs and can hardly find his way out of a bucket." I'd also chatted it up with Mary Stamper and found out that she, Margaret Williams, and Essie Cunningham had crossed paths with me that day on Federal Road because they were heading to Spinny's Tea Room for the Women's Club tea. Margaret doesn't like driving the highway, so Doctor Stamper suggested they take the back road. "I'm trying to find out if there's another old guy associated with the other two girls."

"I can check. You need it now?"

I hesitate. Mom's right. I'm obsessed with this especially after feeling like Mister Barkley opened the door for me to look into the murders for his son. However, when I got home last night, she'd stopped in and left part of a pot roast and tacked yet another newspaper article to my fridge—WOMAN LEFT FOR DEAD ON HIGHWAY DIES. This time, she'd highlighted the name in yellow—Phoebe Wells. What does she expect?

"Did you know Alaina Windowski?"

"Well," Kim sighs. "As much as I know any of the staff. I look them up, do the background checks. We passed in the hallway a few times, said hello."

"Did she have any records in her background check?"

"Yes." Kim must see my questioning gaze.

"If she had a record, why did Jack Barkley hire her?"

"The record Alaina had wouldn't be a disqualifying measure to keep her from working here."

"What do you mean?"

"Mister Barkley doesn't hire drug users, people with violent behavior. He does hire staff workers who may have had something in their past that would disqualify them from other jobs—like jail time. Such, he overlooks some offences for qualities they have that could benefit the club."

"Who? He doesn't seem like a humanitarian."

Kim laughs softly. "Like a really intelligent girl who may be a bit weird, but who might be able solve the murders his stepson is being blamed for."

"Okay. That's fair."

"So Alaina had gotten arrested for drunk and disorderly a couple times. You know, he calls that kind of stuff 'college hijinks.' I mean, she wasn't anything like that here. She was pretty quiet at work, did her job."

"It's the same kind of background the other murder victim had—Angel Daugherty." I chew on this a minute. "She was the bookworm type. But she'd been arrested."

"Really?" Kim asks, shrugs it off. "I suppose that kind of behavior would draw in that kind of crowd. My mom used to tell me birds of a feather flock together."

I nod. "Okay, here's my next question. What quality did Alaina have that Mister Barkley overlooked her past?"

"Oh, you are good," Kim praises with a shrew twist to her lips. She holds up a finger. She narrows her eyes at me like she's seeing me differently. "I didn't think you'd ask that. Alaina was going to do the same thing you are doing, babysitting Liam. Are you surprised?"

"I'm surprised you didn't tell me this, Kim. You act like you were keeping this from me," I say a bit quickly.

"I didn't think it was pertinent to the situation, Violet." Kim tips her head to one side. "Or I would have divulged the information. Think about it. Alaina was pretty and she wasn't put off by following Liam to bars and strip clubs. I think Jack Barkley thought it might be a good match. Unfortunately, it was too good of a match on one level and not a good match on keeping him out of trouble."

"Besides that, it isn't pertinent the last person who had my job was murdered?" I narrow my eyes. "It is. And I'm really good at reading people who are lying to me. I've spent my entire life extracting the facts from the little white lies my mom doles out to me. I'm good at picking stuff out of a conversation and getting to the truth. I'm laying that out on the table for one reason. I can't trust my mom. I can't trust my sister. I don't have any friends I can rely on. So since you know my little secrets, I'm asking you *not* to lie to me. Because there's a certain amount of trust I'm throwing out there. And honestly, I'll know if you are deceiving me. And then you've lost my trust."

"I don't think it had anything to do with babysitting Liam. She disappeared before she even started the job."

"So I can assume you're not going to tell me everything that is going on unless I pick up a vibe that somethings wrong and question you about it?" I'm a bit miffed. I know she can see this. "So, I can't trust you."

Kim chews on this a moment. It seems an eternity before she looks up at the ceiling. "I'm not supposed to trust you, Violet. Mister Barkley doesn't know if you'll stick around. To disclose information leaves us vulnerable. For all we know, you're an informant for the cops."

"Seriously? I work at the school library. Kim, I'm not

an idiot. You can find just about anything on anyone. Nevermind." I wheel around, toss my hands out. I've had enough of this game. "I need autopsy reports and other relevant information so I can research this."

"Listen, I know this guy who works over at the community college." Kim tells my back. I turn slowly. "He's got a research grant for forensic science. He gets all the stuff from murder victims from the police and the hospitals—"

"He gets the autopsy reports?"

"I would think."

"I'm not even going to ask how you know this."

"It's fine," Kim says. "It's not a secret. He's like a third cousin on my stepmom's side. He's a distant enough relative he thinks it all right to stare at my boobs at every family reunion, like a fat kid drool-gazes at chocolate cupcakes fresh out of the oven. I heard him bragging about getting the grant at my mom's Easter dinner. He works on high profile murder cases. He has three masters degrees. He makes the rest of us look bad."

"Do you think you can get some information for me?"

Kim writes something down on a little slip of paper and slaps it in my palm. "Here. He works days at Southeastern State College. But he's got some off-campus building on Fourth Street, where he keeps the records. It's an old bank. He had to have all sorts of security—evidence lockers and special bulletproof windows so somebody didn't steal any files." Then she gives me a funny smile. "If you want something from him, his favorite color is bright red and he doesn't get many dates. I'd wear something low cut, if you know what I mean." She sighs deeply and looks up toward the ceiling with a faint smile. "He likes girls in camo too; you know, like those military games dweebs play online."

Chapter 21

"Where to, princess?"

I turn and narrow my eyes at Rocky McDaniel's voice. My knight has ridden in like the evil prince in whatever fairy tale he's conjured up in his mind. His truck is his mighty steed, which has just pulled up beside me on an old state route with his elbow propped on the window and a smug smile on his lips.

"I thought we had an agreement?" I glare at him. "You stay away from me. I stay away from you. Unless, of course, we are working on contract material." I'm leaning hard on the grill of my car, staring guardedly at the engine under the open hood. "Which we aren't doing now." It's like gaping at Chinese handwriting. "You know, the curse and stuff that makes a big ol' country boy like you scared."

"I should be so lucky," Rocky mumbles, puts his truck in park and hops out. "It's not my call. It was Leah's. She was coming back from work and saw you'd broken down. She told me to tell you this: *so now we're even. I don't owe you.* I'm not asking what she meant, but I feel like I'm holding up our family honor by wasting another tank of gas to get yelled at as a thank you for being your in-a-pickle-man. Do you need a tow and a ride?"

"I'm fine. And you realize, again, you're letting the women in your life boss you around."

"That bothers you?" Rocky cracks a smile. He's close enough to close the gap between us in two steps and nudge me with a knuckle. "You want in on it too?"

"Are you asking if I want to boss you around or be a woman in your life?" I feign thinking it out with a tap of forefinger on chin. "It doesn't matter. No, on both."

"Your loss, then." He steps back, looks a little insulted. I know why Leah feels like she has to do me a favor. Now she doesn't owe me from stopping Kim from firing her, which was probably worse than actually getting fired in Leah's eyes. Still, I wouldn't be surprised if Leah hadn't crawled underneath my car and broken something in the middle of the night just to get me back for my most recent prank. I stuck an orange into the muffler of her car. When she hit the gas to leave the school parking lot after work, it burst out like a bomb going off.

"I think it's the carburetor." That was Dave's answer to my car problems two minutes before Rocky drove up. He's one of the white knights who have come to save me. I don't know Dave. He's a man with a compact car who stopped to offer assistance, along with another guy with a gray beard, named Tim, who pulled in behind him in a truck.

"A bad carburetor don't got that bad smell to it. It's a battery she needs." And that would be Gilford offering up his advice. "I had one of these, boys. I know'd this car."

I can't make out anything that looks broken. I'm not sure what smells like burnt popcorn. That's my opinion when Rocky pulls up in his truck. He narrows his eyes at my tiny camo short-shorts, red tank top, and high heel, open toe sandals. I've even donned a camo ballcap backward that I borrowed from my cousin Renée. Okay, it isn't my usual attire. But I had a plan when I pulled my car off the side of the road to text Mister Barkley and tell him I was going to be late. I made the mistake of turning off my car. It didn't restart. He asked me why I wasn't using the little red car he leased and I told him I could hardly park it in my driveway. I would be the talk of the neighborhood and have to answer to my mom about exactly how I managed to lease a brand new, red Corvette on a librarian's salary.

I'm not sure that I'm more discomfited by the fact Rocky is an hour and fifteen minutes away from any point I would expect him to be right now or that he's seeing me in something other than a prudent skirt and blouse.

"I'm calling a tow truck." Rocky shooed my knights away like a dragon's fiery breath frightens crusaders from a battlefield. I'm left with sliding into his truck and wishing I could pull the edges of my short-short camo shorts down more toward my knees. I have to wonder why Leah didn't shove her anger aside and simply given me a ride.

"Quit looking at me like that." I give him sideways, stink-eye because he's giving me this up and down, fatherly *you-ain't-leavin'-my-house-dressed-like-that* gaze.

"Oh, okay, Rosie, I'm not supposed to think it is odd you are dressed like sugar, like you were waiting for a hundred horny flies to come soaring in—"

"Horny? Did you just say horny?" I laugh a husky laugh and roll my eyes. "You've got no right to judge me. I can wear what I want."

"I'm not judging," Rocky says with one finger tapping on his head. "Last month, you were wearing dresses to your knees. This month, you're like a twelfth grader at her first girls gone wild spring break. I mean, you've got all *that*—" he waves a hand at my cleavage. "—long legs, and half your butt showing. And you can use it to your advantage. I just don't think you have the tools to handle the attention you're getting from wearing it—the wrong kind of attention."

He offends me. "Stop, I'm getting out. I'm not a stupid virgin, butt wipe. I'll call somebody else to pick me up," I growl. I push my hand on the door.

He rubs his cheeks, looks up at the roof of his truck. "A virgin. Did you just say that?" He waggles his head like a bull getting ready to take on the world. "Phew. Nevermind. Where were you heading? I'll take you there."

"No."

"Don't make me fail your Mauer side of the family, McGuire. I'm already the black sheep in mine for trying to help you with the ATV. They are all waiting for the curse to start again, unsaid or not."

"I'm a Mauer. And not true. I know your family was patting your back for a job well done when *you* stole my daddy's ATV. They think it was my cousin who was driving and you beat the crap out of him. If you're investing in guns and military vehicles, there isn't going to be a World War III. Because there is no curse."

"Please. I don't want you to call the idiot who left you at the strip club last month. I'm assuming it is the same person who dumped you on the front steps of the high school. I won't ask. You don't have to tell me anything. We'll part ways, I'll offend you with some hurtful remark and my obligation is complete. The curse will be evaded for yet another day. Tell me where you need to go."

Where is Rayville, which is about fourteen miles of Rocky interrogating me about my intentions and me lying every step of the way.

"So you're getting pictures for this book you're writing and the library you're going to has them?" Rocky asks me five minutes into the conversation.

"Yeah." Of course not; I'm heading to Kim's cousin's on her mom's side and begging for autopsy reports.

"So you're back to *not* talking again."

"Yes. You're the one who shunned me when Leah came that night. Besides, you're a big tattletale. If I say anything, you'll tell Nicky and Nicky will tell my mom."

"Okay, that's a fair assumption," Rocky nods. "What

if I keep it between us? You can add it as an—what is it you add to our contract to make something *not* count?"

"It's an amendment. It just serves to make changes to the original contract. I'm not making an assumption. It is an established fact you go running to my sister every time I do something you believe is outside my comfort zone—"

"God, I love when you talk big people talk," he says that with a sly smile. I think he's being sarcastic. "Especially wearing that." He waggles a hand at me. I look down, try to digest what he is saying. Sometimes, I think we are from two different worlds, speaking two separate languages. "It's like you're geeky smart and trashy sexy at the same time. You're like every redneck boy's dream. People look at us and think, *dude I bet she's not your wife, but you're getting some.*"

I feel my heart drop. It's quite possibly the meanest, most sexist thing he's ever said to me. Rocky huffs a laugh.

"You realize what you just inadvertently called me, right?"

"What do you mean?"

"Well, in less than twelve words, you quite possibly insulted me on three different levels, including calling me trashy, insinuating I'm a whore, and implying I wasn't good enough to be your wife."

He rubs his chin, gives me a grin. I suppose he's used to getting away with this stuff with other girls. I'm not so charmed by him right now. "Can you spell it out for me?" he asks, with a twitch of his lip. "I still don't get it."

"Yes. G-O-T-O-H-E-L-L," I spell out for him. "Back to the addendum, I'm not changing it. I like it better when I'm *not* talking to you. You're mean. You hurt my feelings."

Rocky's smile drops. "Are you serious? I thought you were kidding. I don't talk to anybody but you like that."

"I know. So stop. It is mean and hurtful."

"Rosie, you just never smile, so I can't read how you're feeling." He looks as earnest as I've ever seen him. Still, I'm waiting to be the butt end of another one of his jokes. "I'm just trying to joke it off, you know, like what you said—a defense mechanism. I know every word that comes out of my mouth must sound stupid to you."

"Okay, I do smile." I roll my eyes, then a force a big-toothed grin. "And I don't think you sound stupid."

"That's not a real smile." Rocky takes a quick look at the road, then leans toward me. Right then, he reaches out a hand and tickles my side. I jerk and giggle spontaneously.

"*That*, Rosie, is a smile." He grins while mine slips away. Rocky slides back to both hands on the steering wheel. I rub goosepimples from my arms.

"Are you going to use information I give you as leverage against me?" I sit back in the seat, crossing my arms.

"What?" Rocky stabs me with a glare. "You mean I'll use it against you at some point? You don't trust me at all. How long have I known you, Rosie?"

"Since kindergarten, Miss Thompson's class. I bit you. You bit me back. It was probably the first time we had contact considering the long-standing family feud—"

"—since your something-or-other did something to my something-or-other," Rocky looks all cocky for bringing up the history, then he gets this strange tilt to his head like he's suddenly realized something.

"My something-or-other was named Hannah and yours was George."

"I know the story. But right now, you're not sitting on your daddy's property. We're forty minutes away. Common ground. It's not a war zone. Wait, you remember biting me?"

"It is always common ground when it is convenient for you. And I remember a lot more than you think."

"Does your mom know? Is that what's going on? You're remembering the old stuff before the accident?" The accident is code word for disappearing for two days and coming home with a dent in my head.

"I've always remembered biting you. It's the stuff right around the time of the accident I'd forget. Even that comes in bits and pieces sometimes. It just freaks mom out when I say anything about the past and then have to ask her even a question a normal person wouldn't remember. So— you asked me if I trusted you. Can I?" I turn in the seat so I'm looking right at him. "Because you're the last person I *should* trust. For one reason, you try to sabotage every effort I take to be friends with you, because of that stupid curse. I know that," I assure him. "But of all the people I know now, that I've met in the last month—if I look at them, I can't say that every one of them doesn't have an ulterior motive. I don't know. I really, *really* don't know them. I know you, though. For forever. I sit at Sunday lunch with you every week. I sing three people over from you in the choir. I know stuff about you like you like to fish late at night and you think minnows work better than worms. I disagree, of course, worms are better—"

"What's your point?"

"I don't know. Maybe far worse than any backlash from a stupid curse is us not being friends. Because I know you better than probably anybody else. I do know that you only watch football with Bobby because it's better than sitting and listening to my mom and Nicky gossip." I eye Rocky cautiously. He's tapping his fingers on his steering wheel as he drives, taking in what I'm saying and looking over once in a while. "You yawn way too much and you fidget with your watch the entire time. You don't spay your mama cat because you like to have kittens around your barn and you like it when people stop by with their little kids to adopt one because they see the sign you put out on your lawn. You like chocolate, hate the smell of your neighbor's pigs; but you think your own, Gus, doesn't stink. I know you like the color orange because you like that burnt orange t-shirt that my sister doesn't let you wear. And before that, she wouldn't let you wear that orange-red button up shirt or buy the orange truck. I know you like to sing in the choir with Tangy because your voices blend so well together, hers is high, yours is low. I don't think you even like her. You just like to sing with her. And you want to work for the fire department. Teaching is too dull for you, too—everyday. You like the rush of adrenaline when you're out on a run—"

"How do you know all that?"

"You sit up on the couch when the phone rings and you're on call with your elbows on your knees just waiting, waiting, waiting." I shrug. "You get a spanked-puppy look when you jump up to get it and my sister gives you the mean-eye for it." I nibble on my lip. "You get this twinkle in your eye when you sing with Tangy, but her shrill talking voice makes you cringe. I know if your family saw you with me right now, they'd shit a brick. Your uncle and your cousin, would probably come over and shove you around and you'd take it because you always have—" I take a breath. "I saw the bruises when you were a kid. I don't know crap about any of my new friends. Then again, I haven't had any friends in a long time except for my cat and my guinea pig. You can probably see the reason better than me." I hold my hands out in front of me. "Regardless, maybe you're the last person I should trust." And after I pour my heart out, all's he says is, "That's a lot to digest."

Chapter 22

"So you're Frankie, right?" It scares me how good I've gotten at flirting considering two months ago, I stuttered when my stepdad said hello to me over his breakfast newspaper. I suppose it comes with being so perceptive and being forced to deal with Liam's abusive nature. Maybe it's the Adtraxin making me tired. Now I've cut back, I'm feeling more awake.

I'm leaning over what used to be a front counter to Rayville Local Bank. I've got my elbows propped up and my camo shorts clad butt pushed out and my arms hugging my chest to make my size 34 boobs look at least a size 36 in the bright red tank top and lacy black bra underneath. I can see a flash of Rocky's truck parked outside while he gets ready to leave. I swear he's got his cell phone up, pointing at me. I make a quick flip off with my middle finger to Rocky's truck before I turn my attention to a scrawny man ambling up to the counter. He smells like bubblegum and deodorant.

"Yes, I am." He's twenty-something with a round face and scruffy hair that looks like he's been sitting in front of a computer and rolling his fingers through the top over and over. When he comes over, I stand on my tippy toes and scrub the top of his head.

"Your hair is sticking up. It's cute." I giggle, lean in to push my boobs close to him. "Kim said you could help me."

"You need me to fix your computer?"

"No, silly," I giggle. "I need some autopsy reports."

"I can't do that. I have certain protocols I have to follow. Some of it is considered evidence and not public information yet. I can't make that call. The police do."

"*Can't* or *won't*?" I cock my head to the side and give him the same begging look Baby Cakes gives me when I open up a can of his beloved tuna fish. "Please, please, please." I push a little piece of paper toward him. It has Angel Daugherty, Alaina Windowski, and Phoebe Wells printed on the front. "These three. I promise nobody will see them but me. Nobody."

"I can't." He pushes the paper back. I look over his shoulder, try to latch on to anything that might convince him to give me a copy of them. *Ah ha*. My eyes stop at a particular framed picture settled on a little desk to one side. Another thing Frankie likes is to show off is his office online. I pulled up his social network page and honed in on that picture last night at two in the morning. It took me one hour and forty minutes of scanning the internet to figure out who the old guy with fluffy white George Washington hair could possibly be. "Oh, is that Cesare Beccaria?" I remark. "He's the Italian criminologist, right?" I round the front counter while Frankie blinks wildly at me and tries to stop me with his hands out. I bypass him, walk over to the little frame and pick it up. "He believed freewill allows people to make their own choices, right?"

"Uh huh." Frankie stares hard at my legs, blinks his way up to my face. He keeps swiping at the top of his head over and over like there's a fly up there and he is swatting it away.

"He's so cool," I whisper. "I mean, I'm thinking that, if he was alive now, he would be, like, the *hottest* guy in the world, right? I like smart guys. It's such a turn on. The boys I date, they are stupid. I mean, they think Isaac Newton invented cookies. They don't know how to treat a girl, right?" I look around the room, pull in close enough our bare arms touch. "Look, I'm getting goosebumps just knowing you've got a grant to work on in, what is it?"

"Forensic science improvement and cyber forensics."

"So what's your research about, Frankie? Tell me."

Two hours and fifty-four minutes later, I'm walking out of the old Rayville Local Bank with three folders full of evidence Frankie copied for me and a plethora of facts and data I wheedled out of him between sexy conversation. Rocky's sitting in his truck a block away. I know he drove around the town square three times; I watched him pass. Now he's leaning back in the seat like he's taking a nap. When he sees me, he looks up, leans over, and opens the door for me. It took three hours listening to Frankie rant on about his grant application process, four pictures of me and Frankie on his cell phone he's sending to his brother because his brother sells cars in Cincinnati and tells him hot girls don't hang around with geeks, and me tugging a few times on my shirt hem while announcing it was awfully warm in there.

"You could have warned me it was going to take three hours," Rocky barks. "What were you doing?"

"Using all *this—*" I wave my hand in front of me like Rocky did when I got into his truck. "—to get what I want. Did you take a picture of me when you left?"

"Why would I do that?"

"I don't know. Blackmail? Are you going to show it to my sister?"

Rocky's got a furrow in his brow. He looks down to the folders I've piled on my lap. "No. You're goofy. What do you got there?"

I eye him warily, then let my expression drop. "Hold up your hand, pinky finger out," I tell Rocky. "You're making a pinky finger promise to me." He does what I say, wiggles his little finger at me. I latch on and shake it. "Say: I promise not to repeat anything I'm told by Rosie Mauer."

"I promise not to repeat anything I'm told by Rosie Mauer," he repeats with a slightly bored look to his face. "I won't. I don't tell your sister shit. She doesn't tell me anything anymore. So I've—"

"And I promise not to divulge any confidential information she tells me *to anyone*. I promise from the bottom of my cold, dark heart—"

"You know I'm not going to say that."

"You say it or I won't tell you my secret," I warn with a pompous whisper. "Say: and I promise not to divulge any confidential information she tells me. I promise from the bottom of my cold, dark heart that I will put a gun to my head and die before I reveal Rosaline Ray Mauer's secrets. Say it, Rocky Archibald McDaniel."

I think he is going to pull away. There's this long lull where his cold, blue eyes just stare past the thick lenses of my glasses I'd just popped back on my face and to my own dingy poo-green eyes. He's expressionless. "Okay, I promise not to divulge any confidential information she tells me. I promise from the bottom of my cold, *dark* heart that I'll put a gun to my head and die before I reveal Rosaline Ray Mauer's secrets."

I nod in approval. He doesn't release my finger. We're just sitting in the nearly silent truck, pinkies latched.

"I really don't talk to Nicky anymore. We're like different people. She's got her friends and I've got—" He hard-sighs. "I've got my TV and an occasional game of pool at the bar. What I'm saying is— that I won't tell her."

"Okay."

"Since we're being honest for the moment; you don't think I'm too dumb to be a fireman... do you?" Rocky asks. His voice is deep, quiet, unsure.

"Why would you say that?" I mirror his almost-whisper.

"I just figured you'd know and you'd tell me the truth. You're the smartest person I know and you are, for all intents and purposes as far as our families are concerned, my nemesis—" he forces a wane grin. "So you'd be the first to point out my flaws like putting my elbows on the dinner table while I'm eating."

"Or pelting me with marbles."

"Right." Still, our fingers linger. "So—?"

"I could draw this out, my foe," I feign my superwoman look at the ceiling of his truck. "But I won't." I let my finger drop and look at him straight in the eye. Then I reach out my hand and let it rest on that muscle bulge on his arm (okay, with ulterior motives). His eyes follow. "You're strong here—" Then I reach up and tug on his hair just above his ear. "You're strong here. Kindness is not a weakness. It is a strength. And you are kind. Well, except to me when you're pelting me with marbles. And you've got a college degree. And perhaps people let you slide with your grades, but they wouldn't have if you didn't have the raw intelligence. I will say this only once and I'll deny it in the future should it arise, but you call me out on every stupid thing I say. And if you're relying on Nicky's advice, I wouldn't. She's just scared you'll get hurt or leave her. Don't let that hold you back. You're a big guy, a kind guy. A strong guy on so many levels. You'll make a great fireman."

"You're not just saying that?"

"Of course not," I actually wink at Rocky and he gives me a curious tip to his head. I imagine him sitting in one of Mom's book club readings and all the women doe-eying him and imagining him in a fireman's suit with his shirt off, like the men on the covers of their stories. Book club eye candy, that's what he is to them. I tell him that in a roundabout way. "Besides, you'd look good in the fireman suspenders. No offense."

"None taken."

"Are we done with our pep talk?" I ask him. "Do you want me to punch you in the arm so I don't evoke the curse thing? Or I could add an amendment to our contract—"

"No." He glares at me, gives me a sad smile. Mixed emotions. That's not a new one with Rocky. He gets it when he makes fun of me. I suppose if the guy's so empathetic, it comes with the territory. Then his hand reaches out. His forefinger delicately alights on my Aunt Roo's necklace.

"What's that?"

I tuck my chin like I'm looking at the chain. I pick up the charm and poke the little keys myself. "It was my Aunt Roo's necklace. My daddy found it and gave it to me. I'm not sure what the B means. Maybe Bob or Bill."

"What do the keys unlock?"

"My daddy gave me a chest of my Aunt Roo's things. One opened the lock to the chest. The other, her diary."

"Sounds like a mystery or something."

I don't answer. I'm not sure if I divulged too much information to the enemy already. He could be Nicky's spy. However, he's the only one who has shown any interest beyond thinking I'm a crazy time bomb getting ready to explode. There's a lull, so I pat the folders in my lap.

"Okay, these are autopsy reports on the girls who have been murdered in a sixty mile radius in the last two years," I tell him while I pick up the folders one at a time. "All the technical information about the deaths of Angel Daugherty, Alaina Windowski, and Phoebe Wells—all girls who might have been involved in the same crime." I stop. There's a fourth folder. "Oh—" I don't say anything at first. I lean over, push my glasses up my nose to keep them from sliding. "There's a fourth folder. I didn't notice Frankie had another one—" I blink at the name: Caroline Stamper.

"What?" Rocky notices my abrupt silence.

"I don't know. This is strange. There's a folder here with Caroline Stamper's name on it." I look from the folder to Rocky. "Didn't Doctor Stamper have a girl that was killed by a drunk driver or something? It was an accident, right? I thought they knew who did it."

"Yeah, I heard my mom talking about it. She knew her in high school. She got hit by a car or something."

"Or not?" I ask. "Because she wouldn't be in Frankie's files if there wasn't a question as to her cause of death—it was sudden and violent—and she was given an autopsy." I open the folder, peer at the copy of an autopsy report. It is dated September 10, 1977. It is faded, but I can barely make out the chicken scratch writing. "It says her cause of death was homicide." I let my finger slide down and pause at a copy of a note stuck to the report. It says INQUEST DENIED. REPORTS STATE AUTO ACCIDENT. "Well, that's odd. It looks like she was in a car wreck." There's nothing more in the folder. I sigh and realize Rocky is peering at me before he turns his attention to the windshield. "Maybe it was just an accident he made the copy for me unless—" I tap my chin. "I don't know. There was something similar with the other deaths."

"Are you saying there might be a serial killer?" Rocky gets right to the point.

"Well, yes, if I'm basing my theory on FBI criteria for a serial killer, which has been dramatically reduced to murdering two or more people. They don't need a motive and it doesn't have to be over any period of time or by any specific method." I pause for dramatic effect. "It just has to be the same person, obviously. I'm not sure the police would believe it. It didn't even appear the guy I got the autopsy reports from this afternoon saw any similarities or even knew about Aunt Roo disappearing. But about a year after Aunt Roo vanished, Gina Lee Channel came up missing."

"Gina—Channel? From this part of Ohio? Why haven't I ever heard about her? You'd think it would be big news, like your aunt."

"She was from here. And, yes, I found a newspaper article about it tucked into my choir robe. You only heard about my Aunt Roo because you knew my family and her disappearance was in local newspapers. It hardly showed up in any regional newspapers. She was considered a runaway. Gina Channel appears to have the same dilemma except local enforcement agencies believed a family member killed her. However, they never found enough evidence to support any certain murderer. That was the reason I put up the flyer at the gas station and then—"

"The guy left you the paper sack with the backpack."

"Uh huh," I nod in agreement. "Gina's mom was a single parent, about eighteen or nineteen years-old. The two lived by themselves in the subsidized apartments in Laurel Grove. The paper said that Gina's mom tucked her into bed at ten o'clock. Then she went down to grab a soda from the pop machine on the first floor and stopped to talk with a few people. She went back upstairs, took a shower and got ready for bed. When she peeked in Gina's room, the girl was gone."

"I still don't understand why this isn't something blasted in the news then or even now with the other girls coming up murdered."

"They looked for her about three weeks and started pointing a finger at the mom, said a kid just doesn't disappear into thin air. I guess they interrogated her hard and it freaked her out so much, she went loopy and eventually left town. Then the police started harassing the family, pointing fingers at all of them until it got so bad, I think they all moved away. Instead of investigating other options or finding the reason she disappeared, the local police just swept it under the rug. There were lots of suspects, people who the cops think were involved in the murder. There are lots of what they call *people of interest* who are just the people they want to talk to about the murders. Just like my aunt. You see the similarities?"

It's true. Frankie told me that although there are three girls with slightly similar circumstances, there wasn't enough evidence to link them to one killer. When the federal government came in with a team to investigate three years ago for three girls with similar types of deaths over a series of forty years, they felt the number of fatalities in a region with two community colleges was consistent with other areas of like population. I explain this to Rocky, then add: "Okay, so here's what Frankie said were the statistics last year," I say, tugging up a folder and looking at a scrawled note I'd written on top. "There's almost 16,000 homicides a year. That's five per population of 100,000. Almost 11,000 of those are from firearms. The rest are miscellaneous like poisoning and assault. But the guy I just talked to told me this: Alaina Windowski, Angel Daugherty, and Phoebe Wells all ended up dead by blunt force trauma to the backs of their heads. That is where they believe the similarities end. Alaina was also shot. Angel had bruises on her back and belly. Phoebe was beaten with fists. They didn't have anything else in common. Angel was wrapped in a blanket and dropped in the quarry. Alaina was shot and left for dead in the woods. Phoebe was left on the highway. Aunt Roo and the 2 year-old girl were never even found so they could find any similarities. No body, no murder. They could not conclude it was a single murderer."

"And maybe Doctor Stamper's daughter."

"I suppose. But again, Rocky, remember what I said about the criteria the FBI states makes up a serial killer—two or more murders by the same person. That's it. But they have no clue who killed any of them."

"So, you're trying to tie them all together?" Rocky asks me quietly while he straightens himself in the driver's seat and turns on the ignition to the truck.

"Yes. I don't agree with the authorities." I pat the folders with my fingers. "And it brings me to the conclusion that someone in the police did it or is covering for the person, or persons, who did."

"I'm going to say this. I don't want you to get mad—" he starts. And I know what he's going to say. He's going to tell me I'm putting myself in danger, stepping on police grounds that aren't for civilians or goofy librarians.

But he doesn't. "It's because you came home that day with a big bump on your head, isn't it?"

"I think so," I answer. He shifts the truck into gear, gives me a questioning furrow of his brow. "I mean, there's some part of me that keeps pushing me to dig deeper and no, before you ask, I don't remember what happened. But it's like there is that part of me that remembers and it is whispering to the rest of me to figure it out. I feel like there's this missing link between all these dead girls and me."

"You believe you were supposed to be murdered, too, by this—" he hesitates, "—serial killer?"

"I do. Although Caroline Stamper's death was deemed an accident, I am wondering if something about her death was covered up and maybe she is a part of this too."

He nods his head, looks out his window. Then Rocky turns back to me. "Well, don't get hurt figuring it out, okay?" He reaches over and raps a knuckle on the top of my head. My eyes cross looking up. He chuckles. "Because you're smart up here too." Then he chucks my scrawny shoulder. "But you're tiny everywhere else."

"Like a bunny," I gripe. "I know."

"Yeah, a bunny. But a frigging rabid one."

Chapter 23

I'm practicing a sexy strut Mister Barkley's assistant, Kim, says would be more appropriate for riding Mister Barkley's arm when he introduces himself to the patrons with me in tow. It isn't easy. It's like tiptoe-balancing along a curb, trying to equalize the weight so I don't fall off. Nicky was always the one who jumped up on the curb next to the sidewalk when we walked to school. She could steady herself for two blocks. Me, I'd take three steps and end up flat on my face. Whenever I tried, I had to latch on to her shoulder to keep from falling. Even then, it might only be from one driveway to the next before I would lose my balance.

For the past few weeks when I work from Thursday through Saturday evenings, I help seat guests and chat it up with them. If walking in heels without stumbling isn't hard enough, I'm used to Nicky stepping in front of me, taking over the conversation when it lags. Now, it's just me. I'm forced to walk around with Mister Barkley table to table greeting his guests before his son works his way out of bed and meets me at the country club around six or seven.

It started when Mister Barkley pulled me aside after what he has deemed my Violet Remodeling. "You're smart, right?" he asked me. "I mean, I know you are, but Kim says you're good at deciphering people's intentions—like you can tell if they are lying."

I had smiled my new Violet smile, nodded. "Yes. I guess I am. It's not magic, just reading people—"

"Good." He leans in, his whisper close to my ear. "Harry Goodman is here. He wants me to invest in a waterpark in Cincinnati. It sounds like a sweet deal."

I follow his eyes to a gray-haired man with pink

cheeks talking loudly to the others at his table. "Well, I don't know if I'm that good at it. I just use my instincts and—" I sigh, tug my eyes away. I suppose I've been furiously studying crimes and criminal intent since I stumbled on a book in the Laurel Grove Library in fifth grade that was misplaced in the children's section. *The Dark Secrets of a Serial Killer* had both terrified and mesmerized me under the blanket with my flashlight. My first horror story. "Yes, I suppose I'm not bad at it. But I'd be better if I had my own laptop in my office."

"A laptop," Mister Barkley nibbles on his bottom lip. I stare at him, narrow my eyes.

"Yes. My office is dank and there's nothing but a steel desk, a computer, and a dusty concrete floor. It's dark and smells like the old gym and makes me feel like I'm in a prison cell. I can't look up stuff about these girls who are murdered on a piece of paper and that's all that is on my desk, a ream of plain white paper Kim plopped on there and a pen I brought from home." I sigh, watch him work harder on his lip. "You're indicating you're uncertain like you don't want to get me that computer." I point out.

"What?"

"Biting your lip means you are uncertain."

"Damn," he mutters, reaching up absently and touching his lip. He starts to tug a bit on that lower lip and stops like he knows I'm accessing his action. "Let's see what you can tell me about Harry Goodman."

So, Mister Barkley never actually says he's going to buy me a laptop. Yet, he makes me talk and sit with some of his associates. I laugh at their jokes, reach out a hand and touch them softly on the arm. I lean in, ask a question and the old guys, they tell me all about their lives. It is new to me, being placed in the spotlight.

Mister Barkley has all the men stand when I walk up like I'm some celebrity and they look at me with these funny puppy gazes because they all want to please him. Some just know he's rich and want to rub elbows with him. Others, they remember him from what he calls his glory days, when he was The Ghost Host on national TV. I have to wring my hands together to keep from wincing when I get really close to people. I'm not used to being the center of attention all of a sudden.

Greeting people. Flirting. I never used to do that. Now, it is becoming my new thing. Like hesitating before a closed door when a man walks up, so he automatically opens it for me. That was the trick all along, I suppose. Well, at least when I'm at the Crystal Springs Country Club. Outside of there, I'm still maintaining what Liam Dubois laughingly called my goody-goody, geek life.

I suppose I'd call myself a good girl. I'm not necessarily a goody two-shoes. The latter would imply I'm virtuous. I'm not. I've lied once or twice to Officer Tipton with the Laurel Grove Police Department and told him I wasn't speeding when I was most certainly going ten miles over the school zone limit. I don't, however, jump into bed with every guy who tells me I'm beautiful.

However, I ended up with a brand new laptop on my desk the next day, after I told Mister Barkley that Harry Goodman had six failed real estate investments. I picked that up because he kept pausing and looking away every time Mister Barkley asked him a question about the apartments he'd buy and rent out. I looked him up on my phone, found he also had two aliases. There's a cute little rag carpet under my desk and the drab walls that were gray are now a pleasantly deep tan. Kim even hung a couple random pictures up on the walls.

Chapter 24

I've also even learned new strategies for my battles with Rocky and Leah.

"Hey, Rocky," I purr, soft and sexy while I'm walking the hallway from lunchroom to library a week and a half later. I stop long enough to put my hands on my hips and take a superwoman stance where the vent on the ceiling sends out a cool breeze of air. I feel it whipping around my hair. "I'm just back from saving the world from destruction," I tell him smugly, "while you were grading math tests, I was taking on the evils of the world."

"I was in the lunchroom."

"So I've heard. But—I'm not so sure. One of my minions told me you were sneaking hot pepper flakes into my tea. So are you my archenemy or my ally?" Mindy Carter, the eleventh grade know-it-all and self-appointed classroom tattletale left me an encrypted message in my purse. Of course, by the time I translated her message, written in ancient Greek, I'd taken a sip of ginger-chamomile tea laced with pepper and burnt the first three layers of taste buds off my tongue.

Rocky comes to a complete standstill while I pass and wiggles his head like he's shaking off a fly. "Only time will tell, I *th*uppose," he replies with a lisp.

"So, this is the way it is going to play out between you and me?" I ask him like I don't let it bother me. "Enemies holding tiny plastic swords to poke at each other just enough to sting, not enough to kill. Better than using the real ones, right?" I pause, and produce the little binder I've got tucked between ribs and elbow. "Because here is the binder for the next set of study tools. It is empty, save one object cut into a puzzle that must be put together so you can decipher the secret message written on it. The message will tell you where the study papers are located."

Rocky stares at me, then drops his eyes to the binder. I don't know if I've ever seen him this perplexed. "A puzzle?" He opens the binder to expose pieces of plastic in the sleeve. It is a plastic knife cut into ten pieces.

"Yes, you can either use the puzzle to demonstrate your disaffection for me or solve the cryptic note and get the study papers."

"Disaffection's bad, right?"

"It means hostility."

"Okay." He looks up as the bell for class rings. "I think I can do this. Not poke you with plastic, I mean. Decode or decipher or whatever."

I know he can. I saw him running the other morning at dawn. He almost passed me on Whitehall Road outside town running the other direction. I had to smash myself to a building so he didn't see me. I think Rocky is following the workout guidelines I sent to his phone for the fitness section of the test.

"You better figure it out. It is not a part of the testing material for the fireman position, but by deciphering it, you show you have the ability to solve complex subjects. And that, Mister McDaniel, is in the test."

Rocky loses some luster for a second, then shakes it off and turns to leave. He obviously hasn't been back to his classroom yet. He would be powder white if he had. I sprinkled two plastic bottles of baby powder into a small Easter basket I bought in the dollar store clearance aisle. Then, while Rocky was monitoring the lunchroom, I balanced it between door and frame of his classroom. He is always the first one into the room. It's one of the five paybacks in return for the slingshot incident. Twice, I stole his keys and locked them in his truck. I put Vaseline around the rim of his ballcap. And I slipped a pair of slinky pink panties into his classroom desk.

"You've lost weight, haven't you?" I ask him.

"Huh?" he yelps and nearly walks into the lockers on his left. A couple heads turn to look his way while his shoulder bounces hard against an open room door. "I mean," he looks right to left as he gets his balance and hangs on to the door, staring at it like he's surprised it's there before he tries to move to the next door, which is his classroom. "Yeah. You can tell?" He stops, nods quietly. "I— I did."

"Yes, I can tell." I just smile and roll my eyes. I know that really sends him left of center because even while I shove my glasses up my nose and pivot, he is staring at me walking away. He's always the cool one. I'm always the one bumbling around. At least, for once, I managed to turn the cards on him. Because two seconds later, I hear him gasp as he's bathed in baby powder. But I just walk away, keeping my smug snicker to myself while I hear loud laughter roll down the hallway; the students' reaction to their teacher covered in white.

Chapter 25

I'm having a difficult time juggling my two lives. At school yesterday, I flirted with Vice Principal Walters who sucked it in like a kid dives into a chocolate ice cream cone. Now he keeps eyeing me with a funny curl to his lips. I got six dozen roses delivered to my desk yesterday along with two teddy bears. Mister Barkley said they came to the country club from a couple admirers. Admirers from where? I asked him. He said one was from Harry Goodman, the guy who wanted him to invest in the waterparks. Both had MISS VIOLET written on pretty cards, so I know they weren't from the same person who sent the yellow or blue roses.

At the country club, I forgot to take off my clunky glasses. I can't figure out if I'm more comfortable in muck boots or high heels and half the time, I have to stop and make sure I'm not shoving on the muck boots when I head to the country club or high heels when I go to Daddy's house to help him mow. I wish there was a happy medium somewhere between. The only time I'm not juggling dual personalities is when I'm by myself. And I like wearing the expensive four-hundred dollar dresses Mister Barkley buys me, which I certainly can't afford on a part-time librarian's salary. I can just stare mesmerized at my mouth for ten minutes in the mirror wearing the cherry red lipstick.

I'm walking the line right now because I'm wearing a nice dress *and* my sweater and glasses when I drive past Troublesome Creek Road that would led me to my daddy's house and toward Raccoon Hollow Road. I suppose it really is my happy medium now. I like the dresses. I also like to hide behind my glasses and my old, tatty sweater.

But it's straight off County Road 57. In my whole life, I don't think I've ever gone this way other than a forced ride on the school bus. It's where the McDaniels live and I suppose it was like the forbidden zone, the place us McGuires couldn't cross and the McDaniels would drive a straight line past heading to town. We didn't go straight down by Raccoon Hollow. They didn't swing right up Troublesome Creek Road. If no war zones were crossed, we could all just grumble about each other in the confines of our home or have an occasional fight in a bar or at school.

But I'm crossing the forbidden zone right now in my high heels and sweater. They've got twelve rusted and banged-up mobile homes sprawled out along the roadway leading up to the top of the hill where a shabby doublewide mobile home is tucked somewhere in old pines. There's old trucks, overgrown grass, and junk stuck between roadway and broken porches. This particular doublewide belongs to Johnny McDaniel, who is Leah and Colton's dad, and Rocky's uncle. The land has been in his family for a couple hundred years, since they used to run the old iron furnaces up here during the Civil War. The mobile homes belong to his kids, cousins, and brothers who claim a bit of the land too.

It's the last dirt drive before the land becomes forest for miles. It's a short ramble of car into the dark pines before I stop just short of the doublewide and get out. I'm not even all the way standing before a big, hulking man with slumped shoulders and a buttoned-up flannel greets me at his porch. He's got teeny eyes and a flat line glare.

"Mister McDaniel, I'm Miss Mauer, the librarian from the high school. I'm looking for Colton. Is he here?"

"I know you. You're Ray McGuire's girl. I seen you grow up. What you doing up here? My boy in trouble?"

"Colton borrowed a book from me. I want it back."

"Borrowed or stole? That boy ain't worth the pants I

buy him. He ain't here. He's staying at his sister's up the other hill."

The new me wants to turn really quickly, wave a hand, and leave. I suppose I've already far surpassed proper neighbor-hating etiquette by even getting out of my car. I do start to nod. Then I stop. "He's too smart for his classes, that's why he doesn't do well."

"You being disrespectful? That don't make sense."

"No, sir. I just think you should know," I consider how best to phrase my thoughts. "They always put him in the lower level classes—"

"With the dumb kids."

"I—don't know about calling them dumb, but they have different levels at the school. Since he was in elementary school, nobody bothered to test him, I assume, because—well, I've got to be honest, in local school systems, they aren't always trained to pick these things out."

"And you can? Why's a librarian see it and not the teachers?"

"I work with Colton to help him catch up with the rest. He has a mild form of what is called dyslexia."

"You're saying he's retarded?"

"No, sir. I am saying that on the rapid naming tests I tried on him, to see how quickly he can read words, he was incredibly slow. I've been working on stuff like slowing him down, allowing him to think out each word. It seems to be working. When he wants to apply himself, he has done some incredible things. This should have been caught in elementary school. It wasn't. So, Colton and I are doing triple time to catch him up." I stop and take a breath. "Mister McDaniel, my mom does this to me all the time— she treats me differently than my sister because my daddy's from—here—" I wave my hand. "I know she doesn't mean it.

But I see it. The school system is the same. It's like they look at kids in the same way they look at science fair projects. The rich kids, they can afford the glitter and expensive markers for the posters. Their parents aren't working three jobs and they are around to do half the project, make copies of pictures, and buy the pretty glitter pens to dress it up. They stand out, they win. The rest of us—"

"The rest of us," Mister McDaniel waves me away with his hand. "Get and go before I let loose my dog. You're disrespecting me just by comparing your life with mine. Look at you, all dressed up like a Barbie Doll, colleged up, and working at that school, like all the rest of your family— does your mama know you're here?"

"No."

"She'd call every cop in the state to come get you out of here, wouldn't she?" Mister McDaniel sneers. "And your daddy'd be over here with a shotgun. You need to git."

I stare at him. "You think I *wanted* to be a librarian?" I interrupt him. "You want your son working in the quarry or a coal mine? I'm just saying, I never wanted to work in a library; I had dreams. And maybe Colton does too. He can do more."

"It's fine with me. I worked in a coal mine."

"And how'd that work out for you?" I ask flatly. Oh, that was the wrong thing to say. I'm coming to terms that I've got a snarky side now too. And it is getting me into trouble more often than not. I wanted to ask him why the police thought he had something to do with the dead girls. Crud. Mister McDaniel takes a step forward and I realize I'm standing in the middle of his grown-up, broken dreams. He just doesn't want to admit it, doesn't need it pointed out by a girl from *town*. Maybe he wanted to be an astronaut, a cop, or even manage the gas station downtown. He never did. My eyes, they get wide and I hustle myself back into my car. He cussed at me until I hit the end of the driveway. Then all's I heard was my tires grinding in the gravel.

I don't get far. Just a quarter mile down the road, I pass Rocky's house. It's a teeny-tiny, elderly one-level house painted white, but the yard is clean and the lawn mowed. There's an old red truck outside and a newer one near the house. I recognize the old one. It's Colton's truck, and I can see a flash of his red-blonde hair while he leans his skinny coveralls-clad body over the open hood next to Rocky. I jam on the brakes, skid a few feet and come to a stop. I back up and watch both heads peer around the hood of the truck. I read Colton's lips. He's saying: *oh, shit* to his cousin.

"Hey, Rosie," Rocky steps around from the truck with a curious gaze while he wipes his grubby hands with an old red washcloth. He scrubs his hair with his hands quickly, looks down at his shabby coveralls. Then he gives my dress a wary look. "What brings you up to this side of the hollow?"

"I'm looking for Colton. His dad said he wasn't home."

"Because—?"

"He borrowed something from me. I need it back."

Rocky looks back and forth from me to Colton, who is pretending to peer under the hood at something incredibly fascinating. "Okay—" Rocky draws the word out, then turns to Colton. "Colton, you know what she's talking about?"

"Yeah." Out pops his head. I expected him to lie.

"You want to go get it?" Rocky says slowly to him.

"I'll bring it to school on Monday. It's up at Leah's. I think T's still there." T. It stands for Theodore. Theodore Tyler, that is. He's Leah's on-again and off-again boyfriend and the local weed dealer. He's somewhere in his forties and scrawny. He wears sagging jeans and a ballcap backwards on his head like he's a wannabe; trying to look nineteen, Hip Hop, and cool. He walks around and greets everybody with this nasally voice saying: "Hey-ya, babe. Hoo hoo." I mean, who does that past fourteen?

But T's also hot-headed and meaner than a raccoon caught in a tree with a coon dog baying underneath. Mom always points out when he gets arrested in the Laurel Grove Tribune. She says something like: *Theodore Tyler. Isn't that Rocky's cousin's fiancé? Oh, how in the world did Rocky turn out so well with a family like that? God knows.*

"Well, why don't you take a walk up the hill? See if his car's there. If it's not, go get the—" Rocky looks at me with questioning eyes, trying to extract the information.

"Book." I finish for him. Then Rocky repeats it while Colton stabs him with bored eyes.

"Really, dude," Rocky urges him on with a hand. "Come on."

Colton makes a grand sigh and trudges toward the road. "You might want to park your car. It might be a few minutes," Rocky tells me and so I pull up into his dirt driveway. It shouldn't be awkward around Rocky. I've known him since we were kids. But I'm on the McDaniel's side of the warzone right now, stuffed in the trenches with an enemy and praying someone I know doesn't drive past and see me standing here. I tell myself that ten times before I get out of the car and lean against it while he rambles over to a wall made of concrete stones beneath a raggedy basketball court.

"Don't mind him," he tells me, jabbing his head toward the road Colton is walking. "I'm trying to be there for him. He's not getting along with his dad so he's staying with Leah. T's been giving him hell too, so he doesn't even want to go there." He picks up a can of soda and takes a sip. "You want a drink?" he asks me, extending his hand from across the expanse. "I don't have cooties."

"Cooties," I repeat. "I've traded spit with you before, Rocky," I point out hoarsely like I haven't talked in three months. He tips his head sideways, like he's unsure what I'm referencing. "Sixth grade," I go on. "At Haley Compton's birthday party. Two minutes in the closet. You were out in thirty seconds."

"God, you remember that?"

"It's hard to forget your first kiss," I mumble, feeling like an idiot. Yes, I remember. Haley had a little closet in her musty-smelling basement where the party was being held. It had old coats hanging and she pushed them aside so there was just enough room for two people to sit on two vinyl-covered footstools. We would spin a soda bottle and whoever the bottle top landed on, had to spend two minutes inside with the person who had spun the bottle. I about died when Rocky's spin had landed on me. Kelsey Wright whined he cheated and didn't spin it hard enough. She was always following around Rocky and flirting.

"Yeah, I remember. It was my first kiss too." Rocky holds out the soda. I wave it away, shake my head. "I asked you if you wanted to kiss and you shook your head back and forth. There was a little light in the closet. Your eyes were huge and you looked like you were going to cry. I did it anyway. One big, wet smack."

"Yeah, I didn't see it coming. I don't remember it being wet. I just remember everybody staring at us when we came out and Kelsey was crying on the steps."

"She knew I had a crush on you."

"On me?" I laugh, feel my cheeks turn red and look at

my hands working around and around each other. "I hung around with the nosepickers, Rocky. I know better."

"Not in sixth grade, you didn't. It was before—"

Before. I shrink back. *Before.* I hate that saying. It makes me shudder. *Before.* It's like my life started and finished in eighth grade. Everything earlier than May 20th of that year was normal. Everything after, well, my life was akilter, out of balance, changed.

"Aw, crud. I'm sorry. Forget I said that." Rocky must be able to read my face. I feel the blood run from it like water from an upturned bottle.

"No, it's all right," I whisper. "I don't think about that anymore." Yes, I do. All the time lately. Little memories pop into my head that weren't there before. It's like they've been hiding and I can't decide if they are new, old, or imagined. Last night I woke up in a cold sweat. I dreamed I was sitting in the back of a car. There was an old lady's head in front of me. She didn't turn. But she said to me: *Just so you know. He always forgets to tell the girls that it's going to hurt for just a second. At least the first time. Sometimes it takes him a couple times. I'll try to get him to be quick.* I stared at the round, gray head, then dropped my eyes. There was a shovel at my feet. I saw dried blood on the blade. I was woozy with fear. My entire body was numb when I awakened.

I look up. Rocky's eyeballing me and quickly turns away. "Did you decode the information in the binder?" I ask him, trying to change the subject.

"I got the puzzle done. It's one of the plastic knives they use at church picnics."

"Uh huh."

"Is that a hint?" He reaches out, catches me off-guard with a tickle to my ribs again. "Because I haven't figured out the message written on it."

I giggle. Damn him. Rocky is cocky, staring down at me. "Oh, yeah, Rosie smiles! Now give me a hint. I'll give you something I found that shows I got problem solving skills too."

I'm curious. "You just have to unscramble the words."

"Okay." Rocky taps his forefingers in the air. "Hang on a second." He holds up a finger and then disappears past his screen door. He's only gone maybe forty seconds before he comes back out, holding a newspaper clipping in his hand. "I found another girl who died about the same time you were gone." He hands me the newspaper. "Look."

I catch his gaze before my eyes drop to the paper in my fingers. "Anna Petoskey," I whisper, reading the caption at the top that says: MISSING GIRL, ANNA PETOSKEY, FOUND DEAD OUTSIDE SANDUSKY. I remember reading about her in the newspaper, after I came home from the hospital. Mom gasped when she read the article, kept looking at me funny.

"Where'd you get this, Rocky?"

"I found it looking through some old boxes in my shed. I thought maybe it would help you. Mom kept it. She used to go to school with this girl's mom before they moved up north. Her name was Tina Long. That was the fifteen year-old girl murdered right after you came home—" The screen door opens again. I look up to see Lynn McDaniel, Rocky's mom, peering out the door.

"Well, lookey there! Rocky said you was out here. Give me a sec to grab my cigs and I'll come out." She waves a skinny hand at me and disappears again.

Rocky stares expressionlessly at the door. I can almost see the sinking feeling in his chest. I know he about

dies whenever his mom shows up at some function of my
own mom's. He doesn't say it aloud, but she's what my
mom calls *quite the character,* which means she's out of
Mom's radar range of what she would consider normal.
Rocky's eyes meet mine reluctantly and he sighs softly, like
he wishes he could sweep her under the nearest rug.

"Rosie, can I ask you something before she comes
back out?" Rocky's real serious as he stops right there in the
conversation. He doesn't wait for me to answer. "Are you on
drugs or something?"

"What? No!" I contort my face to express the
ridiculousness of his question.

"I'm sorry." He shakes his head and looks at Colton's
truck, like he'd rather be working under the hood than
having this conversation. "You've just been acting like a
different person. You're usually quiet and—and there's
nothing wrong with that. But you came in to school drunk
the other day. You've been talking to people again."

"I wasn't *that* drunk. I just fell to sleep in the limo."

"Rosie, are you listening to what you're saying? Since
when do you hang out with partyers in a limousine?"
Rocky's voice is calm, but he's got this strangely urgent look
in his eyes. "You didn't even do it at the high school prom.
You're having a conversation with me now like a normal
person. Two months ago, you couldn't even look me in the
eye, much less talk to me."

"I should go. Thanks for the article." I wave the
newspaper clipping, nod to my car. "Just tell Colton to bring
the book to school."

"Oh, don't go. Just forget I said that." He extends a
hand starts to touch my arm and stops. I look at his fingers
dangling there. I know he's a little hesitant about touching
me. He has good reason. At Mom's Sunday lunch last week,

Rocky was sitting on the side of the hot tub. He asked Nicky to put some suntan lotion on his back so he didn't get a sunburn. Nicky tossed the suntan lotion bottle at me, told me to do it because I'd been staring at him like a creep all day anyway. I might as well feel him up and get my jollies because I'd probably been dreaming about it half my life. I had faltered, so stunned by her words that I just stood there juggling the bottle with big eyes, trying not to imagine my fingers sliding along his skin. *Oh, quit being such a baby. Rocky thinks you're bugly. You know what bugly is? It is butt ugly.* She'd gotten up with a cackle and strutted toward the house. Rocky had cleared his throat in the following dead silence. I started to shake the lotion and flipped open the lid. *You probably shouldn't,* Rocky had said and his face was as red as mine beneath his freckles. *She's in a bad mood today.* But I'd squirted the lotion into my palm and did it anyways, rubbed it across his back in the awkward quiet. Then out of nowhere, he says: *She's wrong about the bugly thing, I don't think you look like a butt at all.* We laughed clumsily and I know I put way too much lotion on him. His entire back was a creamy mess and the harder I rubbed, the more it seemed to just slop all over. I'd finally stood back and handed him a towel. *Well, she was right about me feeling you up,* I told him. *I always wondered what it would be like. Now I know.*

Rocky had just started to toss the towel over his shoulders. He just came to a complete standstill and looked up at me. *Wow, I don't even know how to address that,* he told me before he chuckled. That must be lingering in his mind when he looks at his fingers dangling there today because he stuffs them quickly into his pockets. "Just tell me what's going on. We're worried."

"Leave that poor girl alone." The hoarse croaking voice belongs to his mom. Both Rocky and I crane our necks toward the porch and the thick cloud of cigarette smoke disappearing into a film while the screen door shuts hard. Lynn McDaniel plops down in a lawn chair on the porch. She smiles and waves a hand at me. "Gabby says you make better brownies than her Auntie Lynn. It's got to be the magic spoon you wave around it." Mom told me she used to be beautiful when she was younger and before she started drinking beer by the case a night.

"Hey, Missus McDaniel," I greet her with a little wave of my fingers. I laugh. "Yeah, I think everything's better with a little magic witch dust." Rocky is squinting at me, so I explain. "Leah told her I was a witch. I told her I wasn't, but we kid about it, me and Gabby." Lynn waves a fly away herself, sits back in the chair and huffs a deep laugh.

"Don't call me Missus McDaniel baby, it makes me feel old. Call me Lynn like everybody else."

"When did you make brownies with Gabby?" Rocky is eyeing me carefully.

"Usually Sundays, Mondays, and Tuesdays. You drop her at Nicky's when you work at the station. Nicky drops her at Rosie's," Lynn speaks for me. "That's what Gabby tells me." Then she nods to me. "That's a pretty dress. Too pretty to be wearing up to Johnny's. He give you hell?"

"Yes, sounded just like my daddy. All growl; no bite."

"You got out of there quick, though, didn't you?" she laughs, digging into her purse. She stuffs another cigarette between her lips.

"Uh huh. He had the same look my daddy has when he's insulted by what I say. I was afraid he might come out with an old flyswatter and give me a spanking."

She pats a fold up aluminum lawn chair next to her. "Come up here and sit with me while you wait for Colton. That boy's slower than butter in December."

"No, Mom, she's probably got to get going," Rocky says with an odd urgency in his eyes. It's almost like I can hear them screaming, *don't do it, don't do it!* But anything's better than being chastised, like a six year-old, by my sister's kind-of boyfriend. I give him a little tip to my chin, daring him to stop me. He just gets this funny purse of his lips like he's not sure what to do. I strut right up and plop down.

"So what's this book all about? Why's my boy been making a mess of all my boxes I got stored in his shed?" Lynn asks me, still digging in her purse and mumbling about her losing her lighter again. I pick up the lighter from the table. She chuckles the same chuckle Rocky has while I flick it on the tip. She takes a puff-puff.

"I used to light my papaw's cigarettes until he quit smoking. If Mom knew I did that, she would have keeled over and died."

"Your mom's a funny one. She used to—"

"No, Mom, please don't go on," Rocky interrupts. He's standing there at the truck, gaping at us frantically as if we're two little girls standing on the edge of a railroad track holding hands. He's waiting for her to drag me across in front of a train.

"Oh, Rocky, she's not as naïve as you say all the time," Lynn declares. I blink. He calls me naive? Ug. "So what's so big about this book that sends a Hatfield up to the McCoy side of the fence? Because last I checked, that feud between the McGuires and the McDaniels is still going on," she says. "I heard tell your daddy stuck up twenty signs with No Trespassing on them. Rocky's daddy, Big Jake, and Johnny went down, turned them around, and put their names on them, so they looked like they were on our side of the fence."

"Then my daddy shot them all with his rifle. I think my mamaw could not have said it any different than he cut off his nose to spite his face. Daddy paid ten bucks a piece for those signs."

"And Johnny spent three hours and twenty bucks worth of staples for his staple gun to turn them around," Lynn adds, snickering. "And he staple-gunned Big Jake's thumb while he was holding the sign for him and Big Jake cussed for an hour about that." We both laugh. Rocky does not.

"To answer your question," I say, "the book belonged to my Aunt Roo. It was her diary."

"Why'd Colton have it?"

"I got a box of her things." I sniff past the thick scent of cigarettes on Lynn's clothing. "I just thought I'd see if there was anything the same with her disappearing along with the three girls they've found dead outside town. And now Anna Petoskey, back when I was in middle school."

"Is that why you're acting weird?" Rocky pipes up.

"What's weird about her?" his mom asks, taking a big puff.

"Where do you want me to start?" He leans his rear against the truck and folds his arms, looks over to where Colton has just come into view trudging up the dirt road. Damn, Rocky's a fine specimen of a man. He looks like a male model for a mechanics magazine settled in there on the front of the truck. "She went from knee-length dresses to—that—" He points up at my hemline, which ends well above my knees. "She used to whisper one-word sentences and now she's doling out her opinion on everything under the sun and without anyone asking her! Isn't that enough?"

I rip my eyes from the Rocky candy and turn my eyes away at the sound of Colton's tennis shoes grinding in the driveway. He's got the diary in his right hand and some papers in the left. He steps right up, hands the diary to me. "Here, it was pretty boring. Girl stuff. Maybe there's something more, but I didn't see anything," he says, shoving it into my hands. He hesitates, then fans his face with the papers. "And here's the stuff you asked for."

I'm curious while I reach out and take three or four pieces of eight and a half by eleven pieces of paper from his fingers. Quietly, I turn them over and take a look. The first sheet of paper has copies of newspaper articles on it.

"Those are about your aunt," he tells me. "There isn't much. It's just a picture of a missing persons poster somebody'd put up on a telephone pole in town somewhere and her mom standing next to it."

I peer at the image. My mamaw's standing there with her mouth open like she's in mid-sentence talking to the reporter. She's got an arm out, pointing to the poster. It says: *Missing. Rosaline McGuire. Age 17.* I can't read the rest. The words kind of melt into the newspaper.

"I remember all that going on." Lynn leans in, holds her arm up above her head so the cigarette doesn't burn me. "It was after Johnny and Ray wrecked their trucks racing."

"Racing?" I look up at her; I have no clue what she's talking about. "I never heard that."

"I'm sure there's a lot of shenanigans you haven't heard about your daddy and Johnny," Lynn sniggers. "I could tell you so many stories about the trouble they got into, it would make your head spin."

"Look at the next page," Colton ignores her, pokes a finger at the papers. "I'd never heard of that race either until I read the diary. On one of the pages, your aunt talks about six or seven people she knew racing—"

"It was in all the papers," Lynn interrupts me delving

into the papers. "It was because of the wreck that the Stamper girl was found."

"Huh?" Rocky and I both say at the same time.

"Caroline Stamper," Colton adds for her. "They called her Carrie. Doctor Stamper's daughter." I see a shadow slip up and cover the papers. Rocky comes up beside Colton and leans over the papers I'm holding. Colton made a copy of the newspaper. In big, bold letters it states: RACING TEENS. GIRL DIES IN WRECK ON CO RD 57.

I look at Rocky. His eyes meet mine like we already know this secret. "Carrie Stamper," I repeat. "I have a copy of the coroner's report. It just said she was in an accident. So it was a wreck?"

"Naw, she was sixteen or seventeen that year; 1977. September. School just started. And that ain't how she died." Lynn puffs her cigarette. I gaze at a face shot of a girl, probably a high school yearbook picture. She's pretty with wide eyes and shoulder-length light hair and the fake smile put on for school photographs.

"How'd she die?" I ask.

"People just want to forget, honey." Lynn snubs her cigarette on a makeshift ashtray made from an old coffee can. "They don't know rightly. The police, they thought she fell out of the back of Ray or Johnny's truck when they were racing. Then, she got hit by the truck behind. That weren't the case at all. We was all skipping school, Johnny, me, and our friends. The cops called it a race. We were just getting out of school and trying to get as far away from it as we could. Ray and his friends had the same idea. But it weren't like it is now, where you kids all hang out together, don't care whose family is whose. Forty years ago, there'd be no way in hell you'd be sitting on Rocky's porch here."

"Well, I suppose I wouldn't now if I didn't need the

diary." I tell her bluntly. I look over at Rocky. He's got that deadpan stare at me again. "I should go," I tell Lynn. I like her. "So, you're saying Carrie *wasn't* killed in the wreck? She wasn't with you guys?"

"Nope. There weren't no wreck. I think Johnny hit Ray's truck, bumped it a little, and it went into the guardrail. But that was when they heard the cops coming and was trying to get out of there. That's when the cops found Carrie lying down the road."

"So, she could have been a murder victim too?"

Lynn shifts uncomfortably in her chair. "It were blamed on us kids. Nobody ever pressed no charges. But we carried the brunt of Carrie's death. That's why nobody talks about it. I don't want to talk about it."

Chapter 26

"Mom, did you know my Aunt Roo well?"

"No, sweetie, I didn't." Mom is washing dishes in the sink. I'm sitting at her kitchen table, a small wooden one with five chairs around it. "Did you hear about Gayle Heath's daughter?" Her back is to me and she is wearing a knee-length skirt and a white blouse. She's got her sleeves rolled to her elbows and she is wearing baby blue rubber gloves so the dishwashing liquid doesn't dry out her hands.

"No—" I start, because I know she's going to tell me regardless if I want to hear or not.

"She got a DUI in Memphis. A DUI." Mom turns. "You know what that is, don't you, honey? Driving under the influence of alcohol. She came from a good family and look at her. She was always such a sweet girl."

"She is still probably a sweet girl. You shouldn't be so critical."

"Are you drinking, Rosie?" She gets a concerned tip to her chin before she turns back to the sink. "You don't go to the dance halls—"

"They are called clubs, Mom, and no I don't." I rest my elbows on the table and look up at Bobby, who is sitting across from me, holding the newspaper up in front of his face and pretending to read. He peers out every now and then when one of our voices rises and looks back and forth between my mom and me like he's reading our faces, seeing if he should excuse himself to perform some meaningless task in another room before our conversation turns to a fight. For someone who was a cop and whose job was to break up brawls, he sure likes to avoid our confrontations.

"I'm sure that's what Kaylee Heath told her mother, too." Mom draws out a breath. "Oh, and I can't tell you how glad I am you didn't take that job for Jack Barkley. You've heard his newest thing, haven't you?" She doesn't wait for me to answer. "Margret Timmons who is in my gardening club goes there a few times a month. Her husband makes a mint selling real estate. They have a membership there. "

Oh. I stare at my fingernails, pretend to clean one. I try to think of a way to change the subject to something, anything else.

"Well," Mom goes on. "He's got a new girlfriend and she's not a day over twenty. The rumor is he met her at a spa in Mexico. He waltzes around, teasing she's his little niece from California, but everybody knows better—"

"Mom, enough on the gossip," I murmur.

"I just want you to know you dodged a bullet on that one, sweetie pie," Mom says. "He might be winning her over with diamonds and trinkets, but at the end of the day, he's just using her to feel young again. And it's not making him any younger. He's such a scoundrel. He bought her a red Corvette. What does a girl have to do to get a brand spanking new, red Corvette?"

I can answer that for my mom—get dumped at a strip club at midnight and follow around a twenty-one year-old drunk, sadistic psychopath. However, I don't say it aloud. "A scoundrel," I repeat instead, giggling. "Like a pirate with his booty? Mom, when was the last time anybody used the word *scoundrel*?"

"You laugh, Rosie, but I've seen what happens to girls like that. They burn out like candles." She's got the worried glaze to her eyes and tip of her chin. "Nicky said a friend of hers saw the young woman with two other men."

"Mom, it isn't any of our business. I'm sure they are looking deeper into the relationship than needs to be," I mumble. "She probably *is* his niece. You and your friends gossip too much."

"It just worries me that you defend someone like that, like you think it is okay."

"Mom, the world needs all kinds of people. Not all of them can live up to your standards." I sniff. "Can you quit avoiding my question?" I mutter. "Did you know my aunt?"

"Well, let's just say your aunt was one of those girls, Rosaline Mauer." Mom straightens her back, pushes up her chin. "That's what I'm trying to tell you, in a nice way. Why do you have to push and push until people say things they don't want to say?"

I narrow my eyes at her; because I am trying to get some common ground with the girls who have been murdered, that's why. I don't tell her that. But on the way home from Rocky's, I got on the phone and called four of the men who had been suspects. Each of them asked how I got their names. I told them flat out: it's public information.

Two, who were local Laurel Grove residents, hung up on me. However, Troy White told me he dated Alaina two years ago. They broke up and hadn't seen each other since. He'd had a domestic dispute with his ex-wife six months ago and they pulled his file, figured since the cops got called to his house over a fight with his ex-wife, he might also be a murderer. He wasn't. Zane Jacobs, the second who talked to me, worked at the Crazy Fiddle. He was the bartender and knew both the girls from their separate visits there. He claimed the owner of the bar gave the cops a copy of the video tapes from the cameras located in two corners of the bar. He had an alibi. The video showed him working there all night on both occasions.

From the coroner's reports I got from Frankie, I could see Alaina, Angel and Phoebe had been killed by blunt force trauma to the back of their heads. So I'm trying to extricate information out of my mom and Bobby about Carrie Stamper and my aunt. I don't want to jump right in considering my mom thinks I'm bat shit crazy anyway about these crimes.

"I mean, she was a few years older than me," Mom tells me. "We didn't run in the same circle. I just heard she was sneaking around with more than a few boyfriends."

Yeah, I know what that means. Aunt Roo was what my mom calls *from the redneck side of town;* Mom, on the other hand, was from well-to-do section of suburbs on the other side of town. After looking at the files of the girls I got from Frankie, I'm trying to establish a common ground.

"So you don't know why she would have left—like run away or anything. I mean, everybody thought she got murdered, didn't they?"

Mom turns, looks at Bobby who is seated at the table across from me. He shuffles the paper and looks over top the front page. "You want me to answer this one, Gracie?" Bobby asks her. I'm curious. They lock eyes like they've got some big secret.

"Maybe you should."

Bobby sighs, puts down his paper, and addresses me with his eyes. "Okay, so I was a rookie cop when your aunt disappeared. I only worked part-time. You know, back then, you didn't need a whole lot of college or training, like they require now. I was fresh out of high school, just started working at the Laurel Grove Police Department when Rosaline McGuire came up missing." He looks at me, offers up a gentle smile. "So it was like a Friday night about seven and we get a call from your grandma, Paula McGuire. She's frantic because your Aunt Rosaline didn't come home from school." He picks up a coffee settled near his elbow, takes a sip. "So Arnold Kinney's the officer on duty—"

"Is that Timmy Kinney's dad?" I interrupt. "The one I went to school with who is a police officer now?"

"It was his grandfather. Arnold was—well, old school. He did things like they used to back in the 1950s, instead of by the book. He tended to wave off anybody who had money—let them off a ticket and just gave them a verbal warning. Anybody who was, well, from what he considered the other side of the tracks, the lower class, he was hard on them, dragged them into the station, and questioned them."

"Like my daddy's side of the family."

"You got it." He shoots me with a forefinger and thumb, then shifts in his seat uncomfortably. "I mean, not that I think that at all, Rosie."

"I know." Only, he does make remarks once in a while about dirtbags out on Troublesome Creek. I let it slide.

"So, what I'm getting at is that your grandma called. I remember Arnold laughed and rolled his eyes at all of us. He kept telling her that she'd probably run off."

"That's what everybody thought," Mom adds. "I mean, Rosaline was wild—like a little kitten that would scratch you when you least expected it. She didn't do anything to hurt anybody, just didn't seem to have that little thing in her brain that told her to be careful. She got into trouble at school, smoking in the bathroom and fighting at the football games."

"Aunt Roo got in fights?" I chew on this a minute. I've heard my dad swap stories with my uncles, recalling what my mamaw called *little mischiefs,* like my aunt driving down High Top Hill to see if the tires would come off the ground. One time, he said she'd gotten drunk behind the bleachers. But no one's ever compared her to a feral cat.

Mom wiggles her hands out of the rubber gloves,

turns around, and rests her rear on the sink. "Child, that girl was out of control most of the time. She chewed gum in class, snuck around with all the boys."

"Oh, *that's* a crime—" I mumble sarcastically.

"Regardless," Bobby holds up a hand like he's coming between two cats getting ready to fight. "When Arnie answered the phone at the police station, he treated the situation like it was of no great concern. He told your grandma we had a three day waiting period before we began looking for a girl of her age. She was probably with a boy."

"Okay so, what happened after three days?"

Mom looks at Bobby and they both turn to me with strangely solemn eyes. "Well," Mom says. "Arnie went to Holy Trinity Church that Sunday and mentioned your aunt was missing. It wasn't like: *we have a girl missing and does anybody know where she is?* It was: *that little, skanky girl from Troublesome Creek ran off.*"

"There were rumors that she got pregnant—that she ran away," Bobby says. "Dorothy Hewitt, who worked at the drugstore, said she saw her in Crystal Springs two weeks later. The rumors were flying. It was almost like everybody was trying to shame the McGuire's for raising a girl who would run off like that."

"It was never treated like she could have been kidnapped, Rosie," Mom says. "I remember her smoking cigarettes when she waited for the bus. It was kind of like we all expected she'd run off or get hurt by some man she met up with. She'd go out drinking all the time."

"So was it the same when I didn't come home that day?" I ask. "Did you look for me?"

"Your mom did everything she was supposed to do once she thought you were missing," Bobby tells me, like he is defending her. "But you have to understand, she thought you'd gone to a friend's house for an overnight."

"You don't remember, do you?"

I don't want to tell her I do remember some things. I remember getting mad at her because she didn't want me hanging around Rocky and she knew I was sneak-seeing him. She didn't want me hanging around with Kylee. She told me not to walk out the door when I got mad. I remember screaming her she should be happy, I wasn't hanging with Rocky anymore.

"So did my Aunt Roo know Carrie Stamper?"

"Sweetheart, I'm asking that you just let this all go. For me. For all of those who don't want old, sad memories drudged up. Doctor Stamper was so good to us when you were fourteen, so kind and understanding. Do you remember going to her office a couple times a week to talk to her?" Mom is tipping her head to the side.

"Of course. How could I forget? You know how hard it was to sit outside her office in ninth grade and everyone knew I was in therapy?"

"Do you know that Mary Stamper has gotten acclaims all across the United States for her progresses in children's psychology?"

"Well, I remember when she subbed my kindergarten class, she wouldn't let me go to the bathroom after I asked three times with my hand waving in the air. She made me pee my pants."

"Oh, you're making that up. She would never do that."

Yes, she did. I remember sitting in the puddle of pee, still holding up my hand so I followed the rules. And then, I remember having to walk down the aisle while she reprimanded in a soft, gruff voice and the pee dribbled down my leg and on to the floor. I had to wear plastic pants all that year.

"Are you all right, sweetie?"

Bad memories. I'm rubbing the back of my head, don't even realize I am doing it.

"Oh, yeah," I say and drop my fingers. "I'm just getting a headache. It must be getting ready to rain."

"Rosie, can we talk for a minute?"

It is only ten minutes later, Mom excuses herself to go to the bathroom. Bobby leans back at the table, makes a hard-lean to the left until she disappears up the stairway.

He smiles way too big. I nod slowly and watch him shift in the kitchen chair.

"Sometimes it's better to just walk away," he says softly. "And not take a stick and tap at the hornet's nest."

I mull this over a moment in my mind while I stare at him blankly, Rosie-style. I'm finding people think I'm a bit childlike with my dumb stare. Such, they end up divulging a few supplementary bits and pieces just by making their explanation more detailed, like they are breaking it down for a four year-old.

"Hornet's nest?" I ask leadingly.

"Yeah, um," Bobby appears to be considering his words carefully. Or maybe he is dumbing them down. "Back in the day, there were some whispers Arnold Kinney could have put more effort into finding your aunt and solving the crimes. Folks up on Troublesome Creek tended to believe that he was covering for somebody. Word got out and Arnold, he started harassing your grandpa on your daddy's side. He'd have us pull your grandpa and your dad over for going two miles over the speed limit. He was knocking on the doors of Johnny McDaniel's house every day for dogs barking and someone allegedly hearing guns going off."

"Why didn't anybody stop him?"

"Because he was the law. I was just a rookie," Bobby shifts uncomfortably. "We were all just doing our job, doing what our boss told us to do. I figured, I didn't want him getting mad at me and the finger started pointing my direction or at my parents."

"Do you think he knew what happened to my aunt?"

"No, I don't. But I also don't think he was bright enough, or had the right tools, to solve a crime of that magnitude. It was job security for him, taking the public eyes off his ineptness, pointing the finger at everybody else, and making it appear that the girls weren't murdered. They deemed Carrie Stamper a hit and run. Your aunt was a runaway."

"And Anna Petoskey?" I say, keeping a blank face.

"Anna Petoskey," Bobby lets out a deep huff of air. "I remember that name. I remember it well. She was the only one in a long list of girls we checked out around the state who had any details that were similar. It was a knock on the noggin." He bumps his head with his knuckles. "But that's a common way of killing someone."

"Lastly, Gina Channel."

"How do you know about her?"

"A little bird."

"Was it the same little bird who killed himself at the gas station the other night?"

"The homeless man? No."

Bobby eyes me with a funny twist. Is he testing me? He shifts uncomfortably. "Okay, I didn't give you this. I'll deny it if your mom finds out. Follow me out to the car."

I do as he says. It's almost like we're creeping past the bathroom where Mom is inside. When he gets to his car, Bobby reaches into the window and opens his glovebox.

Within, he tugs out a clear plastic baggie. He holds the re-sealable end carefully and wiggles it so it opens. Then, he reaches in with his index finger and thumb. "This has bugged me since I found it. I've carried it with me for no other reason than I thought, at some point, I'd step up and look into it deeper after Arnold Kinney retired." He tugs out a tiny square piece of paper that has been folded several times. Then, he takes out a leather bracelet with a snap. I try not to let out a breath. It's a perfect match of my Aunt Roo's bracelet with DIES IRAE hand tooled on it.

"Do you know what that is?" Bobby asks.

"My Aunt Rosie had one of these too," I say and look up at Bobby. He thrusts out his hand so I take it. He's staring intensely at me when I inspect it closely. I feel like he's trying to read my expression.

"Hmm," he mumbles. "That's interesting. Did someone give it to you?"

"No, I've just always had it," I lie. I get this odd sensation of distrust I've never felt before. I don't want to tell him I got it in the chest Daddy gave me. It's like he's analyzing me, scrutinizing my reaction. Maybe it's just rubbed off on me from my daddy. He always gets a guarded look when I mention Bobby's name. Or maybe my daddy does that to any police officer. My papaw tells me it comes with the territory. The folks on Troublesome Creek Road distrust police officers. It always seems when something goes wrong in town, the finger gets pointed toward those few who live outside the bounds like the McDaniels and the McGuires.

I take the paper, unwrap it fold by fold until within, I see a gold heart-shaped dog tag. It is only as big as my thumb while I hold it there. "Rosie," Bobby says softly while he looks over my shoulder toward the house. "I couldn't do anything when your aunt disappeared. I was young and—

and I regret I didn't stick up for what I thought was right. But I didn't. What is done is done. Maybe these things will help your—quest."

In handmade scrawl from a sharp object, the dog tag is engraved with: *Please return me to T. White. 467 White's Farm Road. Laurel Grove, Ohio*

"You're hiding something." I just say it, don't look up to acknowledge him. He doesn't seem surprised.

"Ah, that's our Rosie, just saying how she feels—out loud," he chuckles. Then his smile drops. "This discussion and these things—" he pauses, and when I look up, he's gazing warily toward the house. "We need to keep them between you and me, you understand?"

"Yes."

"I don't want your mom to know I'm supporting your desire to find your aunt. But there's one more thing I need you to know and you're going to have to pretend like you didn't hear it now and you didn't hear it from me. I heard it from someone who would get into trouble if they knew I told anyone else. But I just got the news this morning; your father and Rocky's Uncle Johnny were persons of interest back when Carrie Stamper was found dead. They were at the scene, although they adamantly claimed they had nothing to do with her death. Their names were eventually scratched off the list. I knew that and didn't think much of it because there were literally dozens of men who were looked into at that point. Everybody seemed to be under surveillance when it was going on. But now their names are coming up again. Johnny's a regular at the Crazy Fiddle Country Tavern, where Angel Daugherty was known to get a drink. Your dad works at the country club, where Alaina Windowski came up missing. From what I've heard inside the department, your dad and Rocky's uncle are at the top of the list."

Chapter 27

The day Bobby gave me the dog tag and leather bracelet, I take them home and plop them on my table. I feel sick to my tummy. *Dies Irae*, I quickly learn from an online dictionary, is an old hymn sung in a Mass for the dead. The words mean *day of wrath*. I find it intriguing that the hymn is about judgement day. I don't know if Daddy knows he's a suspect. I start to pick up the phone to call him but I put it back down. I'm not sure I want to cross that line with him, even if I could coax something out to help solve the murders.

Instead, I try to focus on what is in front of me. I feel like I'm staring up at the sky on a clear night. Each star is a person and each person could be a suspect. But everybody looks the same. I could reach out and pluck a star from the sky, randomly pick a person from the phone book. One by one, I could search their background, find their alibi. Ten years from now, there's still a million stars, a million suspects dangling over my head. Maybe something about them is a clue. Maybe whoever owned the dog tag knows where Gina Channel disappeared to or knows what happened to Carrie Stamper. And maybe, it will be the one piece of puzzle missing from the box that will be the defining clue to solve the murders.

Bobby said he found the paper, bracelet, and dog tag in Arnold Kinney's garbage can when he was tossing the wadded up papers, used tissues, and coffee-stained Styrofoam cups in the dumpster behind the police station. He said taking out the trash was one of the duties of a rookie cop at Laurel Grove Police Station. The tag slid loudly down the metal garbage can where it caught in a crumpled piece of paper, then plunked hard into a brown cardboard box in the dumpster. Only seconds later, the leather bracelet plopped next to it.

He had watched its descent from can to cardboard box. He shook the garbage can and started to turn. It was a sudden urge, a gut feeling he needed to turn around, reach into the dumpster, and snatch up the dog tag with the crumpled paper around it. So he did. He knew if he left it, he'd lay awake all night wondering why he had seen Arnold Kinney return from the coroner's office, tug items from a manila envelope with both Gina Channel's and Carrie Stamper's names on it and toss them in the trash.

Weeks later, he watched Arnold Kinney hand over an envelope to Gina's mother. It only had Gina's name on it. The second envelope with both Carrie's name and Gina's name had disappeared. In Gina's envelope was a pair of shorts, a pair of panties, and a t-shirt, the three things that were lying on Gina's bed the night she disappeared. He didn't recall a dog tag in the evidence and didn't believe it was among Gina's things. He felt it might have to do with Carrie Stamper. But the specific reason his boss had an envelope with evidence from both the girls together, as if there were similarities and may be linked, he didn't know.

But it isn't the dog tag that's caught my eye. It is the little piece of paper with a bunch of random letters scribbled on it like a three year-old's first copies of the alphabet—VRHVMLTOV SZEVIHGLGG. 696 is written along one side. To most people it would be unsystematic listing of letters and a few numbers tossed in. To me, it is the same secret code my daddy and I used to share. It stands for 414 Eisenogle-Haverstott Road.

And while I plugged the address into the computer, it came up with an owner by the name of Jay Richard Cooper, I take in a breath. Beneath random listings of similar addresses for voter registrants and home listings, there is also a local police page with mug shots of known drug and alcohol offenders. A Jay Richard Cooper is listed on the page for having several DUIs. I rub my hand over my forehead. The bearded, glassy-eyed man staring back at me is the same man who handed me my Aunt Roo's monkey backpack. My mind is reeling when I hear the sound of a car in my driveway. I put down the crumpled paper and stand while I walk to my front door and open it up.

"Oh. You're home." It is blonde-haired, blue-eyed Kayla from Kayla's Hometown Florist. She's just getting ready to rest a single rose on my front porch. She stops, holds it in the air. "This is for you," she says. It is orange and wrapped in green tissue paper.

"Who sent it?" I take it in my fingers.

"Don't know. I just get an envelope in my box with your name and your address and this time, it was with a fifty dollar tip. Pretty good for delivering a single rose."

I sigh while she straightens herself and rests both arms on her hips. "So, what does it mean this time?"

"Well, funny you should ask. I looked it up. Orange means desire. So somebody's wanting to get to know you—better and intimately. It's a pretty sexy rose."

I sigh. "I suppose, Kayla, it depends on who is sending it. If it is the creepy guy who picks his nose while he takes out his garbage and who lives in the house on the corner, maybe not." She thinks it is funny. I'm not so sure.

"It can also mean someone's proud of you." She shrugs. My sense of humor is lacking while I watch her leave. I hold the rose in my hand. I wonder who is sending them. Rocky? Bobby? My mom? My sister? Mister Barkley? That's my circle of friends and family. Who would be proud of me? Daddy? I have to assume it's him. I chew on this a second. It fuels my desire to figure out who is killing the girls, what happened to my Aunt Rosie. So I grab my keys, the address and my phone. Then I take off toward 414 Eisenogle-Haverstott Road.

Chapter 28

I'm really wishing I had not made a sharp veer on Raccoon Hollow Road and passed Leah McDaniel's house, seen her outside with Colton who was filling up a push mower with gas from a plastic milk jug. Still, I stop, wave her over. "We need to talk," I tell her. She gives me a deadpan stare and tells me she doesn't have to talk to me.

"Go to hell, Rosie," she calls out over the mower.

I say, "Okay, then when your dad ends up in the electric chair, don't come crying to me." It was enough to get her attention and she narrows her eyes. "I'm making an offer. We've got something in common."

"What, because you turned him into the cops?"

"I didn't turn him into the cops. Because, quite honestly, I don't think he did it. There's something going on. I don't know what. But I think I might know who may have been killing those girls—and I don't know your daddy much," I say. "However, I do know that he helped pull my sister out of a ditch last January. She was in the middle of nowhere, by herself, and it was after dark. She was the premise for every horror movie I've watched and he even gave her a blanket while she sat in his truck. So, I'm thinking the cops are barking up the wrong tree for your dad and for mine."

"Your dad too?" she asks. I nod. And I get out of my car, slam the door behind me. Then I stomp across the knee-high grass toward her. I don't know if it is the shock that I didn't hightail it out of there Rosie-style or she just doesn't have time to react. But Leah stands right there while I come up and stop three steps away.

"It's like this," I huff. Colton is still holding the milk jug over the mower and it is empty while his eyes veer back and forth between us. "Your dad and my dad have become the prime suspects in the murders of two girls. I can almost guarantee that they are going to pit them against each other. And if they have to use us to do it, they will. Now, I would suggest you go for a ride with me."

"Go for a ride? Where?"

"To break into a possible murderer's house."

So thirty-eight minutes later, Colton is driving up and down the main road in my car with Gabby in tow. Leah's playing sidekick to me. The door to Jay Cooper's mobile home is unlocked. The cracked bottom drags roughly over wet, orange-brown shag carpet. I look upward. There's a big carrot-colored stain on the ceiling where rusty water from the dilapidated roof has leaked inside. I sniff. I'm enveloped in the rancid reek of pee and stale cigarette smoke. It is silent, save the angry *bang-bang* of wind blowing against the few remaining pieces of aluminum siding used for skirting along the outside of the trailer. I still ask if anybody is home. Then I wait until the count of ten.

I use my hip to force the door open. Looking around, it is tough to believe anybody has lived here. But there are signs. There's an ash tray made from a plastic bottle filled with brown cigarette butts and an olive green coffee cup with WOLRD'S BEST DAD hand-painted in white beneath the brim. Then I nearly faint dead away. There's the sound of a man's voice. I freeze, clasp my arms to my chest. Crackle-crackle-pop. There is a boombox plugged into an outlet on a ramshackle table built into the wall. The voices are coming from the speaker. Still, I wait and wait like I'm frozen in time. Then, when I only hear the staticky sound of music fade in and out, I make my move inside.

"Listen, I don't have all day." Leah is standing with

her left foot on the third and highest rickety step leading straight to the doorframe. Her right foot is planted at the lowest step so she is straddling the place where the middle step has fallen through to the ground. "Are we besties now, Weird Wosie?" Leah asks in a baby voice. "Oh, I forgot. You're not going to tattle on me at work, are you, and tell them I called you that?" She shakes her head, scoots up behind me, and shoves the door open with her plump shoulder. "Enter, my princess." She holds out an arm and waves it to the living room. "Tell me again, so I know when they book us into the jail at the Laurel Grove Police Department, what are we looking for—or who?"

"It's not *who*. The guy who owned the trailer is in sixty pieces on a cold slab in the morgue. I know. I saw him get hit by a truck. I think he killed the girl they found in the ditch, the one at the quarry and the one on Route 32. Maybe, he killed my aunt and Carrie Stamper. I want to find some evidence before the cops do."

"Carrie Stamper? Is she related to Doctor Stamper?"

"Yeah. She died right before my aunt."

"Great, so you're telling me we're looking for dead bodies? And your reasoning behind that? Because we all know how good you are at screwing things up."

"Gosh, Leah, you're more critical than my charming, manipulating, narcissistic sociopath sister," I groan.

"Yeah, and did it also occur to you the only thing scarier than a narcissistic sociopath would be being their victim?"

"I'm new at this. I've never broken into a house before." I hold up my hands, exposing the little cheap plastic gloves while we walk inside. "At least I remembered these."

"Are those from a hair coloring kit?"

"Yeah, it's all I had." I'd dug them out of my Rio Color Warm Honey Brown Hair Color Kit. "I would suggest you don't touch anything and leave fingerprints."

"Like they could find fingerprints in here?" Leah waves a hand in front of her nose. "This is a hoarder's paradise."

"Hoarding can be set off by a traumatic event," I disclose. "I would think if a traumatic event triggers hoarding, it could also trigger a murdering spree." I look around the little living room in front of us. The room is stacked with old cardboard boxes with newspapers and magazines piled on top. There's a kitchen to the left with a counter that is also nearly hidden by stacks of clothing, a couple TV sets, tools, and an odd array of suitcases and outdated computer monitors.

I slip through the maze of boxes, pass an old orange-flowered couch and note: "At least he color-coordinated." I look up and Leah is just hard-staring me.

"I liked it better when you didn't talk," she tells me making a sweep of the room with her eyes. "*Oh, Leah, you'd be so cute if you put your hair up,*" she mimics my voice in a high pitch. I did bring that up in conversation in the car. "*If you don't like your janitor job, go back to college. You should try my face wash. It helps get rid of the pimples on my forehead*—do you *ever* shut up? Do you drive your friends nuts with all that or are they just like you?"

"You're not my friend. I'm not your friend," I tell her while I flip open the lid of a box and peek inside. There's old, yellowed newspapers and mouse poop. "We are just two people with a common denominator—"

"That's math, right?"

"In our case, it's the fact we're in different situations, but we have one underlying thing in common. We want to find out who murdered those girls so we can get the cops off our dads' asses." I'm weaving my way through to the right and a hallway that has a door at the end. I have to walk sideways to get past the long line of plastic milk crates. I pass a bathroom and the toilet is filled with sewage so it is brimming over the top. I choke back a gag and I crane my neck to see her following four steps behind. "Besides, I don't have any friends, so I don't know."

That shuts her up. I get to the door, test the knob. It's locked. "Crap on a stick," I mutter giving it a good bang with my shoulder. The rank odor of a backed-up toilet is making me nauseous. The squishy sound of leaking sewage and the orange stain on the ceiling is making me squeamish.

"Move, princess," Leah pushes herself around me. She reaches up to the top of a frame around the door, runs her hand along it until she stops. "Bingo. Same place I hide the key to Gabby's room in case she locks me out." She gives me a haughty tip of her chin, shoves the key into the knob. "Hope there's not a booby trap with a gun on the other side."

"People *do* that?" I ask as she gives the door a little shove. "I mean, wouldn't they get shot if—"

"Oh, shit!"

Leah sees the string before I do. She turns, shoves me down by the shoulders just as the sound of a shotgun blast shatters the air. My heart bounces wildly in my chest while she bears down on me and the door explodes into wood splinters flying through the air.

"Damn you!" she screams at me. She uses my chest and face as a surface to push herself upward, then gives me a hard kick in the hip while I start to stand. "This is stupid, so stupid! You're going to get us killed! That idiot really *did* tie a wire around the trigger of the shotgun. What the hell do you think he's hiding in here? He rigged it to the door knob. Do you get that? He set you up? Did it not occur to you that a guy so crazy he's murdering girls and walking in front of trucks would possibly have a hidden agenda regarding giving you his address?"

"He didn't give me his address. Bobby Vandevenne did," I mutter. "My mom's husband."

"You think he set you up?"

"No, of course not." I rub my face, turn to look through the now open doorway. "I mean, why would he do it? It was a code he gave me. I just assumed he couldn't decrypt the code—oh—shit. Maybe he did."

She stops. Leah must see the blank expression on my face. The door is tilted sideways, cheap wood peeling back and exposing the bedroom inside. Wind from a broken window is scattering pieces of paper from one end of the room to the other. The walls are damp and patches of the plaster ceiling are dangling inches from our heads. The carpet is sopped. There is an odor of dirty dishrags.

But on the other side and past the dust I'm waving away with my hand, there's a perfectly-made bed with frilly lace at the bottom and little pink princesses on the comforter. There's a nightstand that was once hand-decorated with blue unicorns, and a beautifully painted castle on the wood siding of one wall. And then, there's a wall dotted with bits and pieces of paper and pictures, some that have fallen and are scattered across the floor and the bed. There are newspaper clippings fluttering with the breeze and tied together with fishing line.

"You're freaking crazy," Leah whispers.

"I like crazy better than weird," I decide out loud, not really paying attention to her. I march across the broken door and into the room. The three walls that aren't painted with a castle are a pretty, little-girl pink. There's a closet without a door and two red plastic bins stacked inside. But the pictures. I walk straight up to one pink wall, take it all in. There are about twenty pictures of young women scattered around. Some are probably sixteen or seventeen, others maybe in their mid-twenties. Some are actual Polaroid pictures, others are cut from newspapers or copies of newspaper pictures.

I lean forward, pick up a picture at the end of the bed. "That's Angel Dougherty," I point to a newer cut out from a newspaper. "She's the one they found in the quarry." I snatch up another. This picture was cut from a yearbook.

"Oh, crud, that's Alaina Windowski," Leah says, stepping up toward the wall. There's a picture curled and she's pushed it straight with her fingers. "It's got her name written on it. What is this?" Leah whispers right behind me. I jump. She sniffs a laugh. "A fricking wall of pictures of all the girls he murdered or is going to murder?"

"*Was*," I remind her. "He's dead." I barely look up. I blink at a pile of images settled in the center of the bed. "Oh, I think that's my dad."

Leah turns and picks up my dad's picture. Then her eyes widen to the next picture. "That's *my* dad. What the hell?" Leah asks.

I narrow my eyes at a third picture beside her dad's picture. I poke a finger at it. "That's the guy who killed himself, who owned this trailer—Jay Cooper." I look at Leah. "Why would he put his picture with theirs? They are suspects," I answer myself. "I suppose, on the flip side, it could be like those police boards they have on TV." I blow a puff of air from my lips. "*If you're dead, you can't talk. And they don't know your secrets.* That's what he said to me right before he walked in front of a semi. Maybe he meant the cops. Maybe he was trying to solve the murders, not come up with a list of girls *he* killed. Maybe he did it because he was a suspect." The stench of the trailer trickles into my nostrils. "I can't be in here any longer. It stinks. We need to gather it all up and take it with us."

Leah snaps to attention. "We're taking this with us?"

"You want the cops to find this?"

"They probably should. I mean, I know you want to see the good in all people, princess, but most likely this Cooper dude wasn't no amateur detective. The guy that lived here was probably a serial killer. We can give this to the cops and they'll know it wasn't our dads—"

"Everybody tells me I don't have common sense," I say softly to Leah, take in her wide eyes. For the first time, she is listening to me earnestly. "Oh, I've got brains, but I don't have street smarts. I lack all that stuff that makes me fun to be around and normal to everybody else. In its place, I have a surplus of the ability to put together broken and faulty codes, problems, and equations and make them whole." I hold my hand out. "I have looked at enough stuff in the deaths to know that there are pieces unaccounted for. Those missing pieces had to be physically taken from someone so the puzzle can't be put together."

"Dumb it up for me, Weird Wosie."

"It's like when Nicky and I were little; I liked jigsaw puzzles. She'd think it was funny to steal a couple pieces of the ones I was working on so I couldn't finish them." I narrow my eyes. I think it is sinking in with Leah. "I think Arnold Kinney, Timmy Kinney's grandfather, took pieces of this murder puzzle for some reason. He was a cop, and I think the other cops will cover for him, just like Bobby tells me they don't give each other speeding tickets. I think Bobby might be a part of this too. He figured I'd come in here, get my chest blown out, and—"

"*Why* would he do it?" Leah asks, bewildered. "Why would he set you up? Does he have a beef with you nobody knows about?"

"Not that I know of, although I have been looking into the murders. We've got to put all the pieces together on our own or maybe they'll just take them away one by one so they will never be solved. And our dads will be stuck in some prison for something they didn't do."

"Well, there's your reason." Leah looks up at the ceiling, then down again. "Somebody knows you got the brains to solve it. If you're wrong, I'm going to kill you."

"Okay, fine." I sigh, trying to make light of the situation. "But you're probably going to have to anyway. You saved my butt from getting shot at the door. You probably incited the McDaniel-McGuire curse."

"Oh, shut up. Don't give me any excuses."

I'm not sure if Leah believes that curse like Rocky does. She acts like she's walking on egg shells around me right now already. So, everything *is* fine for about twenty minutes while we silently and delicately pick up pictures and peel some of the newspaper clippings off the wall and place them in a plastic container we had dumped of its contents. It's a slow process. Each one is placed on the wall with clear tape stuck to the back of it. The paper wants to rip if pulled too hard.

"You know, I don't have any friends either," Leah says out of the blue. "I'm just saying maybe you're not a loser or anything. And T, he's a prison guard. He beats the crap out of me and screws the girls he deals to if they can't afford to pay."

I squint at the room. It's getting dark enough I'm having a difficult time making out the plastic bins in the closet. "We better speed this up. It's almost dark."

"Um, you still get those nosebleeds when you freak out about something?" She asks suddenly. "I remember you bleeding at school." She pulls her phone from her back pocket and turns on the flashlight, lets it spread across the wall. It's almost bare.

"Sometimes. Not as much. Rocky says he thinks it's mostly when my mom and Nicky are around. Does that tell you something about my family?"

Leah huffs a laugh. "Rocky tells you that?"

"Well, it's the only time I'm around him, when he's at Mom's or Nicky's." I look up carefully. "He's the only one who seems to know how to walk me down off the wall, help me calm down. That's why I told him he should be a fireman."

Leah looks up, hard-stares me. It's almost ten seconds before she finally growls, "That's all he needs, another Mauer bitch telling him what to do."

"I don't tell Rocky what to do." I laugh softly, like she's joking. "He wants to do it. He just won't because he gets no support. He's good at it. I tell him he's good at it. Because nobody else does. You don't. He makes me feel safe when the whole world feels like it is exploding around me, so I thought I should help him achieve his dream."

"His dream?" Leah snickers. "Rocky has a dream?"

"Yes. But do you see why you don't know? You guys laugh at him."

"He told you that too, did he?"

"No. I just know. My daddy's family laughs at me because they don't understand me."

"We understand Rocky," Leah replies quickly.

"Did you know he wants to be a full-time fireman?"

"He's a teacher. He gets good pay."

"And you bus tables at the country club. Are you living the dream?"

She snorts at me. I think she's working up a wry retort. Instead, she ducks her head, pokes a finger at the window. "Hey, there's a car pulling up the drive. It's not your car."

"What?" I ask. My face flushes. I can see headlights. It is the oozy shade of nine o'clock where it's darker, but not completely black. "Okay, grab whatever and we need to get out." Frantically, I snatch up a pile of papers on the floor by the wall. Leah is doing the same, ripping off the last three pictures and stuffing them into the bin.

One second, Leah is lugging the bin over her head to make it down the hallway. The next, we hear the slam of a car door. "Back door, back door," she whispers frantically. Her eyes are wide, her steps are like tippy-toe marches. Leah knows her way around a mobile home, wags her head toward the kitchen. I can see a door, but doubt we can get there in time. There's boxes and rolls of carpet and a broken fish tank stacked up in front of it. In one moment of horrid realization, I remember we left the door ajar. Steps. I can hear footsteps on the porch.

Leah is whispering, *go, go, go!* And I'm trying to silently slip through the maze of junk. I can hear my shirt sliding across boxes, hear my heart pounding, pounding, pounding. Leah stops at the back door, shoves the bin at me, and nearly silently unstacks the boxes and aquarium from the door. I see her duck down, I follow and she works her fingers along the knob, tugging it open just as the front door shifts to open wider.

"Slide," she mouths to me and I watch her disappear through the crack she's making large enough for me to shove the bin outside. Then, the front door opens wide and

I freeze, trying to camouflage myself in the pile of musty-smelling, damp clothing piled in a knee-high mound next to my elbow.

I can't see Leah. I hunker there, knowing the sound of my heart is surely loud enough for the shadow at the doorway to hear even as it shoves the door open wide. *Who the heck is it?* I want to turn my head to see, know I can't. I start counting to keep myself from shaking, from moving while the shadow slips back out. I rub my nose. I know it is going to start bleeding. Whoever it is will find me in a puddle of my nosebleed blood—it slips back in again and the sound of clothing slapping against boxes scrapes the air.

Then there is the swish-swish of liquid, something akin to the sound the almost-empty laundry detergent bottle makes when I shake it up before I add it to the dispenser in the washing machine. This goes on for maybe five minutes. I don't know if someone is there. I only know that I count to one hundred, then two hundred. I hear footsteps where Leah left out the door behind me. I know they aren't hers. They are hard and followed by the scent of gasoline. Oh, no.

I wait again for the footsteps to leave, then duck and scramble to get out the crack in the door where Leah vanished. I squish up between door and frame, look wildly around. Gray and shadows, that's all I see. I hear someone gruffly yelling from the front of the trailer, but I can't focus on what they are saying as I hone in on an old wooden outbuilding. I take a breath, break into a jog in the shadows of two old pine trees. I hear the car tires digging into the mud-gravel. I smell smoke. I turn slightly, blink once. Then the next thing I know, there's an explosion. I'm belly-skidding across the grass with my hands on my ears and my mouth screaming with no sound.

Chapter 29

I get pulled over the next day. I'm not speeding. My car still sounds like it is taking its last dying breath, so I've been taking my sweet time about three miles per hour below the speed limit. Timmy Kinney stands there with his chubby hands on my car window frame and takes a long, hard swallow while his eyes seem to memorize every inch of the inside of my car.

"I wasn't speeding."

"Didn't say you were, Rosie," he says, almost warily. He's got these funky looking lips that flap like a duck. It annoys me. "You got a problem with cops?"

"No."

"Good. We need you to come down to the police station and answer some questions."

Now I'm the one swallowing hard. "Questions—about what? I don't have time." I am completely freaking out inside. SOMEONE SAW COLTON DRIVING MY CAR UP AND DOWN THE STATE ROUTE. THEY KNOW I BROKE INTO JAY COOPER'S HOUSE! Leah and I had made it to the car in stunned silence. Colton was freaking out. He said fire trucks for every surrounding county had passed him while he was driving around and around waiting for us. There were sirens everywhere. There were two other mobile home fires that afternoon and a brush fire in some surrounding forest.

"You follow me down there. I'll discuss it with you. Before you say no, I would highly recommend that you reconsider your decision. Otherwise, it might be construed that you are an accessory to a crime."

"What crime?" I stutter. I'M GOING TO BE ARRESTED. I'M GOING TO DIE IN PRISON—

For three hours, I sit in the waiting room of the police station, my belly jumping like wild rabbits are trying to get out. I know they are watching me. I see them escort Johnny McDaniels from a room. He notices me, glares at me with angry eyes. I wonder if they are testing me. Maybe they are testing him. I see it on the crime shows. It's one of the underhanded things cops do to make bad people (and maybe good people) confess to a crime they may or may not have committed.

Then, I'm finally escorted to a tiny, dank room with bare walls, there's three chairs and a camera in one corner.

"I'm going to ask you questions. You need to answer them honestly." Timmy says. He tells me to sit down in an orange vinyl chair with rips in the material. He has a female officer sit across from me. My heart is pounding. Do they know I've got a fake ID with Violet Popovich on it? "If you don't, it can be conceived you may be helping the criminal hide his crime—"

"Sweetie, do you want a drink?" the female officer gives Timmy a roll of her eyes and smiles at me. I glance at her and then back to Timmy. Okay, I've read some of Bobby's books. They are trying to manipulate me emotionally. I've just got to hold on tight. I've done nothing wrong. Nothing.

"No, thank you." I whisper through parched lips and turn to Timmy. "I don't know any criminals," I mutter. I swallow hard. Timmy Kinney stretches his arms over his head, like he's getting ready for battle. I choose to don my Rosie exterior and use my Violet knowhow to get out of whatever mess someone has left for me.

"Sorry about that, didn't mean to come on so strong," Timmy does this coyote-teeth smile. He leans back in the seat. He looks at the female officer. "She knows me. We grew up together, went to the same school—" So he spends about five minutes pretending we've got something in common. We don't. He used to call me Weird Wosie, just like the rest of them.

"Your sister dates Rocky McDaniel, is that correct?"

"Yes."

"Has he ever mentioned anyone in his family owning guns, axes, or knives?"

"Everybody has guns, axes, and knives, Timmy." I shake my head. "Everybody up there hunts and logs."

"Have you seen any gasoline containers at Rocky McDaniel's house? Or perhaps explosive materials?"

"Rocky wants to be a full-time fireman. If you're implying he would start a fire, that's silly. He puts them out." I nibble on my lip. Timmy looks at the female officer, gives her a knowing nod and a smile. Bobby. I think of Bobby. He told me that cops will lie to get you to confess to something. They'll do whatever conniving thing it takes to deceive you, to pin a crime on you. He told me not to say anything, ask for a lawyer. They'll push you until you get confused. Then you say something stupid. I look up, take in the little video camera.

"Rosie," Timmy starts to rise. "There's been a series of arson fires in the area. They are to an extent that it is believed they are started by someone who is familiar with how fire burns—perhaps someone with a hero complex." Timmy shifts in his seat.

I nibble on my lip. Fires. Were there fires with each of the murders? And is he implying that Rocky would do such a thing? I keep a straight face. "If you are talking about the hero syndrome, where someone creates a horrific and desperate situation so they can resolve it—like starting a fire so they can be the first on the scene to put it out, you're looking at the wrong person. There are certain behaviors those with hero syndrome have and one is constant recognition. Rocky is so humble, he lets my sister take the praise from Mom for putting the dishes in the dishwasher even when he does it. Are you more worried about fires than the murders going on?"

"They are all isolated incidents."

"Oh, okay," I nod my head. "Not to point out flaws in your theory, but I'd watch where you point a finger, Officer Kinney. If I'm correct, you were the first on the scene at Alaina Windowski's murder site."

"How'd you know that?"

"It was in the newspaper. My Aunt Kay said you were interviewed." I pluck my lip. "And—" I cock my chin and look to the video camera knowingly. "I saw you in a picture helping pull Angel Daugherty's body from the quarry. Let me ask you something, Officer Kinney, do you feel like your friends have to depend on you in a pinch?"

"Excuse me?"

"It's just one of the signs I noticed you fulfill that is notable in people with hero syndrome. Policemen, especially those in a long line of police figures in the family, have a high need to prove their prowess to their elders—"

"Enough," Timmy Kinney stands up. He's tugging at his collar nervously, then leans over. "I don't know what you're trying to do, manipulating my words. It won't work."

"Am I done here? I don't know anything or anybody who would murder someone."

"No, you're not done." Timmy Kinney says. "Rocky McDaniel says you know something about what's going on."

"Rocky said that? So, I'm under arrest? Because if I am, I want a lawyer. If I'm not, I'm done."

I know I'm knuckling my nose, waiting for it to start bleeding. My heart is racing and I feel like I can't swallow.

Maybe Timmy Kinney sees the signs, remembers an episode or two from high school. Because he leaves for a minute, then returns and opens the door with his back, swinging an arm out toward the hallway. "You're free to go."

I'm sweating bullets when I burst through the doors of the Laurel Grove Police Department. The fresh spring air envelopes me. Fires. Were there fires at the same time as the murders? Was there a murder while Leah and I went to the trailer? I stop. Oh, shit. We were the ones supposed to be murdered. Trust. I suddenly feel it slipping through my fingers. I can feel their eyes on me, peeling back some layer of skin, making me feel vulnerable. I know they are waiting for me to pick up my phone, call somebody. I smell cigarette smoke, follow the vapor with my eyes. I pause just short of my car, look three cars over to the big, white truck settled beneath a tree. Johnny McDaniel. He's glowering at me. I jump into my car, breathe, breathe, breathe. Then he flicks his cigarette in my direction and drives off. I feel a chill slip across my shoulders. I wonder what he told them.

I'm shaking so badly as I leave the police department, I know everyone is staring at me like I am hiding a deadly secret. I'm two inches away from a panic attack and multiplying numbers in my head, like Rocky has me do. My fingers are playing on my thigh until I get to the car and then it's on the steering wheel. I'm so upset, I stop in to get a soda to settle my stomach and Bucky asks me why I'm so pale.

I start crying then, right at the front counter, and in front of one of the other employees working. A thirty-something woman with stale eyes, waves Bucky away and tells him to take a break. We sit down at a rickety picnic table sitting on the concrete slab next to a dumpster behind the gas station and I poke at the lukewarm, wrinkled hotdog Bucky shoved at me. I tell him about the cops questioning me and the mobile home and how somebody blew it up. I tell him I've got a hundred suspects roaming around my head and I can't seem to focus enough on any one of them to cross them off my list. "It's like crazy town in here right now," I complain waving my hands over my head wildly.

Bucky looks at me and says: "So what kind of evidence, other than the pictures, do you have?"

"I've got a couple leather bracelets and a dog tag with an address on it—the Whites," I answer. "Tommy White. His family owns the big stables outside town."

Bucky tells me to focus on Tommy White and see what I can find out first. Then, one person at a time, work through each. If nothing pans out with it, look at the bracelets next.

"Okay, that's fine. But if I start asking around about things, eventually it is going to get back to the cops, who are already questioning me, and my family, who already thinks I'm crazy. Or my dad who would crap a thousand bricks if he knew I was dabbling in police stuff. I'm at that place where I've got to start asking people questions. But normal people don't do that, just cops."

"So, don't really tell them what you're there for," Bucky says. Then he smiles. "You know, like if you need to find out more information on a gun that somebody used to kill another person, go to Savings Hunting Supply and start out by telling them you're looking to hunt turkey this fall. Then work it into the conversation. It always works on the late night crime TV shows."

He also asks me if I would be interested in going out for a beer sometime. I tell him I might. I doubt I will, though. Not sure if Mom would approve and I know she'd hear about a local boy if I went out with him.

Chapter 30

Okay, so plans devised on late night crime TV shows may not necessarily work in real life. Maybe I just didn't think my strategy out enough or consider all the different ways my idea could go wrong. I'm usually all about the statistics; I can calculate my plan and the different outcomes associated with the plan with pretty precise ending results. Not so today. Because there were two fundamental problems from the start. One is having what my sister calls a *type,* a certain attraction to a specific type of person that can basically strike you dumb with delight. And the second is dragging along a sidekick whose sole interest is to acquire comedic entertainment from the plan and who will do just about anything to get it.

"Ma'am, are you all right?"

I realize these particular flaws Wednesday at four in the afternoon. I'm splayed, spread eagle, on the ground in a small pasture and blinking up at the shadow of a cowboy hat above me. I went from balancing myself on a stationary horse to laying on the ground after I gave it a swift kick in the rips and it lurched forward in a dead run. After that, I somersaulted off the back of the horse and landed where I am now.

Just to my left, my self-appointed bodyguard-slash-sidekick Rocky McDaniel is leaning over me a wooden riding arena fence, staring down at me. "Hey, Rosie," Rocky chuckles. "What do you call somebody who wears cowboy clothes" he asks, without waiting for an answer. "Ranch dressing. Get it?" No, I don't get it, just like the twelve other stupid horse jokes he's been pulling off his cell phone for the last ten minutes and tossing at me.

"*Umll.*" I say and it doesn't even sound like a

recognizable burble. It sounds more like I'm spitting up in my mouth. I wanted to tell the cowboy I have an IQ of 142. I wanted to say something grandiose and witty to show off my intellectual prowess. I, in the least, wanted to say a simple word. Even a *yes*, would suffice. But no, *my type* is standing overtop me in cowboy boots, a Stetson, and a southern drawl that is still giving me goosepimples even though I think I've broken every bone in my body. So instead of appearing like a normal person, I'm struck dumb.

So, while I'm lying on my back and trying to get past the realization I've got a type, Rocky is almost blue in the face, he's laughing so hard. He stops long enough to say, "I think she's fine." He can hardly get those four words out between heaving guffaws.

The cowboy extends a hand and tows me upward. He gives Rocky a sideways and questioning gaze while I try to wipe the shame from my face.

"Rocky, stop," I mutter, my eyes glaring upward. The man's got tears running down his cheeks.

"I can't. That was the funniest thing I've ever seen a McGuire do!"

Well, it certainly had to be the most embarrassing. See, I devised this scheme to get information about the dog tag Bobby had slipped into my fingers at Mom's. T. White stands for Tommy White and the address: *467 White's Farm Road* is the address to White Family Horse Stables, LLC. I mean, I didn't want to walk into another trap, if Bobby had actually set one up for me at Jay Cooper's trailer. In my mind, my plan was flawless. It was as simple as walking into White Family Horse Stables, LLC and pretending I am interested in buying and boarding a horse. Such, during conversation, I would bring up my dad and my aunt going to school with Tommy, then lead into finding out how well he knew Carrie Stamper. And perhaps, I would wrestle out information about the dog tag and why Carrie or Gina may have possessed it.

My great plan was doomed from the start. Simply donning a cowboy hat and wearing cowboy boots, a cute, little over-the-shoulder polka dot top, and tight, ripped blue jeans, like the girls in the spring clothing issue of *Whoa, Cowgirl Magazine* doesn't necessarily make me a good rider. Rocky isn't helping either.

Why is he with me? I can sum it up in just a few sentences after I confronted Rocky while I was standing in line at Reynold's Hometown Grocery Store, juggling a box of cat litter, a loaf of bread, and a box of cheap wine, two hours earlier. They were working on the ATM at the bank after hours so I couldn't get cash. So I had to go down to the grocery store and use my debit card. The checkout screen always asks me if I want cash back, but I have to make a purchase first. Hence the kitty litter, bread, and wine.

Rocky has this funny grin on his face: "You *lol*?" He asked.

"Laughing out loud?" I retorted, unsure.

"No, I'm sorry. I thought I was speaking your language. Lol is redneck for low on liquor."

I looked at my wine. Crud. "Go to hell."

"What are you wearing? You gonna tear your best dress huntin' coon?" He asks, eyeing my cute little cowgirl outfit. And so, I reply with, "No. None of your damn business." Rocky blinked like he can't believe I said such a thing to him. "Oh, is there something the matter?"

And such, I laid him flat with a long whisper-screaming barrage about Timmy Kinney dragging me into the police station and telling me Rocky said I knew something about the murders. Everybody in line was leaning in getting an earful of me telling him a pinky promise must mean nothing to him. Rocky stood back, tipped his head to one side and threw his arms out. "You're kidding me, right?" he'd muttered, offended. "Why would they think that? I never talk to Timmy Kinney; he's an ass. And I would not break a pinky promise with you."

He'd been fumbling with a chocolate candy bar. He just slapped it back on the rack with a hurt look and stomped out. So Missus Myers, who used to be my first grade teacher and who was also two people back in line gave me a pucker-lipped scowl. I ended up flopping my groceries on the checkout counter and stomping out to apologize.

"I told Timmy Kinney it was more likely him doing it than you, Rocky McDaniel." I stand in front of his truck and yell at him. "I may not be full-blooded redneck, but I know the code—we don't name names, even it is our enemies. Which is more than your uncle did with the cops when he called them about me riding the ATV. And just so you know, Bobby Vandevenne tried to get me killed. So I'm definitely not talking to cops."

He'd laughed and told me he thought I was nuts. I said I could prove to him I wasn't. Dumb move. Somehow, he ended up extracting my plan out of me, hopped into my car before I could stop him, and riding along for the show, berating me with stuff like: "Why shouldn't you do this? Well, for one, Rosie, you can't ride a horse. Two, you could just ask the guy instead of being sneaky and—"

"You can't ride a horse, can you?"

Tommy White's youngest son, Ben, is the cowboy staring down at me, arms akimbo and shifting his hat back and forth on his head. He's thirty-something and could have walked straight out of an old western movie. He's clean-shaven, sweet country boy pretty, and probably trying to figure out how a girl with an IQ of ten was able to drive a car from town to his dad's farm.

"No, not really. I wanted to ask your dad something about how he might know how somebody could have gotten this old dog tag."

"So why didn't you just ask?"

ARRRR! Rocky's laughing out loud at this one. "Yeah, Rosie, why didn't you just ask?"

I suppose I got the last laugh. Twenty minutes later, I'm climbing on a big horse in front of Ben. Rocky's got this pursed-lip pucker going like he just went from sucking on a piece of sweet candy and switched to a sour pickle. However, he is dropping my car off at the store where he left his parked. Ben is going to take me to the grocery store and drop me off after he shows me something on top of the hill that might answer my question. Rocky stopped shit-grinning me when he saw me sneak-wave my middle finger at him while I leaned hard into Ben's chest. *Bitch,* I mouth to him, just like Colton does to me in the library when he's supposed to be reading.

It's a long climb up the hill in the direction of the little family cemetery tucked into some old pines. Ben tells me they buried their family members up there until about twenty years ago. Now they bury their dead at the big Laurel Grove Cemetery outside town. But next to the old cemetery, they buried their family pets and this is what Ben wants to show me. It is a tiny section of land with five or six white wooden crosses and a few homemade gravestones.

"This is where Tank was buried. He was one good Shetland sheepdog. But he got the name Tank because my grandpa used to call him the most *cantankerous* dog he'd ever met. I remember he bit the crap out of us when we were kids." Ben reaches out and points to a little mound in the dirt. "He used to round up the cows for folks coming to ride at the barn just for fun. But he wouldn't just stop there. He'd try to round up all the kids watching too." I see an old cross about knee-high that has fallen over. "Dad got Tank in the 1960s. He was eighteen when he died, around 1977 or 1978. He was really sick. Dad had to put him to sleep."

"Why would someone have his tag?" I wonder. It's comfortable stuffed in Ben's chest, his arms lounging on my legs while he holds the reins.

"I dunno. Who had it? I mean, I would assume they dug it up. Or maybe a raccoon or something dragged it off. How about we go see if it's been dug up?" He nudges me forward, then jumps off the horse. He helps me off with gentle hands on my waist.

"Is there a specific reason you're trying to figure this out?" Ben asks me while he hunkers down on one knee and pokes at the little mound in front of the dog's grave. I lean my hands on my knees and look down at him. He smiles, adjusts his hat, and I get that wet-noodle-brain feeling again.

"Huh?" I mumble, then turn away, so I can come back to my senses. "There was a girl killed and another little girl who vanished around the time my Aunt Rosie came up missing forty years ago. One of the girls had the dog tag."

"Well, that's just downright weird," Ben pushes himself to his feet. "I can't tell if this has been dug up or not. It almost looks like something was digging in here recently. But we've had a lot of rain. Can I ask you why you're so interested in figuring out why a dead girl had a dead dog's tag in her pocket? And how it ended up in your hands?"

I laugh while I stare at the soil at our feet. "Only if

you can keep a secret."

"Oh, I'm good at that. I have six sisters."

"My Aunt Roo disappeared about eight months after a girl named Carrie Stamper was found dead. Then I found that another little girl named Gina Channel came up missing. They never found my aunt or Gina; don't know what happened to either one. Most people don't know what that does to a family. They don't understand. But with ours, it kind of puts a big tear down the middle that never goes away." I try to shrug it off.

"I had an aunt who died, J.C. She's buried right over there." Ben points a finger to the cemetery nearby. He nudges me with his knuckle and I laugh to myself. I feel like he's herding me with his hand toward the fence. "It was like, 1982. She was playing in the backyard on one of those old rusted swing sets." We stop at a small gate and he opens it with a creaking groan. "My grandma was putting up the clothes to dry and went inside to get some more laundry pins to hang up sheets. When she came back out, J.C. was gone. They found her drowned in the Stamper's pond."

"The—Stamper's pond?"

"Yeah, their farm abuts ours. It's in the valley. They grow crops like corn and soybeans. We're on the hill. We've got dairy cattle and horses. This is J.C.'s grave."

We stop just short of her grave. The grass around it has been recently mowed and I squat down and brush away the flecks of cut grass sticking to the headstone. It just says: Janie Cayce White. Our Little Girl. May 21, 1982.

"May 21st," I whisper, eyeing the date on the headstone. I turn, look up to Ben. "That's odd. It is the same month and day Gina Channel disappeared."

"Who?"

"A little girl that disappeared a year after my aunt."

Just then, my fingers graze something soft and I snap my hand back in a knee-jerk response.

"Gotcha a snake?" Ben chuckles. I shiver, then peer downward at the brown object my fingers had touched.

"No," I say. I reach down, pick up a leather bracelet and hold it so I can read the lettering. *Dies Irae* is burnt into the leather. "Oh, my. My aunt had one of these." I rise and wiggle it to get the grass clippings off. Then I hold it aloft to Ben. "And so did Carrie or Gina. Do you know why she had this with her on her headstone? I mean, was it a thing at one of the churches or were they given out at bible school, I wonder?" I rub my chin. "I looked it up and it is a hymn about death and the end of days, and is a warning to make amends. You know, Judgement Day. They used to give us little snap bracelets and rubber bracelets at Sunday school with the Psalms on them. I've never seen one that's this—dark, you know?"

Ben sniffs a laugh. "I suppose it depends on how much your church does the scare factor thing. Some will go to pretty great lengths to brainwash their congregations into believing the devil's gonna get them if they don't be good."

"But my aunt was a teenager."

"Even to little kids. There's a church right down the road that does a haunted house thing and kids walk through different levels of Hell. I honestly can't think there is anything more disturbing than that. But I don't know. I can ask my dad."

I place the bracelet back on the headstone and mull this over in my mind. I ask Ben to take me down the wooded trail so I can see where the property overlooks the Stamper's property. We ride for fifteen minutes and he stops at the top of a high hill and points a little to the right and down. I see part of a brown tin roof that isn't quite hidden by big, old maples trees. I see a couple outbuildings, a barn, and an old John Deere tractor parked in a gravel driveway.

I want to get closer but we can't take the horse down the embankment. Ben helps me slide off and I scramble down the wild rose infested hillside and stop just short of a yard with mowed grass that looks a week old. I stick to the shadows of the woodland. As I pick tiny rose thorns from my forearms, the crow of a rooster parts the quiet, riding it while I take in the sweet scent of flowers in the air and I feel—strange. My cheeks are slightly numb. My eyes skim from left to right. Why do I feel so horrible now? My gaze stops at a barn that has been renovated into a two car garage. The barn. I stare at it, feel my stomach getting queasier and queasier. *It's time to go to the barn.* I remember the voice. It is the same one that creeps in once in a while and just out of reach. I absently rub the back of my head. Then, the sound of a screen door slamming sends me clambering back up the hillside. I am curiously out of breath, sweating profusely.

"You all right, Rosie?" Ben asks me while he stretches out a calloused hand and hauls me back up in front of him.

"Yeah, I'm fine." But no, I'm lying. I'm not.

Later that evening, Ben gives me a call. "I talked to Dad about that bracelet on J.C.'s grave," he tells me. "He said he got it at a funeral, if you can believe that. I asked him the reason they'd give out bracelets. He said it was just so the friends of the family would remember the person who died. He thought maybe somebody in his family might have put it on her grave. He didn't remember doing it. But he said he couldn't remember what he did with his.

Probably tossed it."

"Did he say whose funeral it was?"

"Naw, he didn't. He was kind of elusive talking about it. But he did say that there used to be a little cross on Tank's grave. When he died, Dad hung his collar on it. The tag was still on the collar. So it could have been dragged off easily." Ben clears his throat. "Hey, that guy you were with this afternoon, is he your boyfriend? You dating him or anything?"

"No," I snicker.

"You just hang out, then?" he goes on. "Because he's a big guy and I don't want to get beat up if I ask you out. He looked kind of mad when he left."

"You wouldn't take a hit for me?"

"I would. Just asking."

Chapter 31

The name on the business card says: EMMANUEL GARCIA-FABRICANTES E IMPORTADORES DE VEHÍCULOS-EURO-ASSOCI. What does that mean? I turn it over in my fingers while I sit at the front desk of the high school office. I'm manning the office until Principal Cunningham's office secretary, Jenna, finishes taking notes for the after-school teacher's meeting in the conference room. I'm listening to Principal Cunningham drone on about some upcoming testing. Sadly, I know more about the tests than he does because I'm the one stuck monitoring them. But I'm just a lowly part-time librarian, lunchroom attendant/after-school detention monitor—oh, and next week, the testing monitor. I don't even attend their stupid meetings.

I'm daydreaming and thinking about my stepdad. I'm trying not to lounge on the idea he set me up to be in that trailer when someone poured gasoline on it and lit it on fire. Colton saw a black car with two people inside. Bobby doesn't have a black car. His sister owns one though. And there are probably ten people I know of who do too. I called Mom when I got home. Bobby had gone out for a beer and to watch a baseball game at Skids Sports Bar in Rayville. She asked why I needed to know. I told her I thought I passed him going to the store. I called Skids Sports Bar and the girl who answered the phone laughed when I described Bobby and asked if he was at the bar. She said I described ninety percent of the men there.

Liam was in a bad mood the next three days and did nothing but drag me from bar to bar and glare at me with angry eyes. I'm even less focused now after taking the ride with Ben White, and it isn't just because I found his Aunt J.C.'s picture and an obituary in the pile of clippings Leah and I had gotten from Jay Cooper's trailer. I'd added her underneath Tommy White's picture. I typed in May 21 on my browser search bar to see if there is more than just coincidence with the dates of death. There's nothing worth noting, considering the only exciting thing that seemed to happen on the date was Charles Lindbergh landing in Paris after crossing the Atlantic.

Now I'm in a foul mood sitting alone in the office like Liam's sulky blues rubbed off on me. I have gotten twenty texts from Emmanuel. I think he is telling me he is out of the country, but he wants to see me again. My life is complicated enough. Do I really want to work a guy into the mix who doesn't even speak English? Maybe not. Because the next morning after Leah and I broke into Jay Cooper's house, I found out from the TV there was a rash of fires all over the county—six in all. All of them were abandoned houses or mobile homes. Somebody was trying to get rid of that information Jay Cooper had in his bedroom. Nobody even seems to know that he owned that mobile home or has tied it together with the murders. It is perplexing. I can't help but think there is, of course, one person who knew— Bobby Vandevenne.

I'm not getting much sleep. So, more often than not, my mind flows to the mysterious man I met babysitting Liam. Emmanuel. *My* Emmanuel. Sexy. He was so pretty, with black hair and dark skin and these cinnamon-colored eyes. And tall. *Tall, dark, and handsome;* that's what my mom would have pulled out of her closetful of sayings she gets from her Tuesday evening book club. Just thinking of him right now and the kisses he left on my lips and neck, they make my tummy jiggle.

On the back of the business card, in pretty handwriting, is *Llamame, the beautiful.* I'm getting the feeling that *the beautiful* was the extent of Emmanuel's

English vocabulary. He just kept saying it over and over the night I met him. I vaguely remember clambering up on his lap, kissing him in the back seat, and reciting the only word I know in Spanish, which was *mi caramelo*. Mi caramelo. My mom used to buy these chocolate candies online shaped like teeny-tiny hearts and filled with liqueur. Well, until she served them as a treat at the women's bible study at church and found out they had alcohol in them. I remember the tiny pink boxes filled with the chocolates she used to set on the table and they had Mi Caramelo written on the top. I suppose Emmanuel is my little boy candy my mom would never approve of and that makes him even more enticing.

I don't know what good it would do to call him, considering the disadvantage we have with the language barrier. So while I sit at the front desk manning the office, daydreaming, and feeling left out, I text him with the cell phone Jack gave me for work. *Hey, mi caramelo.* That's all I put. And maybe, I'm thinking, I should have put all that behind me.

Hey, the beautiful.

And there we stopped. There is a glass wall partition surrounding the office. I look up, take in my image between the foyer wall and the desk. I knew I should have thought this one out. I look at my frumpy dress, self-consciously push the glasses up the bridge of my nose. He probably wouldn't think I was so beautiful today, the girl who is so low on the school staff totem pole, she's hardly visible above the ground. I mean, this is the real me, isn't it? Me with fat, black glasses and drab, dowdy clothes, and a raggedy black-sweater-pacifier I wrap around myself to feel safe. Me with a face doused in tiny tan freckles and my hair a bit uncombed, pulled back, and with a few strands laying across my brow so I don't have to look anyone directly in the eyes.

Ugh. I lay my cell phone down, listen to it ting once. I ignore it, feel my face redden for even thinking my pretty mystery man would be interested. What kind of relationship is based on secrets, lies, and a girl who (underneath a shell of pretty clothes and thick makeup) isn't the girl the boy thinks she is? *Ting*. It goes again. *Ting. Ting. Ting.*

"Well, you're popular today."

"Huh?" I jump, startled, and look up. It is the delivery driver from Gentry Supplies that brings in the office supplies. I blink.

"You're Miss Mauer, am I right? The one who usually works in the library?"

"Oh, yeah." I mumble, forcing a smile and looking over my shoulder. "There's a staff meeting."

"You're not staff?"

"I'm—not important staff, I guess," I shrug with a drab smile.

"Well, somebody thinks you're important." He jabs a thumb toward the door. "I just dropped off a whole bunch of packages in the library for you." He leans in, holds up a clipboard for me to sign. "You must have a fan club." He laughs like he's being funny while I sign next to the X.

I turn my attention to my cell phone. It has a map on it and directions. *Encuéntrate conmigo esta noche, a las las siete en punto.* I'm somewhat curious. Siete. It is seven. The text and twelve others before it are from Emmanuel. *We meet, yes?* He writes that each time and there's a long line of Spanish words I don't have a clue what they mean. I can guess. It's a map to meet. He could be a murderer. It is outside my comfort zone.

But isn't everything? Ben White kept lingering at his truck door after he opened it for me when he dropped me at my car at Reynold's Hometown Grocery Store. I suppose being thirty-something and cowboy pretty, he's got a heads-up on how to sneak in a three minute make out session in a grocery store parking lot, between the shopping cart corrals and Dorothy Wayne's old Cadillac and still make it look hot. Because he did. Ben smooshed me up against his open truck door and the seat and nearly bent me over double. After the third round and a car honking on its way past, I slipped under his arm and flit out to the parking lot like a butterfly flapping away from a playful kitten.

I look over my shoulder now through the glass partition where the teachers are having their meeting. It feels like my entire existence to this point is like the faint image of myself reflecting off the glass on this side. And those on the other side, they are clearly defined. Nobody treats them like second hand clothes or a ghost in the room.

So I turn back to my phone, rest my elbows on the front desk. It was thrilling, kissing in the grocery store parking lot, exciting because somebody I knew might see us. For a shy girl like me, who is always under the watchful gaze of a mom and sister, I find it liberating. So much so, I quickly write: *Yes. Siete. Si.* Just as I send the text, the same kind of common sense kicks in as what left me sprinting away from Ben and back to my car. I actually feel a bead of sweat dribble down my forehead. I swallow hard, work up the nerve, then text Liam on his phone.

Going to meet with Emmanuel at seven. Is he safe?

Nothing. As the teachers start spilling out of the meeting, I nibble on my lower lip. I suppose the concept of asking Liam to appraise someone's moral character might be a bit flawed. When Jenna returns, I make my way back to the library. The hallways are quiet except for a few stray students who stay after school for sports. *Ting.*

I pull my phone up, shove the glasses up the bridge of my nose and peer at the message.

I'll send over a car. Did you get all that crap that got delivered here yesterday and today? Maybe you should temper the flirting. Gentry Supply was here to drop off toilet paper, said he could drop those off at the school—

"Flirting?" I mutter to myself, taking a step and reaching for the library door. I don't flirt. It's not until I open the door to the library I come to a complete standstill. Oh, crud. When the Gentry's Supplies truck driver said he delivered something for me, I didn't think it was actually for *me*.

My eyes are wide while I peer around the quiet room. There must be twenty dozen roses and a human-size teddy bear. Five piles, each from a different man I met either with Liam, or walking around with Mister Barkley. There's heart -shaped chocolate boxes—oh, Mi Caramelos. I take a steadying breath. I certainly don't need Principal Cunningham seeing all this spread around the room after flopping out of the limousine in the parking lot. So I do the only thing I can think of because I can't walk down the hallway with armloads of roses; start stuffing everything out the library room window ten feet down to the little patch of dead grass between a parking lot and the building before I bring my car around to the back parking lot and load them in.

I swear, nothing ever goes as planned. Just as I'm shoving the chubby teddy bear with a big red bow and a blank smile through the window with every ounce of energy I've got, I see a hand come up and latch on to one fuzzy paw and tug hard. I lean slightly, cringe just as it comes tumbling out at the feet of Rocky McDaniel.

"I was just out finishing up with ball practice," he remarks, nodding toward the baseball field. "Then I saw stuff flying out the library window. You know, I wanted to make a smart remark about you being in a pickle again.

You're always tripping over your feet, figuring out you've got your choir robe inside-out halfway through the service, being stranded in the parking lot of a strip club at midnight, stuff like that. But this one takes the cake. Are you practicing a fire drill with your stuffed animals?" Rocky chuckles. "I mean, how often do you see somebody throwing candy, flowers, and a life-size bear out a high school library window?" He rubs his fingers on his chin. "Be careful how you answer. This one's definitely going to come up at some future discussion of things that starts like—*no, I've got the best one on Rosie getting caught doing something she shouldn't be—*" He's got this deadpan gaze staring up at me while he hugs the teddy bear around the waist. He's standing over a pile of roses with green wrapping paper around the stems and he's popping a little chocolate candy into his mouth. Rocky smacks his lips, nods in approval. "What's up, Rosie? You've got a secret admirer?"

I grit my teeth. "Does this look secret to you?"

"Is this one guy or ten sending you stuff?" Rocky retorts quickly, poking a box on the ground with the toe of his tennis shoe.

I peer out the window, take Rocky in. "I don't know."

"You don't know." He sniffs and grunts. "Because I've got to be honest. I'm wondering what a girl's gotta do to deserve all this from all those guys and *not know.*"

"What's it to you?" I snap back. "Go away." God, that man irks me. I reach around, snatch up the nearest thick book and launch it out the window at him. It is no mean feat. The window opens outward in an arc. I have to swing a bit to the left and lean hard into it to get it to soar in his direction. It bounces off his shoulder, flops hard on the ground.

"Ow, Rosie! That hurt." He's rubbing his shoulder.

"Then don't imply I'm a slut."

"Says the girl who took off riding sexy-style with a cowboy. You know Chuck Wayne?"

"Yeah, why?"

"Because he was sitting in his wife's car while you two made out in a White's Farms truck. With those tinted windows, I guess you didn't see him? How do I know this? His son, Daniel, works with me at the fire department and within twenty minutes of Ben White bending you over his truck hood, everybody in a thirty mile radius knew. What the hell was that all about? You frigging left me with your car and didn't get home until ten!"

"I don't like being laughed at, Rocky." I nibble on my lip and mull over his words. "And how do you know I didn't get home until ten?"

"I drove past your house because your mom was trying to find you." Rocky shakes his head. "Girl, you've got to quit flirting. You're getting a reputation."

"I don't flirt." I blink down at him. He's got a smug slit to his lips and a cocky swagger to his shoulder.

"You're kidding. Yes, you flirt. The guy at the gas station begged me for your phone number the other day. Tim King asked me to change places with him in the choir seating so he could be next to you last Sunday. I watched you loll over the guy's counter in Rayville, and two boys in my fourth period class damn near knocked themselves out leaning over their desks to watch you go by because you've got this new strut that looks sexy even in a knee-length grandma skirt." Rocky holds up his hands. "Just saying. Yes, you flirt."

There's a small bookshelf next to me with archaic hardbacks we sell to the students for a nickel a piece. Nobody ever buys them. However, I put them to use. I pick up six or seven in my arms and slam them down on the windowsill, snatch one up and start launching them one by one at Rocky.

None of them hit him and Rocky starts laughing like it's a game. He's too quick, backing up so I have to lean hard against the window with my hip smashed against a solid piece of aluminum window frame. It is awkward. That's when I lean forward a bit too hard and feel myself tumbling off-balance. Two seconds later, I'm falling head-first, following the last book resting on the window sill.

It's only ten feet down, but I think if Rocky hadn't dumped the teddy bear and caught me somewhere between the waist and my ribs, I would have gotten one heck of a bump on my noggin. My legs splay in the air over his head and Rocky takes six steps backward, so I didn't hit the ground. Instead, he just crumples with me on top and we make an inelegant pile on the grass with my head awkwardly close to his crotch and my skirt flopped up to my belly and exposing my skin from bare ankle to the elastic waistbands of my blue polka dot panties.

I grunt and tug down my skirt. Rocky gives me a hard shove off his belly and into a mound of roses.

"Dammit, Rosie!" he gruffs, swiping the dirt off his khaki pants while he stands up and looks around. "And don't tell me that was a part of my training, catching you as you fall out the window." He reaches out a hand like he's going to help me up. I decline and stand on my own, cheeks burning hot as I readjust my clothing.

"You were the one who started making fun of me, Rocky," I retort. "And I'm not a slut. Maybe I'm just fun to hang around, did you think of that? Because five men seem to think so. Six, counting the cowboy." I hold up my hands, let my eyes take in the chocolates dappling the green grass like muddy brown hearts. "And rich ones at that. In fact,

Emmanuel thought so enough he gave me a—"

"A whole lot of chocolates," Rocky reaches down, picks up a little paper attached to a box laid open with the contents falling out. He looks at it. "Do you speak Spanish?"

"Not well."

"I don't think you know the language at all, or the language of love if you're just tossing his stuff out the window. You took French in high school, right?"

"Yeah, so?"

"So you can read this note?"

"No. It doesn't matter. We don't talk much. It's more—"

"Physical?" Rocky rolls his eyes. "Well, it doesn't appear he thinks so. *Mi hermosa mujer con los ojos de las flores,* that's what it says. It means; my beautiful woman with the eyes of flowers. And after, it says: Te amo—"

"So?"

"So he loves you."

"So?" I spat back. I know my cheeks are gaining a deeper shade of crimson.

Rocky just shakes his head, drops his hand with the note. He stares at me long and hard. Then he shakes his head like my daddy does when I make a nasty remark about how stupid it is hunting a little, innocent deer.

"Don't lead guys on, Rosie."

"You're my stupid sister's boyfriend. I don't have to listen to your stupid-ass advice. So, don't tell me how to live my life—"

"I'm not her boyfriend!" Rocky almost yells. I step back. He blinks and shakes his head. "I mean—well, your life is tangled up with my life because of your stupid sister, Rosie, so you don't have a damn choice!"

"So untangle it." I say softly and with a cocky waggle

to my shoulders. "Untangle it. Leave me alone. Stay *away* from me."

Chapter 32

When I was twelve, I snuck-read a spicy historical romance novel that was passed secretly from hand to hand by my cabin roommates at the five day summer camp Mom made me attend on Lake Erie, so she could take a week-long cruise with a boyfriend. It was a chubby girl named Myra who'd snuck her mom's book into her suitcase, then doled the paperback out to eager pre-teenage eyes like a shrewd camp counselor with an eye for money doles out secret pieces of chocolate cake at a fat kid camp.

Of course, I only skipped around to the parts with carefully crimped pages. But I was sucked in. I know it was more than eight times, I read the tantalizing moments of passion for Sofia Fischer, American spy during World War II, and Finn Weber, her secret lover. My favorite excerpt was a short, but very descriptive, moment when Sofia realizes Finn is a German soldier and rips his clothes off in mad passionate anger on the rooftop of a burned-out building.

It was a coming-of-age moment for me; the heroine's sensual escapades mirrored my own prepubescent adventure at camp that summer. Of course, to the girls listening on the other side of the shower house, Gabriella's rooftop romp hardly compared to my clumsy seven-minute make-out session with skinny, pimple-faced Gibby Pike. His kisses were wet and he smelled like sour towels. But in my mind, it was full out passion and adventure—we dared to get caught by one of the counselors.

My boring life resumed that year after camp ended and more mirrored a Rated G social studies textbook version of everyday life in Germany in the 1940s. And I did go from reading silly girl books to diving into how-to manuals and journals on scientific discoveries. I can't say I ever felt that heart-pumping arousal of emotion except for an occasional naughty thought about Rocky McDaniel when he took his shirt off to get into mom's pool. And yet, fifteen years later, I'm sitting at a table at a restaurant along a boardwalk in Miami Beach, Florida, wondering how the heck I got from Point A to Point B in my usually incredibly unromantic, non-fiction boring life.

This is how it started. "You didn't have to do this," I told Rusty Rossi in the car, when he pulled into my driveway two hours earlier. "I could have driven my car. I mean, it's not the prettiest, but it would get me there." It's another one of the small limousines Mister Barkley leases.

I mean, I was having my doubts. I was supposed to be at my mom's usual dinner. I told her I had a sore throat. Rusty has two of his cousins in tow in the front seat and wearing what I can only surmise are the only suits they have in their closet for use at occasional weddings or funerals. They are angry-whispering to each other when I get into the car. Then they both narrow their gazes, eye me up and down. Their suits are gray-striped, out of style, and the two look more like Italian mobsters from a 1920s movie than bodyguards. They are buff, like him, and have the same, dumb-ape expression on their faces as he does. He tells me they were the only help he could find at such short notice and they were a little spicy about having to be hauled away from the baseball game on TV. But I'm not to worry. They are carrying pistols. Great.

"The map you sent Liam was to a private airport. He said his dad would kill him if you got kidnapped to some foreign country to be a part of some sex trade. We're just—security."

"For me or for Liam?"

He'd laughed until he had to get on to the small

private jet. Yes, we all sat down on padded leather seats and Emmanuel is nowhere to be seen. There is only one silent man with a clipboard that keeps staring at me like I've got a time bomb hidden in my belly and I'm going to explode. I have no clue where we were going. And yet, I'm strangely calm about this adventure. I suppose I felt I needed to have the appearance of knowing what I'm doing because Rusty's two cousins are silent and staring at me with mildly reproachful twists to their lips for the entire flight. On the contrary, by the time we touched down two hours and forty-eight minutes later in Florida, I was sure I was being kidnapped and sold as a fourth wife to some creepy old man in South America.

Not so. Emmanuel must have rented an entire restaurant. He surprises me by jumping out as I walk past an open door. I yelp and he laughed so hard he had to hold his hands around his belly. We were the only ones there, barring Rusty's two cousins, Salvatore and Vincent, and several well-armed guards eyeing me as suspiciously as a mother with a newborn eyes a six year-old with a runny nose getting ready to sneeze on her baby. It is vacant except one table with candles in the center. I've got a view of the ocean. He's waiting for me, Emmanuel is, with another couple dozen roses. I'm not sure if I'm relieved or more scared that he's invested so much money in me, he's expecting me to shit hearts and hundred dollar bills.

"The Violet," he whispers to me as he kisses my cheeks in welcome. Should I find it strange, he's shaking like an autumn leaf when he pulls out my chair for me? "The beautiful."

"Mi caramelo," I whisper in return. Holy crap, and in less than two minutes, I'm flirting as badly as Tangy Cunningham plays sexy with Rocky in the teacher's lounge after Nicky leaves. We can't understand each other. So I just look into his cinnamon-colored eyes until we both laugh. We play tic-tac-toe on a napkin and sip wine and I have him put his hands on mine and we play the hand-slap game.

His hands are soft, not at all like my daddy's hard-working hands. A couple times, he reaches out and latches on to my forearm. I scoot my chair around, sit next to him and pretend there isn't a serving staff staring at us while we kiss.

The idea I should be home lying in bed with Baby Cakes tucked in my arm and reading a book from my tablet makes this evening feel off-center. Halfway through the meal, Emmanuel pulls out his phone and opens up a translator.

I am proud like you, he tells me. *You know, boo!* Oh, I think he likes to scare me. He laughs hard again.

Montémonos en una montaña rusa. This is fun, I return. But he sniffs a laugh and makes a roller coaster ride gesture with his hand. I suppose the translation is off.

I ask him where he lives.

"Lima."

"Lima, Ohio?" I ask. He thinks this is hilarious and laughs.

"No, Lima, Peru."

"That's a long way from my home," I say softly. I like him. I don't know. I feel like a ragamuffin that got swept up from the street by a prince and gets to play princess for a few moments of time. I give him a sad smile. He returns it, although I know he has no clue what I said.

After the meal, we take a walk on the beach, hold hands. I take off my shoes, dip my feet in the water. I'm strangely aware we are being followed by my makeshift bodyguards and his well-armed ones. It doesn't leave room for much more than a kiss. Far too soon, I realize it's two in the morning. I have to be at work by eight.

Two minutes before I get on the private jet, he stands with me on the small concrete walkway. Emmanuel kisses me and places a box in my hands. "A gift." A gift. It is a diamond pendant with two violet gemstones on either side of the stone, then two cinnamon-colored stones beside them. I stare at the opened box and shake my head. "I can't accept this, Emmanuel."

"Tengo ojos marrones," he points to his eyes and then the cinnamon-colored gemstone. Then he points to the violet gemstone. "Violet's eyes, yes?" I nod and look up. It is beautiful. He kisses me so softly, it is little more than a touch. It tickles. He won't take no for an answer and gently shoves me toward the steps. For a long time on the flight home, I stare at the diamond. I should feel lucky. I don't. I just feel like a fraud, a cheap version of a high-end retail store doll sitting on a shelf in the dollar store. The color of my gemstone should be dull brown like my eyes without the violet contacts.

"If you don't want that," Vincent offers with a teasing smile from his seat across from me. "I can take it off your hands."

Salvatore laughs. "So this was fun. Do we get to do this again?"

I don't know what to tell him. This is what little girls dream of, isn't it? How many fantasize getting transformed from an ugly and awkward geek to a beautiful princess who is swept off her feet by a dark, handsome, and rich stranger? A lot, I suppose. Even me.

Chapter 33

The restaurant is packed. It is always crowded when they have the seafood buffet. I hate feeling like I'm being smooshed into a pigsty. However, once a month, Mom likes to treat Nicolette and me to a Tuesday dinner at the Rolling River Boat Dock Restaurant overlooking the Ohio River. She loves shellfish, I don't; it makes me break out in hives.

The restaurant is loud and middleclass swanky with white linen tablecloths, silverware wrapped in cloth napkins and tables shoved too close together on red-carpeted flooring. It's the kind of place swarming with families dressed in mall-bought khakis and twenty-dollar skirts. To make matters worse, my mother invited Robby Pierson along. He's wearing a white shirt buttoned to his chin and dark dress pants. His hair is slicked back with what looks like motor oil. When we went to sit down, Mom made a quick skip to the right so I'm shoved right next to him at the table. "I know you two will have so much to talk about," she grins at me. No, I don't think so, other than I'm wrapping my sweater around me like a two year-old cuddles a blanky while he keeps patting the asthma inhaler in his breast pocket like a baby coddles a pacifier. He smells like dollar store aftershave, peanut butter, and hand sanitizer.

"We came for the seafood buffet," Mom tells me when the waitress takes my order and I ask for a side salad. I feel like a little kid and I know the waitress, whose eyes fall to mine, must be thinking the same thing because she looks at me like I might be a bit slow in thinking. "You can get soup and salad anytime." Mom looks up at the waitress. "She'll take the seafood buffet too."

I snatch up the collar to my sweater and tug it up a bit. It's my comfort zone and it is nice to be able to still slip inside when I'm not at the country club or following Liam around.

"You're going to waste away to nothing," Mom mewls, poking my arm where I've got a little bicep forming from working out. I can still hide under long-sleeved shirts at home while cool spring days creep along toward summer. "You've lost weight."

No, actually, I've gained muscle. I don't tell her that. I've gone from a dizzy, run-stumbling a quarter mile every morning at a heavy gasp to a five mile a day hard run. And I also had a breakthrough last Tuesday making me a little cocky. Norma Edwards, Jack Barkley's cardio-kickboxing coach has been beating the crap out of me from one end of the gym mat to the other since the first day we met. Boom, boom, boom and I'm lying flat and sprawled and trying to hold back the tears creeping up to my eyes while she taunts me with: *Bam, prissy missy, you're out!* Everybody snickers it up while she does this stupid dance around the floor. I mean, it is five times a lesson and it had begun to damage my self-confidence a bit, crush what little ego I've been able to conjure up walking around as Violet with her four-hundred dollar dresses, high heels, and makeup.

No, I suppose in retrospect, it is more than a bit. Because while I am lying there after each public trouncing as Norma's personal punching bag, I remember all the times Leah McDaniel and her rough and tumble friends used to push, poke, and make fun of me. Their nickname for me when it wasn't Weird Wosie was Dinky, short for dweeb and stinky. I think I was like a bottle of champagne popping its cork at noon on Friday. It wasn't pretty, but when Norma turned around for her usual beat-the-crap-out-of-prissy-bitch dance, I stood up and ran across the mat, jumped on her back and just started waling on her. She went down hard on her belly, with a grunt that knocked the air out of her. It took two of the workout room attendants to pull me off while I pounded her back with my gloves. Shawna Young who works in the kitchen secretly told me later that Norma's been knocking staff over in training forever. It's the first time any of them ever caught her off-guard. In fact, they took their time coming over to help Norma.

So all week, I was incredibly anxious about working out with her. I'm waiting for her payback. Then Wednesday passes and Thursday passes. I'm thinking, man, she just must be proud of me for teaching me so well. But then, by Friday, I realize she's just waiting for a crowd.

"Sweetie, you look tired. Is your throat still hurting? You're sleeping all right, aren't you?" Mom leans into me at the table while she sips a glass of red wine, shoves my thoughts away. She asks me this every time. But I know my eyes are puffy-tired and have black rings beneath. No, I didn't get any sleep. I went from jet to limo to driveway, changed my clothes and ran out the door for work. I almost fell asleep at my desk trying to dig up any information I can find on the car race Lynn mentioned.

I see her eyeing my necklace warily. "Oh, that's a pretty necklace." I exchanged Aunt Roo's today for the one Emmanuel gave me. "Is that one of Grandma Mauer's?"

"No, I got it online."

"I'd rather see her waste money on a necklace, mom," Nicky is sitting across from me, blows her straw cover at me. "Than that stupid cat of hers." It hits me in the forehead. I see Nicky lean forward, narrow her gaze where the straw cover hit me. I make a quick push of my glasses over my eye just as Robby starts staring at it. I get the feeling he's seeing something that the makeup won't cover today, the teeny traces of a black eye. Norma's retaliation on Friday. But it wasn't as much the black eye as the humiliation of the crowd watching—

A plate drops and everybody jumps. Nicky swings her head over and sits up straight, my eye forgotten. There's a private dinner in a side room and she seems quite interested in the clientele. "Look, that's Mayor Pritchard and his wife," she whispers loudly across the table. "Gosh, how old is she? Sixteen?"

Everybody turns and I groan inwardly at their wide eyes like he's some sort of celebrity. That family prances around like kings and queens wanting to be waited upon. They have an entourage of twenty or so politically-bound fans and attendants who flock around them, like seagulls hovering over a kid with a French fry held aloft. I know. They took a tour of the country club last week, the whole lot of them assessing it for his daughter's wedding and reception aloud like a pack of wolves yowl and bark evaluating a moose for a meal. Mister Barkley was so livid with their outspoken criticisms including a few crumbs left on the floor just outside the kitchen doors, he nearly had Kim escort them out. And no, Mayor Pritchard's wife isn't sixteen. She's thirty, but she's had so many facelifts, she looks like a mannequin with a perpetual pulled-back smile.

"His daughter is getting married," Nicky hiss-whispers with wide eyes like the Queen of England has entered the room. "It's probably their engagement dinner!"

"Hmmm," is all Mom says, her eyes not veering from the chain dangling around my neck. "Another man who always has a young woman by his side."

"It's called a trophy wife," Nicky slides in a giggle before Mom starts in on her gossip about Jack Barkley and his alleged young niece-whore. Me, of course, and thank God she's not pointing a finger at me. Then I realize while I take a sip of my water, Robby Pierson is still staring at my eye.

"Do you have a black eye?"

"No. It's my cheap mascara."

"No, it looks like—a black eye." He points at it. Nicky stares at me and Mom stares at me and Rocky looks from Nicky to Mom and then back again. "How'd you do that?"

"Did I do that?" Rocky says right out of the blue. I snap my eyes over to his, but before I can say anything, he leans over the table a bit, like he's situating himself. "You don't have to cover for me, Rosie. I'm so sorry." He turns to Mom. "I was helping her load some books from the school library and she ran right into a stack I was carrying."

"That's not your fault," Nicky snickers. "If she was the one who walked into it, it's her fault. You apologize too much for things you didn't do."

I look at Rocky. He apologizes to Nicky and everybody laughs lightly. Then he turns away, like the conversation is over. I'm not so sure why he covered for me. Mom starts telling me that if I would have put ice on it right away, it wouldn't be so bad. But I didn't get it from books. No, not at all, and I'm not star struck by the mayor and his entourage like my mom and sister. They made me mad during their tour at the country club; that's how I got my black eye. Well, and being a bit cocky after I tackled Norma and made her bite the gym mat—

"Oh, I've got a good one for you." Rocky's voice shoves my memory away at the table, but not for long. "You're talking about the Pritchards and I got invited along last Friday to the Crystal Springs Country Club with them."

"Yeah, we know," Nicky is shaking her head, slapping his words away with her hand even before he can finish, "We all know about your little adventure."

I didn't know. I freeze, swallow hard, snap my eyes

up to Rocky. Rocky was with the Pritchards on Friday? I almost choke on the lettuce I was stuffing into my mouth. Did he see me? Was that why he covered for me?

"Your sister doesn't. Your mom doesn't," he says, looks at her like a pup with his nose slapped. "Come on, Nicky, if I get a job in Crystal Springs, I could get a membership. The mayor told me he is trying to get reduced rate memberships there for city employees."

"And he hasn't offered you a job there yet, Rocky," Nicky reminds him.

"Yeah, well, maybe. I talked to him about it."

"He gets people asking him for stuff all the time," Nicky adds. Rocky shrugs it off.

He looks at me. "Rosie, it's *so* cool in there. You'd like it. You can swim. And they've got boxing," He gets this funny smile to his lips. Is he hinting he saw me?

"So how does a teacher from Laurel Grove get to be wined and country clubbed by a mayor?" Robby asks. He is playing his finger along the sweat on his water glass. "Because, man, I want to be a teacher then."

"I literally got a cat out of his mom's tree," Rocky laughs. "Along with his mom."

Everybody laughs but Nicky, who shakes her head. "Hey, he's not kidding."

"I was on call and somebody phoned in that there was an old lady in a tree off Main Street. We drove out there, lights flashing and sure enough Mayor Pritchard's eighty-two year-old mother had climbed up in a tree to get her cat down. The cat jumped down when she gets up there, but she got stuck. I climbed up, carried her down."

"Then he gets a call. It's Mayor Pritchard wanting to thank him for doing it. Blah, blah, blah," Nicky continues for him. "He invites him to supper at the country club after he does a tour for his daughter's wedding." She keeps looking at her watch.

"So, let me tell you something funny that happened while I was there at the country club with his family—"

"Not again, Rocky," Nicky groans. "I've heard you tell the story a hundred times this weekend. At the restaurant, to your buddies, at church. Don't listen to it. It's about a couple women who box at the country club. He's told it to everybody he comes into contact. It's his new go-to story."

"Let him tell his story." Mom hushes Nicky with her hands and leans into the table toward Rocky. "Tell us."

"So it goes like this," Rocky starts. "Jack Barkley's got a new girlfriend. She's like twenty or something. Rides his arm around the country club like she won't let go."

"I told you." Mom points a finger at me.

Everybody's enrapt and he knows it so he draws out his story. "The rumors are she's Russian. He tells everybody she's his niece, then he does this wink-wink thing." Rocky winks twice as illustration. In retrospect, I did notice Jack Barkley winking. More often than not, he has the audacity to hand me off to some old dude while he goes to talk to someone else. Hell, no wonder those men fawn all over me. I'm going to have a talk with Jack Barkley about insinuating I'm his lover and one he's more than happy to pass off to the next old guy who is interested in a little affair on the side. "But that's beside the point," Rocky goes on. "I was walking beside Janine Pritchard and she was giving me all the latest scandal in Crystal Springs. She also told me the girl's name is Violet and didn't grow up in town. But she's something else. Just something else." Rocky shakes his head slightly and gets this funny smile on his lips. I see Nicky's eyes narrow. I think she's jealous.

"Yeah, I heard she's *something else*," Nicky mutters.

"Nicky's *something else*," Mom interrupts quickly and reaches out and pats Nicky's arm. "Go on, Rocky."

"So, the boxing coach used to date Jack Barkley and the two women have this competition going on."

Oh, my, I can see Rocky's side of the story is going to be biased, so my side of the story goes like this: So, I guess there's a whole lot of guys who like to watch girls fight. I asked Norma Edwards what was up with that. There's always a small group that swarms into the weight room at the country club whenever we start boxing. It's like they're waiting for us to start. Norma just laughed at me. I mean, I don't really like to watch men fight or, for that matter, people fight at all. It makes me uncomfortable, probably because Leah McDaniel bullied me all the time. I box with Norma because Mister Barkley says I have to do it as part of my work schedule. I didn't understand until Friday he had a hidden agenda. He was making me do it for the audience outside the one-way glass window in the workout room.

But I've taken on this kind of smart-alecky, snarky attitude at work. I think it's come from too much time hanging out with Liam. Everything I say, he has some snotty retort, like jokes tossed around on a nightly sitcom. I almost wait for the canned laughter after each of his remarks.

"They're the ones that make sure you get a paycheck every week, Popovich," Norma had grunted to me low on her breath when she saw me wince at the crowd after I'd knocked her on the mat on Friday. I thought we were done. I mean, my plan was hightailing it out of there after my little payback because I know Norma's going to wale on me next time we spar. But Norma, she wanted to settle up and she wasn't letting me leave until everybody saw she could lay me on my ass.

She nods. "We better go a few more minutes."

And this is where the payback comes in. I looked up and I had a good feeling they'd wound the mayor and his entourage through at the exact moment we started our boxing session, just so they could see the show. Mister Barkley is giving us a bob of his head and he's got a ton of people lining up around the mats. Rumor straight from Kim's lips says that Liam is friends with Mayor Pritchard's daughter somehow, and he nearly begged his dad to let them have the wedding at the country club. However, Mayor Pritchard and Jack Barkley are on completely opposite ends, politically. And Jack takes his politics very seriously. To make matters worse, Mayor Pritchard owns a house in Jack's gated community, so my boss has to cater to his foe's every need. Mayor Pritchard utilizes the country club for political parties and courts rich supporters by throwing huge wedding receptions in their honor, just to get under Jack Barkley's skin. Like the wedding tour on Friday.

"We should sell tickets," I mumbled back at Norma through my mouth guard. It sounded more like: *We shubb shell shickets*. But she understands.

"You keep dressing like that and Mister Barkley might," she answered. "Then again, I suppose, in a way, you already are. I'm assuming that's why he has his little tour in here now."

I look down. It's what I always wear in the gym—a tank top and short elastic shorts. I roll my eyes.

"All right, one more round," Norma gets into her stance. And we bang each other around for another twenty minutes. She's always telling me, with a serious purse to her lips beneath her face guard, to show off my skills: *Now, you've got to hit harder* and *pull a good right*.

And I was still a little cockier and teasing her like: *Gonna kick your ass again. Gonna kick your ass again*, in a sing-song voice while I bounced around on my feet with my fists jabbing in front of my face.

That's what I was doing when I actually did get a good punch in on Friday and right in front of the crowd. It made her keel to the right and do a funny twist to her feet. There was even light clapping. When she threw up her gloves and told me we're done, I made the stupid move of bounding around her in a circle with a little dance. "Oh, I kicked your ass. I kicked your ass," I was joking with her. She didn't think it was so funny.

BOOM! Okay, so Norma doesn't have a sense of humor. She hauls off and punches my left cheek with a slam that sent my face flying west and my body east. I just free fell straight back and she came stomping over to me and stood with her arms akimbo and her gloves resting on her waist. "What you got to say about that now, Popovich?"

"*You* kicked *my* ass, *you* kicked *my* ass," I spit out my mouth guard and mewled in that sing-song voice from my position, which is now on my back and sprawled spread-eagle on the floor.

The entire room erupted in laughter. I didn't think it was so funny. Now I know why Mister Barkley hates the Pritchards. Rocky's story to my family's delight is no different except for his voice taking a high pitch when he repeats my words: *You kicked my ass, you kicked my ass.*

I blanch, try to force a chuckle and make an awkward attempt to read Rocky's eyes. Is he toying with me?

At the same time, Robby Pierson leans into me, blasting out a laugh and says, "I like you because you're quiet like a little house mouse, Rosie Rose. Even your laugh. You and me, we need to go out."

And I don't like him because he's creepy like a scrawny outside cat ready to pounce on me, the house mouse. So I didn't mind at all when the waitress leans over

Rocky at that exact moment and he bumps the glass she's trying to refill. It spills some on his pants. He stands up too quickly, shakes the entire table and sends my sister's glass of soda careening right into his lap and Mom's ice tea splashing on to the front of Nicolette's blouse.

I walk with Nicolette into the bathroom and help her soak up the brown-colored tea stain from her shirt.

"I don't know what is wrong with him," she is mumbling to me. "Rocky is so laid back, but lately he's being such a bumbling idiot." She sighs and holds her hands out. "Um, I know the waitress was flirting with Rocky. That's why he spilled the drink." Nicolette looks up and her eyes skid to a halt when they meet mine. Her head tips slightly. I don't know what she sees, but she looks away quickly. "It doesn't bother me. I just wanted you to know that. We've decided to date other people. I'm not so sure he's not dating that Violet girl. I know she's supposed to be with Jack Barkley, but I heard she gets around. She's got a guy from Mexico. Rocky's never home and he's been to the country club three times and he talks about her all the time and how beautiful she is. Please don't tell Mom. She's already seeing Doctor Stamper trying to deal with *stuff*. God knows what."

"Mom's seeing Doctor Stamper?" I careen right over the fact she thinks Rocky is crushing on Violet.

"I don't know. She just calls it 'old baggage', whatever that means." She rolls her eyes and grunts a chuckle. Then my sister, drops her smile and her voice, reaches out a hand to latch on to my arm. "Listen, you need to know this. Tim Kinney caught me after church, said you need to watch what you say and who you say it to. You're treading on thin ice telling people his dad had something to do with the murders and he might be covering for him."

"I never said that."

"You can lie all you want. But Bobby pulled me aside and said you told him the same thing. That's who Tim said he heard it from." I stand there in a daze, watching her leave.

Chapter 34

"You didn't have to shoot the tires on the limo, Violet," Liam complains. Violet. It still catches me off-guard. "It's coming out of your paycheck! You could have killed us!"

"Yeah, how about we talk to your daddy about that?" I spit back. "I'm sure between us, *you're* the one who is going to get the paddling." But honestly, and in my defense, I had *every* right to shoot the tires. For the third time, Liam tricks me into getting out of the car. This time, he tells me he's going to throw up. He's got this bleach blonde on his arm tonight who is annoying beyond belief. She's number seventeen in the same amount of days. She's a dingbat like all the rest; that's the kind of girl he likes. She giggles hilariously at every word coming out of Liam's mouth.

Between her laughter and hitting three bars where Liam drank three whiskeys and four beers, who would give it a second thought? Not me. I slide out of my seat at lightning speed, then stand there, waiting for him to puke on my shoes. The door of the limo closes behind me. Off they drive, in a spray of dust and ditzy blonde's stupid giggles. I walk toward the limo and it drives up a couple feet every time I almost get to the bumper. So, when it drives off in the usual grand finale before disappearing, I take out the little pistol my daddy got me. I hold it aloft and bang, bang. Two tires on the limousine are flatter than pancakes made without baking powder.

Now Liam's coming down from being snake-spitting angry as we sit inside a little all-night diner while the limo driver figures out how to get new tires at two o'clock in the morning.

"You won't leave me again, will you?" I ask him with

a cock of my chin. The blonde laughs and I shudder, turn to her, and tell her to shut up. I call her Yellow Purse because she's got this screaming-canary-yellow pocketbook that doesn't match her dress. She gets a sad look on her face and a pout to her chin and smashes herself up to Liam in the booth. "Make her stop, puppy," she whines. Puppy. I want to strangle her.

Liam ignores her, but still wraps an arm around her shoulders. He gave her his jacket. Me, I have to wear goosepimples. "You're a bitch. And no, I won't. Because you won't be in the car anymore, *Miss Violet*. When I get to the office tomorrow, I'm talking to my dad. Your ass is fired."

"Yeah, well, we'll see about that."

"I'd fire you," the blonde pipes up.

"Shut up!" Both Liam and I say it at the same time. She blinks this wide eyed stare, like Mister Baby Cakes when I've run out of cat food at ten at night and the grocery store is closed until morning. Then she excuses herself to the bathroom.

"Liam," I sigh, staring at the top of the head of the young man across from me tapping on his cell phone. "This isn't a game. This isn't fun for me. My dad was brought in for questioning by the cops. Someone tried to blow me up in a trailer. I don't need more stress. I've got three and a half weeks left on my contract with your stepdad. Can you give me a break for that amount of time?"

"Lay off, Violet. You got me alibis. As far as I'm concerned, you can get the hell out of my life," he sneers. "I really don't want to be around you. I'm not kidding. I'm getting my stepdad to find somebody else to be my warden. Just bugger off. You're more annoying than—what's her name?" He jabs a thumb toward the bathrooms.

"I don't know." I abruptly feel alone. "She's *your* date. How the hell can you not know her name?"

"You're kidding me, right? It's no worse than you hanging around with the guy who runs the biggest drug cartel in South America."

"What?"

"You didn't know that?" Liam snickers. "Yeah, I thought you'd be smart enough to look up the guys you're dating. I figured you overlooked it."

"I've been too busy looking up the girls *you* dated, Liam," I say in a sulky voice. I don't believe him. He's grouchy and mean. I don't know why. I'd rather be home with Mister Baby Cakes watching some stupid show than here. So I go to the restroom, open the door. I can hear someone talking. It's Yellow Purse. I think it's strange she is standing in a stall to call somebody on the phone.

"—so I can't. There has been no point I could put it in his drink, you get that? I'm not a freaking magician. I'm scared I'll get caught. He's not drunk and there's some chick with him," she is whisper-yelling. "No, I haven't been alone—" She stops cold. I assume she is getting yelled at on the other end because I can make out a voice, but I can't make out the words. "—because it is harder than I thought. Okay, I'll do it. I know."

I close the door hard behind me and stand there in the bathroom. I hear a bit of clatter, like I caught the girl off -guard and she dropped her phone. It makes a lazy bounce-bounce just three inches outside the stall door. I'm one step away and snatch it up. Then I step back. I see her slowly opening the door, peering out.

"So, do you want to tell me why you're putting something in Liam's drink?"

I suppose I didn't think she'd answer. My heart was thumping, so I assume my body knew before my mind, she was going to put up a fight. I did not, however, expect to see a tiny pistol sliding between door and frame. "Back off. Give me my phone." Suddenly her voice isn't so ditzy; she's slipping through with the kind of assured swagger Norma Edwards had before I cardio-boxed her butt on the ground that day.

I blink, then react like any half-lunatic, paranoid person would do if they suddenly realized they were going to get shot in a dilapidated bathroom of a diner off the highway and her churchy mom would hear all the sordid and dirty details of why and how that happened. I jerk up my knee and kick the door so hard it slams back on the girl inside. Then while it swings back open and she falls rear-first into the toilet, I grab the door with my hands and bash it three more times on her hands. The first time, the pistol goes right and her knuckles smack into the wall. The second time I do it hard enough to squeeze it from her fingers. Needless to say, she drops the pistol and just sits there between toilet and wall with her arms over her head.

"Don't—don't!" she is yowling. Her little yellow pocketbook is open next to her heel. "I didn't *want* to do it. It was just a crushed up sleeping pill! That's what they said."

I nod at her purse. There's a little wallet opened up. Inside, I can see her driver's license. "Slide your purse over," I tell her. "Is it inside?"

She falls back. "Yes. In a plastic bag."

"Who told you to do this?"

"I owe a bunch of weed money to Tag Williams. He's got a shop in Marshfield and a big one in Columbus. He told me to do it. I swear."

I lean over, snatch up the gun and purse. I don't take my eyes off her while I delve around inside. Just the half-open wallet and a little baggie with white powder in it.

"Here's how it works—" I tug out her driver's license, peek at her name before towing out a couple credit cards and a ten dollar bill. "Lydia Murphy, that's your name?" She doesn't answer. So I go on, "I'm going to walk out of here. You don't come out for ten minutes. If you do what I say, I'll send these little tokens of our trust back to you in three days. If not, I'm taking every last dime and sending the driver's license and the gun to the cops."

I pivot and exit the restroom, let the door close slowly behind me. I pause long enough to drag out one credit card that I flip across the room. "So you can get home," I mutter while I feel a sudden urgency to get back to Liam. I'm almost running when I get to his table. He's still sitting there, staring at his phone like he's in mid-text.

"We're leaving. Now. Come on."

"What? The car isn't here yet. Where's my date?"

"Liam," I lean over so I am in his face. "The girl you've been dragging around all night is trying to drug you. I heard her talking to someone on her cell phone in the bathroom. I took her purse. She's got something in a baggie, said somebody was making her do it. Unless you want to go to the next level of someone framing you for murder, we've got to get out of here. Because I can almost guarantee they are planning on murdering this girl so you'll wake up next to a dead girl tomorrow."

"What?" He's looking back and forth between my eyes like he thinks she's going to burst through the doors and I'm going to yell it was a big joke. I feel like I'm dealing with a rebellious thirteen year-old while Liam looks away for a split second, down to the floor.

"This is not a joke." I sigh. "I'm leaving. You can stay with the girl who was trying to kill you or go with the girl who is trying to keep you alive, but I'm not dragging you out of here kicking and screaming."

Chapter 35

"All right, Rosie," Rocky yells at me. "Ready to play some ball?"

Don't say the rest. That's what my mind is groaning because I'm in a cruddy mood today. I got one hour of sleep last night before my sister and her go-to guy come barging into my house without knocking. I'm sprawled on the couch with Liam's head in my lap.

It was one big blowout. Rusty Rossi finally returned with his own car and, since it was on the way, he dropped me off at my house, first assuring me he would take Liam straight home. Liam decided he needs to come into my house and use the bathroom. He was coming down off another quarter bottle of rum and bickered at me all the way in and even while I puttered around my living room waiting for him to finish.

The conversation was like: "You know what? You don't get it, do you? I don't *care* if I live or die. I'm worthless. I don't have a job. I don't want to work. My stepdad's right when he says I'm nothing but empty baggage he got stuck with when my mom left—" He'd made a funny sniffing sound from behind the bathroom door. "Hell, my mom didn't even want me."

"If your stepdad didn't want you, he wouldn't have hired me to look out for you." I vaguely remember growling at him while I opened up the usual feast of tuna fish for Baby Cakes and started calling him.

Liam comes staggering out of the bathroom. "Are you an idiot, Rosie?" he laughs with a snarky twist of his lips. "Really? Look at you! *You* as a bodyguard? You're crawling around the floor looking for a damn cat!"

"I can't find him."

"When you walked into Jack's office, I saw his eyes light up. He was sitting on a pot of gold. You were backward and uncoordinated. You couldn't swat a fly and kill it. He wanted you to fail."

I was hurt. I didn't let on while I stopped and peered under the couch. "Why would he want me to fail?"

"Then I'm out of the picture and it ain't his fault," he said in a tone like he was talking to a child. "You know, it was my mom that had all the money and the country club, right? He's not my real dad. So, that money will be mine when I turn twenty-four. Or his, if I'm not around."

"Well, I proved him wrong, didn't I?" I muttered. "Because I saved your ass tonight. Maybe if you just stepped back a minute and showed him you might be an asset to his business, he'd take an interest in you. Show some initiative." That's when I see a bit of kitty cat tail. I reached out and tickled it with my fingers. "Baby Cakes, come on—" It didn't budge. I stopped, turned to Liam. "He's dead."

"Who's dead?"

"Baby Cakes, you dumbass son of a bitch!"

I guess I just lost it when I saw Baby Cakes dead. Liam scrabbled around my cabinets, desperate to find some wine to help calm me down—you know, because booze cures all as far as he's concerned. I had a bottle of rum I got as a gag gift from my sister one Christmas, a two-liter bottle of diet soda that had lost all its fizz, and two buddies that hated to see a girl sobbing over a dead best friend.

At four in the morning, and in the pouring rain, Rusty Rossi and Liam Dubois boxed up Mister Baby Cakes in the shoe box that housed my favorite pair of high heels. Then, the two dug a super-size hole in my garden. Ten minutes later, my neighbor called the cops. I was singing Amazing Grace at the top of my lungs with two off-key, rum

-soaked men singing along with arms around each other's shoulders, like they were in the ending of an old black and white movie, singing Christmas carols while the camera panned through the credits.

After a long, slightly slurred explanation of the death and burial, the cops told us to just go inside and finish the wake. I tossed most of our clothes into the dryer and dug out some of my outfits for Liam and Rusty to wear. We hunkered down with an old movie while I sniffled and rummaged through the yellow purse I'd nabbed from Liam's date. The next thing I remember is waking up to my sister gasping. Rusty Rossi is at my feet and we're still in our casual clothing. My eyes pop open and I blink to two sets of shocked eyes staring back at me from across the room. The bottle of rum falls from my fingers and makes a loud clank to the floor. Both Nicky and Rocky had stumbled to a complete and utterly stunned stop.

"Oh." Nicolette mumbled, speechless. "Um." And Rocky added a little advice to hers with something that sounds like a soft *uh uh*. I don't know what that means. "You missed church," Nicolette finally muttered. "Mom was—um, worried. And—and she's having Robby Pierson over so you can get to know him better." I'm assuming it looked like we had a drag queen orgy last night because Liam is wearing my puffy pink slippers and my matching bathrobe. Rusty had a blanket draped around him like a Roman emperor.

"Oh, please not Robby Pierson," I groaned. Then I turned and looked at Liam. "Why are you wearing my dress?" He was wearing my dress. Oh, my head hurt.

"I don't remember." Liam cringed too. He rose up just enough to give me a goofy grin. Then he vomited all over my carpet and Rocky's church shoes.

Liam and Rusty dug their clothes out of the dryer and left. I pulled on a pair of shorts and a t-shirt and dragged myself to Nicolette's car for lunch at my mom's. And I know the last part about the shirts versus skins is going to be shouted too because he knows I have a hangover and I don't want my mom to find out. She just thinks I overslept.

So, that's why Rocky yells if I want to play a game, to push my hangover over the edge. *He* recognized Liam, even if my sister didn't. He's heard the rumors of the playboy, partying stepson of Jack Barkley. "Shirts versus skins! You be skins. Let's go."

Oh, I feel it singe along my back. Boom. Boom. My head feels like it is sitting in a vice. Why does it annoy me so much? I look down at the sprinkle of goosebumps running up my arm.

"Okay." So I stand up, wriggle out of my t-shirt, and stand there in my bra. It's a cute one, too, with black lace and silk. Rocky just drops the ball. Boom. Boom. Boom-boom-boom. Robby Pierson makes this funny gasping sound and we all stand there while I scoop up the ball. "So let's go, bitches." I'm not a very good basketball player. My hands are tiny. I can't jump. It doesn't matter. Rocky doesn't come at me for the ball. He snatches up my t-shirt from the concrete driveway and shoves it against my chest like he's dousing a fire.

"Rosie!" he whisper-shouts at me. "Dammit! What is wrong with you? Are you nuts?"

"Yeah." I slap at his hands. "Yeah, I am. So leave me alone!" I'm watching Robby turn a pale blue before he pulls out his inhaler and stuffs it between his lips. "I hate you. I hate all of you. You have no clue what it's like to be me!"

It should have ended there. But I stomped into Mom's sunroom and ran pell-mell into Bobby reaching for a beer in the little refrigerator. I'm still stewing when he turns and gives me one of his classic sympathetic smiles like he understands me or something.

"Rosie, simmer down a little."

"Excuse me?" I stop, step back. A layer of chills runs up my spine.

"Well, I mean, you need to sit down a minute and take a breath. You're going to upset your mom."

"Take a breath." I repeat, grinding my teeth. "Maybe my last—breath? Like the one I would have taken if I hadn't gotten out of that trailer before it exploded?" I look him in his eye. It is the hardest thing, I think, I've ever done, confronting him so impulsively. Maybe I wouldn't have done it otherwise, I would have just avoided him, Rosie-style, for the rest of my life. But I'm in a surly Violet-mood and ready to fight and he's standing there. Bobby tips his head like he doesn't know what I'm talking about. He's lying. I see him turn his head toward the open doorway. Mom's somewhere beyond.

"What trailer?" He leans in, the beer clasped in his fingers.

"Yeah, Bobby, you play stupid." I watch him stand up straight then, try to read my face. I swear he is watching his stance so I can't read it. "I think you set me up so I was in there. What do you say to that?"

"Rosie, I don't know what you're talking about. What trailer?" He appears to think about it. "One of the trailers that caught on fire outside town? You're acting—a bit loopy today."

"Sweetie, what is going on out there?"

Bobby shifts quickly. He gives me one last strangely blank stare. "Nothing, hon," he says as Mom rounds the corner. "We just bumped into each other."

"I'm not feeling good. I'm going home."

It should have ended there. Rocky got called out on an ambulance run. Nicolette drove me home and I sniffled into a tissue I tugged from her glove box. I told her about Mister Baby Cakes dying and it seemed to satisfy her need to figure out why I went nuts and took off my shirt in the driveway. She told me Robby Pierson had an asthma attack right after. I could have killed him.

She drops me off and runs. My house is lonely and messy. I avoid the couch where I found Baby Cakes. There's potato chip bags with chips flung out on the floor and a piece of pizza between couch cushions. Liam drank a six pack of soda and just dropped the cans on the floor. It amazes me that three people could have made this much of a mess.

When I get to the bedroom with the sweeper, I stop. I gaze at the walls as I stand in the threshold between hallway and room. I know I'm becoming obsessive, the pictures Leah and I took from Jay Cooper's mobile home. I'd used sticky tape to carefully place them in lines on the larger wall above the wooden headboard of my bed. I borrowed an old overhead projector from the high school that probably hadn't been used in fifteen years. I made a small map and threw the image on the overhead so it showed up on the wall to my left. Then, I took little pins from an old sewing kit I bought at a yard sale and stuck a little Post It Note to each place a dead girl had been found that was on Jay's list of images.

They weren't nameless faces; some were alive. I found them in the phone book and online. I jotted their phone numbers and addresses on little notes and added them to Jay's list beside each. These people all lived in different areas. I couldn't quite figure out what was tying them—*us*—all together. I sigh and I walked into the kitchen, pick up my purse to examine the little baggie with the powder for Liam. I blanch, search around inside desperately. It's gone.

I'm trying to think, did I put it somewhere else? Then I remember I'd slung my purse over the chair in my mom's kitchen, left it there while I was outside. Somebody at the house went through my purse. But who? Bobby? Mom?

There's a knock on the door. I wince. Nobody ever comes to visit me. I peer out of the curtain. Lynn, Rocky's mom, is standing on my porch with Leah not two steps behind. I can't help but feel my heart make a quick jump-stab. Is Rocky dead? She's never come here. I almost throw open the door.

"Is everything okay?" I ask frantically.

Lynn just takes a long draw of a cigarette, then tosses it down on the ground, steps on it. "You tell me, baby girl," she says in her throaty voice. "Rocky called. He said he was worried. Nicky texted him. You shouldn't be alone."

"Me?" I ask, opening the door wider.

"The sirens on the firetruck was loud. But it sounded like he said you lost that cat of yours—"

"Oh, Baby Cakes." I nod. I'm strangely fascinated by the thought Rocky called his mom to come over and sit with me. "I'm just surprised. Rocky hates my cat." I wave the two on inside and close the door with both my hands. "He said he was spoiled and he scratched Rocky."

"Well, he likes you. Like the girl, like the cat."

"I don't think he's much on liking me either, Lynn." I fumble with a laugh while I point to the couch. I feel almost guilty, like I should be in mourning. "He's cursed with me because of Nicky. I'm sure he's gotten some flak for picking me up or dropping me off from his dad because Nicky asked him to do it."

"Cursed," she grunts a deep laugh and I think she's going to plop down until I see her head wag a little sideways. "What's that?"

"Oh." I'm so hungover, I forgot to close the door to my room. "It's just—stuff. I've been kind of collecting information on the girls that have been missing—"

"Because of her aunt," Leah offers as she rolls her eyes, comes inside. "And Dad. Her dad got dragged down to the cop station too."

"I heard tell. You know something about this?" Lynn asks Leah. I notice she eyes her cautiously. Leah tosses it aside with a shrug while Lynn heads down the hallway. "You better not let your daddy find out you two have been hanging out."

"We're not hanging out, Aunt Lynn." Leah's eyes scrape across me. I cringe. My bedroom looks like somebody shook a police evidence locker. There's pictures, newspaper clippings, and tatty-edged notes laying everywhere. Lynn stops just one step into the bedroom and looks around. Two more steps and Lynn's fingers are reaching down to the stack of pictures.

"I found this box of pictures and stuff—" I start, looking at Leah, who gives a teeny shake of her head as if she doesn't want me to divulge we were both there.

"Found," Lynn repeats and picks up one small stack. Lynn glances at me, to Leah, and back at the pictures.

"Yeah, but it's like a puzzle without any matching borders. I tried to put them in order of age and stuff to find out if they have anything in common," I mutter, desperately trying to get her out of my room. "You want some coffee? We can sit on the back porch—"

"This is Tina Long," she says while she peers at the

pictures. "Oh, and Jenny Parker." She flips through a couple more. "I went to school with all these kids. There's Junior Todd and Davie—" She just stops there, flips back through. Then she looks at me with a thoughtful frown. "Is Johnny and your daddy somewhere in this pile?"

"Yeah, how'd you know?"

"Well, here," she says. And Lynn starts slapping the pictures down one beside the other. "You can't figure it out because you got them in the wrong order."

"What do you mean?"

"It ain't by age they need to be grouped, necessarily," she grunts. "You got to know the kids we used to hang with to figure it out. Johnny's friends go on one side, Ray's old buddies on the other. Watch, girls."

So we watch her lay the pictures out on my bed. One by one, she places six images out and then she lays a second set of seven images next to them. "These are Johnny's friends," she tells me, pointing at one side. "And these are your daddy's friends. They have one thing in common, sweetie. If you put them all together, these are the kids that were in the car race I was telling you about. I wouldn't of seen it if we hadn't talked about it."

I gaze at the images, feeling the realization sweep over me. My eyes veer to the stack of old yearbook pictures. I grab them up, thumb through until I find a few that look like a succession of the same face by age. "Okay, who is this?" I ask Lynn. She takes the image from my fingers and looks hard at it.

"That's Cindy Kent," she says, poking her finger at the picture of a little girl with two front teeth missing. "Probably kindergarten or first grade. She was in my class."

There are four of Cindy in grade school and two from high school that I lay beneath the image Lynn had first set down. "Okay, this is the age progression of each," I say. "Right?" I thumb through a few more. Leah is oddly quiet. I'm so used to her scathing remarks for everything I do, I keep turning to her, expecting some mean retort. But her lips are just pursed a bit tightly, her cheeks a bit pale. "The pictures you put down are the images of Johnny and Ray's friends in high school. I got some by my pillow of adults."

Twenty minutes later, I've grabbed some sticky tack from my kitchen drawer, I've climbed on my bed, and I'm pasting up pictures above my headboard. There are thirteen adult faces staring at me. Seven were from my daddy's truck and on the other side, there are six from Johnny McDaniel's truck. Beneath my daddy's picture, I tack my picture along with my age progression from kindergarten through my senior year in high school Jay Cooper must have cut out of old yearbooks. I do the same for Leah, slipping her image under her daddy's, and that's when Lynn stops me with a hand patting my ankle.

"Rosie, where did you get all these pictures?" Lynn asks me softly. It is almost a whisper.

I come to a standstill. "Will you promise you won't tell anybody?"

"No, I won't tell."

"I snuck into a guy named Jay Cooper's trailer—"

"Jay—" she murmurs the name and I'm reminded of the wispy feel of butterfly wings.

"You know him?"

"Not well," she says softly. "I think he dropped out of high school. He was maybe four or five years older than us, but he still hung out with Johnny sometimes. I think he used to buy the boys beer and cigarettes."

"I thought he might have been the one who murdered the girls found at the quarry and Federal Road."

"Well, I don't know so much about that. He weren't that kind of guy. Besides, he's been in jail, sweetie—"

"Jail?"

"Yeah," Lynn tells me. "He was in for four or five years, I think. He broke into somebody's house. I saw he got out a few months ago. When them girls was killed last year, he was incarcerated."

"Well, that's one less suspect; if he was in jail, he couldn't have killed Alaina and Angel." I rub my chin. I puff out my lips, slide off the bed and go to my closet. I tug out the paper sack and the monkey backpack inside. She takes the backpack in her hands. "Jay gave me this. It was my aunt's."

Lynn is just rolling the backpack around in her hands. "Secrets. There's so many of them."

"What do you mean?" Leah steps up, pushes her finger on the soft nose of the monkey. Her voice isn't like its usual, the bounce of a ping pong ball on a tin roof.

"I remember this backpack," Lynn tells me softly. "Rosie always wore it. She hung it off the back of her chair in English class. I used to poke it with a pen and leave little marks on it—see?" Lynn holds out the backpack. On the blue denim, she pokes a knobby knuckled finger at little deep blue freckles. "Then one day, I was jabbing my pen in it like always, she turns around real quick. I thought she was gonna slug me. I got all ready, had my hands in fists. I mean, that's kind of how the McGuires and the McDaniels always took care of things." She stops, gives us each a gaze. "Like you two right now, huh? And I was dating Big Jake, Johnny's brother, even back then. So, being his girlfriend, I figured I had to carry on the torch with your aunt and her kin. I mean, Big Jake and Johnny were always fighting it out with your daddy, Ray." Lynn rolls her fingers on the fur of the monkey's head. She sighs deeply. "Oh, where was I?" she asks herself. "Um, yeah, she turned around and snapped, *I know Johnny's secret.*"

"What'd she mean?" I ask with bated breath.

"I don't know, baby." Lynn is staring hard at the monkey. "I don't know. I didn't ask. I mean, she could have just been bluffing to get me to stop. But—" She clears her throat, hands the monkey back to me and shrugs.

"But what?"

Lynn hard-stares me. She looks just like Rocky in the eyes. She might be rough around the edges, but her eyes are gentle and kind. "I didn't get to ask Johnny. That was just a day and a half before Rosaline disappeared. Nobody talked about. They was scared somebody'd tell the cops and fingers would start pointing."

I strut over to my aunt's box and I tug out her leather bracelet. Then, I pick up the one Bobby gave me from Gina or Carrie. I hold them aloft and walk over to Lynn. "So I suppose you don't know anything about these."

Leah's eyes flash toward Lynn. Lynn reaches out coolly and lets her fingers play on one dangling bracelet.

"Where'd you get these, Rosie?"

"One was in a box of stuff daddy gave me that belonged to my aunt. The other, my mom's husband gave me. He said it was in an envelope with Gina Channel's and Carrie Stamper's name on it. He found it in the garbage after Timmy Kinney's grandpa dumped it in there."

"I don't know. Maybe you should ask Jay."

"I can't," I say flatly. "Jay is dead. He was the guy who got killed himself on the highway the other day."

"Jay's dead?" Lynn closes her eyes. She buried her face in her hands. "I don't know nothing about nothing. I don't know nothing at all."

Chapter 36

"—dead," I say. "Dead, dead, dead." I'm poking four images with my finger. They are the daughters of four of the teens that were in Johnny and my dad's trucks.

"This is what you guys had in the plastic tubs when I picked you up at that trailer?" That's Colton McDaniel. I called Leah and was surprised she came. She had Colton and Gabby in tow. I settled Gabby in front of the TV with some ice cream. Colton had followed us into the room and was leaning against the frame of the door looking bored while he texted somebody until I said the word *dead*.

"All these pictures were on a wall in the mobile home we broke into. The guy that lived there had like some sort of makeshift police evidence board. You've seen them on the crime TV shows, right? You know, when they've got somebody murdered or maybe a serial killer and they put pictures of suspects up along the board to figure out who did the crime," I explain. He nods. "So, when Leah and I found them in the bedroom, they were blown off the wall. Your Aunt Lynn sorted through a bunch of pictures and helped to figure out what all of these people had in common. She said it was a truck race."

"You don't think it is a crazy serial killer board?" Colton asks. "That Cooper guy had to have done it. He knew too much, right? He killed those girls, then killed himself."

"No. He was in jail when most of the murders occurred. I checked his record out. The guy was what they call a career criminal. It's petty stuff, but he's spent one out of every two years of his life in jail. "

"Where'd you get these extra pictures?" Leah interrupts. Her eyes are glued to my bedroom wall and a whole new set of images lining the bottom.

"I cut them out of the newspapers and yearbooks. Some I copied online. These are all the female children of the people who were in your dad's truck and my dad's truck that were racing that day. But they weren't going out specifically to race, as your Aunt Lynn implied. They were racing each other to get to a dead girl first, not going somewhere to compete in a race. It was rumored around the school a dead girl was lying on County Road 57."

"A dead girl?" Colton perked up, his eyes snapping to mine. "That's sick. My dad did that?"

"In high school—"

"Like you've never done stupid stuff," Leah scoffs. "You keep your big mouth closed about this, you hear?"

"Regardless," I interrupt while Colton flips her his middle finger. "They all wanted to see if it was true. As soon as Johnny heard my dad was going to go take a look, he gathered all his friends. They took off at the same time." Leah steps forward so I am staring at the back of her head, watching her take in the pictures one by one. "And when they go there, sure enough, there was a dead girl in the road; it was Carrie Stamper."

"I wonder why nobody saw her before that." Leah's brow is furrowed. "That's weird, right?"

"No, the county road was closed back then. There was a bridge out that never got fixed after a flood." I point out. "I read it in an old newspaper. It's also the reason both truckloads of kids couldn't get away when they saw the cops coming. They were stuck in that dead end. Because the two truckloads of kids were there, the cops just assumed something happened while they were there that killed her."

"Or they set it up. It sounds suspicious, right?" Colton remarks.

"I agree. It could be the cops or somebody else or

maybe nobody at all. Surely, somebody would have noticed that the body had gone through rigor mortis or not. If she was stiff, they would have known she wasn't in a recent accident." I tap at the folder Frankie had slipped in with the others. "But I've got her autopsy report. It doesn't say anything about it. However, here is what I need to stress: strangely, each of those students who were in those vehicles have had a girl from their immediate family killed in a freak accident."

"Like they are cursed?"

I watch her squint, trying to absorb what I am pointing out to her. "Cursed? I don't know. Look at the dates under each." I point to a little note of the dates each died. Each was within two to three days of May 21. Only one is not, other than Carrie Stamper—Phoebe Wells.

"They all happened around May 21sth?" Colton asks, the phone dropping to his side. "That's when summer starts, right? The solstice? Is it a cult?"

"That's an idea," I answer. "There were seven people in your daddy's truck that went to see the dead girl. There were seven in my dad's truck—"

"There were seven in *my* dad's truck?" Leah interrupts. "I remember you saying there were six."

"Hold on. Let me get to that." I tell her. "I believe that since that day, each of these people on both sides has had a young girl die unexpectedly in what most people would call freak accidents. It has taken some digging because some of these people have married and divorced and some have more than one daughter."

"Was the accident on May 21st or 22nd?" Leah asks.

"No. But something happened at that time tying all of these families in. But what? I don't know. I think someone is murdering these girls and if we can find what event coincides with May 21st or 22nd, we'll have the tie."

Her eyes jerk to mine. "Are you sure? I mean, how did you find this?"

How did I find this? I rub my face. It really was kind of a fluke. I haven't gotten anywhere with the murders. There's no evidence, nothing that ties Alaina Windowski, Angel Daugherty, and Phoebe Wells together. There was nothing left at the scenes, no blood trails. I even found out from Frankie in Rayville that they couldn't trace the black garbage bags Angel was wrapped inside because they are so common. I can understand why the cops are stumped. So I decided to simply step away and work on my aunt's disappearance. And the puzzle started to fall into place when I startled one of Johnny McDaniel's old friends so badly, I think she thought I was a ghost come to haunt her if she didn't divulge the truth.

I was standing on the concrete porch step of a small ranch house thirty-two miles from Laurel Grove. I'd shown up at the last known address of Cindy Kent-Riddell, one of the girls who Lynn pointed out in the picture as being in John McDaniel's truck the night of the race. I know she probably didn't hang around with my Aunt Roo since she was friends with Johnny. Still, maybe she knows something. It was worth a try—

"Hi, my name's Rosie—"

The woman who opened the door had gasped and wavered. Even through the screen, I watched her face drain of color; she was the same shade of spoiled milk. "I'm Rosie Mauer," I continue quickly watching her fingers slap on her lips. "My aunt was Rosie McGuire from Laurel Grove. I'm trying to find some people who went to school with my aunt and see if they know anything about her disappearance."

The woman was in her late fifties. She was wearing

cat-eye glasses and wiggled them down off her nose, closed her eyes like she was thanking God she wasn't staring at the dead Rosie, my aunt.

"You must be—Ray's girl, right? God, you look just like his sister! Caught me off guard." She laughed softly and dropped her hand to her chest, like she was feeling her heart pound. "My heart's racing. I thought I was seeing a ghost."

"People tell me that all the time," I agreed, then added, "You say *ghost*. I'm assuming you think she died?"

"Rosie? I don't know. They never found her, did they? Do people just disappear and they're never found?" she asked me and slipped out the screen door to the porch. She was ogling me. For a moment, I swore she was going to reach out and touch me just to make sure I was alive.

"Well, in a typical year's time, there's like 500,000 missing persons cases in the U.S. But most of those are cancelled leaving about 2,000 actually unresolved. At any given time, there are 40,000 remains of people that are unidentified. People show up all the time who had been missing for ten years or twenty years." I smiled. "I'm hoping my aunt is one of the living statistics, but after forty years, the odds are slim. Can you shed any light on the situation?"

"Wow, that's a lot to digest," she laughs softly. "I don't know what they've told you about her. I don't know what I could tell you. I mean, she was a normal girl. She got into some fights at school. I remember that. I remember she used to blow spit wads at the teachers' backs when they'd turn to write on the chalk board."

"Let me be more specific; you rode in Johnny's truck in a race before my aunt came up missing, is that right?"

"You're not sending this stuff to a lawyer, are you?"

"No, not at all. My dad thinks I'm the smartest thing

since Einstein. He's been shoving her stuff at me and asking me to figure it out. My dad, he's—"

"Ray McGuire. I remember him." She got a dreamy smile on her lips and a faraway gaze, just like my mom gets when she says his name. "I bet he looks the same, huh?"

"I suppose," I shrugged. "Regardless, he needs closure. I'm hoping to dig something up that might either help us find out if she ran away or if she is, um, dead."

"Everybody said it was a race. It wasn't." Cindy had freckles on her nose, she reminded me of an elf. "When we got to school that morning, everybody was whispering there was a dead girl off an old county road—"

I took in a breath. My heart started pounding. Did I hear her correctly? "It *wasn't* a race?"

"Well, there *was* a race, but it was to get to the dead girl. When you say it like that, it sounds really gross, kids racing to see some dead person. But it was what it was. Kids do weird stuff. It's like part of the brain is shut off—"

"It's a part of the brain called the amygdala," I told her. "It's what helps us all make decisions. It isn't fully developed in teenagers, so their emotional and impulsive behavior doesn't function as well as their parents. It's the no fear zone and reason their car insurance is so high and they do stupid stuff like ride bikes off concrete ramps." I sighed. "And the reason they think seeing a dead person is cool."

"Well, when you put it that way, I don't feel like I have to hide it away like we were all nuts." Cindy relaxed.

"No, you were being kids and kids are weird. Everybody does it. Maybe they don't get the chance to check out a dead person, but most kids are curious enough to think it would be an adventure."

"That's nice to know," she answered. "You know, we didn't know who it was. We just heard it was a girl and she was dead and lying on the road."

"County Road 57." I let out a puff of air. "And it was Carrie Stamper, right?"

"Yeah. We found out after." Cindy leaned in, looked behind her at the screen door. I knew she saw my mouth open wide with a million questions. She held up a hand. "Let me tell you what I know, first." She pointed to a couple wicker rocking chairs on the porch. "Sit for a second."

We both sat down and Cindy got me a soda before she leaned her back to her chair and rocked a bit. "So at lunch, we decide to skip the last period of classes to go check it out. Carrie didn't show up for school that day, or the day before. But nobody really thought anything. We figured she'd just gotten sick. We hadn't put two and two together. Still, it was so macabre, the idea that a dead girl was on the road. I don't think we really thought we'd find her. It's like going to a graveyard on Halloween and thinking you'll scare yourself by seeing a ghost. It's not going to *really* happen."

"So my dad and Johnny McDaniel—"

"They both had rides, so everybody piled into them. We took off to see who could get there first." Cindy sighs. "I remember her lying there, like she was asleep—"

"So you *saw* Carrie Stamper?"

"Yeah, before the cops and the truancy officer showed up." She turned her attention back to me. "The principal saw us leaving and called the cops. He didn't know where we were going, just that we were skipping."

"How about Jay Cooper? Was he with you guys?" I remember his words. *She were so pretty, lying there. I thought you'd want to know she weren't hurting no more.* His words are almost the same as Cindy's.

"Yeah, Jay was there. We picked him up. He was

going to get us beer."

Oh, so I bet that's what he was talking about. Why would he tell my aunt she wasn't hurting anymore? Why didn't Lynn tell me he was in Johnny's truck? "But my aunt wasn't there, right?"

"No. She was sick, I think."

"And Carrie was dead, right? You're sure."

"Yeah, her eyes were open and kind of dry."

"Did she have blood on the back of her head?" I asked, rubbing the back of my own head with my hand.

Cindy Kent-Riddell grimaced. "Oh, my God," she whispered, pushed her hands up to her face. "I'll never be able to wipe that out of my mind."

"So, she *did* have blood—?"

"Honey, when we got there—saw the body just lying there kind of half-on and half-off the gravel edge of the road and the grass, your daddy had just parked. There were six or seven people jumping out of the back of his truck and we started jumping out of Johnny's. It was like a race to get to her. I remember thinking it was a joke, she was going to jump up. She was pale, and lying with her hands folded under her chin, like she was asleep." A dribble of sweat eased along Cindy's temple. "We all got to her and were standing over her and I remember looking down, ready to laugh. It was a big joke Johnny had set it up, right? Ray stuck out his foot and pushed her with the toe of his boot. She was stiffer than a board."

"She was stiff? Like rigor mortis had set in? That usually takes four or five hours."

"Yeah. She was rock hard. Then all of a sudden, this bubble of blood comes oozing out of the back of her head and she makes this *gronking* sound. I could see where the dark blood had already dried under her. One of the girls screamed. It was—Tina Long, I think. It was horrible."

"Do you know anybody who would have wanted to hurt Carrie?" I asked softly.

"Kill her? No. Maybe there were a lot of people who said she was stuck up. Her parents were really into pushing her to get good grades, be a doctor or something. She liked hanging out with your aunt."

"Who told you guys about her lying on the road?"

"Everybody knew. Everybody was talking about it. I don't know where it started."

"But you obviously know something—"

"Baby, this isn't something you want to get your hands dirty with," she whispered, looking long and hard into my eyes. "Just let it go. It was hell on us kids and the parents for weeks after we showed up there. We were all in counseling for months. Everybody kept saying we'd gotten cursed because Ray and Johnny had showed up there at the same time." She stopped rocking a minute, plucked at her lip. "You know about the curse between your daddy's family and Johnny's, right?"

"Yeah."

"I'm not superstitious. But I wouldn't stir that pot again, bring it up. Bad things happen. It happened to us."

"It sounds like it happened before all you got together, not after."

"That's a thought," Cindy muttered. But she didn't look convinced. "But if it was, the universe was bringing us together to make it happen." Or someone else was doing it so they thought it was the curse. I didn't think I was going to convince Cindy of that, though. Instead I thanked her for the soda and started to leave.

"One more thing; somebody told me my aunt said that Johnnie McDaniel had a secret—"

She laughed. "That boy probably had lots of secrets, sweetie. I think he was fooling around with half the freshman girls. He smoked. He drank."

"But why would my aunt know?" I asked her quickly. She didn't get along with his family.

"Who knows? Maybe she was just making it up. Rosie liked to stir up trouble." I saw her wave me away and start in the door. I turned as well, set my eyes on my car.

"Hey." Cindy calls out to me when I'm almost halfway to my car.

"Yeah?"

"It was like three weeks before she came up missing. I walked out of the school to meet my mom in the parking lot for a dentist appointment. Rosie and Johnny were getting into Johnny's truck." I turn, tip my head. "They weren't acting like they hated each other and not like they acted at school. Rosie was giggling and Johnny was poking her in the ribs like he was flirting. Rosie ducked down really quickly when she saw my mom walking toward the school. I never said anything, didn't want to get beat up by her. She was hot-headed." Cindy dropped her chin. "You know, I always wondered if your dad or your grandpa found out and—you know, got mad enough to kill your aunt."

"Not my dad."

"Naw, maybe not your dad. Listen, sweetie, just let sleeping dogs lie. Bringing up this stuff will just make it worse on folks. All of this is just weird coincidences. I lost my little girl ten years ago. Every time somebody brings her accident up, it sends me reeling for weeks."

"I'm sorry about that." I told her. "Hey, do you remember who told you about the dead girl on the road?"

"I don't know. I think Ben Sefton told me."

"Ben Sefton," I sighed. "And you don't know where

he heard it?"

"No. I didn't ask."

"Can you give me a list of all the people in the cars?"

She hesitated, then complied. I waited patiently while she jotted down two separate lists, tapped the nubby eraser on the paper once in a while.

"You ever see one of these bracelets before?"

She was silent while I held up the little leather bracelet. "It's one of the bracelets they passed out at Carrie's funeral," she said softly. Then she looked up while her fingers played along the leather. "We all had them. Kind of a way to remember her." Cindy ran a hand through her hair. "Did anybody tell you that her parents showed up while we were there? Heard the call on a CB radio."

"No."

"Her mom started screaming, crying and wailing and blaming us for killing Carrie. We stayed there just staring at her, not sure what to do. Johnny, he tried to tell her we didn't have anything to do with it. But she wouldn't listen. We just took off, scared." Cindy sighed. "She got over it though. It was Doctor Stamper who passed out the bracelets right after Carrie's funeral. She said she wanted us to have something to remind us of Carrie. She apologized, said she was sorry for reacting like she did." She rolled her finger along the writing. "Dies Irae. I remember Doctor Stamper telling us it meant friendship or something. I think we all just wanted to forget, though. Then your aunt disappeared and Jay's little girl came up missing."

I drew in a breath. "Jay—Cooper's little girl?"

"Yeah." She held up the paper she had stopped writing on. "I put his name on here. She was the one who lived down at the welfare housing in town. I don't know her name. I just know he had her in high school and the girl's parents never let her marry him."

"Gina Channel?"

"Yeah. Sounds right."

It occurs to me, right then, where the link is. I mean it was an idea, but I could almost guarantee that everyone who had one of those bracelets, who was at the scene of Carrie's accident, has a daughter who was murdered.

I'm exhausted; I don't know why. If my aunt was not in the trucks, maybe her disappearance has nothing to do with the murder of the girls. Or maybe she was murdered because she was my dad's sister. I pulled out of the driveway, stopped at the first gas station on the road. I didn't ask Cindy how her daughter died. I looked it up. Her name was Halley Riddel. She was sixteen and coming home from her first job; her first night driving home alone. The police reported it was simply a mistake made by a new driver—she overcompensated when making a turn on the steep curve on Tinton-Robinson Road. She went off the road and they found her a day later, her gold compact car had gone over a huge embankment between Crystal Springs and Laurel Grove. It was hidden in the scrubby grass and brush. I'm not so sure myself. These strange accidents and murders all seemed to happen after Carrie was found dead. So, I made a mental note to look deeper into any deaths before Carrie to see if there were any similar.

Just as I drive off, I get a frantic call from Liam. "Did you read the newspaper today?"

"No, I've been busy."

"That girl who tried to drug me. Her name was Lydia Murphy. They found her dead in a ditch, ten miles from the little diner we stopped in on State Route 50. You think anybody saw us with her?" Liam's voice comes out in puffs of breath.

"I don't know, Liam. Shit." I scrub my face. "The waitress saw us. Everybody in that diner saw us." I bite down on my lip. "But they all saw us leave without her, right? And Rusty can corroborate—"

"Speak English, dammit! What's corroborate?"

"He can confirm the two of us left without her."

"But we were alone walking while we were waiting for Rusty." Rusty. He was gone a long time looking for a car. Crap, that's all I need. One more suspect.

"Are you there? What are we going to do?"

I sigh. "I don't know. I'm working on it, Liam. Let me think. Just let me piece some things together."

Chapter 37

"So, you believe everybody in the two trucks has a girl who was murdered." Leah's hand walks down the path of each of the pictures from the riders in the trucks to their child who was killed. "Did they all die the same way?"

"Yes, I think I'm sitting on the cusp of figuring it out right now. That's why I wanted you here. No, they aren't all the same. There are some drownings, hit and runs, and blunt force traumas. My aunt was never found, so I have to assume her death would be accomplished to make the others appear freak accidents to the police. It's the same with Lydia Murphy, who was just found in a ditch. Jay Cooper must have figured something out. That's why he made the list. It was his daughter who was the link, Gina Channel. She disappeared just like my aunt," I explain. "It was like boom! It hit me right then that he knew something and maybe Bobby or whoever caught the trailer on fire knew something that would link them to the murders. I just don't know what or even who."

"I think the timing was too perfect with you and Leah inside to be a coincidence." Colton kneels on the edge of my bed. "Two birds with one stone, right?" He points to Leah beneath Johnny's picture, then my picture beneath my daddy's. "You two are the only ones who are still alive, right?"

"That would be true if they thought I would actually be with her." I say softly. "But we have never hung around each other. The odds were slim I'd ask her to go with me."

"If Jay Cooper knew," Leah says. "I wonder why he didn't tell somebody."

"Maybe he did." I reply. "Maybe they didn't listen or threatened to kill him. He told me *'if you're dead, you can't* talk. *And they don't know your secrets.*' He could have been afraid the murderer would find out he had enough clues to know who killed the girls and that they would find a way to murder him. I'm assuming he figured out I'd be next on the list. That's why he gave me the pack. He may have been telling me to run like hell. I don't know. By the way, your Aunt Lynn managed to leave out the seventh person in your dad's truck. You know, the extra person you asked about. It was Jay Cooper. She also lied to me when she said she didn't know anything about the leather bracelet. Cindy Kent told me Doctor Stamper gave one to each of the kids who came to the funeral and that she thought were Carrie's friends; the ones in the trucks."

"She did?"

"Yeah. I don't know who to believe anymore. I'm just wondering if there isn't more, some big secret that all of them are keeping like a pact. My aunt wasn't in the trucks, but she had one. So I can't tie her in. Here look—" I reach down and bring up a newspaper article I had found on the internet. "One of the guys in your dad's truck was Billy Eaton. I was staring at his name on the wall, racking my brain. I look him up online and found a newspaper archive from the Athens Ohio Tribune." I hand the newspaper to Leah. It reads: *ANGIE DUNN. AGE 14. HIT AND RUN VICTIM IN MOVIE THEATRE PARKING LOT DIES. The driver in the hit and run death of an Albany teen hit last Saturday night when exiting the local theatre is still at large. Dunn's friends stated they left the theatre at ten o'clock. Dunn had been balancing on a curb along the sidewalk and stumbled. An early model station wagon, black, later identified as a vehicle stolen from Wagner's Gas Station in Parkersburg, WV was later found in a ditch near Chauncey—*

"Okay, now check *this* out." That's when I hold up my

cell phone for Leah. I'd stopped in at the gas station, asked Bucky to research some of the people on my list. It wasn't even three hours later that he texted me back.

"Look at this. I had a friend research this for me."

"A friend?" The corner of her mouth quirks into a half smile as she takes the phone from my fingers. I watch Colton take three steps and stop behind Leah to read over her shoulder. "I thought you didn't have any friends."

"Yeah, I've met a few recently." I don't tell her she's one. I see her eyes dart to mine before she reads the text:

Looked up the names of the people you gave me. So far, I've found these strange deaths:

John McDaniel Vehicle: Jenny Parker. Now Jenny Barger. Katylynn Barger was her daughter. Died March 1991. Found dead in bathtub May 22, 1991.

John McDaniel Vehicle: Tina Long. Now Tina Murphy. Anna Petoskey. 15 Born 1988 died in March 2003 CAME UP MISSING then was found on a beach at East Harbor State Park.

John McDaniel Vehicle: William (Billy) Eaton. Daughter, Angela Dunn, age 14. Hit and run May 22, 1994

Ray McGuire Vehicle: Arthur Todd Junior. Mina Todd. Walked in sleep and fell from roof of home in Lansing Michigan where mother lived. 1989 age 9.

Stopping here. Got to stock. But you're right. There were fires with each. Sets of three. Some were abandoned homes. Some were grass fires.

Colton has finished reading, I see him scanning the wall with a serious purse to his lips.

"I'm going to check on Gabby." Leah turns. I think she's trying to absorb all of this. I also think it hit her like a belly punch when she saw our pictures on the wall.

"Are you all right?" I ask as she passes the threshold

of the doorway.

"No," her voice sounds hollow. "No, not at all. We're on that damn list. At some point, somebody's—"

"Maybe. Maybe not." I hold up a finger. "Don't you see? The difference between all these dead girls and us? We *know*. They didn't. We can watch for it coming."

"For how long?"

"I don't know," I groan. "Until I can figure it out. Why don't you take Gabby and go hide out for a while?"

"A month, a year?" Leah rubs her face. "I can't even afford to take my kid to a fast food place, much less on an extended vacation."

I wait for her to leave. Now Colton's sober. He lowers his voice, "You know, sometimes she says she wants to die after T comes over and beats the crap out of her. Whenever something good happens to my sister, something bad happens. She's getting laid off at the school."

"Her, too, huh?" I ask him. He nods. "Like a curse." I let out a puff of air. "And it isn't because she's ever been nice to any of us McGuires."

"You're getting laid off?" Colton tips his head to the side. "Why you?"

"Because my job isn't needed."

"Who told you that? Miss Cunningham? She's a bitch," Colton shakes his head. "You're the only teacher that's not a shit."

"I'm not a teacher, Colton."

"Yeah, you are. You're Mindy's teacher and mine. Those other teachers are butts." He waves a hand in the air. "I'm quitting school. There's no way in hell I'm sitting in a class all day, like I used to before you worked in the library." It's quite possibly the only nice thing Colton has ever said to me.

"So, I guess this is like a puzzle, Colton," I tell him, pointing to the wall. "You're good at solving them. You know, you could work on doing this kind of stuff for a living. It's not boring. It's fascinating, figuring out where all those little faces go and how/when they died. Now, I just have to figure out who killed them."

"I don't know. The other Miss Mauer says I'd be better off learning a trade, going to vocational school." He shrugs. "Doesn't matter. My dad, he can't afford to pay the electric much less for college. So where do the new dead girls fit in?" Colton asks. "Or do they?"

I stare at him long and hard. I'm not fighting with him over an education today. I sigh and turn my attention to the wall. "I haven't even gotten that far yet. I've still got some I haven't identified. I mean, I just got all this information today. It is a work in progress. I assume they are related somehow. I mean, it's nothing more than a hypothesis, if you want the technical term—"

"So, it's true?"

"No, a hypothesis is just speculation; you know, an assumption that could explain a reason and is based on just a little bit of information. There could be hundreds of hypotheses to a situation. Like when Mister Cunningham was trying to figure out which of you was smoking in the bathroom at school. Based on the smell of your clothes and the snarky look on your face last week, he hypothesized it was you."

"It *wasn't* me."

"Well, his second hypothesis was that Josh Baer was the one with the cigarettes; he also stank like cigarette smoke and had a snarky look on his face. So, when you've got a hypothesis, you test it, see if there is proof behind it. If you've got enough evidence to find proof and justify it, then you have a theory. Mister Cunningham chose Josh to test his theory. Such, the evidence was the three packs of cigarettes found in Josh's locker. So—when there is evidence to support the hypothesis, it becomes a theory. Mister Cunningham's guess became theory."

"Oh." He looks at me blandly. "Well, whatever, but that's Bailey Sefton," Colton shakes his head, looks away. He points at a picture near my bed post. "You remember her? She went to school with me until tenth grade."

"Went?"

"She killed herself two years ago. There were three kids who committed suicide that year. Bailey was one of them. Two were in high school. One was in seventh grade."

"Yeah, I remember. Bailey Sefton." My eyes walk down the pictures. I stop at one boy on the end of Johnny McDaniel's side. "Well, there's Ben Sefton." I snatch up my computer, type in the names. Sure enough, Bailey was Ben's daughter. She used a .22 caliber pistol to kill herself. There's a forum talking about her death. They found her—

"They found Bailey's body at the quarry," I whisper.

"What does that mean?" Colton furrows his brow while he leans over with his hands on his knees peering at the pictures.

"That's where Angel Dougherty was found."

"Miss Mauer, this is one of the girls who committed suicide too." Colton's voice is quiet while he uses his index finger and thumb to pinch the curled sides of another picture back. "I didn't know her that well, but her first name was Tianna." He turns and looks at me. I see the realization on his face. I drop my eyes to my computer, perform a search for: Bailey Sefton, Tianna, suicide. I scan the results. And I see an online newspaper: *Rash of Suicides Leaves Community in Stunned Mourning. It is quiet in two little towns just west of Crystal Springs, Ohio—Coal Grove and East Milton. Over the course of five weeks, three young girls have taken their lives—Tianna Lynn of Coal Grove, and Bailey Sefton and Kelsey Savings, who was only thirteen years-old. Local school psychologist, Mary Stamper, has been taking on extra hours counseling students with grief management. She states suicide in children is on the rise, and most parents and teachers don't have the proper tools to detect depression. "The signs of depression aren't always easy to detect in our children," Stamper states at a news conference recently. "A child might appear happy and then suddenly, parents find themselves wondering what went wrong—" Local police state the girls were acting alone in each incidence—*

"Colton, get the sticky tack and put Tianna Lynn under Davie Lynn. Davie was in my daddy's truck."

Colton blinks at me and nods. Then he quietly picks up the sticky tack on my bed stand and the picture of Tianna before he knee-walks across the bed and sticks the girl's picture beneath her father's. I flip through the news articles, find the obituary for Kelsey Savings. She found the key to Larry Saving's gun locker and shot herself with his hunting rifle. And sure enough, the town of Crystal Springs put on a marathon benefit for Kelsey, complete with a picture of her smiling face.

I step over to the side of the bed, lean and point to the matching newspaper picture in the random pile. "That's Kelsey Savings. She was the thirteen year-old who committed suicide. She goes under Linda Savings on my dad's side." He looks back, gives me this long and lingering gaze. His lips have lost the usually smart-alecky grin.

"It wasn't suicide, was it?" he asks me in a hoarse voice. "Wait. Are you hypothesizing they were *murdered*?"

Ah, it does sink in. "I am. You? To people who don't know what we know, it almost sounds like a suicide pact. But with this information, and the fact they all committed suicide around the same date, May 22nd; I would speculate that is correct. If this is freaking you out, you can stop."

"No, I don't want to stop."

"Oh, holy hell—" I whisper. "Hold that thought. It's the quarry." I take off to my kitchen, snatch up the newspaper article my mom left on my refrigerator. I ramble back in, holding it up for Colton to see. "Here's the link."

"The quarry?"

"No, I mean, the quarry helped me link Bailey to Angel because I remembered Angel was found there. But by identifying the girls who allegedly committed suicide, you helped me find that link to the three girls found dead recently—or—or at least one. It's their parents."

Angel Daugherty from South Milan, whose obituary my mom pasted on my refrigerator, was the daughter of Johnny Baker. Johnny Baker was in my dad's truck that night. And Phoebe Wells who had been attacked on State Route 32 just a month and a half ago was the daughter of Michelle McCorkle. I found her obituary and her mom's name mentioned as one of the survivors.

"Miss Mauer?"

I'm standing back, taking in the wall, thinking my head is going to explode with this new information when Colton interrupts my thoughts.

"Yeah?"

"You've got one picture left." He's pointing to a lone image of a young woman, a recent addition to my list. "Where does she go?"

"Her name is Lydia Murphy. She's not from Ohio, didn't grow up here. Her family is from Massachusetts." I had just cut her picture from today's newspaper. "She was found dead along the highway. I don't know where she fits in. Just like my aunt, who wasn't in the trucks. And Alaina Windowski. They are what keeps me thinking this is all random. I mean, even Phoebe Wells is off a bit—she wasn't killed on May 21st."

"Did you hear what you just said, Miss Mauer?" Colton's eyes are wide. "The random death or disappearance is what shifts your focus away from the murders in front of you. What if those three were killed as a tactic to make the police look someplace else so there isn't something common? I mean, the main objective of the killer is murder. I would think as long as their target died, they might go off track a little so they don't get caught."

Chapter 38

I've got a lover. It is *my caramelo*, Emmanuel. It sounds funny saying it. And nobody would believe me if I told them I'm dating a guy that flies me out in private jets to wherever he's working. Twice this week, I've been to New York. Once, I went to a resort in New Jersey, and another time, somewhere along the coast of California.

I haven't seen any drugs. I think Liam is lying. Besides, I'm willing to let certain things slide right now. Being with Emmanuel helps ease the pain in a quiet house without Baby Cakes. It takes my mind off all the dead girls on my wall and knowing me and Leah are next. Just before Leah and Colton left that night, Leah asked me if I was going to go to the police. She didn't ask *when;* she asked *if.* I know why. Because knowing all this opened the door for the cops to point a finger at our dads. Because they don't want a finger pointed at one of their own. Bobby? Arnold Kinney? We're the only ones alive. I told them we should wait a week. Maybe I can figure out who it is then, problem solved. Leah reminded me that if I don't say anything and they murder us, nobody may ever know.

I'm beginning to enjoy having a secret life. Nobody harasses me about staying out too late or wearing a dress that my mom would call too slinky. On Saturday, I spent all day in Mexico. On Sunday morning, Mom asked me how I got a sunburn. It had been a cloudy week in Ohio. I shrugged and told her it must be a rash, I ate shrimp for supper last night. Mom doesn't question me farther, tells me how bad tanning beds are for the skin. However, Nicky eyes me suspiciously all day. And Rocky eyes her eying me. I suppose I have that after-sex glow about me. Maybe she can pick it up. Maybe he can too. I can't stop grinning either.

Emmanuel, he is so passionate. He likes to surprise me. I mean, it isn't just unanticipated gifts, like a teddy bears and rings. He has a thing about jumping out around corners to startle me into a yelp. He hides and then jumps out at me. He gives me little cans with a fake snakes in them, and he thinks it is funny to shock me with a little hand-shake shocker. He once even pretended he was going to jump out of the plane we were flying in.

But what Emmanuel lacks in maturity, he makes up for in passion. He is constantly touching me, kissing me, and on our first night together, he laid hundreds of fresh rose petals on the bed. He knows *where* to kiss me. I get goosepimples when he tickles the back of my neck with his lips. He knows *how* to kiss me. They aren't soft and gentle. They are well-placed, thought out, hard, and sensual. And I don't have to feel awkward in my Violet skin, even while we are pulling the petals our of our hair. And yet, the entire time I worry my violet-colored eye contacts will pop out. I'm troubled he'll discover I'm just a backwards daughter of a southern Ohio redneck, not some mysterious woman who he feels he always has to poke words into the translator on his phone and guess who I am.

"A spy?" he asked me the other day. "A dancer? Warrior?" He rolled his finger along the hard bump of muscle on my arm I've gotten from working out at the country club five days a week. "A movie star?"

A spy, I liked that. Of course, if he had watched me dig out an old guitar from my closet on Thursday afternoon and drive an hour and a half to Williams Easy Pawn in Columbus, he would believe it. I've got a beanie hat on my head, jeans on my legs, t-shirt on my top, and a pair of wire-rimmed glasses I bought at the Laurel Grove Dollar Store. Emmanuel would probably say I was a spy. Mom would call me crazy.

Once again, I'm out of my comfort zone and stretching my legs to the point my chest feels tight with anxiety. It's not just the clothing that's so different from my style. Tag Williams's store is on the cruddy side of town, surrounded by old brick buildings and crackled concrete sidewalks. Online, it says he sells musical instruments, jewelry, guns, and flat screen TVs. He pays cash for gold.

His store is stuffy and it isn't much more than a worn glass counter running from one end of the room to the other. It's four walls of hanging guitars, computers on shelves, and stuff I've seen at yard sales crammed in every nook and cranny. There's a dusty deer head on the wall. When I walk through the doorway, he greets me with a grunt while he watches a show on an old TV settled on the wall.

"Bein' a rock star ain't working out for you, baby?" he drawls while I lug the guitar up and slap it on the counter. "What you got to sell?"

"Um, my guitar. I'm making more money working at a gas station selling pita pockets and gas than I'm making singing at cruddy bars. I got rent to pay and a six year-old to feed," I tell him. "What can you give for this thing?"

"Twenty bucks. I got ten of them up on the walls. Same thing." He points upward with a gnarled finger; sure enough, there are guitars hanging an inch apart all the way from one end to the other.

It's probably worth about a hundred and twenty, my old guitar. At least that's how much the same guitars were going for at two of the online auctions. Mom bought it new when I was in the seventh grade and had to have it, it was probably over four hundred dollars.

"It's my bread and butter. Can't take less than a hundred," I lie. I know he'll never give me that much for it.

"Sorry, baby. Can't do it."

I nod, start to leave, then turn around. "I really need the money. You're not hiring here, are you?"

"How bad you need the cash?"

"Are you asking how far I'd go to feed my kid?" I laugh sarcastically. Wow, this is coming way too easily for me. "Because we're down to one jar of peanut butter in the cabinet and a spoiled jug of milk in the 'fridge."

"I need errands run. You up for something like that?"

"Sure. I'll do what it takes." I sigh, lift the little sack I've got dangling in my fingers. I wiggle out the little wallet and ID card for Lydia Murphy and hold it up for Tag to see. "Kind of like the stuff Lydia did?"

Tag pales, making the dark circles under his eyes look red-brown. "No, shit. Are you a cop?"

"You know they found her body on State Route 32 in Adams County, right?"

"I saw the news."

"What's Lydia's story? Who'd want to kill her?"

"You're a cop, aren't you?" Tag slams a fist on his counter. "Damn! I *knew* this was going to happen." He looks up, pokes a finger at me. "You can tell your boss I didn't have anything to do with it. I just gave her name to somebody who gave me five hundred bucks to find a messenger. Once that paper leaves my hand, it ain't no different than somebody passing off a babysitting job to a fourteen year-old. I contract, that's *all*."

"Unless it isn't a babysitting job," I point out. "And the phone number you gave the fourteen year-old belongs to a murderer."

"I got no way of knowing that. I get some people coming in here to find old records or roller skates or to sell their guitars for money to put gas in their cars." He leans over the edge of the counter, pokes a finger at the

WILLIAM'S EASY PAWN sign. "I get others looking for somebody to run an errand for them, provide a delivery service." He cranes his neck over his shoulder, uses his pencil to tap a dusty sign that says: WILLIAMS EXPRESS DELIVERY. "Sometimes when the former needs a lot of money and the latter will pay enough, the two worlds collide." Tag sits back, sighs with his chubby elbows folded over his chest. "This old guy, he comes in and he has an errand. That girl, Lydia, she comes in and needs cash. I think, well, I can fix these two up and make them both happy. That's all."

"Except your former is desperate for cash and your latter is going to break the law and doesn't want to get caught." He doesn't answer, just looks up to the little TV blaring above his counter.

"That's all I'm saying. Bring it on. I got clean hands."

"Who was it?" I'm trying to play it cool. But Lydia Murphy is not fitting into any of the categories of girls on my wall. No family member was in my dad's car, none were in Johnny's. The only link I think I can use to connect it is that someone was trying to set up Liam again, make it appear he was the killer. I have to assume they are out of the police circle and the information that Liam has alibis now. "I mean, if it's somebody else's fault, what do you have to lose?"

"My life, dammit!" he growls. "The guy just dropped off an envelope with a note and a phone number. I gave it to—what was her name?"

"Lydia."

"Yeah Lydia. And she was supposed to call him, get directions on what he wanted and what she needed to do. Lydia called and said she opened the envelope and there was white stuff in a baggie. She didn't want to touch it. I told her if she didn't do the job, she wasn't getting paid. He gave me five hundred bucks in cash in an envelope for payment. She must have needed the money. Check her cell phone. She must have called them."

"Her cell phone is locked with a password. I can't crack it." I shake my head. I tried every word and number combination I could come up with and none worked. "So what was in the bag?"

He looks at me, expression dropping. "I don't know what was in the bag. I told you that. I was given instructions to hand it off to Lydia."

"And what did this man look like?"

"He was old," Tag holds out his hands to his sides. "He looked like an old guy—gray hair and not much of it. Skinny. He was pretty skinny. I get a million people in here. I don't look at half of them." Tag turns, brings up a white plastic dollar store basket with receipts and keys and an odd array of knickknacks in it. He plops it down and rifles through it. He stops twice and holds up a little piece of receipt with writing. The second one, he slaps down between us, then uses his index finger to push it toward me. "That's it. That's all I got."

I take it. But my eyes move upward to the corner of the room. Surveillance cameras in two of the four corners. "You had video cameras running, too, right?" I watch Tag look upward. He lets out a long breath and his entire body deflates before he nods his head.

"Yeah, and I got that."

Chapter 39

Barry M. Underwood 555-2368. That's all the note says. I called it as a phone number with local area codes. Nothing. I looked up the name, the phone number. Either they were fake or Tag was pulling my leg. I add it to the little imaginary pile of puzzle pieces I'm collecting that don't fit together. It's tacked up above my bed with the rest of the information. I gave Tag my cell phone number. Told him to call me if he remembers anything else; it probably wasn't the smartest move. The beanie cap, jeans, and t-shirt are stuffed into a plastic grocery sack and hidden in my closet.

Oh, and I got eleven minutes of a blurry shadow man in a long black coat and wearing a hat from Tag's dollar store security camera. The face is barely visible and the entire thing is like slow motion. Still, I made a copy of the video tape and then, I watch it on my phone. Over and over, I look at it trying to decipher any characteristics of the shadow man.

"Hey, Rocky's here with Tangy Cunningham. You know that?"

I look up from my phone. Leah is leaning over my shoulder at the table in her waitress uniform and juggling a tray with a water. I'm stuffed tightly into a pocket beside Liam and Janine Pritchard and a wedding party at the country club. Janine is the mayor of Crystal Spring's daughter. She's tall, blonde, and seldom gets the chance to come to the country club because Jack Barkley and Mark Pritchard are on the opposite ends of the political table.

Tonight, however, the daughter of the mayor of Crystal Springs is here. I thought at first, Janine was only socially flirting with Liam because she was mad at her father. I heard father and daughter outside the doors, bickering all the way into the building. On the contrary. Liam pulled me aside and told me he invited Janine and her father, so they could get a taste of a formal wedding reception at the country club. It's a clever move, I suppose, and surprising that he is taking an interest in the business.

"Rocky's here. Did you hear me?"

"Oh. No." It's all I can say while my mind reels with tiny movies of different scenes that are going to play out over the next few days as my secret gets out. I follow her gaze to the fourth table. Oh, my God. Yeah, it is Rocky and he's drinking a beer, leaning inward trying to hear whatever Tangy's saying in the loud room.

Leah swings her arm around, places the water in front of me and her voice is low. "I'm just giving you a heads up so you can maintain that low profile required by the boss." She gives me a snarky smile and a head waggle. I roll my eyes wondering what her ulterior motives are. "By the way, did your sister find Gabby's FBI badge? She's been crying herself to sleep over it."

"Yeah, I've got it in my car. I'll stick it on your windshield if I leave before you." I whisper, trying to drag my gaze from Rocky when she ducks close. "You know I'm the one who watches her when Rocky's on call, right?"

"Yeah, I figured that out when she wanted a guinea pig." She nods.   "You find anything more on the murders?" Leah stares at me sharply.

"Yes and no. I'm trying to tie the girl who was murdered this week into the picture and I can't. Her name was Lydia Murphy."

I get an elbow in my ribs and Leah backs up. It's the bride and she thinks I'm a celebrity niece from wherever Mister Barkley hails and she's drunk-told me that with a toast to the entire crowd at least eight times. Because Liam

SHAY LAWLESS

told her that as a joke and, I think, a ploy to sneak off with Janine and show her the building. But the bride grabbed my hand and has dragged me everywhere, like a kindergartener with a newfound bestie on the playground.

I'm not so comfortable with being in the fold of the pretty, popular girls and her friends are gorgeous. She's dragged me along with her to dance with every song. I just sat down and I'm completely and utterly worn out. That's about the time Leah came sidling up next to me. I've seen her a few times in the last few hours. She's wearing a black skirt and a white blouse, with a white apron overtop. She's working the events tonight for a few extra bucks, helping the caterers serve food and drinks. It's packed. I can hardly hear her over the music.

"I thought you might have figured it out and didn't tell me," Leah grumbled with a grumpy twist to her lips. "Just like you forgot to warn me your daddy dammed up the creek out back of his barn so my daddy can't get water to his cows."

"Yeah, do you want to go there?" I ask her, leaning in so nobody else can hear. "My daddy said your cousin, Troy, tossed a roll of firecrackers into the back of his trailer full of pigs when he drove past—"

She shakes her head. "I might punch you later for that," she says, but she's wearing a faint smile when she bangs my chair hard with her hip. Is she bantering with me or bullying me? I can't tell. She rolls her eyes toward Rocky's table. "You think he'll tell your sister?" Leah asks. She's acting like she's taking an order. I sigh.

"I don't know. Maybe I'll tell on him that he's here with a date." I'm not worried about that at all. I'm worried about what Rocky thinks of me. I groan inwardly. I suppose I should make the best of it. I take a paper napkin and snatch up Leah's pen from her fingers. I write: *Dance with me. I'll make it worth your time.* I close it quickly, give it to Leah. "Here. Give this to him. Tell him the girl at the *big kids table* wants a dance with him."

She gives me a funny glance, then nods. I watch her walk over to Rocky's table. And I see her hand him the napkin, then wag a thumb toward me. Rocky looks up. He squints and leans into Leah. There's a short conversation before she returns to me.

"Um, Rocky says he's flattered. You are pretty. But he's with another girl. He doesn't want to offend her."

"You're kidding me, right?" I look around Leah's arm; I can see Rocky looking over at me. He's got a strangely formal smile on his face that I would like to wipe off with my fist right now. Jerk. "You can tell him he's an ass," I tell Leah.

"Are you sure?" She looks over her shoulder. "Because, *Violet,* I've got to be honest. I don't think he knows it is you with your red highlights and makeup."

"What?" I sniff a laugh. "Yes, he does. He has to know it's me." I pick up my cell phone. It's the work one, but I type in Rocky's cell phone number and text him: *If you could have a wish, what would it be?*

"I really don't think he does," she reiterates, shaking her head. "He asked me *why me?* And then he said *isn't that kind of strange? Was she joking*?"

"Well, he will now. I just texted him. How would Violet know his number?"

Ting. I look down at my phone. It's a reply from Rocky. *I wish I wasn't at this stupid wedding.*

I text back: *Where would you wish to be?*

I look up at Leah who is pretending to take an order. "Because he thinks I just gave it to you?" she sighs. "He *doesn't* know, Violet. You really shouldn't do whatever you're doing. It's mean. And he's going to find out and blow your cover."

"Blow my cover," I giggle. "You make me sound like I'm deep undercover." Leah doesn't laugh along. I read Rocky's next text: *A million miles away. Some Mexican beach.*

I just got back from Mexico. And a beach. I send him a picture of my feet when I was lying down in a lounge chair. You can see my freshly-painted, cherry red toenails, a sandy beach, and the horizon.

Sweet.

Sweet. I've never heard Rocky say that word in that context. I look up and he's giving me a sad smile before Tangy bangs him with her elbow to get his attention. I see her talking to another girl, pumping her head up and down like they are deep in conversation. Rocky gives me an eye roll and a grin, turns away. But before he leaves that night, I get one last text: *Maybe I'll see you around—my friends call me Rock.*

Rock? I giggle a bit to myself. Then I send him a thumbs up emoji.

Chapter 40

I suppose I might be a chicken. But when it comes to my daddy, I'm like a mother hen protecting her chick. At ten after three the next day, I get a call from my daddy. He sounds far away.

"Baby, can you come down to the police station and pick me up?"

"What—?" I start, as my heart drops. "What happened? Are you okay?" And I can't imagine how difficult it must have been for my daddy to tell me he'd been detained by the Laurel Grove Police Department. Officer Timmy Kinney had pulled him over coming home from work yesterday. "I wasn't speeding like he said. And I weren't drunk. But they got my car, said they was going to check it for evidence. I need a ride home."

Evidence. "Was it because of the ATV?" Long silence. "I'll go tell them the truth. I'll tell them I stole it from you."

"Naw, baby, don't do that. It's something else."

It had been a quiet ride back. Daddy was pale and sullen, asked about my job at the country club. He wouldn't answer my questions. When I start to turn off the car to come inside with him, he holds out a hand. "No, Rosie, you need to stay away for a while. Until they get this thing figured out. I don't want you getting involved."

"Involved in what?"

"Junior and I went fishing at the quarry all the time last summer. Right around the time that Daugherty girl was dumped there." Junior Todd. He is a boyhood friend of my daddy's. They've been fishing together since they were old enough to put a worm on a pole.

"Oh, Daddy," I whisper. I push my hand to my lips. I

know why they are picking on him; to pull focus away from Timmy Kinney and Bobby. When I pointed a finger at Timmy Kinney the day he dragged me into the police station, I inadvertently forced them to direct the attention away from the police. "I'm coming with you. I don't care."

"No. That cop, Timmy Kinney, he threatened me. Said he'd drag you down if he saw you with me—so stay away, baby girl. At least until things get back to normal."

"But, Daddy," I try to meet his eyes. I don't want to tell him it's my fault. "I've been finding stuff on the murders since you gave me Aunt Roo's stuff. I think it's because of the truck race between you and Johnny. I've almost got—"
—it figured out.

I don't get to finish. Daddy's head pops up. His eyes are a bit wild and big. "Little girl," he growls gruffly. "Stop. What have you been doing?"

"I thought that's what you wanted. You said maybe I could figure out why Aunt Roo disappeared."

"I wanted you to figure out what you felt was missing between you and your aunt. You're always asking about her. Oh, honey, you've got to stop. You listen to me, do you hear me? You can't be the one holding the stick over the hornet's nest. Not you." He reaches out, latches on to my shoulder. I wince. His fingers are gentle upon my skin, however, his eyes boring into mine show something I have never seen before—fear. "You may be too old to put over my knee, but I'm telling you to stay away!"

"I'll stay away, but you didn't know what happened to Carrie Stamper, did you? You aren't hiding something?"

Daddy literally blanches. His face turns a creamy shade of white; he looks like one of the wax museum figures. "Why you asking that?" he asks hoarsely.

"I don't know. Do you—do you—" I stutter. "Did

somebody you know kill her and make it look like an accident or something?" I ask slowly.

"No," Daddy says sharply. "You could go through a long list of people and I'd tell you the same thing because I don't know nobody who would have killed her or any of them girls who died. And I don't know nobody who'd have killed my sister. Nobody."

"Don't be mad at me," I snatch a bit of hair and chew on it. Daddy's stern look falls and slips into a sad smile.

"Baby, I'm never mad at you. Never."

"You were mad when I lost your ATV."

"Maybe a little," he chides me with a teasing grin. "Stay here a minute. I'll be right back."

I wait in the silence of my car. My mind is whirling with something I can only describe as doubt and angst and all those things Daddy's little girl never wants to see on her kind-hearted, loving father. Fear. He's supposed to be fearless. I realize for the first time in my life, my daddy isn't perfect, isn't superman. It makes me feel small and vulnerable.

His shadow works its way to the shed behind his house. He's gone maybe five minutes before he comes back with a little box in the palm of his hands. He says nothing, but opens the passenger side of the car and sets it on the seat. "You got to hide this somewhere. Don't let the cops have it." I nod dumbly.

"I promise I won't, daddy," I say. "I won't."

"Because the cops, they say it is either me or Johnny who killed those girls. And it weren't me. So you stay away from him, you got me? Because I think he's been putting stuff in my shed to frame me. That, right there, weren't in my shed, Rosie, until a few weeks ago. I know it. Get and go."

SHAY LAWLESS

Chapter 41

"You can't kiss someone in a busy coffee shop and make it look sexy. It's like trying to add a sex scene to a workout tape." I'm sitting in Burbank's Coffee and Books on a comfy leather couch. Rocky is plopped on a recliner next to me, with the fireman's pre-test booklet in his lap. He's still a bit churlish that I called in another 9-1-1 to get him here. He chastised me and said if I keep calling wolf, when a real wolf comes along, he's not going to be there to protect me. I told him I could take care of myself.

"You can make anything sexy if you want." He's feeling a bit cocky right now for figuring out the puzzle I gave him. I don't divulge I know he got help from Mindy Carter, who is in his study hall. But I figure he's utilizing management skills for having her decipher my coded message so he could get here. We've been here almost two hours studying and I think he's probably at his threshold.

"Bull. Not the stuff I like."

"Cop stuff? Crime stuff?"

"Yeah. It's facts and—"

"Okay, try this—" Rocky clasps his hands, leans his elbows on the table. "The detective stares hard at the male corpse on the ground. He doesn't look at the police officer standing next to him. He doesn't have to see the officer. In his mind, she's beautiful with long, black hair sweeping down her back. He imagines her taking off her hat, the dark hair tucked into it, falling down her shoulders. He imagines her slipping off her uniform shirt, even while she eyes the one bullet settled stark and alone next to the victim. *Kiss me,* she says in his mind. *Kiss me.* The detective wants to reach out his hand, clasp hers in his own while he studies the body. But he is, for the moment, more intrigued by something else. There is no wound. How did the man die?"

I realize I'm leaning into the table while he talks. I suppose I'm somewhat surprised I'm intrigued. "Okay, go on," I say, mildly embarrassed when Rocky gets a smug smile on his face. "How are you going to slide something sexy into your story, a kiss or something? And how the hell did he die?"

Rocky holds up a finger, looks right to left and then scoots over to the couch and plops down next to me like he doesn't want anyone to hear. "The detective steps forward, knows the officer follows. He hears her footsteps. *Kiss me,* he hears in his head with every step. It's like she's begging him. *Kiss me. Kiss me.* He squats down next to the body, shakes his head. *He is dead, but what killed him?* His eyes work to the evidence marker while he sees the shadow of the officer hover over him. He feels her warmth when she kneels down next to him. She lays a gentle hand on his shoulder, leans into him so her lips almost brush his ear. *I am to blame for this,* she confesses. *He died of a broken heart.*

"That's not romantic. It's sick." I roll my eyes, twist my lips around. "Kiss me. Kiss me. Who says that?"

"I'm not done." Rocky pokes me in the side and I grunt. "Suddenly, the detective turns, snatches up the officer, and he hears her say—"

"Kiss me—" I interrupt with a giggle.

I can't believe I fell for it. Rocky slides across the couch, grabs me around the small of my back and pulls me toward him. He's got one hand behind my neck and is holding me so tightly, I can hardly breathe when his lips slam on to mine. It's rough and incredibly sexy, my belly makes six little jumps before I realize I haven't taken a breath. I remember counting in my mind, like I used to between the flash of lightening and then the growl of thunder; one-one-thousand, two-one-thousand, three-one-thousand—a trick my mom taught me to tell how far a storm is from where we stood at that moment.

I am somewhere between twelve-one-thousand and thirteen-one-thousand when he releases me. I know I just sit there, staring at him with my lips slightly parted and the same stupid look on my face as Colton McDaniel had the other day, when he accidently ran smack into the glass door in the library. I blink, tip my head to the side and try not to take in the faces around us who might have seen what just happened.

"I need some coffee," I mumble. I know everybody's staring at me while I stand and spill all the papers from my lap. Rocky just sits there, self-righteous and taking it all in. I'm trying to be cool, kneeling on the floor, snatching up the papers blowing here and there from a ceiling fan while the onlookers turn away with little smiles on their faces. What the hell?

"You're just ticked off because I proved a point," Rocky tells me when I sit back down on the couch. I don't tell him the girl who made my coffee leaned in and told me it was the sexiest kiss she'd ever seen in her life. "You liked it. I know you did."

"Oh, my God, Rocky, stop!" I hiss. "Quit being so arrogant. Would you please finish? I've got to get to my waitressing job. You're one chapter away from taking your test and then, you're ready to go."

He holds up both hands and then drops them so he can pick up his book. He still doesn't lose his haughty grin until I say those words.

"What if I don't pass?"

"You'll pass." I don't look up. "You know how to do the math. You know how to answer the questions. You just need to sit back, take a deep breath during the test, and treat it like you did that kiss. You'll blow them away."

His head pops up and that arrogant smirk is back. "It was good, wasn't it?"

"Yeah, if I was the type of girl who liked that kind of stuff." Why the hell am I trying to hide a grin?

But I know the kiss was just superficial. He's been texting Violet non-stop as soon as I leave. And he always ends the conversation with: *See you around. Rock.* I think he's in love with her. I think she's an easy way to boost his ego. I haven't quite figured out how I'm going to broach the subject. I'm in too deep to divulge who I am now, tell him my about my secret life.

Rocky has three weeks until the test in Crystal Springs. I've got a month and a half to figure out how I'm going to get my daddy's ATV back. Nicky told me Bobby told her Timmy Kinney is going to buy it at the auction, just out of spite to whoever left the scene. He's been telling everybody around town he's going to ride it up and down Troublesome Creek, just to rub it in.

Rocky excuses himself. I know he's feigning going to the restroom so he can text Violet. Later, I get six messages. I answer them with a quick snatch of my purse. Don't judge me. I'm smart enough to realize he'd never be with me as Rosie. I'm smart enough to know I can never be with him as Violet. But most of all, I'm bright enough to know I want to be with him on any level and I'm hoping it doesn't end. But I know, soon, it will.

Chapter 42

I'd put off opening it, the box Daddy gave me. I don't know why. I suppose I'm just overwhelmed. It's a wooden box half the size of a shoebox with copper hinges—a miniature pirate's treasure box with a tiny padlock holding it shut. I have to wedge the tool end of a Phillips-head screwdriver between the body and the shackle to break the lock.

Before I even open it, I almost stretch my arm out to call Rocky. I know I shouldn't. I want to share it with him. I mean, I know why. I think inside I've grown to love him. I should have deduced it long ago. I suppose the second I spilled the papers all over the floor at the coffee shop, it sunk in. I probably always have and tossed it out as a crush. I mean, who hasn't had a crush on a sister's boyfriend, right? But I know he's out of my reach, so I've learned to hold those feelings at bay and take what little I get of him—bits and pieces. I mean, I see him every day at school. He's always with my sister. Those little encounters seemed to sate my appetite. I mean, well, I knew he'd never be mine. So I stop, pull my hand back. Instead, I take out my phone, push the little icon with the camera and pull up my pictures with Emmanuel.

Ten, twenty—I think there's forty pictures of him with me. Swimming, dining, hotel rooms. I look at him in the images and wait for the smallest of tingles in my tummy, like I get when I'm around Rocky. Nothing. I think I almost feel like a whore—and the realization sits like the second a sip of spoilt milk hits the tongue. Is that what I am to him? Or is that what he is to me? Because it is just going places and sex. We haven't even bothered to learn each other's languages. I don't know his favorite ride at an amusement park or his mom's name. I don't know his favorite color or his birthday. But I can tell you it drives him crazy when I straddle his hips and ride him like a wild pony.

Fanning through the pictures, I pause on one I took of Emmanuel leaning against a hotel bedroom doorway two minutes after we made a playful bounce on the bed. I realize barring the intimate moments we spend together, there's always someone following us with an arsenal of guns. In the image catching my eye, I see a door slightly ajar I hadn't noticed before. Oh, there's three men with semi-automatics resting on a table and watching us even while we're *alone*.

My cheeks burn. I turn my attention to Aunt Roo's box. It opens wide. I peer inside. There's a little plastic figure of a duck and a pink lip gloss. Then, holy shit, I look at the bottom and there's a half of an instant Polaroid picture. It is cut with a jagged edge. I slip my fingers in, dig it out.

I shove my glasses up the bridge of my nose and I ogle an almost mirror image of myself ten years ago. It is Aunt Roo. She's wearing jean shorts and a t-shirt and giving the camera a peace sign. She's got her right arm flopped lazily over a guy's shoulder. He's got to be Colton's dad. He's wearing jeans and a black t-shirt with JETHRO TULL across the front. He's laughing. My Aunt Roo's laughing. And to her left, there's a blonde haired girl. She's got a slight smile, like she's had enough of all the silly. She's teeny and model perfect. I can see someone next to her, a bit of tan elbow but the rest is ripped off, missing.

So my Aunt Roo was friends with Johnny? I let that thought soak in while I dig to see if the other half of the picture is inside the box. It's not. I wonder why my aunt cut him or her out of the picture. Then I slip over to my bed stand and pick up the copy of the newspaper Colton had made for me about the alleged wreck. I tug it out. The face of Carrie Stamper staring at me from the newspaper is almost an exact duplicate of the face in the Polaroid. I put down the picture. It occurs to me somebody had to be taking the picture and knew the secret they were friends. Someone else is in the picture and had been cut out. I look at the clock. It is six-thirty. I start to rise, thinking I'll just take a drive to Johnny's doublewide and ask him face to face. Just then, there's a knock on my front door. I make a quick exit, close and lock my bedroom door.

"Where have you been?" It's Nicky. She's sliding inside and waving a hand toward the lock I just unlatched. "And why did you deadbolt your door?"

"I always use the deadbolt," I tell her. At least, since I started putting pictures of dead girls up on my wall.

She looks at me warily. Nicky knows better. "You completely missed Mom's cookout at the park!"

"Cookout?"

"Oh, my God! Rosie, what on earth is going on with you? We had a cookout for Mom's birthday this afternoon. I told you this a hundred times."

I stare at the wall, shake my head. I'm sure she didn't. Or maybe I've just been so focused on figuring out the murders, I hadn't stopped long enough to listen.

"Listen, you have missed every Sunday lunch and most of the Tuesdays at the buffet," she tells me. Then Nicky looks up at the ceiling. "Okay, we're going there, I suppose. I didn't want to do this on Mom's birthday. But I'm going to just say it—so what other drugs are you doing?"

"I'm not doing drugs."

"Okay, well, I know you're lying," she sneers. "Because I found a little plastic baggie with—"

"It was *you* who got into my purse?"

"Yes, I got in your purse!" she shouts at me with her hands up. Nicky has a way of flipping her hair with her hand when she's confronting someone. She takes her forefinger and flicks it back, then shakes her head just a bit. She's doing it now while her chin lifts. "And I'll do it again. You're acting nuts. You're acting like a lunatic."

"Stay out of my stuff," I hiss at her. I stand up straight, hold out my hand. "Now, get out."

"No, Rosie, I swear to God I will have you committed to a drug rehab if I have to—Bobby says—"

"I wouldn't listen to him. He tried to murder me—"

"Bobby? You're paranoid, you know that right? Mom's Bobby?" She laughs out loud, a forced cackle that bounces off the walls. "Okay, I gave that baggie to Bobby and he took it and had it analyzed. It had a chemical inside called Rohypnol. Do you know what that is?"

"I said, get out."

"It was crushed up pills. They estimated there were three of them. Roofies. They were frigging roofies, Rosie! Do you know what those are?" she asks me. "It's a drug that has been used to put into people's drinks—a date rape drug. The chemical makes the brain react so the person taking it is less—inhibited. Do you know what happens to school faculty known to have drugs on their person? They get administrative leave. What if they believe you were giving these to students? You could go to jail for twenty years. Are you taking these or was somebody trying to give you these drugs, Rosie? Is one of your cousins dealing to you?"

Oh, that was an emotional slap in the face. I see her eyes roam around the house. She pushes her arm out, veers right around me. "Why's your bedroom door closed? I'm going to tell you this. One of the guys at the fire department saw Colton McDaniel driving your car the other day. Are you dealing to him? Are you—*sleeping* with him?"

"Oh, my—" I can't even speak. I bite down hard on my lip and stomp down the entranceway. "I don't have to answer to you, Nicky—you assume I'm that kind of person just because of my daddy! At least mine comes to see me. Yours hasn't been around since you were eight." My sister is stunned for a moment. She recovers quickly. "Move." She wags her hand at me. I'm between her and my bedroom, blocking her path with my arms.

"Really? *Really*?" she repeats, like she's recapping for dramatic effect. "You know, it's your fault my dad doesn't come around, you manipulating, lying *bitch*. You told Doctor Stamper when you were little that he hit you. Mom kicked him out and had a restraining order placed on him. But you know what Doctor Stamper told me four years ago? She said you show all the signs of a pathological liar *and* a sociopath—you are anti-social and just plain weird. She didn't know it when you were six and showed her the bruises. But she believes you put them there yourself now. Just like when you said you were abducted. You weren't. You ran away and probably hit your head into a wall to get that bump. Doctor Stamper pulled Mom aside and told her all this. That's why she's seeing her. Now, even Bobby thinks we're at the point we need to intervene before this goes too far. Get out of my way."

To think my own sister would shove me aside and wrestle with my bedroom doorknob left me numb. Seeing her turn, blink once, and then shove her shoulder to my door to strike it hard enough to break the cheap lock, leaves me stunned. "Holy shit." That's what she says while she steadies herself and looks up at my bedroom wall.

"Get out!" I scream at her. "Or I swear to God you will be the next picture on that wall!"

Chapter 43

"Talk to me."

I'm sitting on my rock at the edge of the cliff at the abandoned Dell's Fantasyland. I've got a tissue shoved up to my nose and I'm huffing hard. It's evening, almost dark. There's a fog rising up the hillside, slipping between the nooks and crannies of the tall hemlocks there. I'd gotten thirty-two calls from Mom and Nicky before I blocked them on my cellphone. Now it is quiet where I'm standing, no ting, ting, ting of the phone.

I knew Rocky was coming up the trail even before he got there. From my vantage, I could see his truck pull in to the gritty-asphalt parking lot next to my car and watched him get out. With a simple twist, he hit the lock on his key for his truck doors, then ambled to the path. I don't answer him. I'm on the rock about three feet above him. He has to look up and he narrows his eyes.

"Can you look at me?"

"No."

He's weaving his head around trying to see past the glaze of pink on my glasses. "Do you need me to count?" Then he has the audacity to snatch a little at the tissue, like he's checking if my nose is still bleeding.

"No, stop it. It wasn't a bad—attack."

"You don't seem to have them as much in the past few months." Rocky observes. "Of course, you've been avoiding me, your mom, and sister, so maybe I'm right. It's Nicky—" He sees me glaring at him, turning my head and shunning the conversation. His shoulders drop. "Okay, well, I'll talk." Rocky looks up at me and then leans his back on the stone and folds his arms. "By the way, this is common ground, deal?" When I don't answer, he just settles with his back to the stone and follows my gaze out to the town far away. "If you don't remember our pact from eleven years ago, it goes like this: This is common ground. Whoever calls it first, gets the last word and—"

"—whoever gets the last word has to say something nice about the other person," I say blandly. "I remember the code, Rocky." I sigh. "She called me a sociopath. Nicky said Doctor Stamper said I was a frigging sociopath."

"Just finish the pact, Rosie. Do you remember it?"

I do remember. It is there, like it had never left, but I know up until the moment he says it, my mind had shoved it into some dark place, where those memories long forgotten sit and wait for something to pique their interest. Rocky and I sat here long ago. I'd turned thirteen that year, he was fourteen. I think it was probably the first time we could both get this far from our homes all by ourselves. I think the first few weeks we passed coming here, we just walked wide berths around each other. No words were said. I was there first. Rocky would come later on his bike to ride up and down the hill. It was almost unspoken that as soon as he came up the hill, I would leave. Then one day, I stayed and he told me he'd race me to the bottom. I didn't even get a quarter of the way down when I hit a root and went flipping and flying into the brush. Rocky had stopped and helped pull me out and tug out the little rose bush thorns sticking to my skin. He told me he'd never seen a girl not cry after wiping out so hard. I told him I wanted to cry, but there was no way in hell I was going to do it in front of a McDaniel. He thought that was funny. Then we sat down there, and rehashed the story over and over until he made me laugh describing me flying through the air. *We should make this common ground—* that's what Rocky said. *And make a pact—*

"If you remember it," he says now. "Finish it."

"No. You broke it when you turned your back on me, wouldn't be my friend."

"I never stopped being your friend. I just had to be— your friend in a different way."

"Different like making fun of me and hanging with my sister?"

"Sometimes, friends do what they have to do."

"Yeah, right." I sniff a laugh.

"Listen, I've had your back a thousand times between then and now." He points to my eye. "Like the black eye the other day at the restaurant. Fine," he says. "I will say it. Whatever is said on common ground stays between us and never leaves this place. You can tell me anything without being judged. I can tell you anything without being judged."

"No fighting. No saying bad stuff about each other's families," I add. "Just being friends."

"You know, I suppose out of anybody in a million mile radius, you get me, you understand me." He takes in a breath, lets it out in a huff and looks down at his feet. "Nobody in my family is anything like me. None of them went to college, they didn't even try. They look at me like a freak, like I'm trying to be better than them and it's a bad thing." He smiles and looks up. The wind blows pieces of leaves into the air and he swipes them away with a hand. "I know you struggle with the same stuff at your dad's. And I don't have to say how it is at your mom's."

"What's your point?"

"I don't know." Rocky shakes his head back and forth and his body makes a lazy follow. "It's just nice to know there's somebody out there that has the same things going on, I guess." Rocky sniffs a laugh. He looks up and smiles at me. I smile back.

"Rocky, don't compare my life with yours," I tell him with a little twist of my heart. "Nicky told me you're off-again in your long-term, on-again, off-again relationship. And you're already dating Tangy Cunningham."

"Tangy." He chuckles. "It was just a wedding thing in Crystal Springs." He looks up at me. "She knows that. She didn't want to go. Tangy did. I'd have taken you if you weren't working at the restaurant that night. Hey, how's that going?"

I look at him. Of course, he's lying about taking me. However, he's unblinking. There's no teasing in his eyes like he knows my secret. "I like it," I say. "I like the people I work with. So you're tight with the mayor now?"

"Maybe." Rocky turns his eyes toward the horizon. "I told him I would like to work at the Crystal Springs Fire Department fulltime. He says he needs hard workers like me working for the city. He's kind of wining and dining me, says his uncle's in charge right now and getting ready to retire. They're looking for someone he can train to eventually move into the position. I mean, I'd be the low man on the totem pole for a few years but—"

"No, shit." I know my eyes are wide. I look down at him. I'm excited for him, I mean really, really excited. "So, he offered you a job? And you're going to take it? Oh, my God, Rocky! Isn't this always what you wanted?"

"Yeah, but don't tell anybody. I still have to pass the test," he says. He's doing that silly-boy grin right now. "You're the only one who doesn't think I'm crazy. I mean, your sister does. My mom and dad do."

"Rocky, the only thing you lack is confidence. To hell with them."

"Well, I'm not so sure about that. I'm so damn backwards, Rosie. I couldn't fit in at Crystal Springs. It's a high-class place to live. I'm a country boy." Rocky rubs his hand across his face. "It's big houses and big malls. It's people our age clubbing and—I've never learned to dance." He shakes his head. "Let me tell you something. Don't laugh. I'm sitting at the wedding and this beautiful woman asks me to dance; you know I can't dance, but she doesn't know it. There's no way in hell I'm going to tell her I'm mostly redneck blood, because she doesn't get it. So I just blew her off. I mean, maybe I'm just not high class enough to rub elbows with those kind of people, you know? What if they want to come and meet my mom or dad, see my cheap, little house, surrounded by doublewides and trailers with crap all over the yards?"

I think at first, he's setting me up, knowing he's talking about me in Violet clothes. I'm glad he can't see me blanch before I peer downward. Intuition tells me Leah was right. He really didn't recognize me at the wedding.

"Rocky, I'm sure this beautiful woman would see past that stuff. And if she doesn't, she isn't worth it."

"Yeah, well, I blew it. Even if I didn't, I don't want to hurt Nicky."

"Why do you feel so obligated to her?" I ask.

"I don't know. I've always been the fat kid. I mean, girls look right past the fat kid, you know?"

"You're not the fat kid anymore," I shimmy down off the rock. Rocky extends a hand and helps me right myself just before my feet hit the ground.

"Yeah, I'm not. Thanks to you." He pokes me in the arm. "Your sister saw you running one morning when she was heading to school early. She asked me to follow you in the car to make sure you were safe. You kept cutting behind buildings. I couldn't keep up. I thought I'd do it on foot a few times to see the route, so I could catch you when you came out the other side of the buildings." Rocky runs a hand through his hair. I haven't seen him do that cocky sweep since we were kids. He pats his belly. "When I started losing weight, I just kept going with that workout sheet you gave me for the fireman test."

I smile up at him before I tug out the cellphone from my back pocket. I scroll through my music, pick out a song.

"What?"

"You're going to learn to dance so you don't miss out on the girl next time." I set the phone down on a little outcropping of stone and hold out my arms.

Rocky just blinks at me, gets this sheepish grin. "No, sweetie, I appreciate it, but—I mean, I'm not completely backwards, you know. I've kissed more than a few girls. I just don't like to dance."

"Yeah, right," I tease him. But he gets this irritated cast to his eyes looking down at me. "It's common ground. You spoke first. I get the last word." I think, well, he's not going to do it. I really do. But Rocky just lets out a little puff of air and he takes a step forward.

"Okay. But you realize you get the last word all the time, don't you?"

So honestly, a girl called Weird Wosie by her peers doesn't get many chances to glide sexy-style across the floor with a guy at the school dances. Wallflowers usually don't; that's how we get our name. We sit and watch the world go by in our safe little cubbies along the wall. I'm probably not the best teacher in the world. But I don't think it matters so much when Rocky wraps his arms around me and I rest my hands on his ribs and lean into him. I think we probably looked more like two sixth graders at their first junior high dance, awkwardly rocking back and forth in the oozy darkness of a school gym.

Still, we kept going long after the first song ended. Maybe it's because I felt him start to pull away and I snatched a bit of shirt in my fist. He stopped and we rocked there through the second. And the third. Because I caught a whiff of his aftershave with a musky hint. I felt warm and safe in his embrace. Right then, I wasn't Weird Wosie, Violet, or Nicky's odd little sister. I was just me, getting the once in lifetime chance to dance with my crush.

I suppose it was the grumble of thunder tugging us apart. I'm not sure if I pull away or Rocky does first. But I look up at the same time he looks down. "Now there's no excuses for not dancing—"

Rocky leans over right then. He slips his hand beneath my jaw and tips my head up. Do I stop him? No. I know what he's doing even before I feel the softness of his lips graze mine. And oh, holy hell, it's not the kind of kiss a girl gets behind the camp counselor's cabin! It's two gentle pecks and then Rocky scoops me up, pulls me forward with his hand sliding along my back. Oh. My heart is like a hundred horses stampeding and he's enveloping me in this embrace that's sexy as all get out. Well, right before he stops and stands back.

I blink, feel stupid that the words aren't coming. Rocky gets a smug smile. "I just wanted to prove a point."

I try to make a quick recovery. However, he's knocked me back into Weird Wosie shoes.

"What would that be?" I ask him more sharply than I mean to. "That you can get your ass kicked across a hillside by a skinny girl?" Wow, where did that come from? I think it surprises Rocky too. But he plays it cool, rolls his eyes.

"Yeah, that's not it." He's got a funny little grin playing across his lips. "I think I made my point. You're not the only one who read that book on detecting deception."

Damn him. I roll my eyes, "You read that?"

"I did. Did you read the one I gave you?"

"No."

"Well, you should."

We left not a minute later. I shrug and wave a hand in the air. *Winsome Falls.* It's just out of my comfort zone, or rather my interest zone. I hear Rocky's footsteps behind me avoiding the roots on the trail back down the hill. I linger at my car door. "She's just a girl, Rocky."

"Yeah, my mom said the same thing. She says there's a million out there just like her."

"Even if you can't work up the nerve to dance with a girl, you just knock her socks off with one of those kisses."

He snickers, looks discomfited. "Yeah, I'm going to tell your sister I talked you into taking the pictures down."

"She'll know I didn't."

Rocky shakes his head, looks at the ground. "Not if you move them to that walk-in closet you've got and lock the door."

"That's the first place my nosy sister would check. Why are you doing this, Rocky?" I ask, honestly curious.

"You're kidding me, right?" he says. "There's this line in the book I wanted you to read." He isn't looking me in the eyes. "It's after the girl's family takes in the wounded soldier and hides him. Someone in her town finds out and she tries to save him from soldiers who are coming to get him. It goes like this: *If I come with you, they will follow. Right now, they assume you are just a man. But you are more, so much more. Please go. I may never see you on earth again, so wait for me on the sunny side of heaven. Go.*" Rocky rocks back and forth on his heels. "It's beautiful. I'm just looking for somebody who'll wait for me on the sunny side of heaven." Then he tosses it aside with his hand. "Nevermind. We're off common ground. I'm not spelling it out for you. You're smarter than a rocket scientist, girl. You figure it out."

Chapter 44

"Seven minutes and five seconds, six seconds—"

Rocky's cheeks are red when he crests the hill and hears my voice. I click the little stopwatch and lean in to see the numbers. "Seven minutes and seven seconds."

"What the hell, Rosie? Your left leg better be chewed partway off by a wolf or I'm *never* going to answer another 9-1-1 from you again." He's in his school teacher business attire—white button up and dress pants, has his suitcoat laying on his arm. "You called and said you cut your knee. Don't tell me I jogged all the way up this hill and you were just timing me."

"Okay, I won't. But I was. No wolf. It is a part of your testing," I say. "You might look healthy and fit, but your stamina is shit. Well, it was shit. Two weeks ago, it took you nine minutes and ten seconds to do the same distance from the park in town to the water tower. Last week, you were down forty seconds. And yesterday—"

"Woman," Rocky stops just short of the rock I'm perched on, with legs bent and arms hugging my knees and leans over. "You're killing me."

"Technically, I'm doing the opposite. I'm making you fit." I lean over, tug a bottled water from a little cooler. I toss it into his outstretched hands. "Drink. And answer a question. Which tool is greatest at finding a fire in an attic? A pick axe, a sledgehammer, a pike pole."

"Pike pole." Rocky opens the water, takes a swig. "You poke it and turn it so the hook catches and then you jerk it downward. Okay, I'm not going to do this. We need to talk. I know what happened three nights ago after we were up here."

"Forget it. I'm over it. You got the question right. Did you study the knots I gave you?"

"I did study them. I'm not letting you change the subject. You know I had no clue they were going to do it, right?" He narrows his eyes. "You've been avoiding me like I've got chickenpox; you missed two days of school."

"I was sick." I take a little piece of rope from the backpack and wiggle it in front of me. I wasn't sick at all. I am just dodging my mom's side of the family. Everybody's sidestepping what happened when I returned home after standing on the hill with Rocky. I suppose I should have known he was just keeping me busy long enough for Bobby to come over and examine the wall and tear it down, picture by picture. I feel like I built a beautiful castle and the enemy has arrived on a black steed and torn it asunder. But even worse, all my work and all Jay Cooper's work is now in the Laurel Grove Police Department's evidence lockers.

"Are the medications Doctor Stamper put you on making you sick? Nicky said she gave you a lot."

"It doesn't matter," I retort hotly. "And if you continue, I am going to get up and walk away. However, I do not start something I can't finish, so I won't stop with your pre-testing until you become a stupid fireman. So just shut up and do as I ask." Rocky sets down his bottled water on a flat piece of rock. He takes the rope in his hands and I hold out my wrists to him. "Make a handcuff knot. You really hurt my feelings. I trusted you."

"You're hurting my feelings saying I would betray you. I came up here to be with you the other night. *You*, not Nicky. I left Nicky to be with you. If I let anybody down, it's her." Rocky lets out a deep breath, looks skyward. "Rosie, you are the only one who believes in me. I'm trying really hard to believe in you. But I can't let your sister down either." He scrubs his head with both hands. "I don't know what to do. I feel like I'm the captain of a dodgeball team and I'm sparring with the other captain to get the best players. It's my turn to pick one player and you and your sister are standing there and I've got to pick one or the other. And I can't choose."

I look up. He's earnest. I suppose I know the drill. I've played dodgeball enough to know girls like me are the last to get picked, if we get picked at all. It's not just dodgeball or dances or boyfriends. It's life. So I force a smile. "It's all right. Nicky's always been better at dodgeball. I recognize the fact she's the best choice and would accomplish the task at hand, which is winning the game. I wouldn't hold it against you," I tease him. "Let's get this done." Rocky gazes at me, then turns his attention to the rope. It's isn't a simple knot, but he works the rope into two adjustable loops, then thrusts my wrists inside. After, Rocky tightens it with a couple snaps of the rope. I'm bound.

"Good." I start to wiggle my wrists free. "You're like three-quarters of the way done." But Rocky holds up my wrists and looks at them.

"You know, there's a couple hundred things I'd like to get you to do or say while you're under my control."

"Stop," I say impatiently. "We don't have time for playing games. Your test is in less than three weeks. We're cutting it close on two hours a day. I've got twenty-four days of work laid out and you only have twenty-one days—"

"Is there a single grain of passion in here?" He reaches up, knocks my head with his knuckle. "Didn't my kick-ass kiss knock your socks off at the coffee shop?"

"Knock my socks off? You were proving a point. It would be like looking at a magazine with technical images of a naked woman and getting horny."

"That would be porn and yes, it makes me horny." He seems to think it's funny I said the word, and now he's got a lopsided grin like he's holding back a laugh. "You don't see anything sexy, sensual, in this position I've got you in?"

I look down, see his hands holding my bound wrists. "Well, no, not really. Being handcuffed isn't sexy."

"Holy shit, you're a robot. You're a freaking robot the aliens made and stuck you in Rosie's body."

"You're trying to waste time so you don't have to answer more study questions." He hurts my feelings. I try to jerk my arms away. Rocky stops them. He doesn't see the urgency in getting the testing process finished like I do.

"Stop," he says, his voice low. "Be still a second."

"Do you want to pass this test?"

"Can you let me take a one minute break?" He sighs, tips his head. "Please, Rosie, I go to work all day and I study all the stuff you give me all evening and into the night. I've studied more in the last month than I cracked down on the books in college; the formula for perfect productivity is fifty -two minutes of work with seventeen minutes for break."

I grin at him. "You looked that up."

"I did." Rocky looks so proud of himself. He frees one of his hands and taps a finger on my lips. "Last night at one in the morning, I thought my brain was going to explode on the diagrams you designed, but I figured them out. So did I impress you enough; do I get a break?"

"Sure. Sixty seconds."

"Okay. It's a deal. I thought it might be that seventeen minutes suggested for high productivity, but I'll take what I can get." Rocky is swinging my hands just a little, back and forth, back and forth. He's got this shit-eating grin sliding across his lips. "So you get a little break too." He reaches out again and plays his finger along my right arm, gives me goosepimples. "You can be my toy."

"Your toy." I repeat. Why don't I trust his silly grin and why am I blushing like a fourteen year-old?

"Yeah, you really don't have a choice, do you?" he asks me. "You get fifty-two minutes of my full attention, I was an attentive student. Now you have to be *my* attentive student. I should make you read Winsome Falls every fifty-two minutes. But I will show you just a few things from the book, kind of act them out."

"Oh, that would be good," I say sarcastically. And I giggle. Do I giggle? I sound like the silly waitress in the restaurant who served Rocky eleven glasses of water last week in a twenty minute span of time.

He takes my hands and pushes them side by side. "So, Winsome Falls is about a girl who leaves her home right before World War I and comes back to stay with her family. She meets an enemy soldier who got shot. They are from different worlds. But he's lonely, she's lonely." Rocky lets out a soft sigh. "I'm lonely most of the time, are you?"

"Me?" I ask like there is anybody else around. "I guess." I'm surprised Rocky is lonely at any time. He's got his buddies from work, his buddies from church, old buddies from high school, now newer ones where he teaches, and another set from the Laurel Grove Fire Department. "How could you possibly be lonely, Rocky? You're got a million friends."

"I don't know. I feel like I'm missing something." He looks at me, drops the smile. "I figured you might be feeling that way too. And I like hanging out with you." He hard-sighs, tugs me a little so I slide off the rock and stand up in front of him. "See, I don't know why it's so hard to tell you that. If it was anybody else, I'd blow it off if you said you didn't like hanging with me. But you? For some reason, it's not that easy."

"I can sum it up. The curse." I look up at him. My tummy jerks left, then right. I'm looking into his eyes, he's looking into mine. I'm feeling like he's coming on to me. But I need to put on the brakes. Because guys like Rocky, they don't like geeky, awkward, and ugly girls like me. And if he does, it's because he thinks I'm being nice by helping him.

"So you're smart, figure out how to get rid of the curse."

"I'm not a psychiatrist, Rocky." I say softly. "But I know for a fact, all this superstitious crap is based on what's called false cause. It's created by cause and effect. Our families grew up with all the Appalachian superstitions, like black cats being bad luck. Our grandmas passed them down to our moms and dads and then to us. We resort to superstition when we can't figure out why something happens. It's human nature to want to figure out an explanation for what we don't understand. I can't convince you differently. And I'm not telling you your mom and dad were wrong just so I can debunk your beliefs."

"Well, I think it's more than just our parents, Rosie." Rocky's fingers are still gently playing with the rope handcuffs. "It's even worse when people in the school system reinforce the issue."

"What do you mean?"

"All the times you went in to talk to Doctor Stamper, she didn't give you that old story?" Rocky chuckles.

"Yes, she did try to rationalize it to some extent. But she always told me—"

"—not to tell anybody?" Rocky ends for me. He's right. I can remember her telling the story of the curse. I always thought it was because I was from the other side of the tracks, the poor side of town. She was trying to find a common link with me. I think she started every one of our school sessions like that and ended with a wave of her hand and: *But don't tell anybody I told you about that old curse. Not even your friends."*

"Yes, don't tell anybody—" I repeat, looking down. "I've heard of that before."

"Heard of what?"

"It's called—it's called the Streisand Effect. It's when somebody tries to hide something and ultimately it backfires and ends up getting more exposure and more attention. It happens all the time with celebrities, when naked pictures are leaked online and they try to have them taken down. Everybody wants to know what all the hype is about and downloads the naked pictures."

"Make it English for me, Rosie."

"It's like people become almost driven to pass on the information, just because they aren't supposed to. Maybe Doctor Stamper did it on purpose. She cued us all—even our parents—on the curse by knowing if we weren't supposed to talk about it, we would."

"Holy hell, Rosie, you're killing me!"

"You want me to break it down more for you?" I ask, blinking at him.

"No, you're talking all smart and it—does something to me. I'm just giving you a warning. In just a second, I'm going to kiss you because my break is almost up."

But I'm hardly listening. My mind is churning. Doctor Stamper used to tell me the story every time I came into her office if I got in trouble. It was like a threat that we'd wake up the curse if we did bad stuff. She did the same with my mom and my dad. We laugh about it all the time—

There's a moment there where I'm thinking, yeah, sure. Doctor Stamper is from this area. She's superstitious.

But she's a psychologist. Surely, she knows the background of these false notions. Or, what if she is planting this in everybody's head, in two entire generations of students' heads to make them believe all these weird deaths are caused by a curse. As I think back, most of the employees filling the town offices and the school grew up here. They went to Laurel Grove High School. They had Doctor Stamper as their psychology teacher. At the exact moment I'm letting all of this sink in, Rocky leans in snatches me up by the back of the head and pulls my face toward him.

THE KISS. I say it in all caps because, quite possibly, it was the most epic kiss I'd ever had. It wasn't just that I'd sunk my teeth into what could possibly solve the murders and was riding a certain high, but when Rocky McDaniel planted his lips on mine, I think I almost fainted dead away.

"Breathe, Rosie—" Rocky pulls away with a self-assured smile on his lips. I let out a breath and wobble there a second. Rocky tugs on the handcuffs to help right me.

"That good?" he asks.

So I say, "Yeah, yeah, it was good. But oh, shit. Rocky. I keep getting these cues. What if it is Doctor Stamper's murdering everybody? I think it is her."

He doesn't say anything at first, just tips his head to the side like I blew all the wind out of his sails.

"*Yeah, yeah*. What does that mean?" He holds up a hand to keep my words at bay. "No, don't answer that. Doctor Stamper? The lady who gives out free helmets to all the kids every summer?"

"Why does everybody say that?" Oh. Because she does it to make everyone believe she is good and kind. "Rocky, have you ever heard of the Trojan Effect?"

"I've heard of the Rosie Effect. It's when a girl is using too many technical terms and completely disses a guy who just kissed her hoping to knock her socks off."

I glare at him. "I'm on the cusp of figuring out a good theory of a serial killer and you're mad because I didn't jump up and down that you kissed me?"

"Pretty much." He looks mad, wiggles the handcuffs off my wrists. "But whatever. What's the Trojan Effect, Rosie? Because you've got that look in your eyes and I know you're not going to stop until I listen."

"Thank you. But in my defense, it turned you on four minutes ago." He rolls his eyes, but the smug smile comes back. "According to ancient legend, the Greeks offered the city of Troy a gift of a huge wooden horse. The people of Troy dragged it into the city, but it was filled with Greek warriors who waited until darkness. They escaped to unlock the gates to the fortress surrounding them and such, let their own soldiers in to take over the city."

"Dumb up the point you're making for me."

"It was a tactical motive for giving a gift. The poor, poor Stampers—" I wiggle my fingers in quotation marks. "—who lost their daughter and out of their desire to help other children survive, donate helmets to the community year after year. They teach Sunday school at Holy Trinity, they coach baseball. They give gifts to make people trust them. Then, they take over the town and murder the kids in retribution!" Rocky shifts his feet, scratches his head. He looks like he's mulling my words.

"I'm trying to read you," I say to his empty stare. "Either the much anticipated explanation is difficult to digest or—"

"I get it." Rocky replies as flat as a pancake.

"Oh, I ruined the mood, didn't I," I rub my wrists.

"Just a little." He holds his hands out far apart.

"I like you, Rocky, I just... don't know *how* to like

you." I'm not good speaking with my heart. But right there and standing on the threshold of my theory, I'm almost high with it, even if I don't know what to do with it. I supposed I had a mental orgasm and I'm pillow-talking Rocky right now, divulging all those little things I wouldn't say before we got so close. "I suppose I can blame that on the Stampers, too, if my logic is correct. Whenever I'd leave Doctor Stamper's office, she would smile and give me a wink. She'd say, *stay away from those McDaniels. Your mom's head would explode if she saw you anywhere near them.* But beside that, I don't know why a guy with *all that*—" I fan my hand at him. "Would like a girl with all this. Or am I looking too deep into it and I'm just the girl of the moment?"

"I don't know, Rosie. I really don't know the reason. Why does there have to be a justification? I just *feel* that way. You're beautiful. You're smart."

"You think I'm beautiful?"

"Of course." Rocky shoves his hands into his pockets, looks over his shoulder down the hillside. "We should probably go. Somebody's going to see your car there and my truck parked beside it."

I nod and feel sad, like somebody just lobbed a big ball of tears in my chest. Did he not know I waited until the sun started to set to make us meet on the sunny side of the hill? Maybe I should have just grabbed the moment for what it was, enjoyed being the girl on Rocky's arm for the next twenty minutes. It'd be better than nothing at all.

Chapter 45

"You're quiet today." My mom observes when she walks into the kitchen on Sunday. I'm staring into the refrigerator and trying to avoid Rocky and Nicky, who are mumble-bickering in the other room. I shrug.

"You're kidding, right?" I narrow my eyes at her. It doesn't take much. They are puffy from lack of sleep. "I'm just tired." That's an understatement. I can hardly see straight enough to drive.

"It's just the extra pills you're taking. Doctor Stamper said it would make you tired to take two every twelve hours and make you restless at night. I put a prescription for sleeping pills in your purse, too. I hope you're not still upset about me calling her and setting up an appointment. Bobby promised the chief of police, when he handed over the pictures to him, that he would make sure you saw the doctor, as long as they didn't try to get a court order to have you placed into a mental health treatment program. You have to admit, the diagram Nicky described on your bedroom wall is nothing short of what a serial killer would devise. It is abnormal."

"Why do you assume because it's me that it's something a serial killer would use? Did you not consider that it's like the evidence display boards you see on TV?"

"You need to let it go, Rosie."

"Let it go," I repeat blandly. "My own sister betrayed me. Bobby broke into my house without a warrant and nobody thinks there is anything wrong with it. I wouldn't be here right now at all if—" If I didn't think they would have me admitted to some mental health treatment center, like Doctor Stamper told Mom I should be right now.

"If what, dear?" Mom says and pats my arm. "I'll

definitely have Nicky drive you home later, unless you want to stay with me. You are loopy today. Things will get better. Just let the police do their job. Bobby says the man whose home you found the pictures had been diagnosed with schizophrenia when he was quite young. Jay Cooper was his name. Before he dropped out of high school, Mary Stamper was seeing him quite often, she told me."

"I bet she was," I mutter.

"What does that mean, Rosie?" Mom asks, with the cagy eye of one who is playing a game of musical chairs. I am the one hovering near the seat of the last chair, holding off the moment waiting for the music to stop.

"I think Doctor Stamper has something to do with the murders. She's been manipulating all the students in the school system. Maybe she started with her daughter and then just kept going? I think Bobby has something to do—" Oh, why does it sound so farfetched coming out of my mouth in comparison with what I am thinking in my head.

"Stop it!" Mom slaps a hand on the table. "Just stop it! I don't want to hear another misguided notion from that mouth of yours! I heard you yelling at Nicky on the phone over this. Do you know how silly you sound, how irrational your thought process is? You have picked the two most wonderful, rational, and ordinary people and you are trying to make them into monsters because of this *paranoia*. Doctor Stamper has taken care of the mental health of this community for almost fifty years. My Bobby was a police officer for nearly thirty-four years. You want to know my honest opinion? I think you are so afraid the police and people on the task force, like Mary Stamper and Bobby, are going to point the finger at your father, you're making a desperate attempt to point a finger at two innocent people."

"Task force?" I repeat. "Bobby and Mary Stamper are on a task force?"

"Well, of course. They are two pillars of the community." Mom waves a hand at me. "Sweetheart, you've got to quit talking about this. How am I going to convince the school board to let you keep your job if you are slandering Mary's name?"

"I don't want to work there anymore. I'm already working at a restaurant outside Crystal Springs."

"Yes, Rocky told me. It would be fun to visit you while at work."

"Yeah, loads of laughs."

"Rosie, you would make more money at the school than at a waitressing job, even if you have to accept a lower pay range to keep it."

"You're kidding me, right?" I snort a laugh. "I'm not even good enough to get the pay I get now? It is minimum wage, by the way. You think I like being the one who gets all the stuff dumped on her?" I close the refrigerator, turn to face my mom. "I *hate* that job," I hiss. "You know that's all I do, don't you? I've got a teaching degree and I'm a lunch room attendant and a detention monitor. I make copies all day. I babysit the problem students the other teachers are too stupid to teach properly. Mariah Patterson doesn't have a reading list with classic books. Her students should be reading at a high school level. They are at a seventh grade level. You know how I know? I am the one who monitors the tests and figures out their placement. Tangy Cunningham gives the kids a math book and if there's a problem, she sends them to me to help them figure it out. I am training Ginger Childs how to use the computers; she's the computer instructor!"

"That's not very nice." Here comes Nicky, fresh from a fight with Rocky to take Mom's side and lay in on me.

"It's the truth. Nicky," I say flatly, and not without noting my mom's curious expression while she eyes me carefully. "You're no better. You sent Colton McDaniel down for me to babysit. You want to know *why* he acts out in class?"

"Because he's better suited to be working with his hands in a gas station?" she says smartly while Rocky quietly comes up behind her.

"No, Nicky," I spit back. "Because none of the teachers have the tools to keep gifted students busy. He's got an IQ of almost 122. We were on the computers and I had him take an IQ test; he tested twice and higher than 120. What's your IQ again? One-hundred and six?"

"It's just like you to think you know everybody's jobs better than they do."

"No, Nicky. *You're* wrong."

She just stops and takes in a deep breath. Nobody tells Nicky she's wrong. I see my mom's eyes get wide. She's not used to me talking back like this. I'm usually tugging my sweater over my shoulders. Well, screw that. I'm sick of Nicky being mean to Rocky. I'm sick of her yelling at me.

"You're out of control, Rosie," she spits. "You need help. You're certifiably insane. Ask Mary Stamper."

"Because I disagree with you?" I take a step forward, cock up my chin. It feels right. I don't know why. But I feel the fight in me. I remember—I remember long, long ago sticking up for myself to my sister.

"No, Rosie. Because you had a damn serial killer's death list on the wall! What the hell were you doing with that?" she screams with her fists clenched at her sides. "Adding to it?"

"Leave her alone, Nicky. Stop." Rocky's got this funny cock to his chin and his voice booms across the room. I jump. Nicky jumps. Mom's eyes snap to attention. I look up. The entire time he was getting yelled at by Nicky, he hardly said a word. He always just takes it. But right now, I see him giving her the same warning gaze Daddy used to give me when I talked back to him.

"Don't tell me that psycho over there has convinced you she's right. You know that's what psychopaths do, right?" It's like suddenly something registers in her eyes. I see her stare at him, then turn her narrowed eyes to me. Back and forth, she goes before I can see her shoulders start to move angrily with each breath she takes. "Oh, my God. It's Rosie," she mewls.

"What's Rosie?" Mom asks like *oh, my God, what else can my crazy daughter do?*

"The *someone you met* is Rosie?" She throws her hands into the air. "Oh, my God! I should have known! The way you look at her. At every stupid teacher meeting you've ask why she isn't a teacher. I told you why. She's crazy. But your decision making skills in the last year have been equal to a seven year-old! You go and buy a truck. A truck? What are you going to do with a fifty-thousand dollar truck that sits in your driveway because you can't afford a garage? You want to be a fireman? No way. You are *not* dating my sister!" she screams. "You can go out with anybody but her. Anybody. Marry Tangy. Marry your stupid pig. I don't care. But not my sister. She doesn't like you. She's just doing this as some master plan to keep her dad out of jail."

Rocky is looking from mom to Nicky, back and forth and his face is turning a deep, deep shade of red. He doesn't look at me. I see him kind of wagging his head like he's agreeing with her. Then his expression changes. He snaps his head over and lets his eyes rest on me with the same utter distaste the students gaped at the vomit one of their peers spewed all over the floor of the lunchroom last week.

"Rosie? You're kidding, right? Nicky, where do you

come up with this stuff?" Then he laughs and rolls his eyes. "How desperate do you think I am? It's a woman I met at the country club."

"What's going on?" Mom's eyes are wide while I feel my heart just sink. How could he say such a thing? She is looking at Rocky now. "You're seeing other women?" Her head snaps to Nicky. "Is he seeing other women and you're all right with this?"

"Mom, stay out of it!" Nicky yowls. "No, he's not. We're fine. I just got mad. Now he's mad at me."

That's when the bickering starts in the kitchen. Mom and Nicky sound like two cats in a fight and I'm the only one who is standing there in silence, glaring at Rocky and ready to cry. It hurts. He hurt me with his words. He's hurting me with the faraway gaze he gives me, like I'm nothing but crap. I can feel my hands reaching out, snatching up my sweater and wrapping it over my shoulders. I start to back out, can't look at Rocky. I don't even think he notices I've slunk into the living room. None of them do. And they don't even notice I've left.

Or so I thought. Twenty minutes out of the driveway, I hear the ting of my cell phone. When I pause at a stop light, I pick up my phone. It's Rocky. There are probably eight texts from him. I sigh, check the light and see it is still red. Then I open up the text and feel my heart jump. Pictures. One by one they pop up on my phone. They are all of my bedroom wall. He took a picture of each and every image before Bobby tore it down. And the text says: *I'm telling you right now, if we're choosing teams for a game of dodgeball and I know you throw like a girl, I'm going to choose you anyway.*

And I text back: *I don't throw like a girl.*

Chapter 46

"Rocky, stop! My dryer is *fine*." I am standing in the doorway of my tiny utility room housing my washer and dryer. I'm staring at Rocky's back. It's Monday night. He's pulled my dryer away from the wall and he's rolling his hand up and down the drywall behind it. He's pulled off the flexible lint vent, unscrewed the back of the dryer. It is midnight. I wasn't quite asleep when he came pounding at my door.

"Rocky, it's not going to catch on fire. What is up with you?" I ask him. I'm in a ratty t-shirt, no shorts. He caught me off-guard. I tug the shirt down to my thighs, trying to cover my panties. I see his eyes follow, then abruptly snap away.

"You don't know that." He doesn't even turn. He's got some kind of a tool in his hand and he's holding it out toward the electric socket that the dryer was plugged into. "There's always the chance, you know? Your house could catch on fire. There's been eleven fires in the tri-county region, Rosie. Eleven. You could be sleeping and—"

"You put a fire alarm in every room for my Christmas present last year, Rocky. Every neighbor in a ten mile radius will wake up if I light a candle. Even if it does catch fire, you taught me how to get out. Um, I can use my shirt and stuff it around my hand and break a window if I need to, right? You told me that." I sigh. "What's up? I know it isn't my wall catching on fire because there's too much lint in the vent. That's another precaution you warned me about. I clean it every time I do the laundry."

I don't think he's going to stop. But he does, just leaves his hands against the wall and his head falls, chin tucking to chest. "There were three fires tonight, one after another. Two were abandoned houses, one was a trailer. Then just as we're cleaning up, we get this call. Another girl was found dead. Rosie, I thought—I thought it was you. I got called out on it. We were the first on the scene. From behind, she looked like you."

"Another girl? Who—who was it?" I freeze there. Was it Leah? If my theory was correct, we are the only two left. Three more fires. *More fires.* With every rash of fires, there's a murder. Someone's been murdered tonight.

"It wasn't me." Colton's probably right. Another girl was murdered to take the focus off my theory. Who would know about it? "Did you check on Leah?"

"Leah?"

"I mean, she's the one who lives in that trailer. It's a death trap."

"She's at her dad's tonight. Ty came home drunk again." He tips his head. There's something in his eyes. I can see he's hiding something.

"You're not telling me something."

"You told your mom you think it is the Stampers and Bobby who are murdering the girls."

"I do think they've got something to do with it." I walk up and around the dryer.

"Well, your mom went crying to Mary Stamper about what you said. Now she knows. You need to go to the cops." Rocky stands up. There isn't much room for both of us.

"Rocky, you saw what Bobby did to the pictures on my wall. He took them to the cops. They didn't even bother to call me. You heard my mom talking to me. Nobody believes me. The cops will listen to Doctor Stamper, Nicky, and my mom. I'm certifiably nuts in their eyes, a psychopath."

"Okay, so what if somebody tries to come after you?

That could have been you."

"It's not me." I tell him softly. "See? Me." I'm standing there only six inches from him. I only come to his shoulder. "But you believe me, right?" He's looking down. I'm looking up. We have a moment where we are just staring at each other. I see something in his eyes. I'm not sure what it is. I don't know. I've never seen Rocky so upset.

"Yeah. You're not really playing with my head, like Nicky says, right?"

"No. Can I—" I whisper. My voice is so soft, I can hardly hear it. "Can I touch your face?"

He stares at me long and hard. I see him visibly swallow. I'm not sure if he believes me or not. I think he wants to, though. Maybe that has to be enough. "I—yeah, Rosie," he whispers back. And so I reach my fingers to his cheek, slowly let them dribble downward until they stop at his jaw. His skin is rough and soft at the same time. He's got a bit of evening stubble. The tips of my fingers trip over the hairs. I pause, take in a breath. Then I work them down to his neck and then his chest where the button to his shirt is open. I stop. He is just staring at me expressionless, unmoving. I linger there. I want to unbutton his shirt. Maybe just one button. I've seen him a hundred times without a shirt, but it feels like this one action—it means something deeper.

"Can I unbutton your shirt?"

"No." He says that one word hard and deep. Then he scrubs his face with his hand. "Okay, so if I say *no,* does that mean you walk away? You'll never ask again?"

"Yeah, probably."

He pushes my hand down. "You know, I should leave. There's so many things wrong with what I'm thinking right now. And it isn't just because our dads hate each other or I dated your sister. Or that everybody will think I'm crazy for being with you." Rocky pushes past me. "And the—"

"The curse?" I finish for him. He makes it to the door.

"Yeah, that." His back is to me.

"You can touch me," I tell him. He stops.

"Touch you," he repeats to the wall without turning. So I take the three steps to where he's stopped. I can see his elbow working a bit, like he's nervously scrubbing his cheeks again. I step around him, look up and peer at his eyes. He looks down at me, smiles feebly, almost as if he is wearing his Sunday suit and is standing on the edge of a muddy creek that he knows he needs to cross, but he doesn't want to get his clothes dirty. I take his hand and move it to the delicate arch between my jaw and my neck.

"Yes, touch me," I whisper. His fingers just tickle there. "It's why you're here, isn't it?"

He doesn't answer, looks a little pale. Yet, he doesn't move his hand.

"Okay," I say. "So maybe not. But I want you to touch me. Even if you think I'm batshit crazy."

"I can't, Rosie, you know that." He drops his hand, fumbles for his keys in his pocket and starts for the door.

"Can I kiss you?" I ask his back.

There's a long pause. "I—don't think I could stop you if you did, Rosie."

"What's that mean? Rocky, you're a big guy," I laugh softly. "One little push and I'm on my butt on the floor."

"Yeah, big man, little girl," he says softly, turns around. He's three steps away. Now he's got a snarky look on his face. Still, it's a little nervous, a little pale. "You think you could handle all this?" He waves a hand in front of his chest.

I don't answer, I just step up to him. He's taller than me by a lot. I see my little stool I use to reach the jugs of laundry detergent I've got on a little metal shelf. I tug it over with the toe of my foot. Then I take a step up, lift his chin up with my knuckle and kiss him.

Oh, my. It's a soft and gentle kiss. It leaves me with this holy-hell achy feeling in my chest.

"You shouldn't have done that," Rocky whispers gruffly. Now he's mad and he just gives me a gentle shove away with his hand. I step down from the stool. "What the hell were you thinking?" Rocky pivots, almost rams into the doorframe. He stomps off and snatches up his jacket while I follow a few steps behind.

"You kissed me. What's the difference?"

"It's different because—because I wanted it. You didn't. You stopped it going farther. We both want it—now."

"So neither of us will stop. The world didn't swallow itself up, did it?" I ask him. "Because we both want to kiss."

"Rosie, we can't do this. It will go too far. It's not just a kiss with you. Not here. Not now. In the coffee shop, I could stop. Here, I can't." He's got his back to me. I think he's staring at the floor about five steps from my front door. I'm waiting for him to walk out, slam the door. But he just stands there. "So say something," he tells me softly. "Either cry and tell me you're sorry or—"

"Cry? Tell you I'm sorry? Sorry for what?" I snap at him, mean little Chihuahua-style. "I'm not sorry. It was a good kiss. It didn't have to end with you stomping off like a four year-old. You're kidding me, right? Why'd you come here, Rocky? It's what you wanted, wasn't it?" I shake my head. "Okay, I am mad. You come here and tear apart my dryer like—what the hell does that mean? If you think I'm crazy, like Nicky says, and that's stopping you, go fix Nicky's dryer. Go fix my mom's dryer. Go fix Tangy the bitch's dryer." I toss my arms out. "So it's like this. If you walk out that door, don't ever come back in. Period."

"We're on common ground."

"Suddenly, we're on common ground." I snicker. "No, Rocky, you're at my house. Those rules don't apply. I'm sick of them only applying when it is convenient for you. Get the hell out of here. You instigated this. You're stuck on this stupid curse thing. I can't do it. I can't punch you and kiss you. I can't have you kiss me and I turn you away or the other way around. I can't push you and hug you, love and hate you. You either let this go where it wants to go or get out. Just go."

"I didn't instigate *crap*, Rosie, you did." He rolls his eyes. "You about killed that dorky guy, Robby, from church taking off your shirt when we were playing basketball. I wanted to punch him across the room when he kept bad-mouthing you at the restaurant like you're trash. And, holy hell, what's with those little camo shorts and every-redneck-boy's-wet-dream tank top you wore to Rayville?"

"You realize what you're saying, Rocky?" I spat back. "You're a *redneck boy*."

"Yeah, I do. *I'm* not the one who never gets it." Rocky's kind of waggling his head like an angry bull before he turns. I'm not sure if he's battling himself or if he's just mad at me. I see him taking me in, sopping up the angry on my face. Rocky stops three inches from my face, reaches out a hand and I tip my chin up, ready for a fight. "You about killed me when you took off your shirt, standing there in nothing but that pretty—no, *beautiful, beautiful* black, lacy bra and your flat tummy and—shit. I can't get you out of my head. You're sitting like mud—"

"Mud?"

"No," he waggles his head. "Not mud. Just—all around my mind, so I can't think of anything *but* you. You know what I mean, right? I can't stop thinking about you. I can't stop thinking about you being with somebody else." It's a kiss he gives me when he reaches down and cups my jaw. "You don't need to do that—stuff for them, those guys you hang around, you know that, right?"

"I'm a big girl, Rocky. I can handle it. I'm just trying some guys on for size, you know? Different types—I can handle you—"

"You wouldn't know what to do with a guy like me—you're like a freaking bunny rabbit."

"A guy like you? So, you think you're some big, bad wolf?" I snap back. "And I'm a little bunny?" I say in a sarcastic baby voice while I pinch a tiny bit of air between finger and thumb. Screw old Rosie. Hello, Violet. Ain't no boy going to call me a freaking timid bunny anymore and get away with it. I cock my chin. "Bring it on, big guy."

It's like he's been waiting all his life for me to say that. Rocky doesn't even hesitate. Well, maybe he does. He gives the ceiling one last wary gaze, then leans over and takes up the tiny expanse between us. His hand wraps around my shoulder, fingers tickling at the nape of my neck. His touch is soft, firm, gentle. He draws me in, kisses me softly twice. "Sweet Jesus, this is the last thing I should do," he says in a hoarse whisper. The third is a little more passionate like he is figuring if I made it past the first two without springing away like that scared doe, I'm ready for the next step.

I'm not completely new to awkward first attempts at making love. I had an clumsy and unadorned tryst my first year of college. I can't even remember the boy's name.

Twice and hurried, we rolled around the squeaky confines of his bunk bed before his roommates came back to his dorm room. Then we mumbled apologies and went our separate ways. He went to the library. I headed home to mom's. I've been with Emmanuel. It's a different kind of relationship. I don't love him. It's sexy stuff, rolling around and talking nothing to each other because I can't understand a word he says. I was drunk the first time. I spent time worried about asking him what he liked, and then bumbling around to figure it out. Then, we just kind of ended up doing it fast to get it over.

But Rocky and I, we aren't strangers and I'm not drunk. I can't walk away if I make an idiot of myself. Every Sunday morning, I'm going to have to stare him in the eye, take the hymnals from him, and help him stack them in the cupboard. I feel like there's something more intimate between us. It is both calming and terrifying at the same time—

"Don't analyze it," Rocky snickers, and I swear he must have read my mind.

"I can't help it."

"I know, right?"

"So here's how we play this out," I say softly. "I'm going to tell you something I like. Then you tell me something you like. We, um, do that back and forth until we don't need to do it anymore, right?" I don't wait for him to answer. "I like your kisses. The ones that are two times really soft and then a hard one."

"Okay." Rocky takes in a breath, like he's getting ready to take off in a track race.

"It's not a competition," I whisper. "Just do—" Holy shit. He kisses me and my chest explodes with a thousand butterflies. My heart's pounding by the second round of kissing—another two pecks and a really hard kiss, like a man does and not a bumbling college kid. I'm surprised and not a bit dismayed that Rocky is really good at it. It's like he's completely focused on me, assessing my reaction and holy shit, the third time he just reaches under me and picks me up, sets me down on the dryer. My heart is racing and my belly is making jumping bean flip-flops.

"Okay, so I really liked it when you played with my hair when we danced on the hill."

I wiggle my finger so he comes close again. Then I let him kiss me and my fingers roll along the nape of his neck, tickling along to his ear.

"You good?" he whispers in my ear before he grants my next request—Rocky kisses my cheeks and neck and tugs on my shirt, brushes his lips along my shoulder. It tickles and gives me goosebumps.

"Yeah," I whisper back. He smells good—sporty aftershave and sweat.

And he kisses me again and again until Rocky heaves a sigh. "I like sexy stuff whispered in my ear."

"That's not fair. That's a hard one." I tug on my hair nervously. He tells me he likes that too. So I lean up and cup my hand on his ear, tickling the lobe, just like I used to tell secrets to Nicky. "I'm only wearing panties and if you're a good boy, I'll let you see what color they are."

"Oh." Rocky clears his throat while I push his hand down along my waist, tug up my t-shirt so he feels the flesh of my thigh. "If we're going farther than this, we're not doing it in the laundry room, Rosie," he tells me softly, pressing his forehead up to mine. It is an affectionate move, makes my tummy jump. We linger, foreheads touching. My hand is resting on his bare arm. It is muscled with tiny hairs and a dappling of freckles. "If you aren't sure—"

I linger there. I mean, we're at the point of no return. Maybe I'm looking too much into it. It isn't like we can have a normal relationship. Maybe it's like my bounce on the college dorm room bunk bed mattress, meaningless and maybe just doing it so I got past the never-having-done-it. No, not with Rocky. It could never be like that with him.

"Okay, you're hesitating. You don't need to say more," he sighs, but he doesn't move back.

I let my forefinger pat his arm. "I'm not hesitating," I tell him, my voice is hoarse and almost a whisper. "You know, it's like when you go to an amusement park and wait in line for what seems like four hours for that brand new ride you've been dreaming of all summer. And you're at that point where you're finally sitting on the rollercoaster and it tops the first hill. You know it's going to be over soon. You want this moment to last forever. You're anticipating the ride. I like that moment the best, you know." I'm rambling, talking too much. "I like that point right before the thrill—this." I hold out my hands between us. "Rocky, I'm trying to make it last." It's the truth. I'm sitting there on a stupid dryer in my dusty utility room which smells like Bounce Dryer Sheets. I'm feeling something incredible that I've never, ever felt before. It's like I'm standing with my toes on the edge of a cliff and looking down into nothingness or something I've never known. And it is terrifying and exciting both at once.

"So—"

I look up and Rocky's got a little cocky grin on his face. "So let's see how far we can go," I tell him. And he scoops me up again, my legs around his waist and we bang against the hallway walls and door frames in a frantic scuffle of kisses. I let my feet fall to the floor just outside my bedroom so we are face to face.

"Are you stopping?" he asks gruffly.

"No." My heart is pounding so fast, I think my chest is going to explode. I make a hurried wave toward the bedroom. We never even quite make it there, just three feet short of the door with Rocky pressing me against the hallway wall, his hands twined in my hair and my arms around his shoulders.

He wiggles off my shirt. I tug on his and he pulls it over his head. Our bellies touch, my warm skin meets his cooler flesh. Rocky looks me in the eyes, then lets his eyes fall to my little black bra and then to my panties. It's all there is between us, his jeans and my bra and panties. His right hand slips down from my shoulder, tickles along my arm and stops just short of my left breast. He takes in this long breath, lets it out in a puff of air. Just when I think this is going to be a short roller coaster ride, he pauses and looks me in the eyes. "You like the roller coasters. You know, fast and thrilling, yeah?"

"Yeah," I whisper.

"Well, the thrill's over way too fast for me. I like the really high Ferris wheels. I like to go up and feel like I could touch the sky, sit there a little bit and take in the world, over and over. You want to try it?"

"I've only ridden roller coasters, Rocky," I whisper.

He says nothing. Instead, Rocky slips his hand around my back, doesn't stop looking into my eyes. He smiles softly. I smile back. I'm shaking and I don't care if he knows I am. I feel the pressure of my bra clasps release, feel his hands working downward to tug on my panties. My hands are in tight fists on the waist of his pants.

My panties drop. I feel his hands on my bare bottom and then we just fall to the floor. He rolls so he's on top of me, his arms rippling with muscles while he keeps the weight at bay. He's kissing me and I hear myself making funny gasping noises. "Wait, baby, slow down," he whispers to me.

"I can't."

"You can."

I can hardly hold back. I'm trying. He unclasps his jeans, shimmies them down and never makes it out of them. "Just a little longer," Rocky says softly. We move together then, my arms wrapping around his shoulders, kissing his neck until I wrap my legs around his waist. I'm trying not to think about the way he feels, begging myself not to let loose so I can please him. (Did I just say that about a McDaniel?) But I know he's feeling the same way. He keeps holding his breath, gritting his teeth. I can feel the way his fingers are playing on my skin, the way his kisses are gentle and—

"I can't wait, Rocky, I can't—!"

"So, was it worth the wait?"

Two hours later, we're wrapped in warm blankets and lukewarm guilt we both aren't confessing in my bedroom. Rocky's voice is husky. His cheeks are pink. Every time I look up, he gets this boyish half-grin. He keeps staring at me, like he's seeing me in a whole new light. I suppose he is. I ripped my fingernails down his back, begged him in a husky voice to never, ever stop.

"Uh huh." I smile back at him, feel my cheeks get warm with a blush too. "You?"

"Oh, you don't know, Rosie," he says giving me the full grin. Now, his cheeks are a deep rose color. I'm tucked into Rocky's arms, both of them, and he's got one hand slipped behind my head. It's comfortable. We talk about stupid stuff; like roller coasters, the great taste of pink cotton candy at the county fair, and those spinning rides that make Rocky blow chunks three seconds after he gets off. He tickles me softly on the shoulder. I rub my palm across his chest, wiggle my fingers to the soft hairs around his belly button. He chuckles that funny huh-huh chuckle he has. Yet, it is almost like he's afraid to let me go. Do I push away? No. I'm afraid if I pull away, he'll be gone. Or I'll start bumbling around like my usual idiot self and say something dumb. *Oh, God, does he hold Nicky like this?*

With that settling on my mind, like a stale puddle of water left to warm in the August sun, we dose off. I'm not quite asleep when I get the phone call. It's Jack Barkley looking for his son. He screams at me while I step into the hallway until I *yes, sir* him a hundred times and tell him I'll find his son who is not answering his phone.

"I got to go," I whisper to Rocky over the side of the bed. I've got a plastic grocery bag with my school clothes in it dangling from my fingers.

"Who was that?"

"It's just my boss at the restaurant. I forgot I had to take a night shift." Tomorrow's Tuesday. I am praying I find Liam before I got to get to school. I slip on a short dress and modest high heels. I opt out of the Violet makeup, so Rocky doesn't see me in my secret life. "I got to—my boss called."

"Rosie, don't—"

"It's my job."

"Working at the school is your job."

I just stare at him. He knows the truth; I'm getting laid off. It won't be my job when summer rolls around. "Please keep this between us," I say. "You work for the fire department. Surely you know there are risks everybody takes and has to suck it up."

He doesn't answer, just sits up in the bed and nods while he scrubs a hand over his head.

"Rosie. What kind of risks do you take at a restaurant?"

"You know, getting junk under my nails cleaning grease vats—"

Just as I turn, he reaches out and gently snatches my hand. I linger there in mid-pivot, our fingers barely touching. Then, we let go. But the touch on my fingertips, it remains long after.

Chapter 47

I am working in my little office. Liam has his feet propped up on my desk. He's holding a plastic baggie with ice over his eye. He's trying to balance it between the bridge of his nose and cheek. I don't know why; perhaps it is just something to do. He's still drunk. I'm still shaking. It is five in the morning and there are only a handful of security inside the building, nobody else. Technically, I should be safely tucked into bed. It's my night off, but Jack Barkley called and said Liam wasn't answering his phone. I needed to hunt him down. That was four hours ago. I found him.

I tug the cord connecting his cell phone to my computer and disconnect it from the phone. I see him peering out at me from beneath his ice pack while I extend the phone. He leans forward, lets the ice pack drop to his lap and takes the phone in his fingers.

"Are you happy? You've got all my contacts. You can find me anywhere now. Or are you still mad at me?"

"You're kidding me, right?" I ask him. I look at Liam. He's got a cut that runs parallel along the bridge of his nose, a fat lip, and the early onset of a black eye. "You went out, without me, on a Monday night; it was my *only* night off this week. You about got me killed. So, I'll tell you what my mom always says to guilt me. I will forgive, but I *won't* forget." I look up over my computer in the gray room and give him my meanest gaze. "Oh, I'll never forget."

"Oh, that's harsh." Liam makes a ragged sigh. He rolls his finger in the air to add to his sarcastic retort. "Was it the kiss or the—"

"I said you are not to ever mention the kiss." The kiss. Liam Dubois had completely caught me off guard and drunk-kissed me less than forty minutes ago. It was a cold, wet peck of lips smelling of beer and puke and his tongue weaving around in my mouth for the two seconds I was in shock. The kiss was followed by my right fist jamming hard into his ribs and a threat of another much harder bash with the toe of my shoe in his balls if he ever did it again. "Period. You say it again and I'll give you another busted lip."

"You were so badass, Violet, I mean you're like one of those cops on *Real Cops TV, Chasing Bad Boys*. Except you were wearing a dress. Damn, girl." He lifts up his arm, feigns three punches in the air. "*Bam, bam, bam*." He pauses, looks thoughtfully at the ceiling. "Well, then another well-placed *bam* at me."

"You're an idiot when you're drunk. And those guys were so drunk, Liam, they could barely walk."

"Naw, they were managing to kick my butt."

That isn't saying much. I look at him. He's not the kind of man I've ever liked—spoiled, rich, and with the kind of slight muscle that comes from working out sometimes, not all the time, and not from really working. I suppose if I had a secret, it would be that I like redneck guys—the kind that don't take shit and wouldn't let a woman take over their fight once they started it. And Liam had done just that. He'd shrunk back into the shadows as soon as I dug the tip of my high heel shoe into the first crotch. He didn't come out until the bouncers stopped my arms in the air and two seconds before I let the chair in my hands fall to the second's back.

And yes, they were drunk. At least that's what I saw when I walked into Downtown Sally's at two-thirty-eight. I called every bar I could think of while I was charging down the highway trying to find him. Then I stopped and thought it out. It wasn't that difficult. I dug up Crystal Glass's phone number I'd gotten from the strip club and sure enough,

Liam was tossing out twenty dollar bills when I walked into the door. I stopped just short of his table and the two men that looked like they came straight from an insurance salesman meeting complete with suits and ties next to him. They started harassing him and asking if his wifey had come to drag him home. They thought it was funny. Liam did not. He threw a wobbly punch that missed the first man and hit the second in the shoulder. Then both of them started waling on Liam before the bouncers could even make it across the floor. So I started waling on the two men; three well-placed groin kicks, one elbow in the nose, and two Norma Edwards Specials in the jaw left them flopping to the floor.

"You got me frigging kicked out of a strip club, Liam! You know how hard it is to get a woman kicked out of a strip club?"

He guffaws. I can't help but huff a laugh too. It doesn't last long. I'm shaken tonight. The first bar I stopped at was the Crazy Fiddle on my way out of town. It was closing time there. I walked in the door, looked around. It was almost empty, so I turned and went back out into the dark parking lot. Just when I put my fingers on my car door, I felt a hand on my shoulder.

I squeaked a yelp, turned, and realized I was facing Johnny McDaniel. I couldn't move. He was standing half in the dark and half out. I thought this was it, he was going to kill me. My heart was racing so badly, I thought I was going to have a panic attack.

"Stay away from my own," he growled at me. I swallowed hard, just stared at him. "You stay away from my boy and my girl and anybody else that's a McDaniel, you hear me? Or you'll be sorry." He shook my shoulder then and I stepped back hard against my car door. "You hear me?" He yells at me. I hear a car door slam in the parking lot. Johnny snaps his head to the side. There's a couple standing there, taking us in from a stone's throw away. He took a step back, released my shoulder. "You don't want what's coming to you if you start that curse up again, girl. You know another girl come up dead tonight, don't you? Maybe if you don't keep your nose out of stuff, you'll be next. Ask your auntie about that. It ain't good. And I'll do what I can to stop it, stop *you*. So watch your back—"

"Are you afraid I'll find out your secret, Johnny?" I ask, my eyes wide. "Because the only thing between your niece and the murderer is me. Just me. And I'm the only one who doesn't believe you've been murdering girls up and down every road in the county. But I hear tell the cops are right on your ass. So before you go and try to hurt me, I'd think about that." My voice is shaky and too high to be intimidating. However, it gave me enough time to get away. His words unsettled me. I'm not as badass as Liam thinks I am. Or maybe, to a pansy city boy, I am.

Liam is quiet for a few. I think he might have fallen to sleep, but when I look up, he's staring at me.

"I need to tell you something."

"If you're professing your love to me," I mumble, "you already did so twice in my car, which is two times less than you threw up along the side of the road."

"No. I think I've been giving a lady information about you."

"What?" My head shoots up. I stare into his bloodshot gaze. "Who and why?"

Liam laughs. He picks up a pen from my little pencil holder, kicks his feet up on my desk again, and chews on the pen. "You forgot when, where, and why." He notices I'm not returning the laugh. "She's a psychologist. I think that's how my stepdad found you, through her."

"I thought it was through my dad."

"If I can be blunt, there's no way Jack Barkley would hire you with only an endorsement from the guy who runs his shooting range. He may have asked your dad about you, but he wouldn't hire you without a ton of credentials. She said you'd be a positive influence on me. A Doctor Stamper? I went to court for a DUI. The judge let me off if I talked to a shrink. She was the closest one in a fifty mile radius of this boondocks town. I didn't have a choice if I wanted to stay out of jail."

"Why would she ask about me?"

"At first, she just asked who I was hanging out with and when I was hanging out with them," he tells me. "But now, in retrospect, I see she was finagling stuff out of me. It was like she maneuvered the conversation to you. I'm assuming you saw her too, because she knew a lot about you."

"I thought they had an oath of confidentiality. She told you stuff about me?"

"She said if she told me stuff about you, we had a pact that neither of us could tell you. I thought it was strange. But I went along with it. I didn't like you. It's nice to know your enemy's weaknesses."

The tiny office is silent while I stare at him. I feel betrayed. But when was he ever anything but belligerent to me anyway? "Yeah, my mom will go to great lengths to manipulate me."

"I thought your mom didn't know you worked here."

"She probably doesn't know where Doctor Stamper gets her information." I'm quiet for a few minutes. I fiddle with my computer.

"I didn't tell her what your job was. I just told her you wait tables." He's working his head a little to the side like he's trying to read my expression. "You're mad at me, aren't you?"

"Do you care?" I sniff a laugh.

"No, I don't give a shit about anybody—" Liam tosses the pen at me and it bounces off my arm. I don't even look up. Then he does something I don't expect. He stands up, picks up the pen and places it in the little metal container holding the pens. "Yeah, I kind of care. I know it's a secret and stuff. You're kind of like a big, bitchy older sister."

"Secret." I repeat. *I know your secret.* That's what the prank phone caller said. "How long ago did you start your sessions with her?"

"I don't know. It was about a year ago. A long time before you started here."

"Oh, my God," I groan, press my fingers to my temples. I look up. "About the time Alaina Windowski and Angel Daugherty were murdered?"

"Yeah." He ponders this. "I guess so. Why?"

"Do you think Doctor Stamper would be capable of murder?"

He chuckles, rubs his eye with a knuckle and shakes his head. "You're kidding me, right? Dad said she gives out bike helmets to kids every year for free."

I roll my eyes, take in a breath. "She also had a daughter who was murdered right when my aunt came up missing and girls started showing up dead."

"It could be anyone, Violet. I don't even know how you'd prove it even if she did." He rolls his eyes in disbelief.

I rub my face. He's right. But there's something in the back of my mind screaming that maybe I should try. "Why do you think this is funny, huh? How else would anybody know *where* you were so they could set it up to make you look like you were the one murdering girls? Did you tell her about a date with Alaina?"

"She told me about her. Asked if I could help her get a job at the country club instead of working at the strip club."

"And Angel?"

"She introduced us at a wedding." Liam croaks. "And Lydia just showed up at a bar, started coming on to me."

I narrow my eyes. "See, Liam, let me tell you something. I've got a wall of pictures of murdered girls. They are all from a race my dad and another man took in high school with two truckloads of teenagers to see a dead girl. That dead girl was Mary Stamper's daughter. Each one of those teens grew up and had at least one daughter. Each of those daughters has died under mysterious circumstances, except for me and one other girl."

He shifts in his chair. "She gave my dad your recommendation for the job here," he tells me with a gruff voice. "Damn. Who is the other girl?"

"I'm not telling you." I cut him off.

"You don't trust me."

"No, Liam, I don't."

"You should, *Rosie*." He says my name softly and stresses it. He sits up in his seat, then leans slightly forward so he is cupping his face in his palms. "I could have killed you, you know." Liam bursts into a storm of tears. "Three times. She gets in your head, you know? I was three inches from killing you."

"What?"

"Doctor Stamper. She like has a way of manipulating stuff and she freaked me out. She said she could make all my problems go away, all of them. She said she knew I killed those girls. She said if I killed you, she would make all my problems go away. I think she killed them. I do. I know it's crazy—"

"You're not crazy." I feel the sweat beading on my forehead. I only wish the only person who believes me wholeheartedly wasn't a suspect. And one who would think about killing me. "She is. But why are you telling me this now, Liam? I know there has to be an ulterior motive. Or are you just drunk-sad?"

He looks up. His eyes are already tear-swollen. "Because you're the only one besides my stepdad who hasn't dumped me for being the worst side of me. And I think that's the only side there is of me."

"You are a pain in my ass." I take him in for a moment. Then I shake my head.

"I'm a pain in everybody's ass. But I don't get any respect anyway. What's it matter?"

"You know, before I started working here, I blended into the world with as much flair as the wilting honeysuckle growing on the wall in my mom's garden."

Liam sniffs a laugh, breaks a smile. "That's definitely not true anymore. Especially after your kickass moves tonight."

"You realize you don't always have to be a spoiled shit, right?" I ask him returning his smile with a teasing one. "If I can go from Rosie wallflower to kickass Violet, you can change too. Maybe you can show an interest in the country club. My daddy always says you've got to *earn* respect."

Liam looks down at his hands folded in his lap. I expect for him to make a snide remark about my daddy being one of the grounds maintenance workers, so what would he know about earning respect? He doesn't. Instead, Liam shrugs.

"Maybe."

Chapter 48

"Miss Mauer?" I look up from my front desk in the library and blink at Charley Walters and Jake Smythe the next morning. I had stopped long enough to pick up the phone again, weighing the price I'd pay if I told the police what I know. Instead, I stop short with disappointment. I see a text from Rocky to Violet on my work phone. *Hi. Sorry. Got caught at work last night. How goes it? You still want to go out?*

"So, Colton McDaniel says he's helping you work on solving a crime." I jerk my eyes from the phone, set it face down.

"Was he serious?" I take in the two boys. They are similar, like bookends with pimpled faces, wire-rimmed glasses, and teenage gawky. Ug. I'm waiting for them to pull some prank. These two are always coming up with some new joke for the library, like flipping my books upside-down or putting clown faces on the backgrounds of the computers to scare the other students. They are too bright for the AP classes, so Mariah sends them down to the library to play with the computers instead of coming up with more stimulating projects for them.

I nibble on my bottom lip. "Well, kind of. I mean, he did some research from my aunt's diary who has been missing since 1978."

"Can we work on it too?" Charley asks eagerly. "We heard there was another murder. They found a girl in a burned car between the town and the highway."

He's right. They haven't released the girl's name yet, but Rocky told me they already ran her driver's license and she's got a whole bunch of arrests for drug use and prostitution. She was from Columbus and was wrapped in a blanket and stuffed in the trunk of a car. The car was red. I'd say she was easy pickings to use as a ploy to take eyes off of the real killer. And I don't think the red car was chosen on a whim. It was the same make and model as mine.

"I want to go into forensic science," Jake adds. "The experience would look good on my college applications."

What do I have to lose? I ask myself that and shrug. "Okay, sure." I reach into my purse, pull out the receipt with Barry M. Underwood 555-2368 that I got from Tag at the pawn shop. It seems innocent and probably just a ploy to get my attention. "Here." I slap it down on the desk between us. "I got this number. I don't think it's a phone number. I don't know what the meaning is, but it may have to do with the murder of a girl named Lydia. Let me know what you find."

"Lydia Murphy? The girl they found dead from Columbus?" Charley leans in.

I push a finger to my lips. "Hush now. Do you want to help or not?"

"Yeah." They both say, nodding earnestly.

"Go figure out what this clue means."

Johnny's got a secret. It's in the diary. It isn't written in the pages. I find it tucked into a little pocket where the puffy back cover had been slit about two inches along the top edge. "Colton." I wave a hand at Colton McDaniel and he trudges up to the desk.

"Can you please be cool, Miss Mauer." He leans his elbows on my desk so he's an inch away from my face. "I have a reputation to uphold."

"That's right, and it's *such* an admirable one." I hold up both hands. "I'm sorry. That wasn't very nice. No big deal. I just found something cool, thought you'd want to see it." I see his eyes drop to six or seven pages of the diary that had been tugged out.

"What is it?"

"The pages you noticed were missing when you borrowed the book—" I hold up my index fingers as quotation marks. "—the first time."

"No kidding." Colton almost crawls across the table to see them while I delicately unfold them.

"Now who is being uncool?" I mutter while I lean closer, push my glasses up the bridge of my nose. Colton pulls his head back to snub me, then leans over.

"It says—" I squint. "*Johnny's got a secret. He told me. There was a dead girl on the road the other night. He knew she was there. They heard about it from the guy who comes in and does the drug talks at school. Everybody knew about her. I wanted to go see her too, but Johnny said I couldn't. We might get caught. They all got in the cars to go see it—*" I look up at Colton. "Do you see some strange things here?"

"That they knew there was somebody dead and wanted to see her?"

"Well, yeah, that's a no-brainer," I say. "But why would my aunt mention the fact that someone who does the drug talks told them about the body. Who usually does the drug talks now?"

"Officer Hanson," Colton tells me. "He's the cop the school pays to bring his dog down and sniff lockers. Oh, maybe he wanted our dads to go racing down there so someone else got blamed for killing the girl, right?"

"Yes, I've seen Officer Hanson buddying up with the kids he knows are smoking pot to get information from them. Maybe whoever was the drug cop was doing the same with them. If my aunt wasn't lying, how would a cop know before the rest of police that there was a dead girl on the road? Why the heck wouldn't he be doing his job and calling an ambulance or something? So this big secret—"

"Miss Mauer, it wasn't a secret that my dad and your aunt were friends so much."

"What?" I look up. Colton is strangely subdued.

"My dad can't read. That's the secret." He waits for me to say something. I don't. I let his words sink in and before I can question him, Colton reaches into his back pocket and pulls out a folded piece of paper, opens it. It is another small section of my aunt's diary he extends to me. I furrow my brow at Colton. "You took this?"

"I ripped more out when I borrowed it. I didn't think you'd notice because some were already gone. The other pages came out too. That's why they were tucked into the side and I didn't want to give it back. I didn't want you to know. I couldn't fix the jagged edges. I tried to make it look like she did all of them." He points to the paper. "Your aunt wrote a little bit about starting to teach my dad to read. That was his secret. I was worried you'd think he was stupid. You know, the whole thing about us on Raccoon Creek being stupid and all. My dad would die if anybody knew about it. He doesn't know I know about it."

"He has dyslexia too."

"I guess. I just know she said he couldn't read and she couldn't figure out why the words looked different to him. It's like me, I guess."

"I won't tell anybody."

"Leah said you think it's Doctor Stamper who is murdering the girls. She said nobody believes you."

"That's true."

"I don't understand why not. I believe you."

"Can you do me a favor? Can you find out from your dad or aunt who was doing the drug talks back in 1977? I can't ask at the office because they'll wonder why I'm asking. All the files from that time are kept in storage outside town because they were done on paper, not on the computer."

The doors to the library open. I nibble my bottom lip. It's Rocky. We haven't talked since I left to find Liam two nights ago. When I got back home, Rocky had left.

"Hey, I need to talk to Miss Mauer about teacher stuff, Colton." Rocky waves Colton away with his hand. Colton rolls his eyes, shakes his head. But as he pushes away from my desk, he jabs a finger at Rocky's chest.

"What happened to you, dude?" he asks with a grin. "You spill your coffee?"

"Yeah, your sister's up to her old tricks," he answers, making a blind swipe over his shirt. "She must have drilled a few holes in my favorite coffee cup. I poured it in from the carafe and it started streaming out the sides."

"You didn't see the holes?" I ask, as if I can't figure out how he would have fallen for such a trick. I do. It took me nearly a half hour this morning climbing up to the ceiling and unscrewing six lightbulbs after I'd drilled four holes in the coffee mug marked with: WORLDS BEST TEACHER one of his classes had given Rocky two years ago.

"There's a few lights out in the teacher's lounge. So no, it was kind of dark." He waits until Colton is out of earshot, follows him with his eyes, then leans his elbows on my desk and looks at me.

"Miss Mauer, about the other night—"

Yes, what about it? I reach over, slide my work phone into my desk drawer and try not to think about the text he sent to Violet a few minutes ago. "I know. It was a one night stand. You didn't mean to do it. And no, I won't tell anybody." I hold up my hand when he starts to talk. "It's okay. I've got a boyfriend, Rocky," I say. Why did I say that? It makes me sick to my tummy. But Rocky hasn't stopped texting Violet since the wedding. He doesn't like *me*. I know I'm just going to get hurt in the end.

"The guy who sends the chocolates?"

"Yeah." I tap my pencil on the desk. "Leah says you've got a girlfriend anyway. I'm assuming the girl you wanted to dance with. Did you ever get the dance?"

"No" Rocky leans his elbows on the counter, pats his hand twice between us. Then he leans forward so he is six inches from my face. "I'm going to call you out on this one, Rosie. You're manipulating the situation. Don't put words in my mouth. I've spent the last ten years with your sister doing the exact same thing. You're mean. You're meaner than you say Tangy is on any level. I don't honestly think you have a soul-"

"That's harsh."

I think he is going to say more, but my cell phone rings. Just to avoid whatever is happening, I start to snatch it from my drawer. I see it is Liam. I think Rocky sees it too. Rocky stands up straight, gets this faraway look to his eyes and pats his hands on my desk. "Yeah, you just go ahead and get that. Well, that's that," he says. What's that mean?

Chapter 49

"What's it mean, *that's that?*"

Four minutes ago, I pulled into Rocky's driveway. I can hear his truck fan running when I pass the hood, know he just got home too. I walk to his door, knock on it, and stand there until he opens it up. I'd stood there, hearing his footsteps cross the carpet, each pound of his foot on the floor in synchronization to my pounding heart .

He just stands at his door, looking down at me. He doesn't say anything. So I sigh. "Just so you know, I don't know why I said I had a boyfriend. I thought you'd tell me to get rid of him. Here's how I feel: I'm scared about the way I want to see you so badly. I'm terrified my mom will find out. Shit, I'm breaking out in a sweat right now, thinking that my daddy might see my car in your driveway. I've got secrets I can't tell you. And I'm not going to tell you." He just stands there like he is stunned I'm standing there at all, so I go on. "I'm a girly girl. I like dresses. I don't have big boobs or blonde hair or stuff you probably like. I'm not good at basketball, like Nicky. I take pills to control my crazy. But I like you. I like being with you whether it's on my hallway carpet or—sitting in your truck tossing out test questions at you."

"So here we are again," he says, his voice low. He reaches out a hand and lets it slide along my upper arm until his fingers stop just short of the crease of my elbow. Rocky leaves it there, looks down at me with sad-puppy eyes. "I've got forty-five minutes before I've got training at the fire department. What do you want to do?"

"You know what I want to do," I purr while my own lips turn into a grin and I wiggle a forefinger at him. "If you lean down here real close, I'll whisper it to you." He doesn't hesitate, leans over and I push my hand around his neck to tug him close enough I can murmur softly just beside his right ear. "I want to do *you* on the couch, I want to do you on the kitchen floor. And I want to end up in the bed, so tangled up we might not be able to set ourselves free. You think you can do that in forty-three minutes and twelve seconds?"

Holy crap. Yeah, Rocky McDaniel can. He wraps an arm beneath my bottom and lifts me right up like I only weigh ten pounds in his arms. I wrap my legs around his waist. He turns long enough to push the door closed with his shoulder while he smothers me with kisses. We never make it to the kitchen. It ends up being the couch and then, when we don't quite fit, the floor between his little coaster table and the couch.

I can still feel his fingers tangling in my hair at the country club a few hours later. I can still smell his aftershave on my skin. I can still see his eyes when I opened them at just the right moment when we melded together. He'd opened his too. It was a moment that lingers in my mind, his warm, sweet eyes the color of a hot August sky looking at me. "I—" he'd started. He stopped there. *I* what? *I got to stop? I can't do this? I like you. I love you? What?*

But I find out at eight-thirty the same night. There's a ting on my work phone. I pick it up. It's a message for Violet from Rocky. *Hey, how's it going?*

I answer him. We flirt back and forth. When another hour passes, I get a message from Rocky to Rosie.

We need to talk.

Talk?

I can't do this. Too many consequences. It's complicated.

Chapter 50

"This was against my better judgement." This evening, I'm bowling with Kim, Liam, and about three-quarters of the staff who get off work on Friday nights before nine. Kim is sitting across from me while she glances over at Liam knowingly. I'm not quite sure why they all do this on one night a month. But Kim says it is a *thing*, a tradition. They rent half the bowling alley in a town about thirty miles north of Crystal Springs.

I don't know if they like the idea that Liam and I are tagging along or not; they aren't saying. Every once in a while, we get a lingering, wary gaze. Liam keeps elbowing me and rolling his eyes. "I mean, I think everybody has the right to date who they want," Kim goes on with a braced sigh. "But Liam asked me to do this and I know it goes beyond my usual providing a background check on our employees." Kim scoots a piece of paper over to me, an eight and a half by eleven sheet of paper. I glance at her, drop my eyes to the paper, and scan it. "But you're a friend, so I kind of felt okay doing it. I did some background research on the guy you've been seeing, Emmanuel Garcia, AKA Carlos Diaz, or Manuel Alvarez, or Colbert Gonzales. I can keep going. He has sixteen known aliases, probably more. It's about as many as his lawyers can come up with to keep him out of prison. He's loaded, so he can. Violet, he's a part of an international organized crime ring, drug traffickers who prey on Europeans. He's in a gang called No Traces or *Sin rastros*—kind of like The Untraceables."

I look up from the paper, eye Liam, who is deadpan staring at me. Kim looks from him to me. "Go on," I say. I don't show that my heart is dropping. I suppose I knew something was strange with him. He's always disappearing after we spend a couple days together, only to pop up again out of nowhere. Surprise.

"Okay. Do I really need to?" She takes in my straight-faced expression. I know she thinks I don't believe her. It isn't that at all. He just made me feel pretty and desirable. Now I just feel ugly, dirty, and used. "This gang he's in, they traffic cocaine to young people all over Europe. They get these attractive young men like Emmanuel to charm a group of high school or college age people and start dealing drugs to them. They use poorer twenty-somethings as couriers, so they don't get caught themselves. They pop back and forth across the borders so they aren't tracked. I would suppose your Emmanuel has been doing that all over the country." Kim pokes at the paper. "He's a scary guy to be with, like hanging around with an old hand grenade. Somebody wants him dead in every country. If they start shooting and you're holding hands—"

"All right, enough." Liam pats the table with his hands. "She gets it." He's been eyeing me protectively since he told me about his relationship with Doctor Stamper. It's like we share a bond. I think he knows if she knows he told me, he'd be dead. And I feel like we are like Hansel and Gretel, hugging each other close on a kitchen stool while the wicked witch sharpens her knife, getting ready to murder us and add our meat to her stew.

I sit back in my chair, try to act like Kim's report doesn't bother me. But I see Kim and Liam eyeing me like they're trying to read my mood. Finally, Liam seems to conjure up something to change the subject. He tosses a napkin at me and sits up in his chair. "So, you know my stepdad as well as I do. How do I approach the subject?" Liam is mopey tonight; he doesn't want to be here. He's just not the dollar beer and greasy pizza kind of guy. However, I also know he ran into Mayor Pritchard today. The mayor asked if he could talk his stepdad into letting the city workers use the country club facility at a discounted rate like Rocky said at the restaurant. Liam knows, without asking, what Jack's answer will be and it is a *no*.

"Well, considering the local police are still tossing around the idea you are a suspect in killing two girls, I would approach it slowly," I tease him. But he's all serious, so I sigh. "I think it is bold move on the mayor's behalf. He's overlooking the bad publicity that your stepdad is getting over the murder accusations. I'm assuming in the past, he's tried to have ties with Jack politically or socially, and has been turned down. He is utilizing you as a tool at this point. I'm also assuming it is the reason he allowed his daughter to sit with you. He's letting others know he trusts you—another sign he doesn't think you killed those girls."

"That's true."

I realize right then Liam is probably one of the few people who understands me without my having to explain my thoughts on different levels. "So you have to gain your stepdad's trust, Liam. He's a difficult man to please. However, for some reason, he has taken a shine to you. He could have left you in some jail to rot in Cleveland when all this started. Instead, he puts up with your shit. Show him you're not an idiot. Show him you can take things seriously."

"You're kidding, right?"

I groan, shake my head at Liam, who looks like I just shoved a pile of manure in front of him while he glares at me with pursed lips. I wish I hadn't come. The only thing worse than being around a mean Liam is being around a sulky Liam. I'm also thinking about Rocky, wondering what he's doing. For the last two days, I have been texting back and forth with him. He thinks he's texting Violet Popovich.

So the most recent texting goes like this:

What you doing?

Getting ready to go to a meeting. You?

Just sitting here. Bad week. Thinking of you.

Thinking about me? I ask. And a bad week? I think back. Nothing seemed amiss. Well, maybe. I mean, I didn't see him at all, in fact.

I should have danced with u.

The conversation didn't go much farther. It was my turn to bowl. When I came back and Rocky had texted a few chit-chat items, I answered. But over the course of the time between the wedding and now, I think I know everything about him. He likes chocolate bars with raisins and has always wanted to race a car. He hates teaching, likes dark beers, and gets bored going to sports bars. There's at least forty other things I didn't know about Rocky and I suppose I could easily call it his Violet side. And he knows a lot about the Violet side of me. I've sent him a bunch of pictures I took when Emmanuel took me to Disney World and Mexico and a little island resort in Alaska.

So, you have a boyfriend? He asks.

A few. I'm not looking to settle down. You got a girl?

Not really. Kind of. Maybe.

Then, Rocky wrote: *You want to go out to dinner with me?*

I want to avoid that one. I suppose I should have known a relationship built on texting, deception, and lies wouldn't last long. The one thing I do know as Rosie is that Rocky will avoid dancing at all costs. So I text: *Yes. But you have to take me somewhere and dance with me.*

Bam! I feel a hard fist-thump on my right shoulder and I tilt slightly to my left.

"Getting your geek on, Popovich?" It's Norma Edwards. I've tried to avoid her all night. Just as soon as we got out of the cars, she was already dancing around me like she was play-fighting. It isn't a difficult dodge. She's a loud talker and her voice echoes off the walls of the bowling alley. There's no point in the entire building, including the ancient bathroom with a closed door, her exact location can't be pinpointed. "Oh, yeah, that's right. You're a geek all the time." She makes a boisterous hyuck-hyuck laugh and starts jabbing her fists in the air at me when I glare upward.

"Can you leave me alone just one night?" I groan.

Liam says something. I don't turn. My head veers to the right to avoid another bump by Norma. My eyes alight on another group of people because someone got a strike and everyone is hooting and clapping. It's like BAM! I see it when Norma's fist careens into my arm again.

My sister is sitting there. My heart bounces a pitter-patter-oh-shit while the young woman who got the strike does a high five with her, then leans over and gives her a big smack on the lips. Now, it isn't the type of kiss you give a friend. It lingers with their lips together and then, they lock eyes. Nicky's got on ripped jeans, and I see the girl reach out and tickle a little bit of the bare skin sticking out of a hole just above her knee. Nicky giggles and does one of those cutesy gentle slaps of her hands at the girl who feigns being scared. Someone else jumps up and does this funky dance around them with a beer in his hand. Shit on a stick! It's Timmy Kinney. My sister is friends with him? I find that strangely fascinating because not only have I never seen my sister wear ripped jeans, I've never seen her outright giggle like a giddy schoolgirl. Not even when she *was* a schoolgirl.

I'm flustered and slightly irritated while I lazily rub my right arm. I suppose it all comes together then. Because a few weeks ago when I'd gone to Mom's for supper, I'd headed to the upstairs bathroom and I walked in on Nicky and Rocky having a conversation in Nicky's old bedroom. It went like this:

"So how long is it going to take before you make this decision," Rocky asked softly. I started to turn away. I know they didn't realize I'd stopped in to eat. *"Because it's not fair for me to sit around, year after year, waiting so you can keep this secret. I think I've been patient."*

"You've been patient, Rocky, I'm sorry. Everything's going to change. Mom's going to hate me. I'm scared."

"I'm here for you, you know that, right? Either way. You say the word and please, Nicky, say the word—"

I'd back-stepped quietly away then with my eyes slightly closed and my brow furrowed, hoping they wouldn't hear me. I just assumed it was Nicky afraid Mom knew they weren't dating anymore, like she had some big investment in the two up to this point. But now I'm sitting with my eyes wide open. I suppose that's what irritates me, what makes this sudden horrible ache gush up into my chest. I mean, I suppose that's what Rocky meant by: *I can't do this. Too many consequences. It's complicated.* It feels like my whole entire life is being run by my mom or Nicky, except when I have this stupid, secret life. I thought Rocky's indecision was based on me. And when it sinks in, I feel rage at my sister for holding him back, regardless if it was with Violet or Rosie or even Tangy. She's got her own secret life with her own set of friends. And at the end of the day, it's her loyal pup, Rocky, she's hurting.

Almost half-heartedly, I can see Norma's fist coming in for the second round and not a second too late, I snap it up in my own fist and shove it away, deflecting the blow and making her lean to the right. She doesn't fall, just slaps her hands on the table, calls it a geek-move and tweaks my nose instead. I want to kill her. I think I'm going to cry. I don't know why. It's frustrating, knowing it is never going to end because my sister is never going to tell Mom she has a girlfriend and she's never going to marry what Mom calls my sister's *love of her life*. She's buddying up with the same person who dragged me and my daddy into the police station and harassing us.

I stand up quickly, shove myself around Norma. I can't go right. I'm not sure if my sister will recognize me or not in my Violet getup. So I make a hasty retreat to the bathroom. I slam the swinging door to the stall behind me.

I try not to cry into a wad of toilet paper I bunch in my hand. Still the tears drip. I sniffle just as the bathroom door opens. "I'll be right out." I make a few more swipes, flush the toilet.

"I didn't mean to make you cry, Popovich." It's Norma's shadow I see creeping by the stall door. Her voice is subdued. "You're too sensitive. I only pick on you to make you stronger, you know that right?"

"Whatever. I'm a pussy. I know that. Wah-wah-wah, you made me cry. Isn't that what you always say?"

"No, you're not a pussy. Liam says you've kicked ass a couple times defending him. Although, *he* doesn't call it that." Norma leans against the door. I can see the backs of her bowling shoes. "Jack told me from the start his son needed a bodyguard. You know how many girls I beat the shit out of to get to you? Thirty-two. That's a lot of pussies, thirty-two. He told me I had to either quit being so hard on the likes of you all or he'd never have a babysitter for his son. I asked him what the point was if he had one that wasn't tough. Because his boy would end up dead. If it took a hundred, just keep them coming. Eventually, one would stick it out." Norma bounces a little on the door with her butt. I imagine she's folding her tanned, muscled arms across her chest. "So when you came along all geeky and girly-girl with your thick glasses and scaredy-cat stare, I figured, okay here goes number thirty-three. And I told Jack that. He laughed at me, bet me fifty bucks I couldn't make a fighter out of you."

"Great." I swipe my nose with a piece of toilet paper and open the door. "I don't know if I get made fun of more at my job at the high school or at the country club."

Norma's eyes follow me to the sink where I dab the toilet paper under my eyes and pull my lipstick from my purse. "Honestly, the second you jumped on my back at the boxing ring that day and waled on me with those pussy cat paws, I knew you were going to stick it out. You've even got a signature move—a veer, a kick in the shins and two punches with the left arm."

"Thanks. I think," I mumble, rolling the lipstick across my lips.

"And then you run like hell." She stifles a laugh with her fist. "I like it. And you're welcome. I call it the Popovich Shuffle. The only thing you're leaving out is to flip your assailant off. I wouldn't recommend it in my case. Don't think I'm not going to keep beating your ass when we spar."

Right then, the bathroom door opens and I hear laughter. Norma scoots from the stall door, shifts to the side while I slowly drop my hand holding the lipstick. Holy hell, it's Nicky and her date coming in while I peer out of the corner of my eyes at her. It's like time freezes as Nicky gives me a long look, but hardly catches my eye. I close my lipstick with a certain coolness, eye the two up and down, like strangers who just rudely interrupted our chatter. Norma makes another shift to her left waving her hand to the door. "All right, Popovich, get your girly-girl ass back out there and lose a another game to me." I do as she says, make a turn toward the door. And I realize my sister did not recognize me at all.

Chapter 51

I've learned to hate Wednesdays because I actually only get Tuesday evenings off from both my jobs, I dread the day after because I know I won't get a break for an entire week. Wednesday is also the day I help out the staff in the front office, running copies for all the teachers. I can't help but notice each week that Tangy and Mariah hold off all their copying until Wednesday, just to rub it in that I'm the lowest man on the totem pole.

So on Wednesday morning, I'm planted at the copy machine I've wheeled to my library desk. I've got a bad attitude and Winsome Falls opened to page two-hundred and thirty-three. I've got to stand there for six hours and make copies of math sheets for Tangy, English homework for Mariah, and two-hundred and twelve school newspapers with four pages (front and back) each for Meghan Wilder. While I do it, I'm trying to forge through the last three chapters of Rocky's romance book and figure out the key to his fascination with me reading it.

"Miss Mauer." I feel a nudge on my elbow on the last page of the book. I turn around, shove my glasses along the bridge of my nose. I'm staring at Charley Walters and Jake Smythe, who also shove their glasses up the bridge of their noses in perfect synchronization as my own.

"I'm knee deep in drudgery and heartache, boys, what do you need?" I ask them while Charley holds out the little receipt with the numbers on it.

"It's not a phone number," Charley explains while I take it in my fingers. "It's a clue, like in a game. We looked up Barry M. Underwood in a directory online. He was a local artist who painted pictures of covered bridges. He died about ten years ago. But there's a website on his work—"

"The domain name was purchased just three weeks ago," Jake interrupts. He is hugging a laptop, which he plops on to the copy machine and opens it wide to expose a bare, tan website page. "The site was built with one of those cheap free website builders—Bizbo. There are only three pictures on the website. They are all covered bridges."

I squint at the screen, scan down to the bottom where the copyright owner of the website usually places a link. Nothing. "Did you look to see who owns the domain name?"

"Barry M. Underwood." Charley flips the screen, exposes the information on the domain. Sure enough, his name is there. "And that was his correct address. We looked it up on online maps. It's the Underwood History and Art Center. He donated it to the county."

"And you're sure he's dead."

"Yeah. I read the obituary."

I pull the laptop closer to view the three bridges. "I know the second bridge." I poke the screen with my finger. "It's over off Staley Mill Road. My mom has a painting of it on her living room wall." My eyes veer upward to the long shelves of books. "Come with me."

It's an easy find, the shelf housing the historical books for the region in the back of the library. I roll my finger down the spines until I stop at one that says: *Ohio Covered Bridges, Then and Now*. I gently pull it out, turn to the table of contents.

"Staley Mill Covered Bridge." Charley's leaning into my shoulder and he uses a stubby finger to point to page thirty-two. I flip the pages until I come to the Staley Mill Covered Bridge.

"What's that," Jake whispers as the three of us squint at a long line of hand-printed numbers and letters placed in lead pencil just beneath: *EnCt2741cb9c59e6831446c286c-fc6611e3d59cc95834741cb9c59e6831446c286cfc20W9KdvqrgO*

"It looks like an encrypted message."

All three of us jump. I crane my neck, see a third face staring over my shoulder. It's Mindy Carter. You can read her mood by her clothes and makeup, and she has BO, and talks too loud. She doesn't seem to offend Colton. Wherever Mindy is, he isn't far behind; harassing her in the same way an eight year-old will push a little girl that he's crushing on down. It appears he is coming up beside her now. Yesterday, she was anti-hunting and in a foul mood; her mom had to bring in a change of clothes in exchange for the yellow t-shirt she was wearing with a deer flipping off a hunter. Colton hunts from October through February. Even so, I heard him tell her the shirt she had on was cool.

"It is an encrypted message," Mindy announces with a haughty air. "I went to the Columbus Computer Camp last summer. We worked in teams to make a project. I was on the team with a simulated Mars robot. We encrypted messages back and forth to each other, so the other teams didn't figure out our project."

"Shut up and go away, Mindy," Charley sniffs. Colton eyes him warily. I don't know if he imagines he might be in competition with Charley, considering Charley is closer to Mindy's intellectual level and parental financial status. "We don't care."

There's a bit of a competition between Charley and Mindy over maintaining the highest grade point average in the entire school. Rocky always leans in to me when they vie for some new high point on an aptitude test and calls it: *geek wars*.

"Yes, we do." I bump him with my shoulder, look at

Mindy. I'm slightly freaking out and trying not to show it to the four standing there. What may seem like an entertaining scavenger hunt to them is screaming danger to me. It may not occur to them that someone had to come into this library and jotted down the code on the pictures. However, it does to me. It makes me shiver. Mary Stamper has access to the library still—"So, tell me, did the competition get so tense," I go on, "that you learned how to *decrypt* your competitors' messages at any point?"

"I would never cheat, Miss Mauer, you know that," she tells me with a haughty wag of her scrawny shoulders. Then, she slips in a sly smile. "However, I also made sure the other teams could not cheat against us. So I've set up several programs that can single out the usernames and passwords associated with an encrypted message, and such, decrypt most messages within four minutes."

"Awesome," Colton says and he's looking at Mindy with sparkling eyes like she's a rock star. "Can you decrypt this?" He's prodding the book so hard with the knuckle of his right hand, it is bobbing up and down.

"Gimme it." She takes the book from me, struts off across the room. Jake and Charley follow her. Colton looks at me like I just opened the door for Charley and Jake to steal his possible prom date.

"You've kept quiet about my theory of Missus Stamper, right? You need to until I can figure out how to convince the cops to dig deeper into the facts. Right now, they think I'm nuts." I watch Colton nod, then look behind him, the other three leaving, chatting it up like best friends.

"So follow them." I wave a hand toward Mindy.

"I'm not one of them."

"Oh, you may not want to hear this, but your IQ is equivalent to theirs. So, yes, you are. It is the reason you migrate to Mindy, although you would never admit it. Welcome to the club." He just nods once, muttering something under this breath that sounds akin to that old *biiii-tch* all drawn out with the last half out loud and echoing in the room.

At three in the afternoon while I watch the yellow school buses roll into the parking lot, I see Mindy swinging through the glass doors with Jake and Charley in tow. Charley is shaking his head back and forth. He is waving his hands angrily at Mindy. I know all three have AP math right now. I'm wondering how they got out of it.

Mindy starts to speak. I hold up a hand, stop her. "Why are you not in class?" I ask them. "You didn't tell Miss Cunningham what you were doing, did you?"

"Of course not," Charley mumbles. "She's at some sort of teacher enrichment program today."

"Mister McDaniel's covering her class for her," Mindy adds. "I couldn't figure out a math equation. So Miss Cunningham told me to wait until Mister McDaniel got there to get help so Charley and Jake and me were working on decrypting the message. Then when I asked Mister McDaniel for help, he just laughed and said to come down and bother you with whatever we were chatting about. He said a math problem couldn't cause that much commotion."

"He's hot," Mindy giggles. "But smart, he's not. Which is fine, because he just told us to do *whatever* while he took a nap. So, we're here."

Yeah, that sounds like Rocky.

"I came down to tell you the message is well encrypted," Mindy says, plopping her laptop on my desk. "But it would be easier to work on it in the library than the classroom. Somebody went to great lengths for you to find this message and for you to have to work hard to find it," Mindy goes on. "Do you think it might be the person who is abducting and killing the girls? My mom won't let me out the doors past seven because of him."

"*Him.* What makes you believe it is a man?" I ask her. I don't tell them who I believe it is. I'm not having that allegation going around the school. However, if I can find more keys to prove it was her even if they don't know who it is, it will only help my voice should I go to the police. I sigh, type in: *serial killer traits* on my computer keyboard.

"I don't know." She blinks, while I watch the screen come up with the results. I turn the computer toward Mindy and wiggle my fingers at the screen. "Look. It says right here men are *not* the only type of person who kill in numbers. Do you know what that means?"

All three heads shake. A fourth, which appears beside them sniffs a laugh. "That she's sexist?" Colton, who I'm assuming has decided to be the comedian of the group, shoves Jake aside and looks at the computer.

"Hello, Colton, glad you could be of service with the smart remark," I mutter. "But no, I'm saying that you need to think laterally or outside of the box."

"But statistics show that around eighty-percent of serial killers are men," Mindy counters, eyeing Colton suspiciously. "You can't discard fact just to think creatively."

"True." I nod. "But we still need to check all angles regardless. What I'm saying is that although eighty-percent of serial killers are men, that still leaves twenty percent who are women. That's a pretty high percentage of people to leave out if you are going to look into the different behavior and character traits—"

"Criminal profiling. Is that what we're going to do?" Charley's eyes widen like I just handed him a hundred dollar bill. "This is so coolio."

"Nobody says that, coolio," Colton grunts.

"Easy Colton." I hold up my hand. "Because that's what I'd like you guys to work on if you want to help. Trying to convince law enforcement agencies to see outside a book can be difficult." I sigh. "We need to keep this quiet and I'll tell you why. Not just because I'm probably surpassing my authority as a librarian at this school. But every person the cops have pointed a finger at—my dad, John McDaniel, and a few other *males* are highly improbable suspects and I think it is because they have simply exhausted their supply of everything *inside the box*."

"That's why you're doing this, because your dad is a suspect?" Jakes asks. Then he looks at Colton. "And your dad too." Colton nods.

I sigh. "Cops have been thinking *inside* the box and as we can see, the crime isn't solved. They are pointing fingers at a handful of men, but none of them actually fit the serial killer character. But they keep pulling them back in over and over because they want to solve the case. And if it is going to get solved—"

"—we need to do it," Charley mutters.

"Yes, and we need to look *outside* the box." I pat my desk. "But as far as your initial question for the reasoning behind sending the encrypted message, it may be sent to us as a cat and mouse game because the killer wants to watch people working on it. Or it may be something to point us in the wrong direction."

Not to be outdone, Jake is poking something into his phone while Charley peers over his shoulder. I see him squinting at the screen. "Well, so if this site is correct, female serial killers are middle class, Christian, and usually know their victims. Oh, she's someone like a nurse or teacher. And she uses poison more than something violent like a knife or shovel."

"It could be Miss Mauer." Colton grins and pokes me on the hand.

"Thanks, Colton, for the insight." I roll my eyes. "We still can't exclude men, yet," I say. Charley snatches up his phone from his back pocket, then looks up.

"It says here male serial killers do it mainly for domination, sexual violence." He looks up. "The three women that I know of were just found with a wound to the head. I read it in the paper. They weren't, you know, um—hurt in other ways."

"This says women do it for power and money too." Jake adds.

"You two are like dueling banjos," I laugh. "Get and go and write it down for me. Find out if there are certain days the murder was done and the method used to kill and dispose of the bodies." I catch Mindy by the sleeve, pull her over. "This is really creepy stuff. You're okay with this? You think they are okay?" I nod to the boys.

"I watch a lot of forensic science shows. I think I'm okay." She smiles. "I'm more worried about them. I always thought Charley was a serial killer in the making."

I snicker. "So, what math equation do you need help with?"

"Oh, it's not a big deal," she starts to wave me away. Then she shrugs her shoulders and digs a paper from the purse she's got slung on her shoulder. Mindy plops it down and I can see the equation she's stumped on because it has been erased so many times, the paper has a hole in it.

"Can I tell you something?" I ask Mindy, staring at the paper. She shrugs. "It's not that you can't figure out the answer. You just need to change your strategy." I roll my finger along the page and follow the eraser marks that roll a straight line down at every question that has a combination of functions. "Each of these equations have different concepts involved to get the answer, right? And if you look at the paper, you can see by the number of times you've had to erase over and over where you have a difficult time solving that particular part of the problem. It is always the same. You are messing up one simple concept, over and over. Just like solving crimes and looking outside the box, you need to do it with your homework. You get frustrated and you move on. So focus on figuring out what you're doing wrong at that particular point, fix it and apply it to the question you can't figure out."

"Start all over again? But the other ones are right."

"No, they aren't," I tell her. I can see all of the answers are incorrect. She made the exact same mistake on each problem, so her answers are way off. "You're not listening to what they are asking and so you are basing your initial question on probability, not what the actual answer is. You're being just like the local police trying to find suspects to a murder, don't you see? They look at the same suspects because it is easier and they fall into a pattern, just like you're trying to with your problems. Doesn't Miss Cunningham check your work?"

"No, she says I'm smart enough to figure it out."

I sigh and spend a half hour showing Mindy how to correct her mistakes, then she sits down at a table to work on them. At four, I tell her I have to go home and to use the same focus she used on the math problems on decrypting the message.

"Having a geek party? Can I join?"

That's Rocky leaning into me as I round the corner of

the bookshelf five minutes later. I'm getting ready to leave. He's smiling at me while I tug my sweater up over my shoulders. I try not to catch his gaze, but I want to see his eyes. When I look at those twinkling blue eyes, it always makes my tummy tickle. No tummy tickle today. I look at the last button on his plain button-up shirt instead.

"No jocks allowed." I hold up a hand, pass him. "Especially ones who reject me." I know he pauses because I pass his shadow, then I watch as it scoots up beside me. "Who has sex with someone and then writes a text telling them they don't want to see them anymore? Can you please leave?" I look up long enough to shove my glasses up the bridge of my nose.

"Okay." Rocky gives me a sad smile, lays a book down on the counter between us. "I just need to check this book out." He uses two fingers to push it over closer to me. It's a watered-down, high school appropriate book on crime scene investigation. Rocky's got a curious tip to his chin and he's eyeing me hard, like he's waiting for a response.

"Okay, but teachers don't have to sign them out. You can just fill out the sheet right here—" I lean to the right, tap a pen on the white plastic clipboard by my desktop computer, "—and take it with you."

"Okay." Now Rocky's giving me a flat line smile like I just missed the punchline to a joke. He makes a half-hearted snatch of the clipboard, then stops. "Open it."

"Okay." I finally finished Winsome Falls. I've still got no clue what is so significant in the pages Rocky wants me to read. I felt no overwhelming sense of romance, just the victory of finally finishing my first romance since middle school. I open it cautiously, sure that something is going to jump out at me. Instead, I'm staring at a hollow rectangle cut out of the center. Inside is a pretty, miniature bouquet of Lilies of the Valley, its tiny bells bouncing while I stare at them tucked into the cleft.

"Lilies of the Valley means I'm sorry." Now Rocky's face is deep pink from his jawbone, across his cheeks, and all the way to the tips of his ears. He gives me a strange tip of his head, snatches up the book.

"You think dumb flowers are going to make me feel better that you used me? I don't think so. Go away—"

"Yes, I did. Because for one, I *didn't* use you. And, yes, it was stupid what I said. I can't tell if you're just being nice to me or you really like me." He pivots, then stops and turns back around. "I sent you the yellow rose when I figured I could finally tell you I fell in love with you in second grade, when you tripped me on the bus. But I—I just couldn't tell you. The baby blue was just to make an adventure out of it. The orange, they were just because you blow me away with your beauty. Forget it. Just pretend I don't exist. I'm glad I figured it out now."

"So how long have you been covering for my sister?" I spit at his back. That stops him in his tracks. He doesn't budge for almost thirty seconds. "Aw, man." Then Rocky looks up. "How'd you find out?"

"I saw her with her girlfriend."

"Thanks for not telling your mom." Rocky pivots on his feet. "Nicky is afraid she'll freak out."

"Why would I tell her? My sister is entitled to her own life. But I think my sister underestimates my mother's ability to love regardless of our differences in lifestyles or opinions," I say. "Mom just wants everything her way. She's not necessarily intolerant." I sigh. "What about you, Rocky? I mean, as far as I'm concerned, I can't go around ducking and covering with you for the rest of my life, just so my sister can hide the fact she's gay from Mom, just because of some stupid curse and our families fighting all the time. But I get it. I got my own secrets I'm not telling. So make your choice what you want—"

"How long do I have? I mean, to make this decision."

Okay, what kind of question is that? I know he reads my mind right then, the tip of my head and the anger in my eyes. "You just made the decision, Rocky."

"I'm not the one who still has a boyfriend, Rosie."

"How would you know that?"

"Your sister added her cell phone number to the addresses that receive a copy of all your texts on your cell phone. She did it a couple weeks ago when you went to the bathroom at your mom's. It's in your settings. It takes two seconds to add another device."

For a moment, I fall silent. My phone. I cringe. Oh, my private phone. Not my work phone. Not my Violet phone with all my secrets—

"Which phone?"

"Which phone?" he looks at me strangely. "Do you have more than one?"

"No," I lie, relief washing over me. "No, I don't." I bite my lip, change the subject quickly. "Why should I give up my boyfriend? You made it sound like you were embarrassed to be around me at Mom's. If you really mean what you say about me, then you need to hold hands with me in an open room, even when everybody's calling me Weird Wosie behind my back. You've got to be with *just* me—mind, body, and soul. Isn't that what she says in Winsome Falls when the soldier leaves?"

"You—read the book I gave you?" Why does he look so flabbergasted?

"Yeah, I did. Won't admit I liked it though."

Chapter 52

Liam got pulled over for doing sixty miles an hour in a forty-five mile-an-hour zone. Yes, he wasn't going that fast. But Liam Barkley has never driven a car over a hill and hit the gas at the top so it makes his tummy tickle. He did it once and then didn't want to stop. We did it twelve times.

I don't think the cop was as concerned about the speed as much as me standing on the front seat with half my body outside the sunroof and scream-laughing at the top of my lungs. I think the cop also thought we might have stolen the car because he called Mister Barkley who demands that we come back to the country club ASAP.

"I don't know if my son got in more trouble before I hired you or after I hired you, Miss Violet." Mister Barkley is tugging on his tie and walking fast down the hallway an hour later with Liam and I both in pursuit. "It's like having two kids to bail out now."

Liam has chosen the worst possible time to start earning the respect of his stepdad. I don't know what he is thinking when he steers me into my office upon our return and asks me for some information I was researching for him after we went bowling. I'm praying he doesn't go down in a fiery ball after I pumped him up with unicorns and sunshine about proving himself to his stepdad.

"You remember when the mayor asked if we could give the city employees a deal on using the country club?" Liam is trying hard to keep up. I'm two steps behind him and pressing three folders to my chest.

"I said *no*. He's a Democrat."

"He's a Democrat that owns a house on our property," Liam tells Jack Barkley. I was a bit stunned when

Liam video-phoned me to contact the accountants for the country club last night and do some research with them on expansion and membership. He had taken in my surprise. I think he was looking forward to it in the same way I still like to indulge Nicky with the perfect birthday present even though she makes my hackles rise more often than not. I did as he said and he appeared quite pleased. I got off the conference line with them at two in the morning. However, I know this little meeting can go one of two ways—either the both of them walking off into the sunset holding hands or Liam crashing and burning while Jack Barkley drives his stepson off a cliff. But I've noticed in teeny tiny increments since the night Baby Cakes died, Liam actually has a brain, a heart, and a soul hidden somewhere behind the spoiled blackness. Right this moment, he's standing up straighter and has a serious set to his lips. He has a certain confident composure. He doesn't look like the usual spoiled man-child.

I think Jack Barkley notices it too. His jaws are working. Even the thought a Democrat would set foot into his country club could be the tiebreaker decision between sitting in purgatory another ten years or going to heaven. Still, he's narrowing his eyes at his son. "Give me a good reason."

"I did. He owns a house on the country club property. He knows a lot of people in good positions who make a lot of money. Those people could be assets to the country club." Liam looks at me, takes in a short breath before he takes two steps forward so he passes his stepdad. He wheels around, forcing the older man to stop. "Okay," Liam takes a little slip of paper from his breast pocket. "Owen Grimes is Mayor Pritchard's right hand man. He owns an office supply company. He sells his toilet paper for half of what we're paying now."

"It's cheap."

"No, it is better quality. It has really high reviews online." Liam's shoulders are straight. I'm interested in what he has to say. He's never seemed attracted at all to his family's business except to spend the money it earns. "And we need a new parking lot. People have complained that it is buckling near the south entrance. Buddy Carlton's wife is a good friend of Pritchard's wife. He's got a paving company and gets his gravel from his own quarry. It cuts his cost three-quarters." He doesn't take his eyes off his stepdad when he extends his hand to me. "Violet, give me the assessment you wrote up for me." Jack Barkley is trying not to let me read his expression. However, I can see he's intrigued. I catch up and extend my hand, slip Liam the folder. Liam hands it to Jack.

"I asked her to research how this would impact us financially before I brought this to your attention." Liam looks his stepdad in the eyes. "In a nutshell, the investment in the community and the extra income would, by far, exceed any losses we would sustain by giving each city, township, and county employee and their families a highly reduced rate in a yearly membership."

"This place will become a dump if every road worker and police officer and their kids come tramping through these doors." Jack Barkley takes a step to the left, walks around his stepson, and waves the folders in the air thoughtlessly. "We'll talk about this later."

I see Liam turn his attention to me, see whatever dignity I had noticed moments ago wash out on his face and his posture.

Don't stop. I mouth to him while Jack Barkley walks away. *Go.* Liam nods. Then he turns. I watch him catching up to his stepdad again while I try to keep pace too.

"I've already taken that into consideration along with

ten or twelve other issues I thought might impact the country club. If you take a moment to look at the information, you'll see the results. We will build a side entrance to the pool area and gym. The general public won't come in the front doors unless they are here to dine or utilize other services. We will impose a dress code."

"If one thing goes wrong, all those people who could be backing us, are then against us." Jack has his eyes set to his office door. "Now, we are flying under the radar. I have a lot of political ties on the other side of the spectrum. I could lose their business. Did you think of that?"

"I did. Look in the folder and you'll see. I think that instead of trying to cater to certain political groups, you should support them all. If you just cater to some, you lose the others. Just be the guy who smiles at everybody instead of—"

"Why do you care, Liam," Jack finally comes to a halt, pivots on his feet. He stops so fast that Liam nearly careens right into him. "You got money coming from your mommy whether this place thrives or goes under."

"Mommy didn't raise me. You did."

I'm stunned. I look from Liam to Jack and back again. I can't tell if the significance of the situation registers to Jack. They both just stare at each other like they are trying to read each other beneath the indifferent surface. This is usually where I step in for Mister Barkley when he has a business proposal. I know I am walking a fine line here. I don't want to usurp Liam. But if I don't say anything, it will appear like I'm making a statement that, perhaps, it is a bad idea.

"Mister Barkley, he is correct," I shift to the left to see the older man. "I made inquiries and researched the outcome. There are only positive results. Period."

"Okay." Jack turns back around, waggles his head

like he is shooing away flies before he grumbles something about me imposing double trouble on him again. "It's done." He tells Liam with his back to him. "It's your job to work through this whole mess, understand?"

"Yes." Liam turns his head just enough to catch my eye. I see him unload a long breath before he gives me a slightly clumsy grin.

"Well?" he whispers.

Chapter 53

"Boo!"

It's probably bad timing on Emmanuel's part. I mean, considering I'm waiting on hold for Timmy Kinney at the police station. I called the number, talked to the front desk. It is the third time in the last four hours. The first time, he wasn't in the office. The second, I chickened out and hung up. The third time, I'm getting really close to hanging up while there is a long recorded spiel of safety lessons for those on hold while the front desk clerk buzzes him in his office. But Emmanuel jumps out at me while I am working myself up to spill all my beans to Timmy Kinney and getting into my car in the parking lot of the country club. Emmanuel is holding a dozen red roses while I drop the phone. He's scattered petals around my car and even wrote *mi amore,* in what smells like aftershave, on my windshield.

And what do I say while I watch my private cell phone bounce across the asphalt? "Okay, I can't do this." I know he can't understand me, doesn't know I'm scared crapless about calling up the cops and telling them what I know because I don't think they'll believe me. Especially if Bobby has already talked to them. I'm sure he's convinced them I'm crazy.

Then Emmanuel says, in perfect English and with the tainted and cagey stare of someone who's getting dumped. And I imagine, one who isn't used to getting dumped and probably has a gun. "Why not? What we're doing is fun, Violet Popovich."

So he *does* speak English. It makes sense. How can you hire drug mules in America if you don't speak the language? "Come on, baby, I got plans for us." I'm scared shitless of him. I realize that now. All those things Kim told me about Emmanuel are sinking in and if there's even the most minuscule chance Rocky wasn't lying to me and does like me, I'm out of this relationship.

"Get in my car. Let's party. We're not done."

So, I reach into my glovebox and I take out Gabby's little FBI badge and I stand up to face him.

"Well, I'm having fun too," I tell him softly and with a shaky voice. I reach up with my arms around his neck and give him a long, passionate kiss and he's saying: *yeah, yeah, that's it*. Then I pull away, force some tears. "But, I'm not who you think I am. And I did not know who you were until today. So you've got to leave." I whisper to his angry eyes. I hold up the little plastic FBI badge. "The police have been following and their plans are to come for you tonight. They will take you to jail."

"So come with me, out of the country."

And all's I can think about is Rocky repeating the line from his romance book. I'm thinking, if it works for him, maybe it will work for Emmanuel and keep me alive because he doesn't look thrilled I'm breaking up with him in a parking lot after he showered me with gifts. "If I come with you, they will follow. Right now, they only assume you are just a man. But you are more, so much more. Please go. I may never see you on earth again, so wait for me on the sunny side of heaven. Go."

Chapter 54

"Well, baby, sometimes you just got to throw yourself out there and when you do, you skin a knee or two."

That's my daddy's answer to all my woes while he pulls on the cord for his chainsaw. Mine was to take two anxiety pills before I came here today, and I'm looking over my shoulder every two minutes because I have this sneaking feeling Emmanuel is following me. He didn't take the breakup well. He screamed at me in the parking lot until security escorted him out. I don't think he believed me about being in the FBI. He looked a little too long and a little too hard at the plastic badge.

Daddy and I are out in his farthest back field. It's Sunday evening. I skipped Mom's house and church today. I went over to Daddy's to hang out until everybody comes over for supper. We don't talk about the big things—his arrest, figuring out me and Leah are next on a list to die, and maybe being stalked by a guy who is in an international drug cartel. Instead, we daddy-daughter small-talk, like we used to when I was little.

I'm wearing a tank top and shorts and feeling the sunshine on my shoulders and thinking it can't be too long before summer. He's sawing through the bottoms of the new fence posts Johnny McDaniel put up between their properties. I mean, they aren't brand new, the posts. They are just seven foot saplings he cut down and used a post-hole digger to bury them six inches over daddy's property line. The fence is old, rusted barbed wire. I'm reclined on an old, camo-painted ATV with my feet resting on the handlebars, watching my daddy get a smug smile each time he takes a fence post down at the ankles and hoping Johnny isn't barreling up the hill with a loaded shotgun. I've got a mini version of his chainsaw with a pink handle. He'd proudly given it to me for Christmas four years ago. We spent the better half of Christmas day happily sawing down trees for his fireplace.

Daddy got the washed-down version of my horrible last two days, of course. I told him I got my heart broke twice in one week. I lost one boyfriend. And I got a crush on another guy who kind of has a girlfriend and he's out of my league. Of course, Daddy tells me there *ain't no man out of my baby's league.*

"So, this boy who broke your heart that has a kind-of girlfriend," Daddy starts while he pauses to scrub a hand over his brow. "Is it anybody I know?" He's eyeing the sharp chain on his saw and I know he'd use it on Rocky if he knew it was him. "Because there's stuff I can do to guys that hurt my little girl. And what the hell's a kind-of girlfriend? You either got one or you don't."

"I don't know." I say. But I do. It's the kind you sexy-text like Rocky's been doing with Violet all this time. But Daddy doesn't hear me. He's gunning his chain saw, easing it down to the tree and I can bet he's imagining it's the head of the guy who hurt me because he's got a set to his chin and I see woodchips flying everywhere. It's right about then, I get a call. William's Easy Pawn is blinking on my cell phone. I sit up in the seat, slip off, and walk far enough away from my dad's crazy sawing and call the number back. Then I plug my free ear with my finger.

"Listen," It's Tag Williams's voice on the other end. "I don't know who you are or what you're doing. But I guess that Lydia Murphy girl told her roommate she was coming here to pawn off a bunch of gold necklaces she got at a garage sale. And I'm figuring you're not really a cop because the cops came here the other day and gave me hell because I was one of the last ones that seen her alive. They went through everything, tore my place apart like maybe they're thinking I lured her into some back room and killed her or something. I don't need them in my business. I didn't tell them shit. But this has got to stop. Right after the cops leave my shop looking like a bomb exploded, that old man called back. He says he dropped something off for you—"

"Me?"

"Yeah, missy, you. It's a box, it was sitting on the back step of the building this morning."

"Do you know what it could be?"

"Hell, I don't know. He told me not to open it. Said you had to do it. I figured you might know something. But that's why I called. Why don't you come get a look-see?"

"Are you crazy? Why the heck aren't you calling the cops? What if it's some girl's head or something?"

There's a long silence. Then I hear Tag breathe in and breathe out. "Oh, I hadn't thought about that."

"You're kidding me, right? You know this guy murdered Lydia. It *has* to be him."

"I'm not calling the cops because I don't want to die, you get it? I don't have a single doubt in my mind that he will kill me if I go to the cops. I'm thinking you're thinking the same thing, right? This guy is either a serial killer or he's just some messed up crazy. Either way, I don't want him mad at me. So don't judge me, girl. I got grandkids living with me. The cops that were here today, they aren't going to protect me. I'm assuming since you're doing this on your own, you're feeling the same way. I got a good idea they'd think I had something to do with it."

"Did you?"

"Oh, hell no," he huffs. Then his words take on a smart-alecky twist. "Do *you*?"

I wince. "No," I sigh. I stand there, knowing he can

hear the sound of Daddy's chainsaw behind me. Still, I hesitate. I suppose I'm coming face to face with the reason right this moment. "You've seen him, right?"

"Yeah."

"If I showed you a picture of him, could you identify him—*would* you identify him?"

"For you, I would." It is silent on the other end for such a long time. I finally hear him heave a great breath. "He just looks like an old man," Tag grunts. I work my way back to the ATV with my index finger over my right ear to drown out the noise. I hunker back down on the seat. "Doesn't look like he could hurt a fly. You seem like a sweet girl. That Lydia, she was a sweet girl. I read about her in the newspaper. She was only twenty-something and saving up to go back to college. She had to stop to take care of her grandma because her family couldn't afford a nursing home. I'm thinking, you're probably like that girl, right?"

"Well, right now, she's dead. I'm alive."

Just when I say that, I hear the roar of ATVs working their way up the trail on Johnny McDaniel's side of the property. I hang up, see my daddy looking up from his chainsaw with a wary glint to his eyes.

"Crap, daddy," I grunt and slide up in the seat slowly while two ATVs peak at the top of the rugged hillside. There's dust flying and I see them stop less than a stone's throw away. Daddy stands up straight, cocks his chin high and gets this smug smile on his face. I feel my shoulders drop. It's Johnny and Rocky. Each is climbing off an ATV, whipping a leg around and standing up straight before both come swaggering over to the edge of the fence.

"Hey, asshole, you trespassed on my property for the last time," my daddy yells at Johnny. "It ain't happening no more."

"You bastard," Johnny shoves out his chest like a male turkey on display. His eyes veer right to left all the way down twenty-two sawed-off fence stumps to where my daddy's standing with his head held high. "I'm gonna sue your ass! I'm calling the cops! This is a thousand bucks of fence you're ruining, a thousand bucks! Not only are they going to have your damn ATV, I'm going to get your damn *house*!"

It goes on back and forth for about eight minutes while my eyes wander from Johnny to my daddy. Rocky's standing behind his uncle with his mouth in a straight, angry line and his arms crossed. I know for a fact he helped put in that fence. I heard Nicky telling mom it had taken him and Johnny two weeks to get the top of the hillside done. It's only taken daddy two hours and ten minutes to take almost all of it down. Six more posts and the thing is going to tip over, like dominoes, down the hillside, poles flopping forward from the weight of the top of the fence falling.

Rocky's ticked. I can see it in the narrowing of his eyes, but I don't let on. I know better. I just keep my seat on my ATV and wait for Daddy to tell me what to do. I'm tired and grumpy and I'm more than happy to take my irritability out on him and his uncle. I'm half-listening to them bicker back and forth when I hear Johnny McDaniel say something like: *It'll be over my dead body. You cut one more and I'm calling the cops.*

I watch my daddy walk up to the next pole. He leans over, brings his chainsaw to the pole, and chops it right in half.

"Aw, shit," Rocky curses. I see the reason. Johnny's clambering over the fence, and my daddy, he doesn't even wait for Johnny's right boot to make it there. He drops his chainsaw and starts hunkering down like a bull and going at

Johnny with both hands out, trying to shove him back over. Johnny tips sideways, falls into the tangle of fence wire. Then Daddy, he turns right then and in less than four steps he's got *Rocky's* collar in his fist and he's waling on him with full-out punches.

I've never seen my daddy react like this. He's crazy angry. Rocky's trying to block his blows with his palm, trying to hold back the punches.

"Daddy stop it!" I screech and jump off the ATV, try to catch my daddy's arm. "Daddy, please stop!"

"Rosie, get back!" Rocky yells at me. He turns his head toward me for a moment, then gives the sky a hard glare. It is bad timing. Daddy cocks his arm and slugs Rocky in the jaw, sends him backward trip-walking over a freshly cut fence stump. I see him fall, see my daddy laying into him. Rocky's not hitting back. I know he won't because that's my daddy.

I can see blood dripping from my Rocky's nose. It scares me, freaks me out. Blood. My fingers are rolling over the back of my head. Blood. Rocky's blood. I can hear a voice in the back of my head: *It will just hurt the first time, sweetie. See, I remembered to tell you. Just close your eyes.* I huff a breath, desperately push the thought away.

"Johnny, please stop him! Please!" I don't even realize I'm scream-sobbing at Johnny McDaniel, who has rushed past me, shoving me aside. Just as his shadow crosses over Rocky's leg, my daddy stops cold. Johnny bends down, grabbing my daddy by the arm and towing him upward. Daddy's blinking at me like he's looking at a ghost, Johnny's face is dead white while his nephew pushes himself to his feet. It's like a bomb just went off.

I think Rocky is trying to take advantage of the moment that both men are quiet. He pivots on his feet, stands so he's facing his uncle and gives him a solid shove backward. "Let's go. Another day."

"This isn't over, Rocky." My daddy growls. "You stay away from my baby girl."

"Daddy, please stop," I say it softly, shove myself in front of him with my hand on his chest. "Stop."

"He got ahold of you, didn't he? I'll kill him."

"No, you won't. He didn't *get ahold of me*." He makes me sound like one of his female coon hounds in heat and Rocky is the neighbor's mutt sniffing around the back yard. "Daddy, stop. Just leave them alone." It's like my daddy's looking at me, but he's not. It's like he is staring at a stranger. "Don't look at me like that." I see his gaze focusing on my face, watch him take in a breath like he's going to yell at me. He shakes his head like a dog shaking water from his fur. Then he rubs his eyes with his hands. "Go back to the ATV." It's Daddy who pushes a hand on my shoulder and walks me back to my ATV. He doesn't say anything, just steps over to his own ATV and starts it up, nods his head for me to go first. I feel like the worst daughter in the world.

I don't look over at Rocky. I have no clue what is going on between his uncle and himself. I just drive off with Daddy down the hill and wonder what just happened between the four of us.

Chapter 55

"What's wrong with her?"

Aunt Kay is hovering near the kitchen door with a worried wringing of her hands while I pace back and forth, taking in these horrible ragged breaths. "Ray, can't you *do* something?" I can't breathe. I can't think. I just—can't do anything except for cry and I'm doing that a lot with the *hyuck-hyuck* gasps.

I keep squeezing my pill bottle. It was my cousin, Renée's, first reaction to dig them out of my purse and tell me to take them. But I can't. I already took two today because it was my usual day to go to Mom's, even though I didn't go. Doctor Stamper always tells me to never take more than two. I keep telling my daddy that, who keeps pacing with me, over and over while everybody who is waiting for supper keeps giving me cagey peeks through the doorway and asking if I am all right.

"She's having an asthma attack." Daddy looks up at Aunt Kay long enough to wave her away with his hand. He's got a cut on his cheek and one on his chin and he's dabbing it with a piece of toilet paper. "That's what Gracie told me."

"No. Panic attack," I correct him.

"Maybe you should take her to the emergency room. She looks bad, really bad."

"No." I huff with wild-eyes and Daddy's eyes get wide too. "No, Daddy, they only make it worse." And Aunt Kay is making it worse giving my dad a step by step progress of how horribly close to death I look.

"It's been forty minutes, sweetie. There's got to be something I can do. Do you want me to call your mama?"

"NO!" I yelp with even wilder eyes. I've never had an

episode at Daddy's. Ever. Everybody's acting like I've got the crazies here now, too. I feel like I'm going to get sick again. I had to stop twice on the ATV back to the house.

"Please-make-them-stop-staring-at-me." I know my face is as white as a ghost. I know I'm going to eventually faint and they are going to call the squad. I'll die right there sprawled on the floor and everybody will remember me as Ray's little bat-shit crazy daughter who died in front of the kitchen sink on a Sunday afternoon.

Daddy waves them away and tries to get me to sit. "We've got to do something or I'm calling the ambulance."

"Rocky's the only one who can get them to stop." It takes me thirty seconds to gulp that out. "Please get Rocky."

Daddy stares at me long and hard, like he just swallowed a big ol' June bug. "Stay put." He walks out of the room and my cousin, Billy, lumbers in and takes his place. He's probably the only one who my daddy trusts would stop me from walking off the edge of a cliff. He sits and drums his fingers nervously on the tabletop and asks me if I'm going to puke again because it was the cool color of red slushies.

I suppose if strange anomalies and major events were recorded in the annals of the local history books, Rocky McDaniel and Johnny McDaniel, being escorted by Ray McGuire, through his living room and into his kitchen would, most likely, be awarded the topmost position for the last hundred years. I can't imagine the humiliation my father had to face as he walked with them beneath the horrified gazes of his dad and the rest of our clan. If I had not dishonored him enough by losing his ATV to his archenemy, I think I might have disgraced him enough to disown me by having to beg his enemy's nephew to come into his home and save his crazy daughter.

"Hey, Rosie," Rocky hunkers down on one knee in front of the kitchen chair I'm settled in. He looks at Daddy and asks him to get me a couple baggies of ice.

"I'm sorry. I'm so sorry. But it won't go away." My leg is jiggling up and down. I want to die. I think I am.

"No worries." He gives me wide eyes and a stifled grin, like we share some sort of a secret. "You got me out of helping Uncle Johnny clean his guns."

"Oh." I groan. "Was he going to use them on us?"

"I'm teasing." Rocky smiles softly.

I can see Johnny wrestling with figuring out what spot he should plant himself. He leans against the sink and sees my Aunt Kay eying him warily. He works his way to the oven, right when my papaw uses his walker to move into the doorway and lion-glare him. He's lugging his old green oxygen tank in a backpack on his walker. Johnny folds his arms across his chest, watches Papaw scowl cold-fire at my daddy. Johnny looks like a raccoon caught in a chicken cage with my cousin Billy staring him down. Daddy, he looks like a kid that just got caught smoking behind the barn.

"Hey, look at me." Rocky draws my attention away from Johnny. "You ready for some numbers?" he asks, resting his elbow on the table and gently holding on to my arm. "What's the square root of nine-thousand six hundred and four?"

"Ninety-eight."

"What is the longest time someone's held their breath?" He reaches out, takes the ice packs from Daddy. "Put these on your cheeks. Tilt your head down."

"My nose is bleeding, isn't it?"

"A little." He looks up at Daddy, asks him for a towel.

"I think I'm actually going to die this time."

Aunt Kay runs to the bathroom to get one.

"You always say that. You always live. You're going to be fine, Rosie. How many times have we done this?"

"Is that a question? Do I have to answer it correctly?"

"No. I'm estimating a hundred times." He takes my pill bottle so I can take the ice.

"Okay, I think it is like twenty-two minutes and twenty-two seconds." I heave each word.

"You really know that?" Rocky blinks and sits up a bit. "Damn. What type of clouds are storm clouds?"

"Cumulonimbus," I answer. "It comes from the Latin word cumulus, which means heap, and nimbus meaning rain cloud." I huff. "They think I'm a freak now, Rocky."

"No, they don't. It'll blow over. Besides, they are more interested in me and my uncle right now."

"I don't want to be Weird Wosie anymore."

"What is a prime number?" Rocky ignores me, knocks my head with his knuckles. His strong grasp on my arm makes me feel safe again.

"A whole number greater than one whose only two whole-number factors are one and itself." Not so many gulps that time. Aunt Kay comes in the room, wiggles the towel at Rocky. He snatches it and holds it up to my nose. There's like a crowd of my family standing outside the door.

"I like it better when you use your shirt," I try to tease me. He rolls his eyes. I want to die right then, sink into the floor. Whatever it takes to be away from the stares.

"Give me three prime numbers."

"Seven, eleven, and fourteen."

"Smallest animal—"

"You do know I was wrong, right? Fourteen wasn't a prime number." I point out, blinking at him. "Do you really know the answers to these questions or are you just winging it?"

"Are you trying to get out of answering what the smallest animal is?"

"No. It's the white-toothed Pygmy Shrew. It weighs less than an ounce."

"You remember the line from the book I liked?"

"Uh huh. *If I come with you, they will follow,*" I recite. "*Right now, they only assume you are just a man. But you are more, so much more. Please go. I may never see you on earth again, so wait for me on the sunny side of heaven.*"

"Good."

"Yeah," I whisper low, leaning in so only Rocky can hear me. "I used it to break up with my boyfriend."

"My favorite excerpt? I was going to use it in the book club next week. Now it's tainted." Rocky says this loud enough everybody in the kitchen can hear.

"It probably saved my life. He was a drug dealer."

"Only you could tell that story and I wouldn't doubt it for a moment." Rocky chuckles his classic chuckle, wiggles the medicine bottle in his hand. "You're looking less pale already." He looks at it, looks at me. "But maybe you want another one, just to make sure?"

"I can't. I already took two. Doctor Stamper told me I can only take two a day."

"Doctor Stamper?" he asks me slowly. "I thought you said the other day she was the one—" he stops.

"Mom told me if I didn't take the pills and Doctor Stamper's advice, she was going to call an ambulance and have me committed to some crazy hospital." I know he thinks I'm crazy for taking the advice of the same person I am saying is a murderer.

"How about if I call the hospital and see if you can take one more? Maybe it will help."

"Don't leave me." I know everybody hears me. I hear Papaw's walker make a clumpy walk along the linoleum and out of the kitchen, like I've fallen from his graces and he can't even stick around.

"Okay." Rocky wiggles out his phone. He must have the hospital on speed dial, because he doesn't even ask for the phone book. I think I'm less lightheaded, and I see him smiling up at me while he talks to somebody on call there. He waits. Then he gets up. I watch him hold up a forefinger as if telling me to wait while he paces to the far side of the room, reads the pill bottle to the doctor three times.

"You said Doctor Stamper gave you this?" he cranes his neck to look at me. "When did she start prescribing the Adtraxin?"

"When—you know, when I ran away or whatever when I was fourteen. I don't get it at the pharmacy. Mom gets it directly from her."

"You've been taking this particular pill that long?"

"Yes."

"You never had nosebleeds before you started taking it, did you? I mean, I don't remember any."

"No."

"Or anxiety?"

"I don't know. Mom said it was from getting hit on the head, the anxiety and the nosebleeds. That's what Doctor Stamper said. It helped calm me down. It started about the same time. It's what was prescribed for it. I'm going to throw up again."

"Huh?" Rocky asks me. Too late. He starts to stand

and does this little dance backward three steps with his arms waggling in the air. He doesn't get far enough. I spit up on his shoes. Now everybody's rushing to either get out of the kitchen or mop up Rocky while Billy heaves a breath and mutters to Rocky, "Yeah, better you than me."

It's not that funny, but Johnny starts laughing and I hear Daddy chuckling, mimicking Rocky's dance while I gag and Renée shoves a glass of water under my nose. Aunt Kay comes in with another round of towels and mops up Rocky and the floor.

"I'm sorry I puked on you, Rocky."

"I figured it was one more step in my testing." He doesn't even get mad, doesn't swipe it off like it's poison. He makes me smile.

"I haven't been taking the pills regularly in the last few months. I suppose I shouldn't have doubled them up after not taking them. I've been busy. I keep forgetting."

"It's okay. It's what Doctor Hill said for you to do."

"What?"

"Vomit them up. Those pills you're taking are Adtraxin," Rocky says as Daddy hands him a couple paper towels to wipe his shoes. "They are for depression and anxiety in *dogs*. It isn't for human use. He looked it up and three of the fifty side effects if accidently taken by humans are nosebleeds, anxiety, and lethargy. He said it was like an icepick lobotomy in a pill for humans."

"It's a pill for dogs?" My daddy comes up and looks at the pill bottle Rocky is holding up. "Who gave you this?"

"Mom gets them for me. Doctor Stamper's been giving them to me for, like, ten years."

"You're not taking any more, that's for sure." Daddy reaches out and gives Rocky a couple approving pats on the arm. It's the same pleased gesture he'd give me when I was six or seven and ate my peas when I didn't want to eat them. "She's going to be okay?" he asks Rocky anxiously, who looks just as surprised as me.

"Uh, yes. Doctor Hill said to stop taking them. Period. He can see you in his office in a couple days if you want, see how you're feeling." They left the same way they came. It wasn't until Daddy mumbled a thank you and loaded Rocky up with a six pack of pop in his refrigerator as a thank you. Then right before he left, Rocky leans in and says: "You need to call Timmy Kinney. Just pick up the phone and call. Now."

Chapter 56

"Papaw, Daddy said you wanted to talk to me?" It's quiet in the little bedroom where Papaw's sitting on the bed. I can hear the chatter and laughter of the TV blaring just ten steps away.

"Close the door, Rosie."

I shrink back. But I do as he says and quietly push the door closed between bedroom and living room. I think he's going to tell me not to come back to Daddy's. I'm shunned from the family for disgracing his name, for being the weird one, for inviting the enemy into our little fortress.

"Sit with me." He pats the bed next to him. His face is pale and he adjusts the little plastic, oxygen tubing that goes into his nostrils, puts one hand on the little knob on the tank.

"Are you mad at me?" I ask, plopping down next to him on the old, soft comforter. "I'm sorry. I had to have Rocky come. I didn't think Johnny would come too."

"I didn't want to talk to you about nothing like that," Papaw says softly, forces a sad smile. "He looked scared of this old man, didn't he, Johnny did?" Papaw pushes his chin up proudly. "I may be an old man, but I can still make them boys scared-eyed wiggle in their pants! "

"You can." I smile back. He did.

"I didn't listen to her."

"What?" I shift a bit, scoot back on the bed until my feet are barely touching the floor. "You didn't listen to whom?"

"To my Rosie."

"Aunt Rosie? She told you something?" I reach out and touch his hand that's not fiddling with his oxygen tank.

He looks at me, takes my fingers in his own. I wonder if he sees her in me, and that's why he always hesitates when I walk into the room.

"She told me she didn't want to go to school that day she didn't come home. I didn't know why. I just thought she wanted to skip school. She were so bad that year after her little friend got killed. She was smoking and sneaking out."

"Her friend?"

"That little Stamper girl." Papaw is playing with the little dial on his oxygen tank. His eyes are bloodshot. "I know'd she was friends with her at school. We all know'd that even though that mom of hers didn't want her hanging around with the likes of us. She'd come over and listen to music with Rosie once in a while. She were so polite, so quiet. I know Rosie didn't go over to the Stampers, though. We was too poor, too hillbilly for them."

"Do you know why she didn't want to go?"

"Back then, I thought she was just wanting to get out of going to school. She hated riding the bus. She said it stank. I thought, back then, Johnny killed her. I know'd he was hanging with Rosie and that little Stamper girl. I told her to stay away from him. He was trouble." His fingers stop twisting the dial. "Rosie called me from the skating rink to pick her up early that Thursday night in September of '77. She said she was sick. It were the next day, they found Carrie Stamper dead. Rosie was sick all weekend, didn't go to school most of the next week. Then eight months later, Rosie, she don't come home. She were so mad at me that morning. She didn't want to go to school I told her to get her ass out that door. I was sick of it, sick of her bellyaching all the time. I saw from the window. I saw Johnny's car drive past the house a couple times. Slow, really slow. Oh, that made me madder than fire. Then she just screamed at me and slammed the door and left. His car, it never came through again. I know'd he picked her up. My heart's broke. It broke the day my little girl didn't come home. That Doctor Stamper woman—Rosie said she was scared of her."

"Do you think Johnny had something to do with Carrie Stamper's death? With Aunt Roo disappearing?"

"I think Johnny knows something. He ain't telling." Papaw takes out a pack of cigarettes from his breast pocket and opens the top. In one hand, he takes a cigarette. Then he turns the cigarette pack over and a little paper falls out. "Your daddy cleaned my shed for me a couple months ago. I wanted to get rid of all of Rosie's old stuff. It ain't good for an old man to be thinking about the past so much. This is what I found stuffed into the wall. It's ripped-out papers from her diary."

I take the paper hesitantly, stare hard into Papaw's eyes. He doesn't blink, doesn't turn away. I exhale, then open it. It's baby blue with lines and matches the pages of Aunt Roo's diary. The date is September 9, 1977, the day after they found Carrie Stamper.

September 9, 1977

This is the worst day of my life. Me and Carrie were supposed to be at the skating rink tonight for the school skating party. We went to the parking lot to smoke a cigarette and Bobby was there with Lynn, making out in the back seat. Carrie started hanging out with them and saying stuff about me behind her hand. Then they'd laugh. Carrie knows I hate Lynn. And I told Lynn I was going to tell her brother she was hanging out with a narc. Bobby said he could take us all driving around and we could get high. I don't know why I went along. I should have just stayed. But we went to Dell's Hill.

Bobby had some pills and Carrie took one to show off. She started climbing up the rock and fell off. Bobby took me and Lynn back to the skating rink. He said he was going to take Carrie home. Her head was bleeding and she was crying.

September 11, 1977

Carrie's dead. Nobody knows we went riding around on Thursday and I'm too scared to tell them. Her mom wouldn't let her hang out with us. I know they'll send me to jail. Bobby told me to never say anything. I was crying in the hall and Johnny asked me what was wrong and I told him my secret. He's so stupid, he went to see her and took *everybody*. I'm so scared. I got called down to the office and I think Doctor Stamper knows too.

"Some of them pages was rotted to pieces, got wet in the wall. That's all that was left except this—" He reaches into the cigarette pack and tugs one more thing out. It is a piece of Polaroid picture, the missing section that I know would finish the image of my aunt, Johnny, and Carrie standing together.

"It's Lynn McDaniel," I whisper. I can see it, even though Aunt Roo must have jabbed an X across her face and then wrote BITCH over her head. Only her elbow missing. And that would show up next to Johnny in the other image.

"You do something with them. You go and ask Johnny McDaniel if he knows anything."

"You want me to talk to him?"

Papaw pats the papers in my fingers. "You're the smart one in the family. You do what it takes to find my baby girl. Bring her home."

Chapter 57

Dates. Dates. Dates. I sigh, work through the dates of death for each victim again. I'm almost glad Bobby took all the pictures. I chew on my thumbnail as I dig through Aunt Roo's things and spread them on the bed. Papers. The monkey bag, the necklace, the pictures, the bracelet. I stop on the bracelet, rub my finger along the wording DIES IRAE. Judgement Day. Why would Mary Stamper pass out a bracelet about being judged—unless she believed all of those she gave the bracelets to were going to be? Because, perhaps, she thought they were guilty and maybe had something to do with her daughter dying. I run through the computer, start to dig up birthdates. Maybe it is something with—then the *oh-shit* moment hits the second I try to search up an online obituary for Carrie Stamper and I find a picture of Carrie's headstone on a cemetery website.

"Bingo." I whisper. Because the headstone reads: CAROLINE STAMPER. DAUGHTER OF MARY JANE AND ROBERT. BORN: MAY 21, 1960. DIED: September 8, 1977. *May 21st.* There's the date that matches the deaths.

I drive to Rocky's mom's trailer, knock on the door.

"I don't want you around here." That's what she tells me with a blank face and a cigarette dangling from her lips. "Doctor Stamper told Johnny you'd be coming. You'd been telling Colton stuff. She said Colton'd been acting up at school. She says you been giving him weed. You're bad news. You always was. I remember you getting my boy in trouble all the time back when you was little."

"Well, you don't have to like me. I'm trying to keep Johnny out of jail, just like my daddy." I watch her turn slightly, see a hulking shadow behind her and then the hand coming to tug the door open. I balk. It's Rocky's dad, Jake.

He's a huge figure of a man—a Rocky-double, only another hundred or so pounds heavier and a bit of fat where Rocky has muscle. Then I push my chin up.

"Naw," Lynn purrs. "I think when it all comes down to it, you'll throw him under the train, just like your daddy did after Carrie showed up dead. You know Ray, he said Johnny did it."

"Johnny told the cops my daddy did it. They were kids. They were stupid and scared."

"My wife says to get."

"No. I know Johnny's secret. He can't read. Whoopee shit. I know about the race to see the dead girl and that it was Carrie Stamper. I know her birthdate is the date that daughters of girls whose parents were in those two trucks were killed."

Lynn starts to close the door on me. I shove out my foot, stop her cold. "I know who has been murdering the girls. You do too. You were with Carrie the night she died."

"No, I weren't. I didn't have nothing to do with it."

"But you know what happened. You know she took a pill Bobby Vandevenne gave her and she fell. You were there. Bobby was the cop at school who told everybody about the dead girl on the road. He set Johnny and my daddy up to make it look like one of them killed her." I hold up the half of the picture Papaw gave me with Lynn leaning against a truck. I hold up the other half Aunt Roo had in her trunk. I shove them together.

"It's the curse," Lynn snaps. "As soon as your aunt started being friends with Johnny, all hell broke loose. It started it and it ain't gonna never end until all of us are dead and buried. One by one, it's gonna get us."

"It isn't going to get *you*," I growl. "If you don't tell someone the truth, it is Leah and me who are going to die!"

Chapter 58

I miss Rocky. I miss him teasing me about being in a pickle all the time. I mean, he's always in my face at school. He stopped texting Violet, even when I sent him a couple messages. I toss and turn. I wake up at two in the morning to the sound of knuckles on the front door. I clamber through the living room, peer out the little peephole.

"T's at home. Can we crash here?"

I can't help but stare at Colton. He's wiping a bloody tissue beneath his nose. His eyes are a deep red and will probably turn to purple and black in four or five hours.

We. I look over his shoulder and see Leah's car in the shadows of my drive. I'm sure I was on their radar. I'd called Leah and let her know what I found out about Bobby. She'd already had the update from Lynn six hours earlier. "Did you get in a fight?" I ask, opening the door wide and beckoning them in with my hand.

"T's drunk and got mad at Leah. He tried take Gabby, saying he was a better dad than she was a mom." I tug on Colton's shirt sleeve to lead him inside. "Leah grabbed Gabby and we ran. That was a few hours ago. We usually park up at the old amusement park, but the cops were sitting there tonight. We're about out of gas."

"Are you telling her our entire life story?" Leah snaps as she comes up the steps. She's carrying a sleepy-eyed Gabby, who is almost as big as she. I show Leah and Gabby to my guest bedroom and make a bed on the couch for Colton. Now I can't sleep. So I'm lying in bed with my feet on my pillow, staring at the blank wall above my headboard. I take out my phone, think about texting Rocky. I type his phone number three times. I delete each text. I lay in the darkness for a half hour, then I muster up the courage to give him a call.

"Hey, Rocky."

"Rosie?" His voice is normally deep, but it sounds even raspier right now. I suppose I woke him from a dead sleep. I hear his bedsheets swish and know he must be sitting upright. "Are you okay? Is there—"

"I'm fine. I had a bad dream." There's a long silence so I try to play it light. "This is part of your testing, a call in the middle of the night. You'll get a lot of these when you're full-time at Crystal Springs," I tell him. Again, he doesn't say anything. I shouldn't have called. I put him in a bad position at Daddy's. I'm sure even if there was an inkling of fondness, that's gone to dust. "Well, I suppose I just wanted to hear your voice—" That sounded stupid and needy. Crud. "Nevermind. I don't know why I called. I'm sorry." And then there's the longest lull of all. I sit there in the darkness, my face burning hot.

"You feeling better without the pills?"

"Yeah, I suppose."

"Mom was really shook up tonight," Rocky sighs deeply. "She's talking about going to the cops tomorrow. Dad's trying to stop her. He's afraid they'll say it was her, you know? It's just sounds so farfetched, the whole idea that Bobby had anything to do with it, that the Stampers are murderers."

"You think I'm lying too?" I ask raspingly. "I'm hanging up."

"No, I don't. Don't—hang up. You need me to come over? We can just sit and—talk."

Yes, I do. Thinking with my heart and my emotions and the new Violet-Rosie, I'm screaming YES, YES, YES! But Leah, Colton, and Gabby are here and he doesn't know it. There's school in the morning. I'm tired. There's a thousand reasons he shouldn't. But just the single solitary memory of lying wrapped in his arms, smelling the scent of his skin, and feeling his breathes tickle across my hair makes me want to tell him to come.

"You're not answering. I assume it's a no."

"What about the curse? I know you're blinking right now."

"The world didn't implode the last two times we slept together."

"What if I want more? What if you want more?"

"Are you telling me you want more in a relationship than—*sleeping with* me?" Rocky sounds wide awake. "Because, again, you initiated the step we took in that direction."

"What would you say if I did?" I ask. "I don't want to hurt my sister. I don't know how far my daddy's head would explode if he knew. Or if your daddy would kill you. Your mom told me to stay away from you. I know people will talk because you dated my sister. When I look in your eyes, I see you looking back at me and in every case I can think of, I can read people like the back of my hand. But with you, I can't. No, I can. I just *won't*. I question my ability to read you. I sabotage any idea you'd like me back as much as I like you. Like when you came to Daddy's house with your uncle. I'm thinking that's about as near to walking through fire for a woman as it will ever get, a McDaniel stepping through the door of a McGuire house. But then I think that you're just doing it because it's your job to save people. Oh, hell." I don't want my words to come pouring like a flooded creek from my lips. But I can feel it again, that achy-wonderful sensation he leaves in my chest. "When I'm not with you or when you are with some other girl, I feel—like my insides are getting ripped out. So, yeah, I want a relationship with you and more than just friends, more than you showing up at my house or me showing up at yours and ending up rolling around the floor. I'm willing to tear down the brick wall completely—, all two bricks that are left, and build a wall around us if we need to do it."

He does a Rocky-classic chuckle. "Okay. Done."

"What's that mean?" I ask.

"I'm making bricks. Aw, crap, we'll have to finish this later," he sighs. "I've got a *real* 9-1-1 call right now, on the other line. As opposed to the test one you gave me just now." He chuckles. "Got to go. Love you." Click.

What? What? Did he just say *love you?* I put down my phone and wish my wide eyes would slump a little with sleep while that rattles around my brain. I listen for sirens. I think I hear some far away. Now I'm worried about Rocky, which only adds to the anxiety. Maybe he didn't mean to tell me he loves me. I should have stuck an *I love you* into the conversation at the end. I didn't. Then I wonder if it's a fire he's going to right now. Is it time for me and Leah to die? I toss and turn for three hours, look at the clock at 5:30. I can't sleep. I have a half hour before I usually get up.

"Do you sleep?" Colton's voice from behind startles me and I try to muffle my yelp.

"Colton, I thought you were asleep. No, I guess not. I'm thinking about—dead girls." And love. *He loves me?*

"Why is it that when you say that, it doesn't sound as creepy as it would if I said it?"

I laugh softly. "It is creepy. I'm working myself up to go talk to Timmy Kinney this morning. It's time."

"But we didn't get you all the serial killer information? How are you going to show it could be Doctor Stamper? They still aren't going to believe you—"

"Is it normal behavior to be up this late at night?" Leah sticks her head out the door of the guest bedroom. She scrubs her head and pads down the hallway.

"Technically, it is morning." I yawn into my palm. Both Colton and I turn guilty gazes to Leah. She's got her red hair tied up on top of her head in a thick, lazy bun. She's got the same gritty, ill-tempered gaze Baby Cakes would give me after I'd accidentally knocked him off my bed in the middle of the night.

"You look tetchy." I cringe when she does that tip to her chin sideways like a fighter getting ready to walk into a ring. "I figured you were going to ask if it's normal behavior for me to have a seventeen year-old in my bedroom at five in the morning."

"He's eighteen. He can make bad decisions on his own now." Leah grunts, then points a finger at Colton. "And it *would* be a bad decision. And not just because of the curse." His face turns bright red and I tell her to shut up.

"Hey, while you slept like a baby in my guest bedroom, I found out that your Aunt Lynn is thinking about going to the cops."

"A baby? And I knew that." She sniffs. "Uncle Jake and her got in a big fight about it. And, by the way, nobody could sleep like a baby in this house. It's like a zoo. There's three cages of hamsters battling it out over one running wheel and a guinea pig that won't stop whistling."

"I'm sure the hundred dollar a week hotel off the highway next to Downtown Sally's Strip Club has less squealing and squeaking going on," I mutter feeling a little crabby myself. "Well... maybe not." I add a waggle to my neck.

"He's right, Uncle Jake is. Nobody's going to believe you—a retired cop and a school counselor as murderers?

Those two old people, the Stampers, are the kindest people you've ever met. They bring us boxes of food around Christmas. They volunteer at Laurel Grove Park." Leah gives me a wary gaze. "Everything you've told us can be manipulated. All of the girls being killed could just be coincidence. It's Bobby's word against my aunt's that he killed Carrie."

"No, it isn't just that. It is the date their daughter was born—Carrie Stamper. May 21st. If you look at the dates of each death, they are either on May 21st or May 22nd."

"Like—like tomorrow." Colton's face is drained of color when we both turn.

"Is tomorrow the 21st?" I ask.

"Yes, Rosie," Leah answers me and turns quickly to her brother. "Colton, you need to go get ready for school." Leah almost chokes those words out. "Just—just go get dressed or something. Rosie and I need to figure this out."

"I'm not going today. I don't have any clothes, they are all at home. I can't wear the same thing two days in a row."

"You have to go."

"Maybe he's better off here. Maybe we all are for a couple days," I say. "We can hide out and wait for the two days to pass."

"I don't want my little brother anywhere near me if I'm the target of some serial killer. He's safer at school. And I can't get fired from my job." Leah laughs sarcastically. "I can't afford that."

"Can you afford to die?"

I hear a ting on my Violet phone. I lazily pick it up in passing. It says: *Hey, enjoyed getting to know you. But I don't want to lead you on. I've got a girlfriend. Hope you get that dance with someone someday. Rock*

Chapter 59

CHECK YOUR FIRE ALARMS! RASH OF FIRE RUNS LEAVES LOCAL FIRE DEPARTMENT FACING QUESTIONS—IS IT ARSON OR FAULTY WIRING?

Fourteen mobile homes in the tri-county area have been destroyed by fires in the last six months. Fire Inspector, Dean Wilson, states that although each occurred close together in time, it is most likely coincidence. "It seems only natural to assume it is arson," Wilson states. "But these mobile homes were all over forty to fifty years old and built by the Kansas Mobile Home Company. The company went out of business in 1985 because a high ratio of the mobile homes they had wired were done with cheap materials and were recalled. But it was not before there were eight deaths across the Midwest. I believe this is just another case of faulty wiring—

As of this past week, there have been three deaths caused by the fires. Volunteer Fireman, Rocky McDaniel has seen a few of these. We asked him how others can avoid this type of tragedy, "Have a professional check your wiring," Rocky suggests. "Make sure you have fire detectors in every room."

I know the exact moment everything starts going to hell. I'm hugging my phone and letting it sink in that Rocky likes me, *loves* me. For being me and not a bunch of makeup and slinky walk Violet. I'm beginning to think my superstitious kin are right. There really is a curse.

There's a piggy magnet holding up a copy of the article about fire alarms on to my refrigerator. Mom had bought eight of them because Rocky's picture was on the cover with his fireman suspenders dangling at his sides and his hat in the cleft of his arm. She gave two to Rocky to give

SHAY LAWLESS

to his mom, then stored the rest in a box in her closet for future generations of Rocky and Nicky's offspring.

It's not just the newspaper article. There's a blue Post-it note stuck on top that says: *Call William's Pawn Shop ASAP.* It is in cursive, but doesn't have the same twists and curls as Mom's usual writing. It looks familiar, though. Is it Leah's handwriting? I tug on the note and the newspaper article comes with it, the magnet holding it drops downwards, knocking two others loose in its wake.

I'm slightly alarmed she came to my house when I was gone, even as I watch the papers fall. I can imagine her trying the knob on my bedroom door and grinding her teeth when she realizes it is locked and perhaps hiding what my sister saw within. I know she wiggled her nose when she peeked her head into my guest bedroom, and took in the odor of hamster and guinea pig cages. It is discomfiting knowing she is snooping around my home. Again.

"Shit." I curse, bend over as the newspaper articles flutter like dying butterflies toward the floor. I wave my hands to catch them, miss two, and snap one in mid-air between thumb and palm. On that, I fix my gaze. I am staring at the back of the newspaper obituary for Angel Daugherty. ANGEL D. MAY 21. The cursive matches that of the note to call the pawn shop. I make a hasty pick up of the other two newspaper articles. One is for Alaina. I flip it over, stare at the cursive. ALAINA W. MAY 21. It, too, matches. No one knows the dates they died. Except, of course, the killer.

The cursive. Where have I seen it before? I wheel around, make my way to my purse and open it wide. Inside, I see the prescription Mom gave me for the sleeping pills Doctor Stamper recommended. I never took it to the pharmacy. Now I take it out. I reel back, cover my mouth with my hand. The writing matches.

I pick up my landline phone next to the refrigerator to ask my mom if she put those newspaper articles on my refrigerator. The phone is dead. Did I pay the bill?

Leah's still in the shower. Colton has left for school. It's still dark in the living room with the curtains closed. I look at the clock on my cell phone. Tag Williams. He's left six messages on my cell phone. I groan, throw my head back, and call him.

"Yes, what did you need?"

"You need to come and get that package."

"I don't have time." I haven't had time. "Can't you open it and tell me what's inside? If I drive to Columbus, I'm going to be an hour and a half late for school."

"No. You need to come," Tag says hoarsely. "You *have* to come."

I figure out I was set up after I drive to Columbus. I parked my old car a block down the street because there wasn't any parking. I made my way along the buckled sidewalk past a couple closed-up shops with bars on the windows and a newer apartment building.

Tag doesn't say anything when he stands up rigidly and gingerly knuckle-shoves a brown box toward me on the counter. He had been watching TV and settled on an old barstool with the ripped lime green vinyl on top. I've got on a pair of jeans, a t-shirt, and beanie. In another twenty minutes, I'll be parking on the side of the road and slipping on my Rosie school clothes. I feel like at every angle, I've got to hide my identity. I don't know who I am. It was against my better judgement to come here. I don't trust Tag. I stare at him. He stares at me. I know he knows something more than he's saying. I open the box carefully, one flap at a time.

"He left a note this morning and said he'd kill me if I didn't get you here to pick it up."

"What?" My head snaps up. I've got this horrible sensation in my belly while I stand there with my fingers playing on the cardboard lid. "Is—is he *here*?" I'm sweating, feel a wave of heat hit me. "Does he know I'm here?"

"No. I don't—think so. The note was on the door."

"Where's the note now?" I hardly finish saying that when Tag lifts up a little piece of paper with clear tape stuck to it. It's the same writing as my prescription and the notes on the newspapers tacked to my refrigerator. "I should go." I say that because I get this sensation I'm being watched.

"Open it. Please." Tag taps the box. My fingers are numb. There is brown packing paper, which I pull out, one long piece at a time. When I finally drop the last one on the counter, I'm transfixed staring into the depths.

"What is it?"

"It's a pair of tennis shoes with wheels on them."

"What?" Tag leans in, stares into the box while I gently reach my hand inside and lift them out. They appear brand new, blue and red tennis shoes. I turn them over in my hands and look up at Tag.

"You have no clue who this person is?" I ask. "Are you sure these were for me? I mean, I remember wanting these when I was eleven or twelve, but my mom wouldn't get me a pair. She hates fads."

"They've talked to me over the phone. They left an envelope with cash on my back step. It was on my step."

"So is this the guy who came in?" I pull out the Holy Trinity Church directory from ten years ago out of my purse. I flip through the pages, hold up the book, and point to a picture of Rob Stamper. I'm afraid to hear the truth.

"Well, I'll be damned! Yeah, that's him." Then he opens a drawer, removes a pistol and a box of bullets. "Sweetie, you might need this."

I call my mom coming out of the shop. My eyes are flapping around, up and down the block. I'm searching for a car. Maybe it will come up on to the sidewalk and hit me. A freak accident. Maybe the Stampers are going to shoot me.

"Hey Mom, I have a question for you. I need an answer quickly." I'm expecting her to huff out some smart-alecky remark about me not returning a call. Instead I can hardly hear her for the sirens screaming on her end.

"What's going on there?"

"Um, I don't know. Are you okay? Your voice sounds funny. I just stopped to get gas. This is the third firetruck that's gone past. A lady inside said they had a false alarm at the nursing home. But somebody said there's another set of trailers on fire. I had to pull over twice. Where are you?"

I freeze in my tracks. Does no one else associate fire truck sirens with death now? Every time there's a fire, another girl dies. I get this horrid feeling I need to call Leah and Colton. "Real fast, Mom; do you remember when I wanted those tennis shoes with wheels on them?"

"Yes, dear, I remember well. In fact, the entire neighborhood probably recalls it."

"What do you mean by that?"

"You stood out on the front lawn and screamed at me for twenty minutes because I wouldn't buy you a pair. You're not thinking about getting some, are you? If you do, get those elbow and knee pads."

"Did the Stampers live across the street then?"

There's a long hesitation. "Rosie, you have to stop this. Yes, they did. But I don't think you're all right."

"I'm fine. Have you been placing newspaper articles on the murders on my fridge for the few months?" How do you point a finger for murder at a couple who has been embraced by the entire town? If my own mom doesn't believe me, who will?

"Of course not. Where do you come up with these things? You missed choir practice again. Are you at work?"

"No, mom, I don't have time for this."

Now, there's the long silence while I get into my car, start the engine. "Time for *what*?"

"Doctor Stamper and her husband are trying to kill me. Your husband gave Carrie Stamper a drug in high school one night while they were hanging out and she fell and hit her head."

"Does this have something to do with your father calling me about the pills? Because you shouldn't stop taking them. I called Mary Stamper and told her what was going on and she said the doctor at the hospital is a quack. She's been giving kids that medication for years. The new doctors are just out to make a buck through the big pharmaceutical companies. They get kickbacks for the new medications. Yours is inexpensive through her. It is tried and true and safe. I asked your sister and she said Mary *knows her stuff*."

"You know what? Nevermind. You're not going to believe me." I hang up.

At ten-fifteen, I'm pushing through the doors at Laurel Grove High School, almost an hour and ten minutes after the students arrive. When I walk past the front office, Principal Cunningham points a chubby forefinger at me and jabs his thumb toward his office. "Miss Mauer, I need to speak with you a moment." I feel a bit woozy.

"I know I'm late. I locked my keys in the car."

He's shaking his head and in front of him and sitting on his desk is a plastic baggy. He looks at me, then looks at the baggy. I follow his eyes to my jeans and my shirt. I forgot to change. Then Principal Cunningham shakes his head. "In light of the situation, I'll make this quick."

"What—situation?"

He looks at me almost curiously. Then he pats the desk. "It came to my attention you had, in your possession, a narcotic substance. Considering we presumed your story of discovering it, I don't think the subject would have been broached if we did not find this small bag of marijuana in your desk drawer this morning."

"I don't smoke pot. It isn't mine."

"That's not my job to make judgments, it is the court system's." He lets out a puff of air. "However, it is my duty, as the principal, to protect the children within these walls. I believe you are a threat to them. This morning we have two students missing from school—Mindy Carter and Charley Walters. It appears Jake Smythe was receiving texts from the two last night along with Colton McDaniel. They were working with you on some project on serial killers. Is this correct?"

"Well, um, yes. I mean, just in the library."

"Do you know where they are?"

"No. It was just an encrypted message." My hands are shaking. *Just* an encrypted message. I underestimated those students. "I'll figure it out. I'll find them."

"Well, you can figure it out at the police station. Your dismissal from this school will be immediate. Under the circumstances, it had already been discussed at our school board meeting that it is up to me if your uncustomary behavior could be grounds for dismissal. I will be contacting the police department. I would suggest the police station is your next stop. You can explain your case to the authorities searching for the students. Gracie is sending Bobby Vandevenne to make sure you get there safely. Have you spoken with your mother?"

"About two hours ago."

"You should, perhaps, call her again. There has been a bit of an accident—the McDaniel family will be in mourning for quite some time."

Chapter 60

Leah's dead. That's what Mom said. I burst through the door at a dead run. The hospital waiting room is deathly quiet, except for a small TV in the upper right corner of the room on a news channel. It's like the moment I cross the threshold, the air is sucked from the waiting room. My head goes back and forth. There are twenty-some chairs and all are filled. I don't see Mom or Nicky. It's just the McDaniels and they are giving me wry, accusing expressions. Nothing new, I suppose, so I snatch up my phone to text my family, see where they are. There are three calls from Colton. I groan. What could he want? I see three little texts go pop, pop, pop. They are from Mindy.

Miss Mauer. Hello??!! I decrypted the message.

515 Ferris-James Road. Seven steps from mailbox, three feet down.

Colton, Charley, me. Going to check it out.

NO! I text back. *Where? Stop!!*

The next thing I know, I hear feet stomping up toward me. There's another ting. I look up to see Jake McDaniel taking one last and long stride toward me. He had stood up so quickly, his metal chair flies to the left and bangs across the floor. He's huge, a giant of a man with a thick, red beard and stone-cold, blue eyes.

"Get out! You have no place being here," he yell-growls less than an arms-length away from me. He points toward the door. "Get out or, I swear to God, I will pick you up and toss you out!"

"What happened? What's going on?"

"What's going on?" Big Jake takes a huge step toward me, stomping down hard, like he's trying to scare a strange dog off a porch. "My wife is in jail because of you! My niece is dead because of you!" I react the same as the dog, jumping back with wide eyes. Ting! I look down at a text.

"Rosie!" Nicky sweeps down the dim hallway. I can hear the clack of Mom's high heels behind. I'm looking for Bobby to come out next. My hands are shaking. I've got the gun stuffed into the back of my jeans. I peer to the left of Rocky's dad's arm and he steps to the left, eyeing Nicky carefully. "Get her out of her, Nicky," he says gruffly. "There won't be trouble."

"I will. She doesn't know, Jake."

"Know what? What's going on?" I ask and Nicky grabs me hard around the shoulders and tows me to the corner of the room near the hallway. Ting! Mom comes up beside her, dabbing her eyes like she's at a funeral. "Is it Rocky? What's going on?"

I glance at my phone. Leah. Oh, thank God.

Where are you? Leah's message asks.

"What's going on?" Nicky huffs in a low voice at me while she looks over her shoulder. "Put the damn phone down." They are coagulating like blood, the McDaniels, whispering in little groups and staring at us.

I text Leah: *At hospital—Rocky hurt.*

"Will you quit texting?" Nicky scream-whispers. "Why were you not answering your cell phone?"

"Nicky, she needs to leave. This is not a good time nor place to explain the situation. Walk her to her car."

Is he okay? Leah texts back.

I groan inwardly, realize I'd blocked Nicky and Mom when I got mad at them last time for calling. "What the heck is going on?"

I text Leah, *Get to the hospital.*

"Shut up!" Nicky shoves fingers over my lips to stifle me. "Dammit, shut up. There was a fire tonight," Nicky continues quietly and like she's talking to a child.

"I heard the sirens. No. I mean, I went to school for work and Principal Cunningham said there was an emergency."

"Well, Lynn went to the police and confessed she'd taken drugs with Carrie Stamper the night she died. Now, she's in jail. Then—three people—" she lowers her voice further and reaches out to me, pushes a hand on my shoulder, "—died. Rocky tried to get them out. He couldn't. He almost died himself, trying to get them. And then when the police showed up, they accused Rocky of starting the fires to take the focus off his uncle on his murdering spree." I waver, feel woozy and faint. "They are trying to find Johnny McDaniel. He's the one who has been killing the girls, Rosie. Listen to me." She latches on to my arm. "Do you hear me? It was Johnny McDaniel the whole time. Over the years he's murdered other girls, including the one they found in the quarry."

"No." I shake my head. "That's not true. Who died?" I stand starkly still. "Mom? Answer me. Where's Rocky?"

Nicky looks at Mom. "Sweetie, it was Leah and Colton McDaniel. And Gabby."

I stare at her. Is this a joke? "No, Leah's not dead," I tell her. "Neither are the kids. I just talked to them." I shake my head. I see Nicky's eyes get wide like she thinks I'm having some sort of a crazy attack. "You've got to believe me. It isn't Johnny McDaniel killing those girls." My voice is rising. I see Rocky's dad stiffen, turn an eye on me.

"Yes sweetie, he is. It's okay. We'll all get through this. They found one body so far in the trailer. You just need to leave for now while tempers are high."

"But it's not true. I just saw them. They aren't—" I close my eyes. They won't believe me. The body, it has to be T. Leah told me he barged into her trailer last night and wouldn't leave. "Is Rocky all right?"

"They have him in custody, with police outside the emergency room. He is—beside himself with grief," Mom sighs. "Leah's trailer was one of the homes burnt down early this morning. It's gone. Just gone. They are gone. Rocky tried to go inside while it was burning—they've just gotten him into the emergency room—" Mom looks over my shoulder, cocks her head to the side. Relief seems to wash over her. "Nicky. Bobby's here. He'll take care of her."

"No, not Bobby."

"He'll take you home."

I pick up my phone and text Rocky: *Leah, Colton, Gab not in trailer. With me all night. Dead body was T. Rocky, I need you. 9-1-1. Pickle. Big pickle. Now. Waiting room.*

My phone is making that noise again. Pop, pop, pop. Then, ting, ting, ting. I pull it up, look at the map displayed on my screen. 515 Ferris-James Road. I see White's Boarding Farm on a little icon.

"The Stamper's house," I mutter. "Oh, my God. I don't have time for this. The kids are at the Stamper's!"

"Dammit!" Nicky snaps at me, jerks my phone from my hand. "Put the damn phone down and listen to me!"

"Colton isn't dead. Leah and Gabby aren't dead! There is no stupid curse! And I don't have time for this!"

"Bobby!" Mom screeches.

I back up and start for the door. Mom is wringing her hands and Nicky is pawing at me. And I see Bobby stomp forward, his hands waving like he's going to grab me.

Norma Edwards would be proud of me. My first day boxing with her, she knocked me flat on my bottom and stood over top. "You'll hate me now, Popovich, but someday, getting the shit beat out of you will pay off." I didn't think so then while I stared up at two of her; I was wrong.

I don't think Bobby planned on punching me. However, his hand struck out toward my ear to grab me. I started to follow Norma's careful instructions in fighting back; I could hear her grouchy whispers in my ear—*All right, Popovich, lean to the right.* It isn't difficult. She'd pounded them in five days a week, my signature move—that old veer—*now, kick hard at my shins*—but I change it up a bit and instead of the kick in the shins, I slam the toe of my tennis shoes into Bobby's crotch so hard, I think I hear something crackle and pop. *Now, two hits. Bam-bam.* He makes this funny coughing sound while I lift my fists-bam-bam, but by the time my fists are coming back for my first of two left arm punches, he is already kneeling on the floor. It's silent in the waiting room. One of Rocky's uncles is moving forward. I see a nurse tearing down a hallway.

"Get the hell off of me—!" That's Rocky's deep roar. I see his shadow first. He's shoving himself through a set of doors, one officer and a male nurse dressed in blue clinging to his arms. He's like King Kong, swinging them off, rubbing them against the doors. He is wagging his neck, like a bull, looking for me. He catches my eye on the third swing. "You've got to trust me, Rocky," I yell. "Don't—don't let them get me. I—I love you too!" Then, I hear the fire alarm go off, catch just the faint outline of Big Jake McDaniel jerking down the pull station fire alarm mounted on the wall. It's like a wall of McDaniels part ways and fold themselves around my path. And I run like hell.

Chapter 61

On September 9, 1977, Mary Stamper was standing at her kitchen sink, looking out the window. The window was open, the warm breeze slipping through the screen and whipping about the red gingham curtains. She had rubbed her forearms, a layer of goosepimples rising along her flesh. It was eighty degrees outside, but after the record-breaking heat of the previous two months, it almost seemed like the cooler winds of fall were breaking through the blistering barrier of a long, hot summer that seemed unending.

"I remember closing my eyes, drinking in the deepest of breaths of that air and thinking my life had to be simply and utterly perfect." Mary Stamper is telling me this now. She's wearing baby blue yoga pants with pink stripes down the sides and a matching jacket. She is standing on her porch while I get out of a little compact car not ten steps away. I'm strangely intrigued by her story while I feel my left foot touch the sparse grass on the side of the driveway. I'm shaking furiously.

"Where is Mindy, Charley, and Colton, Doctor Stamper?" I interrupt her thoughts and she falls silent long enough to scold me with a glare.

"Don't interrupt me, Rosaline."

"Please. Just tell me where they are."

"Don't waste your time. The police are coming. I called 9-1-1. But it's going to be too late." She warns, rubs her arms. "Listen to me. Are you listening?"

"Yes." But I'm not sure the police are coming. Three miles from the hospital, I passed Leah McDaniel screaming down the highway in her little compact car. I honked and careened to a halt nearly sideways. I told her the cops were going to stop me. I had to trade her cars. I'm sure at this very moment, she is sliding to a stop, surrounded by Laurel Grove police. I am praying she can convince them I'm not a complete nutcase. But I know if they had caught me, stopped me, I wouldn't get here on time.

"I had it all—a good husband, a home, a wonderful daughter," Mary Stamper continues softly, like she hadn't stopped, staring at me with a soft smile parting her lips. The full force of her anger and pain started the moment I blew into her driveway, sliding sideways at seventy miles an hour with Leah's car spewing black ooze from underneath her hood. She knew I was coming. She was standing on the front porch, rubbing her arms with her hands. My own mother had called to warn her. Now, I'm sweating bullets. I hear a child cry out, the low sound of muffled sobbing in the distance. Gabby. Shit. Gabby's with them.

"Doctor Stamper, is that Gabby?" I take a step forward. "You have her too? Let her go, please."

"It's the little girl. I think that's what Colton called her. Gabby. Yes, it's Gabby. She cried so hard when we put the bandana over her eyes I had to slap her." She's wearing a cherry red lipstick, the kind old women don that they think makes them look young, but only makes their skin grayer. "I heard the sirens that day. Those damn sirens. I hate the sound of sirens now. I associate them with death. I almost dread them coming now. But there's a part of me that needs them, wants to hear them right before the kill. So Rob, he starts them for me. The police will be here soon. I wonder if your mother will know the minute, the second— the exact moment when your life goes away. I imagine Carrie cried just like that little girl." She lowers her head, watches the toe of her white tennis shoe kick at the porch wood. "I did. I knew the moment Carrie had died." She sighs deeply, loses the smile and replaces it with a thoughtful gaze toward me. "I felt it. It was an emptiness inside, at the exact time the sirens wailed by. It was the morning of—"

"She didn't die that morning." I take a step toward her. "She'd been dead. She died the night before. Bobby Vandevenne killed her. It was an accident. He gave her a pill and she fell, hit her head. I've got my aunt's diary and she wrote that Carrie—"

"No dear, a mother knows. You're just making it up. It's the bond of mother to child, a deep abiding love. You may not understand that now. You have no children of your own—" And this is where her smile whips around and blends to a sneer like warm butter melting on a piece of hot toast. "And you won't, my dear. Because I won't let you. They killed her, your father and John McDaniel. They ran her over and just left her there like trash."

"No, she was with Bobby Vandevenne. Listen to me, please. It wasn't Johnny or my dad. Bobby Vandevenne killed her!"

"Silly girl. You can't fool me. I know your tricks. We've done this dance before, don't you remember? No, you don't. But you deserve the same panic, horror, and sorrow I felt. Your whole family deserves it and I won't stop until every one of you feels the gut-wrenching pain I felt at the very moment I found her dead."

"Why are you blaming all of us?" I ask her. The moment my voice challenges her, I feel the sudden change in me. My throat feels like invisible hands have wrapped around it, my windpipe starts to restrict. My fingers automatically move to my nose. Shit. I can't remember. I want to remember what happened and I can't. Doctor Stamper ignores the realization settling on my face. She whips up her gun, waggles it at me.

"Nobody told you? I would think with all the digging

you've been doing with that nosy little nose of yours, you'd have figured it out."

She laughs softly. "I've given it to your mother and your father in small increments over the years. Then, as a colleague, your sister. They've confided to me about you. I've told them about your problems, your mental illnesses. You know what that is, don't you?"

"Brain washing?"

"Ah, yes, a classic example of systematic persuasive techniques I picked up in a study on Korean War prisoners. The book is called *The History of Brainwashing in the Twentieth Century*. It's just a wonderful book. There's something incredibly gratifying finding a technique, being able to test it, and then having it perform as expected. You can't imagine my delight when I picked it up the year you were in the newspaper with me. I was able to disassociate you from your peers, get your mother to change your diet so you were constantly deficient in nutrients, and encourage the other children in your classes to criticize your every move so you felt guilt, fear, and exclusion. It's so sad, Gracie Mauer's daughter is psychotic. Now your mommy gets the full force of my anger and feels the pain I've endured."

I know Doctor Stamper has done this to me, years of coding all of us with the stupid curse, years of making everyone believe I'm crazy. I try to stop it. I can't. I feel my heart start to race. "Doctor Stamper, you need to stop this. I know what you've done. You don't have to hurt anyone else. If payback for your daughter dying was what you were looking for, you've paid so many families back—"

"You know what she did, don't you?" She takes two steps off the porch. She has a large, black revolver in her hand.

"I know what *you* did. You spent the last forty years

counseling the kids at the high school, planting seeds in their head about the curse. I know you've been slowly killing the firstborn daughter of every person in those two cars, one by one. And all for nothing. They *didn't* kill her."

"Oh, you're the smart one."

"I was also the one who got away, wasn't I?" I ask in a surly tone. I am standing with my back to the car, closing the door behind me. It's hot against my back. I'm shaking. I'm trying desperately to hold her back. I made the call, like Rocky said. Nobody in the police department picked up the phone. I left a message for extension 102, Timmy Kinney, and while I drove like a bat out of hell toward the Stampers, I told him the story, the whole condensed version, and told him Bobby had also pinned stuff on his grandpa by giving me evidence he'd allegedly thrown away. Then I called my daddy and I told him I needed him. I'm praying he gets the message, they get here soon because I *know* that Mister Stamper will tell those kids he's going to do it fast. But he won't. He'll have them kneel down on the damp floor of the barn. He'll place bandanas over their eyes, so they can't see. He'll draw it out, whistle a little bit, and pat a shoulder. And while they cry and beg for him to let them live, one by one, he'll lift the shovel and smash it into the backs of their heads.

"Let's just say you're the one who we *let* get away."

My head has cleared in the last two days since I went off the medicine. I've twined together the dreams and the hazy memories. I remember bits and pieces. And what I don't remember, I can piece together, a jumbled puzzle with enough answers to know who tried to kill me, who is murdering the girls. I remember kneeling on the ground. There was a brown tarp laying there and covering the floor. It had been carefully stretched out. It would catch any blood. It made a crinkling sound when I knelt there. Mister

Stamper spent five minutes smoothing it out in front of me with is fingers. I remember him hitting me once. But for some reason he over balanced slightly at the same time I heard the whistle of the shovel. I fell flat on my belly, getting just a graze of shovel on the back of my head. And then I had skittered, like a crawdad, across the floor; kicked, screamed, and ran. I dug my fingernails into the old dirt floor and tried to dig my way underneath the barn door while Mister Stamper chased me with the shovel—

"Doctor Stamper, where are the kids?" I ask again. But I know. I see the rear bumper of Colton's truck parked in the small barn to the right, just as Rob Stamper slowly closes the doors. He watches me, gives me a leering grin before he disappears behind the doors. "Don't—don't do this." I hold out my hands. "Please."

"Don't do this? Where were you when —"

"No, there's four kids in there, that would make it uneven. They aren't a part of this—" I try to rationalize with her. I push myself away from the car, ease my way toward the elderly woman. But she's wiry, nimble. For every step I take forward, she takes one step toward the barn. I've got sweat dripping down my forehead and my pistol tucked into the back of my jeans. "You know, Gabby's only nine. We make brownies together. She still plays with my dolls when she comes to my house. I think if her friends knew, they'd make fun of her."

"Rosie, you're manipulating the situation, trying to play on my empathy. You did that a lot when you were in middle school. We talked about this in your sessions, remember."

No, not really. Because psychopathic serial killers have no empathy. I'm trying to get close to her so if I shoot, I kill her. "Colton, he's her uncle. He tries to come off really cool about not going to college and just working in some gas station all his life. That's what everyone is expecting from him. But I caught him looking in the college guides in the library. I think he wants to travel, be an archeologist."

"He's watching you."

"What?" I ask, following Doctor Stamper's gaze. She nods her head. I waver, follow with my eyes.

"Rob, he's watching you. I left you a message on your desk. You had to see it. I had to dig deep with a letter opener to write it."

"You wrote that." I swallow hard. *I'm watching you.* I really had thought Leah scrawled that into the desk because of my pranks.

"Yes, he's waiting. He has to let the Rohypnol that the children took start to do its magic. He's not so quick. It makes it easier on them, just like it made it easier on you, makes them sleepy and uninhibited and forgetful, in your case. The first couple times, the girls cried so hard. Bing! Then I got the idea to drug them."

Rohypnol. Roofies. The date rape drug my sister said was in the baggie Lydia tried to drug Liam with. She must have given me the drug when they abducted me. That's why I could never remember exactly what happened.

"—still, it always hurts a little the first time—"

I swallow hard, look to my right. My eyes widen. I can see a face at the barn window. It's smiling a big-toothed grin at me. He wiggles something next to his head. The shovel. That damn shovel. God, I remember that grin. He played with me. He made me play hide and seek in the barn until the drug began to do its dirty work and before he tried to kill me. But there was nowhere to hide, so he put the bandana over my eyes and toyed with me. *Have you ever played the game Marco Polo?* Dead girls. *I put a bandana around your head and you call Marco and I call Polo and you try to find me.* I didn't know it then, but I suppose he'd done it with others in there.

"It's time for us to finish this, Rosaline."

No. She can't do this. I need more time. I just need five more minutes for my daddy or the cops or somebody to come driving pell-mell down the road to save me. I need five more minutes for the cops to figure out where I went, to try to stop me from going crazy—oh, God. I blink. Mary Stamper is setting me up so it looks like I made up the message to get the kids here. She's going to make it look like I've killed them all, the crazy daughter of Gracie Mauer. It is the ultimate payback for what she thinks was my daddy's cruel blow to her daughter.

Her revolver makes a loud snap. It's like I didn't expect it. One minute Doctor Stamper is talking, the next, she's shooting me. I feel a stinging pain just below the ribs on my left side. I suppose I had expected it all along, I would die. But until I felt that pain and reached down to see the blood flow lazily over my fingers, it didn't quite sink in. It's almost surreal, the sensations. Strangely, I think of riding Daddy's ATV and the sinking feeling the moment it got stuck. I can think of a hundred times I have embarrassed my family, all probably inadvertently bestowed upon me through Doctor Stamper's well thought out plan to torture my family. And now, the ultimate. My Daddy will have to live with the fact his daughter was a murderer. And the Stampers, they will walk away unscathed, again.

I grit my teeth because as the thought process sinks into my brain, so does the pain of her gunshot. It's only three seconds, three breaths. I shift to the left and then to the right, avoiding the next two shots with the squirrely motion Norma Edwards taught me in cardio-kickboxing. Then, I whip out my little pink pistol from the back of my pants, take off the safety like Daddy taught me and I aim it at Doctor Stamper.

"You won't be able to do it, you know," she grins like she is taking in that first taste of spring again. "Stockholm Syndrome. You know what that is, don't you?" She cocks back her revolver, closes one eye as if aiming down the barrel. "You feel a psychological alliance with me. We're alike, the two of us. Because I think we have a bond, don't you? Over the years, I've been the one you've divulged all your secrets to, been there to comfort you when your mom was at your throat. I know, in the back of your mind, you know I helped you get your job at Crystal Springs Country Club. I manipulated Jack Barkley into hiring you, just like I manipulated the police into believing his son killed those girls. Now, if you just let me kill you, I'll tell everyone that it wasn't your fault."

"No, you won't."

"Yes," she says smugly. "Because Mommy's good little girl has done everything she's always been told, hasn't she? And it just took me rolling my eyes that day to get you to buck her shirking the club. Actually, you've been doing everything I say, you realize that now, don't you? When I counselled your mother on how to deal with you, I also told her how to react to you. When I counseled you, I told you how to react to her. Like ping-pong balls, back and forth, back and forth. You'll do everything I say to save your family, save your family's name. Because if it isn't you, it will be your daddy or Liam or John McDaniel. So, put down the gun—"

"You have no clue what is going on in my head, *bitch*," I snarl. "I got you to admit your guilt and take six steps forward so I can't miss the shot." My bullet penetrates Doctor Stamper's skull with a funky kind of snapping sound. There is a boom and a pop. I jerk impulsively, feel the urge to vomit. My heart is pounding and I think I'm going to faint. I'm on the verge of a panic attack. But I don't have time to entertain the thought as Doctor Stamper crumples like a paper doll. Because I hear the screams.

Chapter 62

I'm bleeding. It is warm against my sides, but cooler where it is settled on my shirt and slapping against the skin below my ribs. Textbooks tell you blood doesn't have a smell. It does. It's like the scent of the earth on a warm summer day.

"Shit!" There's a door on the side of the little red barn. I peer inside. There are four of them kneeling on a tarp, hands tied behind their back. Two have bandanas over their eyes—Charley is leaning slightly to his left so his head is almost on Colton's shoulder. Colton's skinny shoulders are bent. The next figure has what looks like a dirty rag over her head. I can tell by the hair brushing her shoulders that it is Mindy. Poor little Gabby is last. She's shivering and shaking, a tiny doll next to the others.

I twist the knob. It's locked. I can see in the window. Holy Hell. I see the shovel in Mister Stamper's hand. I think he probably stopped when he heard the gunshot. I don't know what to do other than shoot the doorknob, like they do in the movies. It seems appropriate. It doesn't work. The bullet just grazes the knob, vanishes into the air.

So I rip off my shirt and stuff it over my fist like Rocky told me to do if I had to break a window and get out of a burning building during a fire. I smash it into the window. It takes two punches before the window breaks and I wiggle my hand to the latch. I'm strangely calm while Mister Stamper walks over and tries to hit my arm and elbow with his shovel.

"Where's Mary?" he demands as my foot shoves the door open and I nearly fall on my face from the force. I'm like a two-stepping cowgirl on a tarp-covered dance floor, trying to catch my balance. Dizzy. Crap on a stick, I'm losing blood. And I'm right where I need to be to bleed to death. All's the Stampers had to do was drag me in there with the others and set me up to look like I'd killed them. The clean up after would be simple.

I'm suddenly basked in browns. I lose a second to feeling faint and come to my senses on my knees.

"I always forget to tell the kids this," Rob Stamper has gone from standing in front of me to being behind Mindy. "It might hurt a little, the first time." He takes long strides over to Colton. "Let's play a game, why don't we? Games make it fun! Who wants to go first?" They are sobbing, chattering, talking and he screams for them to shut up. "When I say Marco, you say Polo." He lifts up the shovel. Colton bucks. It gives me just enough time to bring up the pistol.

"Marco," I say.

"I'm playing with them." Rob Stamper looks at me with a crazy twist to his head.

I'm scrambling in my own blood in slow motion. And that's when I raise my pistol. I mean, he has to know I'm going to shoot him as his shovel rises above Colton's head. Colton can't see. His hands are tied behind his back. I hold the pistol, aim, and let my forefinger drop. I think it should be more difficult stopping this whole mess. But it's not.

"Polo," Rob Stamper mumbles. I pull the trigger and let the gunshots rip. One. Two. Three. And then, Mister Stamper's knees just buckle. His head turns. He looks at me with his mouth agape. Then, he drops dead. And I lay there, painfully aware I'm dying with nothing but my bra covering my chest and wishing I could put my shirt on. Then, the darkness takes away the agony.

Chapter 63

It's been three weeks since I rattled everybody's brains in Laurel Grove, Ohio. It took twenty-three minutes for the ambulance to get to the Stampers' house. Doctor Stamper played her games with a vengeance. She'd told the police she was along the highway heading to Crystal Springs and I was chasing her down. Three of the seven police team force were on the opposite side of town, sirens blaring searching for us.

The air seems stale with it all already. They are digging up the Stamper property, trying to find the remains of my aunt and Gina. They found the bones of a child in the old well. Gina's mother identified the clothing as belonging to her daughter. They also found a tiny chain she wore around her neck. It had once held a dog tag she found while visiting her grandmother's grave at the cemetery on the White's farm property. Her grandmother was Tom White's aunt. Her mother stated when she tucked Gina into her bed every night, she told Gina to take the necklace off and leave it under her pillow, so she didn't strangle herself if it got tangled in her clothing. It had been taken as evidence the night Gina came up missing. It wasn't Arnold Kinney who took the dog tag and bracelet from an evidence locker in 1979. It was Bobby Vandevenne, almost forty years later.

But the mounds of excavated dirt at the Stamper's is old news now, replaced by more pressing scandal. Tangy Cunningham confessed she placed two joints in my desk drawer in the library for Timmy Kinney, so he could have an excuse to arrest me. Tangy's grandpa, Marvin, got arrested for soliciting a prostitute at Downtown Sally's, and then, there's Janine Pritchard's wedding coming up at the country club. I think it is still tough for people to come to terms with the fact that we have been rubbing elbows with serial killers and that one person could brainwash an entire town. My sister's in a tizzy, at least that's what my mom is saying. I'd like to say everything changed with them. It hasn't. I'm still Nicky's odd little sister and Mom has no clue about my secret life or my sister's. I'm not telling her, that's for damn sure. She freaked out enough when I got shot. I don't want to put her over the edge.

Besides, Frankie in Rayville contacted Kim, who contacted Mister Barkley. He wants to join forces with me, pick my brain a little bit about some other serial killings that have not been solved. He thinks Mister Barkley is some kind of an amateur crime task force leader whose staff I am on. I'm sure that is what Jack Barkley insinuated when he talked to Frankie. Such, Mister Barkley suggested I keep my Violet identity so he can play spy, too, for a while.

The school board wants me to stay on as the librarian, lunchroom attendant, after-school detention monitor, *and* as a teacher for a criminal science course next year. Everybody has been acting like little chicks in a barn when the roof blows off in a storm. They are scattering here and there with wide eyes, running willy-nilly trying to figure out why the sky is falling on them. I either get sideways peers or whispers that barely glance off my ears. *Is that her?* They think I can't hear them. I don't know why.

The only one who has cooled a bit on his anger at me is Johnny McDaniel. He came and visited me at the hospital the next day, after he was released from the local jail. He asked for the necklace, the one with the B on it and the two keys. I was wearing it before they had me take it off in surgery to remove the bullet from Doctor Stamper's gun. Daddy was holding it in his pocket. I nodded and he handed it over to Johnny, who said he gave it to Aunt Roo for teaching him to read.

"There's this old Chuck Berry song called Johnny B. Goode about a poor, country boy dreaming about being famous and he does," Johnny told me softly. "She kept telling me if I could read, I could be something someday just like the boy. They had a bunch of necklaces at the fair one year and I wanted to get her one, I couldn't get her a J because maybe somebody'd know we was friends. So I got the B like Johnny's middle letter. She thought it was funny, gave me the nickname of B."

I'm still the weird girl. But now I'm the weird girl with the hot fireman boyfriend and the daddy who is embarrassing me walking around town saying—*you know, that's my little girl who caught them serial killers.*

Wednesday, June 3rd I stood outside the Crystal Springs Eatery and phoned Rocky, told him I think my stitches were coming loose or something and my car wouldn't start and some guy in a white van offered me candy and a ride. It was like the grand finale at the fireworks, I tossed the entire mother lode into the sky and boom! He hauled ass up to save me. I handed him three Number 2 pencils and pointed across the street to the Crystal Springs administrative offices, where they were holding the fireman test in ten minutes.

"Really?" He shifted uncomfortably.

"Really. Because the truth of the matter is, Rocky, you've been smart enough all along. You just needed to realize it. All the tactics I've been using to get you to study were really one big tactic to help you overcome your fear. Do you want the probability you're going to pass this test and get hired in Crystal Springs?" I asked him. He just stared at me. "Okay. You have a seventy-percent chance you'll get an A, an eighty-percent chance you'll get a B. You'll have a hundred percent chance you're going to go into that building and pass the test, period, because I'm going to kick your ass just like I kicked Bobby Vandevenne's if you don't. I'll be standing here waiting for you. Forever, if I have to."

"You did kick ass, baby," he says. Baby? I get that stupid grin on my face because he reaches out and tickles me in the tummy. "I'll do it if you pick out one of the kittens my mama kitty just had in the barn."

I'm not ready to replace Baby Cakes. Still, I nod. "Okay. Now go and take the test. I have an appointment with your cousin in six hours and forty-two minutes."

I do. Because the local police are a bit spicy because one of their own didn't solve the crime. It's a big deal when the Feds come in and start asking questions as to why they didn't solve the crime themselves. Bobby Vandevenne is in jail. He begged my mom to pay his half a million dollar bail and she laughed at him, told him she's using the money for a divorce. Timmy Kinney is on administrative leave until they prove his innocence or guilt for planting the pot in my desk drawer. So on Saturday, Daddy's ATV is going on auction. That's the thanks I get for putting our little town on the map—I mean, it's not like Ohio's even in the top ten states for the number of serial killers.

"Why am I getting a really bad feeling about this?" Liam Dubois is standing with me, rocking back and forth on his heels six hours and forty-two minutes after Rocky's test. He's wearing a pair of light-colored jeans and a white button up shirt. He sticks out like a pale, coddled poodle in a pack of black, ornery pit bulls. We're standing outside the chain link fence at the impound lot of the Laurel Grove Police Station with Leah and Colton. They had the sense to wear dark clothes to steal back my daddy's ATV.

It is dark, a moonless night, and two minutes before

midnight. Leah is holding my daddy's heavy duty bolt cutters in her hands. She keeps lugging them upward toward Liam's waist and saying: "Clip-clip." I think this is her way of flirting with Liam, although he keeps scaredy-cat -eyeing me like he thinks she really might neuter him if he blinks. Heck, maybe she will.

After the initial shock of losing T to the fire, she seems to be adjusting well. She and Gabby have moved in with me temporarily, although my mom says I'm probably going to be stuck with her because *you know how those folks are from over at Raccoon Creek*. Leah, Colton, and I started putting up an above-ground pool for Gabby today. If we don't get arrested and sent to prison tonight, I think we'll have it finished tomorrow.

"Why are you worried? She's the one that always screws stuff up." Leah shrugs.

Of course, if I don't kill Leah before that. "I saved your ass, didn't I?" I sputter at her. "You're alive today because of me!"

"You're not sitting in a prison cell because *I* saved *your* ass," Leah spats. "You know there were six cops surrounding your car because they thought it was you. I had to crawl out the door on my knees with hands on my head. Timmy Kinney patted me down and I think he felt me up."

"I know. It was on all the social networks," Colton sniggers. "Six people had their phones out, taping it." Leah reaches out a fist and slams it on her brother.

"My stepdad gave you fifty-thousand dollars for figuring out who the serial killers were. Buy your dad a new ATV," Liam complains.

"Where's the fun in that?" I ask. "Besides, I have to make a point."

"And what would that be, our illustrious leader in

felony larceny?" Liam sniffs a laugh. "That you're not as smart as you like to make everybody think?"

"That you screw everything up?" Leah repeats. "Didn't I just say that?"

"No," I look back and forth between the two. "That's not my point. My point is that—" I wiggle my fingers at the bolt cutter and point to the padlock on the fence. "I don't know." I do know. I suppose I'm never going to be cool. I'm always going to have a geeky answer. "I just want my daddy to be proud of me for once in my life. Cut the damn lock."

"I liked you better when you were drugged and a psychopath." Leah scuffles two steps forward and sets the bolt cutters on to the lock. "You know that doesn't make sense. You're trying to make your dad proud by becoming a felon." She grunts twice and wrestles with the shackle, then with a loud CLICK the metal snaps. "But I suppose for a McGuire, that's a step up."

"So what's the plan?" Colton asks me.

There is no plan. I've scouted out the premises for the last three days from my perch at Dell's Fantasyland and a pair of high powered telescopic binoculars. It has been pulled out for the auction tomorrow and set to the side of a shed near the front gate. And this is where I stop, take in a deep breath. Barring a bit of dust, the exterior is in perfect condition.

"So this is where I ride off into the sunset," I tell my partners in crime. "All's you need to do is make sure the gate is closed behind me and then take off toward Colton's car." Mindy Carter is picking the trio up around the corner. She's a bit high on life tonight and has been on two dates with Colton. She wrote a paper about decryption and how she helped her teacher catch a serial killer; she has been accepted, as a high school junior, at three colleges already.

And so my plan should work, right? I hop on the ATV and I gun the engine, take off into the night. I stop just short of the impound gate to make sure my team has gotten outside. I give them a geeky thumbs up and I no sooner raise my hand when the engine makes a guttural sputter.

"Oh, shit. Maybe I should have brought a gas can," I mutter while three pairs of eyes snap up to mine. "Can anybody give me a push?" They are all just staring at me dumbly.

"Fine." I pop out my phone, poke a few numbers. "Hey Rocky—"

"Where are you at? Everybody's trying to find you."

"Um, well, I'm—" I start.

"Listen, I'm going to tell you this first—I passed the test! But only because there's *bigger* news."

"Oh!" I feel my heart bounce up and down for him.

"That necklace you gave Uncle Johnny. He was in the newspaper with it, holding it up."

"Yeah, I saw it."

"I guess it was some kind of sign."

"Sign?" I don't have time for a lengthy conversation. Leah and Colton are antsy, running around to grab the handlebars to try to tug the ATV forward. Liam is trying to push the ATV with his rear and whisper-yelling for me to hurry up because he thought he heard a siren.

"Yeah, it was a sign it was safe to come home. She knew Doctor Stamper was nuts. Your aunt, she called your grandpa. Uncle Johnny helped her run away. It's a secret he's been keeping for forty years. He just figured she was dead, since she'd never gotten ahold of him. She's alive!"

"That's cool." I mumble, trying to digest his words.

"That's cool?" Rocky groans loudly. "This is epic."

"At this moment, I'm kind of in a bit of a pickle." I look over. Leah's sitting on the ATV and Liam and Colton are using their backs to push it along the sidewalk at a very slow pace. "You think you can bring something to tow an ATV with and maybe your truck?"